I0847100

BLUE STAR ENTERPRISES

BLUEPRINTS FOR TOMORROW

M. J. MARKGRAF

ISBN: 979-8-88993-069-3

Edited by Cassandra O.
Cover by Ivan Zanchetta

Published 2025 by MoonQuill®
Arlington, VA

www.moonquill.com

TABLE OF CONTENTS

chapter 1

LOCATION: PETROV STATION
SYSTEM: GLIESE 667
DATE: 2392

The aging recycler smiled and stood from his chair to greet his newest customer. "Viktor! It's been far too long. I don't see Svetlana around. Has she finally wised up and found a real man?"

The captain of the *Amophor* rolled his eyes and clasped the man on the back. "She hasn't come to her senses yet, ya old coot."

They both laughed at that before the man motioned for them to sit.

"Have you brought me something interesting? I see your engineer, Mateo, hiding out in the corridor like a kid caught with his hand in a cookie jar."

Viktor rubbed the back of his neck, earning a raised bushy eyebrow from the old man. "It might be more trouble than it's worth," Viktor finally relented under the man's stare.

Yuri leaned back in his chair, the spring squeaking audibly as he did so. He needed time to digest what the captain had told him. Trouble could mean many things. He tried to steer clear of illicit goods, but there was only so much one could do to stay on the straight and narrow on the fringe. Most people didn't come to Petrov Station because they wanted to and not everything that came through his shop had been acquired legally.

Then again, Viktor had never brought him anything other than salvaged scrap before. He decided to roll the dice on this one. "Let me be the judge of that."

Viktor nodded and whistled for his engineer to come in.

The thing following the engineer made Yuri's eyes go wide. "By the stars, what is that thing!"

The eight-foot-tall robot had to duck to fit through the bulkhead that separated his salvage yard from the corridor that ran along the outside of the station.

The Engineer, Mateo, stopped a few feet from the desk and without any signal, the robot stopped behind him.

Yuri grunted as he stood from his seat and walked around the desk to look at the strange machine. He circled it, picking up the strangely flexible arms and letting them fall back into place. Then he ran his hands along the molten scar that bisected the front of the torso from the upper right shoulder past the left hip.

He had seen enough scrap in his life to identify damage caused by a weapon. If he had to guess, either a Gauss turret or a railgun. Judging by the damage, not some dinky little handheld but a true-blue ship weapon. But that wasn't what surprised him.

What surprised him was the fact that the robot hadn't been obliterated by a glancing blow from either weapon. Normally only ship armor was capable of withstanding something like a direct hit from a ship cannon.

Before heading back to his seat, Yuri flicked the crudely attached holo projector on the robot.

"What's with the holo?"

Mateo smiled and punched in a code on the device glued into the damaged portion of the robot. Soon a cartoon face sputtered into being a few inches over the robot's torso. "I figured since it didn't have a head, we could at least give it a face to make it less... *imposing*."

Yuri quirked an eyebrow at that. "I can't say it helps much. Where did you even find something like this?"

The two hesitated and Yuri waved them off. "Never mind, I don't want to know. Just tell me, is it stolen?"

Viktor bristled at the implication, telling Yuri all he needed to know.

"So that's a no. I'm just trying to see what kind of trouble this thing will bring me if I buy it off ya."

"So you want it?" Viktor asked expectantly.

"Maybe," Yuri responded, thinking out loud. "It looks military. Although I've never seen a military robot like it in all my years. Even during my time with the Coalition. Could belong to an STO member, but they didn't really go in for automation."

He would know. The Coalition fought for many years against the Sol Treaty Organization. Then again, it could be a rogue faction, it was hard to say.

"What is it capable of?" Yuri inquired.

"It can fix pretty much anything," Mateo stated.

"Really?" Yuri asked skeptically. "Show me."

He reached into a desk drawer and rifled around until he found what he was looking for. The box he pulled out was rather banged up on the outside, but he opened it and quickly inspected the contents within. He had never quite been able to get the delicate device to work correctly. He turned it around and showed it to Viktor.

The man looked at the box, then back at Yuri with surprise. "A music box?"

Yuri only smiled. "I ain't trusting that hunk of metal on anything serious if it can't fix something like this."

Viktor shrugged. "Robot, fix this device."

The robot bent forward, its agile arms slipping past the men as it picked up the box.

Verifying how delicate the thing could be was another one of Yuri's tests. And it appeared to have quite a gentle touch.

After pulling the box close to itself, it just stood there for a moment, turning the box at different angles.

"How's it see?" Yuri asked, realizing the robot had no sensors that he could locate.

The men shrugged before Mateo spoke up. "I think it uses some form of echolocation or something. My tests were inconclusive."

After about a minute, the thing stopped and beeped.

Mateo walked over and read the screen on the device. "It states insufficient materials available to make repairs. Can it use your printer?"

"Eh, sure. Why not."

As the robot walked over to the printer, the old salvager couldn't help but chuckle.

"What's so funny?" Viktor asked.

"Oh, nothing. I just find it amusing that a robot is able to program an unknown part into my printer. How did you get it working anyway? I can't imagine that damage made it easy."

"That would all be Mateo's doing. I'll let him explain."

"It actually made it quite easy," the Engineer responded as he walked back over. "It exposed the robot's main control pathways."

"So you programmed all of these functions into it?" he asked dubiously, starting to get a sinking suspicion.

The two shared a look and Yuri cursed. "Don't tell me you just reactivated it."

When the two remained quiet, he swore again. "Is it even safe to have around?"

"It should be fine. We've been using it for weeks," Mateo stated. "All of the commands have to go through the holo, which also functions as the control box."

Yuri rubbed his temples. *An unknown robot with unknown programming.*

At least it didn't look like a combat robot. He would have shown the pair the door with a swift boot to the ass if they had brought something like that onto the station, let alone his salvage yard. There wasn't much that got you on the STO's radar faster than black market arms. Having a weapon aboard the station was a good way to get spaced.

Yuri was pulled from his thoughts as a box plunked down on the desk in front of him. He stared at it for a moment before watching the robot return to its location behind Mateo.

He turned the box toward him and opened the cover. A sweet tune started to play as soon as the cover was opened all the way. He smiled sadly as the tune reminded him of his wife who had passed away years ago. The box had been hers since she was a young child. Even though he hated the blasted thing, he couldn't bring himself to get rid of it.

With his decision made, he tenderly closed the box and stuffed it back in the desk drawer. Then he turned toward Captain Viktor. "I'll give you a thousand credits for it."

"You're joking, right? It's worth at least a hundred times that."

"To whom?" the wily old man asked. "There's a reason you brought it to me, instead of taking it further toward the core systems."

"Come on, at least give me ten thousand for it!" Viktor pleaded, not acknowledging the previous point.

"No way. I'm taking all the risks of having this thing around. What if some black ops team comes around looking for it?"

"I very much doubt that's gonna happen!"

"Oh? Are you going to tell me where and how you found it then? You know for my peace of mind." Yuri knew the salvager captain would never give up his locations or contacts. It's how he made his living after all.

"I thought we were friends, Yuri. Fine. How's five thousand? I won't go any lower than that. Anything less and I might as well take my chances at a more populated station."

Yuri smiled. "Alright, five thousand."

The pair shook hands, and Mateo handed him a control wand along with a handwritten manual.

After the pair got their money and left his scrapyard, he tossed the book into the trash. As if he would trust some unknown programming. Even though he wasn't nearly as skilled of a programmer as Mateo, he knew enough to reprogram the module himself. This would ensure there wasn't any latent code in it. He hadn't survived this long by being foolish.

After flashing the module and erasing the code, he began to program his own. It was simplistic, but he only needed the robot to move heavy things around, it wasn't like he needed it to perform brain surgery or anything like that.

The work was off and on over the course of a year, but old Yuri wasn't in any hurry. He also didn't want to put too much time into something if the STO suddenly came asking about it. When nobody showed up and there wasn't a peep about it on the back channels, he finally put his full effort into finishing the programming.

"Move that over there," he stated, pointing at a large manifold.

The robot stood for the first time in a year and tottered over to the large hunk of steel. Its movements were quite jerky, but it did manage to pick up the manifold and move it where it needed to go.

"Good enough," he grunted. The robotics code he used had some self-learning built into it so the movements should smooth out over time.

He gave the thing a series of commands to organize his inventory and allowed it to work.

After supervising it for five minutes he nodded in approval. He hated cleaning and sorting the yard. With this robot, he wouldn't have to worry about that ever again. Now he could simply focus on what he actually enjoyed: fixing things.

* * *

Alexander didn't know when it happened or what it was, but one moment he was staring at a veil of shifting and shimmering lights. He got the impression that it was important somehow, but his mind was having a hard time piecing it together.

He quickly realized that he didn't know where he was or how he had gotten there. He racked his mind for an answer but came up blank. As he tried to search his memories, he found mysterious blank spots. He knew who he was, and that he was born on Earth but little else. There were other memories that floated hazily at the edges of his mind, like he could almost reach out and touch them. When he tried to grasp them, they seemed to fall apart like gossamer.

Fearing the possibility of losing more memories, he stopped trying to pull at the threads that sat tantalizingly just out of his reach. Instead, he stared at the veil of light.

There wasn't much else he could do since he couldn't feel his body. He couldn't even turn away from the lights. He thought he should feel more fear about his situation, but his mind was calm—numb almost.

He didn't have time to explore that thought further as one of the lights drew his attention.

He thought he saw an image for a moment.

chapter 2

LOCATION: PETROV STATION
SYSTEM: GLIESE 667
DATE: UNKNOWN

Alexander focused on the lights and soon another image flashed by. He noted it and mentally started counting the seconds. He wasn't sure if his sense of time was accurate in this place, but he got to the count of ten when the next image flashed by. It was the same count as the previous one and the one before that.

There it was again.

Images flashed by in a repeating pattern every ten seconds. He couldn't quite make the images out as they were there and gone in almost the same instant, but he could still tell there was an image.

If someone blinked, they would miss it. Thankfully it didn't seem he needed to blink, or maybe he didn't have eyelids. That thought made him a bit uncomfortable until he remembered he wasn't feeling any pain. He wasn't feeling anything, if he was honest with himself. Perhaps this was all some weird dream.

Although, if it was some strange dream, he didn't feel like he was in control of it at all.

There was only him and the stream of light. He knew it was a stream because the images always flashed in from above and vanished below.

The one time he tried to look away from the stream, he found it surrounded him. All except for a dark section that felt like his mind had been shoved into an old CRT television displaying only static. It made his mind feel weird, so he avoided looking at that section.

Time was also peculiar in that place, and he sometimes found himself blanking out for an undetermined amount of time before coming back. He only knew this was happening because of the lights. They weren't uniform. When he blanked out and came back, they jerked suddenly like someone had hit the skip ahead button on a video.

One time he came back, and the entire field of light was replaced by an angry red. The red was swept away before he could even contemplate what it meant.

Red was usually bad. It only happened once and never repeated itself, so he figured it wasn't something he needed to worry about. Instead, he enjoyed the rather pastel color field made up of blues, pinks, yellows, greens, and purples that streamed through the darkness.

It might have been pretty if he wasn't stuck staring at it since he had awoken. The appeal had quickly faded.

Alexander thought about it further and wondered if he had awoken. He thought that was what clued him in to the colors, but his mind was so full of holes and hazy areas, that he couldn't even say if he was awake or still dreaming by that point.

After a bit of thinking, he decided that what he was experiencing was real. Mostly because it was too boring to be a dream, even a lucid one. Why the hell did he remember what a lucid dream was when he couldn't even say for certain it was a dream?

Alexander could only hope the holes would repair themselves with time. He could already feel the feathery bits at the edge of his awareness firming up. If those could fix themselves, certainly the rest would follow.

* * *

"I'm a robot!"

The realization came as quite a shock to Alexander when he finally figured out how to turn the slow slideshow of images into something more coherent.

With the lack of external stimuli, it was impossible to tell if what he was seeing was himself moving about or some remote camera view.

He was certain the curtain of light was some strange data stream, but that epiphany only brought on more questions.

He remembered at least bits and pieces of growing up. Most of those memories had come back from the feathery edges of his mind. The only problem was the holes remained, and he could tell at least a month had gone by since he awoke in this strange place. With no further improvement to his condition, he couldn't rely on his missing memories to help him out.

All he could do was stare at the video as his "body" moved heavy machinery about. He saw other humans occasionally, but the video quality wasn't the greatest. Although it was slightly improving as the weeks wore on.

He wondered if it was less him figuring out the image issue as it was the body fixing itself.

That was just another mystery added to the pile of questions he already had. Another being 'where the hell was he?' As far as he could see, everything was metal. Maybe it was some strange warehouse or lab. That might explain why his mind was trapped in this body.

Why him? Nothing in his memory led him to believe he was anyone of importance or intellect. Did he have some tragic accident? Maybe someone sold his comatose body for science?

He did vaguely recall people doing that and their loved ones ending up as testing dummies for the military.

That didn't feel quite right though. If Alexander had been stuffed in some sort of military robot project, why was he stuck moving hunks of scrap metal around?

He sighed. There was no point letting his thoughts tumble down an endless well of questions. Especially when he had no answers and no way to get them. He needed to focus on what mattered most: regaining control of his body. Once he did that, then he could figure out what was going on.

* * *

Time seemed to whip by as Alexander paid attention to every detail. Slowly his vision of the world expanded as the curtain of light became a panoramic view of the world. All except the dark void that cut across what he thought of as his front.

However, it was strange. Alexander could see everything at once. His mind was perfectly capable of taking in the entirety of his visual space without having to turn around or focus on a certain point.

When he thought about it, his mind seemed to go fuzzy, so he tried not to focus on why he could see everything at the same time.

With his new view of the world, he found out what he looked like thanks to a mirrored piece of junk he was hauling about. Or at least what the body he was in looked like.

It was an ugly robot. Something straight out of some alien horror film. There was no head, because why have a head on a robot? The arms were long and articulated, looking like some sort of segmented bug carapace. They moved more like a snake than any robotic arm he had any memory of. The legs were much the same way, ending in wide conical feet. The body looked a bit like a deformed egg. It tapered at the hips where the legs attached to the sides but then ballooned out toward the top where the arms attached along where the shoulders would be.

The only thing that stood out from the painfully black exterior of the machine was a long gash that ran from the upper left to the bottom right of the torso. It looked like something very violent had melted its way through his body. The damage also coincided with the blacked-out area in his vision, and though he didn't see any cameras or other protruding sensors on the robot, so he had no idea how he was able to see at all.

There was one last thing he noticed: a box.

It looked to have been jammed into the jagged rent in the body and haphazardly glued into place. The piece of technology was different from the rest of the robot, while he didn't know what the box was, it looked vaguely familiar to other technologies from his scattered memories. It had blinking lights, beat-up old paint, and some unknown words that could have been Cyrillic but were too distorted in the reflection to read. That was good.

When he first saw the reflection, he nearly freaked out. As freaked out as his apathetic mind could get anyway.

The reason for his concern was simple. He thought maybe he had been abducted by aliens and stuffed into this body to work as a mindless slave. Knowing that humans were involved really didn't make his situation any better, but at least he understood the motivations of humans.

The next thing he learned was that he was in space. More accurately, he was on a space station.

It was an eye-opening experience to watch the massive bay doors open while being left in an airless chamber as a massive ship came to dock. The ship wasn't like anything he had ever seen back on Earth. Either humanity had been hiding this technology, or a whole lot of time had passed since he was a self-ambulatory human. Yet, not so much time that he couldn't recognize certain design elements of the ship.

It used some form of projected thrust engine that produced a bright blue flame. There were also stabilizing jets around the ship that burped out little cones of fire or compressed gas. They were too small and too far away for him to get a clear view.

There was also artificial gravity, which blew his mind when he first realized that, but there were no shields. At least, he hadn't seen any indication of shields.

To be fair, he didn't spend a whole lot of time studying the ship. As soon as it landed, the belly clamps released two cargo containers and his job was to empty the things, or at least that's what his body did. Alexander still didn't have any audio so he couldn't tell what the old man who owned him had ordered him to do.

It was clear that nobody treated him like a person, so he assumed they thought he was just a robot. Alexander had to hope that was the case, because if they knew he was a human trapped in this body and still treated him like this... well, that would suck.

* * *

More time went by, and he could finally hear things. Although, the sounds were garbled most of the time.

It was just nice not to be stuck in this soundless void watching the world go by. He finally learned the name of the old man that owned him. It was Yuri, Yuri Sokolov. Although that last part should have been self-evident by the big sign above the door to his salvage yard that read 'Sokolov Repair and Salvage.' To be fair, Alexander had a lot on his mind, and it was an easy thing to overlook.

It also didn't help that Yuri had activated the holo emitter that was glued onto his body as some weird control unit. The stupid thing projected a cartoonish face a few inches in front of him that covered most of his torso. He could still see through it, but it made viewing things a lot harder.

The old man hadn't actually wanted to turn the thing on, but Alexander's form was frightening people, and the Station Council told him to do so.

He didn't think it made him look any less intimidating. If anything, it reminded Alexander of an evil clown or demonic toy. Maybe like a mask that a robber might wear. The council seemed fine with the change, so who was he to argue? Not that he could argue or anything. He may have regained hearing to some degree, but he still had no control over his movements or any ability to speak.

* * *

Dear diary... Just kidding. What would be the point?

He noticed he didn't really forget things so that was one upside to his situation. Plus, who would read a mental diary?

However, something interesting happened. It was interesting enough that if he had a diary, he may have been tempted to write it down. He was moving scrap around like he did every day when some idiot manning a small mobile crane smashed into him.

Not a good way to start his day, especially when he lost.

The crane, being about three times his size and weight, sent him careening across the bay they were working in. It was not a fun experience. However, something in his mind or from the impact seemed to slot into place and he reached out, managing to stop himself.

Flabbergasted at having control, Alexander forgot anything else. Unfortunately, the control vanished shortly after as his view of the world went dark.

He regained consciousness to see a cursing and grumbling Yuri. The man was fumbling with the box in the dead area in his vision.

Alexander had long wondered about that box. It seemed to perform multiple functions. One was obviously a control interface for the old man, it also functioned as a projector. Alexander figured that was its original purpose.

But now... Now he noted it was his interface to the outside world. Which was a problem.

If that box functioned as both an interface and control point, could he even get control of his body back while it was still attached? There was no way he was removing it, especially not if disconnecting it meant being plunged into the dark silence again.

Alexander waited for Yuri to fix him and leave before he tested something out. With a significant effort, he willed one of his fingers to move. It felt like pressing through a thick wall of mud and his mind was growing fuzzy, but he saw one of the digits twitch.

He released the pressure and relaxed his mind as he gave himself a mental high five. He could do this. He could regain control of his body; it was only a matter of time and willpower.

* * *

A little clock in the upper corner of Alexander's vision dinged at him. *Has it been a year already?*

The clock was one of the many little tricks he had picked up since gaining his mobility back. He still pretended to be a dutiful robot since he couldn't speak anyway. Explaining he was a man trapped in this body would have to wait. It wasn't something he wanted to do anyway.

Alexander had realized a few things over this last year.

First off, he was unique. And not just unique as in a human trapped in a robot body. The body itself was unique. He had seen enough human tech from this era to determine that. There hadn't been a single thing that even remotely resembled what he was or what he was made from.

Either old man Sokolov didn't realize this or didn't care, but Alexander wasn't about to wave a huge flag in his face stating, 'I'm unique, cut me up and study me!'

He wanted answers, but he was going to have to find them himself. Thankfully the old scrapper left him to his own devices most of the time. It had taken a bit of effort, studying, and planning, but he had learned how the terminals worked around the yard.

There was internet, but it wasn't exactly like it was back in his day. Most of the information seemed to be locked behind paywalls, but he had learned some stuff.

The first thing he looked up was the actual date. It was 2395. He knew a significant amount of time had passed from his memories of Earth to now, but he wasn't quite ready for just how much.

His last memory was from the mid-2050s. Nearly four hundred years gone, just like *that.*

If he had any strong feelings one way or another, perhaps he would have been upset that everyone he cared for and loved was long dead, but he couldn't even remember anyone from his past, let alone feel anything for their loss. When he thought about his situation, he realized if his mind hadn't been trapped inside this body, he would have died long ago as well. So that was a minor comfort.

The second thing he learned was where he was. Alexander had originally figured he was in some station orbiting Earth or the Moon. Maybe even Mars.

Again, no.

He was in Petrov Station, located somewhere in Gliese 667—wherever the hell that was. Maybe that was something he knew at one time but was now lost to the voids in his memory. He would likely never know the truth about that.

Each new answer generated more questions. He had to put those aside as he had more pressing concerns.

Scanning his surroundings, he found himself alone.

Alexander made his way over to a terminal and began typing. One good thing about being a robot, he was quick and precise. The pages flashed by as he siphoned out a tiny amount of money from Yuri's account and into his own under a fake name.

This was Alexander's great plan to finally get out from under Yuri.

The man was fine, it wasn't like he abused him or anything. It was just that Alexander didn't want to be a functional slave forever, so he needed to work for himself. Even if this new him was a fake persona he had purchased.

It turned out you could buy just about anything if you knew who to talk to. Of course, Alexander didn't know anyone except Yuri. After a year of doing Yuri's work, he had learned the man wasn't as upstanding as he presented himself to be. Some of the people he worked with were fine working around the law.

Alexander derived joy from using Yuri's money to purchase the fake identity. He didn't feel bad about doing so, just thinking of it as his long overdue paycheck.

However, setting up the identity and siphoning off small amounts of money was only the first step, as well as the easiest.

chapter 3

LOCATION: PETROV STATION
SYSTEM: GLIESE 667
DATE: 2397

Years passed for Alexander in the blink of an eye. It was repetitive and dull, especially pretending to still be a dutiful robot.

He hadn't told anyone of his ability to act independently, especially not Yuri. With his situation uncertain, he decided to take a cautious approach to his freedom, so he didn't draw undue attention to his circumstances.

He wasn't in a hurry to escape. The slow approach had worked in his favor so far. It gave him time to see what type of man Yuri truly was.

It turned out he was the type that would sell his mother if the price was right. Yuri wasn't great, but he wasn't the worst person he had run into on this station.

Alexander had carried more than one unmarked box to a set of sketchy individuals over the last two years. If he was given the choice, he would not have associated with those people at all.

He needed to free himself from Yuri's control before the man decided selling him was worth more than keeping him around—not that the man ever seemed to part with any of his junk. Alexander swore the man's collection grew every time he sold some part or component.

The first idea Alexander had about freeing himself was to blackmail the man into selling the robot to his fake persona.

After weeks of thinking about the plan, he decided to scrap the idea. The man he purchased his fake ID from was one of Yuri's connections. The man wasn't stupid, he would ask around and soon find out the ID was fake. Alexander didn't want to start on the slippery slope of committing more crimes to get his way.

True, he had stolen money from the salvage yard owner, but that was repayment for his work and to set up a new life.

With his first plan in the dumpster, he went with a simpler one.

Yuri understood money, so Alexander would simply purchase himself. Of course, that was easier said than done. He had no idea how much money it would take to purchase himself from the cantankerous old man, but he doubted it would be an insignificant amount.

That wasn't the only thing he needed to consider either. Alexander needed a place to stay once he was legally owned by himself.

Since he didn't need to sleep or eat, a small out-of-the-way dwelling would be fine. A small shop would be ideal as that would allow him to continue to earn money the only way he knew how, and that was by repairing things.

When Yuri closed up for the night, Alexander made his way over to the station terminal and logged in with the old man's stolen credentials. He couldn't use his yet in case the station logged who used a terminal. He assumed they would.

Few things were free in the world Alexander had found himself in. Thankfully, business listings were among those. It was probably because they only showed current station assets and not those outside its confines. He would take the small win though.

Petrov Station was designed as a typical ring station from Alexander's memories, which surprised him.

The whole point of designing a ring station was to spin it around a central axis to create gravity. However, the station had normal gravity instead of spin-generated gravity as was clear by them standing on the floor of the ring instead of the outer walls. The only way he could explain this discrepancy was if the station was built or was in the process of being built when humanity discovered a way to generate artificial gravity without the need for spinning stuff. He didn't actually know what that process was, but it did intrigue him.

At least he finally understood why all the doors looked to have been slapped in as an afterthought. If they were meant to be accessed from the outer wall and had to be cut out and reoriented, it would certainly explain the patchwork.

Yuri's shop was on the third ring. It was designated as an industrial ring along with the fourth and fifth rings of the station. The sixth through eighth rings were commerce and housing. The ninth and tenth were upper class housing and control.

After a quick look through available spaces, Alexander realized he couldn't afford even the smallest space on the third ring with the money he had squirreled away over the past years. He winced internally at this.

Setting his sights a little lower, literally in this case, he looked into the second ring.

It seemed even in space, you couldn't get away from the destitute. The second ring was where those as well as orphaned children were housed. Although, you wouldn't know that by looking at the station map.

On the map, the second ring was simply labeled overflow and storage. Nobody lived on the first ring. That was reserved for reclamation systems, power generation, oxygen generation, and water storage.

There wasn't even a lift to that ring except the one through the core and Alexander knew only station personnel had access to the core. He didn't want to live in the noisy power generation area anyway.

That left the second ring as the only viable option for him.

It wasn't ideal. Being down there would certainly limit his ability to earn money. Then again, fewer prying eyes and less demand for the spaces down there would mean he wouldn't need to earn as much anyway.

After swiping through the properties for rent in that ring, he settled on a small storage room with a door to a secondary closet within it. He assumed someone had added a wall in there at one time to partition the space. What that reason was, he couldn't say. It served his purposes fine. Best of all, it was within his small budget.

The unit wasn't very big, maybe twenty feet by thirty. The closet was probably big enough for him to stick some shelves along the walls and barely stand inside, but it would work. He would make it work because there wasn't any other choice.

Alexander recorded the information. During the day when he was out for a delivery, he would access a terminal outside of the salvage yard and purchase the lease on the property using his fake identity.

With that out of the way, he switched the terminal to Yuri's personal library. It was where all the old man's digital purchases went. A man as old as Yuri had quite a few. Less than a quarter of them were for actual service manuals. The less said about those other purchases, the better.

Alexander picked the next service manual in the list and began scanning it. He did one manual a night to ensure he understood all of the content within.

So many things had changed since the twenty-first century that he was lost the first time he stumbled upon the trove of gold. Thankfully, it wasn't so alien that he couldn't grasp the basics. It was good he could comprehend the technology because it was going to be his only way to earn a living. The more he read, the better he seemed to be able to piece together the next.

He wondered if his mind was helping him. The dark spots in his memory had never recovered, but maybe he was once an engineer or mechanic.

When he finished one of the manuals, he seemed to just understand the concept or device the manual was created for. It was almost instinctual to the point that he sometimes thought of ways of improving the designs. Other times he would come across some component from another manual and realize it could be used to improve a different device.

It was something he really wanted to test, but he couldn't until he was free of Yuri.

The night passed by quickly. Alexander turned off the terminal and went back to where he usually stood.

Yuri arrived no more than half an hour later, grumbling something under his breath.

"He's late," Alexander heard the man say. The man complained about a lot of things, so this was no surprise.

Alexander just stood in his normal spot as he watched and listened.

Soon the communicator that Yuri carried beeped.

"You're late," Yuri cursed the person on the other end.

There was muted shouting from the other side that Alexander couldn't pick up, but he saw Yuri pull the device away from his ear.

"Don't get pissy with me!" Yuri shouted back. "I agreed to be the go-between for this deal because I owed you one. I don't care if you ran into trouble getting here."

More garbled speech came through from the other end, but the person must have stopped shouting as Yuri kept the device up to his head this time.

"Yeah, yeah," the older man responded. "Just have the crate ready, my bot will be there shortly." Then he clicked off the device before stuffing it back in a pocket. "Ingrate."

"Robot, go to hangar 415 and retrieve the crate. Then bring it to hangar 512. And be quick about it."

Alexander started moving as he whistled internally. He had been sent to the fourth ring on various occasions for deliveries or retrievals. It was the most heavily trafficked ring as it catered to mid-sized and smaller ships. The fifth ring, however, catered to the large ships and luxury craft. As such it only had a dozen hangars. The big ships simply docked at massive unloading ports that stuck out like towers from the station.

That meant this crate, whatever was in it, was going to someone important. By the clandestine way Yuri was handling it, probably highly illegal as well. Alexander just gave a mental sigh.

* * *

Hangar 415 was easy enough to locate. Alexander had been there numerous times. He even recognized the ship and the nervously pacing man near a very futuristic-looking box. Everything about this situation screamed 'turn around' to Alexander, but if he did that, he would give himself away.

He forced those thoughts away as his feet clanked against the deck. The captain of the ship finally noticed his approach, not that he had been stealthy or quiet by any means. Although he found he could be both if he chose to be.

"Finally! Hurry up already. My client is waiting for this crate, and he doesn't appreciate tardiness."

Alexander didn't hurry. He kept the same sedate pace that he always did. The annoyed look on the captain's face helped smooth over his annoyance at having to be the errand boy for whatever illegal nonsense this was.

The crate wasn't very large, about the size of a party cooler from Earth, but it was heavy if his whining servos were to be believed. Not that they made any actual noise, it was all digital. He had learned to sort of read the digital feedback that scrolled past his vision. He still didn't understand most of it even after two full years, but he got the gist of it. It was clear his body possessed a vast array of sensors and functionality that he simply couldn't tap into, or that was damaged by whatever had caused the large, melted scar across his body.

"Be very careful with that," the captain stated, putting his arm on Alexander's causing him to pause. "The stuff in there is very delicate."

Alexander remained stationary, waiting for the man to remove his arm. It wasn't because he wanted to but because the damn interface Yuri had built into his body prevented him from moving when he was in contact with a person. While he had regained control of his body for the most part, Yuri improperly reinstalling the control unit put constraints in place to prevent him from accidentally or purposefully hurting anyone. Not that he ever would.

"Gah, why am I even bothering? You're just a stupid robot, you wouldn't understand anyway. Just hurry along." He removed his hand and waved in dismissal.

Alexander turned and walked out of the hangar, carrying his load.

Finding the other hangar took a bit of time. It was clear across the other end of the station on the fifth ring. The people he passed up here stepped aside and stared at him. They weren't used to seeing him like the crews on the third and fourth rings were.

Alexander ignored their stares and whispers as he trudged along the ring to his destination.

Unlike the hangars on the lower floors, Hangar 512 was richly appointed, or at least the entryway was.

Alexander was forced to pause in the entry as a woman behind a desk contacted someone else.

Shortly a brick of a man stepped through an inner door. The individual was kitted in full body armor and was equipped with a shock baton. Alexander was pretty sure the man would have preferred to carry something more lethal, but weapons were highly regulated according to the station laws he had read.

The man waved a device over the crate, and it gave a happy little beep. "Alright, bring it in."

Technically, Alexander could have left the box there, he had fulfilled his orders, but he was curious to see what type of ship the wealthy flew.

He followed the man into the more spartan hangar. The ship resembled luxury yachts from back on Earth but converted into space-going versions.

They were all elegant lines and sharp edges to make them look sleek and imposing. He supposed he shouldn't be surprised by that. Those designs had been popular with the rich for a reason.

The squat armored man walked up the ship's ramp, but Alexander stopped short of it. For the first time, he thanked the restrictions built into the control box.

"Don't just stand there, bring it aboard," the man urged.

Alexander set the box down at the edge of the ramp and stood. Then his little box chimed in reply. "This unit is forbidden from setting foot aboard another vessel. The contract has been fulfilled. Thank you and have a nice day."

After the overly cheerful voice finished, Alexander turned around and left.

It wasn't the first time he had been asked to board another ship. It seemed to happen almost any time he did these sketchy deliveries for Yuri. If the old coot wasn't so paranoid, Alexander probably would have been carted away and sold before he had ever regained full use of his body. He kept up the charade of complying because it told him who was trustworthy and who wasn't.

chapter 4

After his eventful delivery on the fifth ring, a few weeks went by in blissful peace. Alexander's only concern during that time was reading more technical documents and moving scrap along with other deliveries.

The work was dull, sure, but he didn't mind. Every day brought him closer to his goal of freedom.

That bliss was shattered as a hurried set of steps neared the entry. It was a good thing his body had excellent hearing. Even so, Alexander had to rush to log out of the terminal and return to his spot before Yuri ran into the salvage yard bay. It would not have been good if the man caught him away from his assigned spot.

The man had a panicked look on his face as he sprinted across the entry area and into the room he used as his office. It was impressive given the man was probably in his eighties. Alexander had never seen the old man move so quickly or seem so flustered.

He could hear muffled cursing as items crashed to the ground from inside the room.

After only ten minutes, Yuri rushed out carrying a duffel bag. "I knew I shouldn't have taken that damn job!" The man spat as he hurried over toward Alexander.

Fearing he had been caught, Alexander stiffened. What could he do if he had been discovered, kill the guy? *That... That wasn't going to happen.* Alexander wasn't a killer. During his moment of indecision, the man had made it to him and set down his duffel bag. Then he reached into a dirty pocket on his overalls and fished out a data disk.

When the man didn't call him out, some of the tension left him. Alexander had seen the digital storage devices before but hadn't ever used any of them. They looked like quarters, only with completely blank faces.

The man shoved the tiny disk into the control module glued to his chest.

"Greetings," the same mechanical yet somehow cheerful voice that accompanied all of the communications from the box responded.

"I have given you a list of responsibilities ordered by priority. You are to continue to carry these out until I return."

"I understand," the voice repeated.

An actual calendar appeared inside Alexander's mental space with a list of duties for each day. As he read through the ridiculous list of tasks, he also watched Yuri.

The man inserted a credit stick into the terminal Alexander had only just logged off from. From his vantage point, he could clearly see the man emptying his bank account into the digital wallet. He only left enough for what seemed like a month's worth of operating expenses for the yard.

Either Yuri wasn't coming back, or he expected to be back within a month. Neither option was great for him.

There was a moment where he thought it would be beneficial to let the older man in on his secret, but rationality quickly pushed that thought to the back of his mind. Even if he didn't mind Yuri, he certainly didn't trust the man. There was no way Alexander wanted to get caught up in whatever nonsense had him so flustered that he was packing for a one-month trip in the middle of the night.

Yuri Sokolov, the old man and owner of Sokolov Repair and Salvage, stopped at the exit, taking one more longing look at his life before vanishing down the corridor.

The man hadn't even shut the door in his haste to leave. Waiting a few minutes to make sure the man was truly gone, Alexander went over to close the door, but the program Yuri had installed beeped at him.

"Deviation from assigned tasks. Please remain in place until your next assignment is scheduled."

The robotic voice repeated this message with every step. Alexander sighed mentally, that was going to get old fast.

He closed the door and returned to his spot near the wall. He had tried just standing still but every thirty seconds the voice would repeat itself if he wasn't where the dumb program wanted him to be.

It obviously wasn't an AI but some sort of tracker or assistant that Yuri had modified. He wondered briefly why the man hadn't bothered installing it until that moment. Then again, maybe Yuri knew how annoying it was and didn't want to listen to the thing constantly yammering either.

Alexander attempted to remove the disk from the control box, but paranoid Yuri had added preventative measures to block him from attempting it. To be fair, the man was right. Of course, Alexander already knew of these hard-coded rules. He had explored most of the features and rules that prevented him from doing certain things over the years. Part of getting his freedom was knowing what he could and couldn't do.

It wasn't that he couldn't bypass most of them by now, but some were stubbornly ingrained in the device. Alexander couldn't afford to damage the control module either. It was literally the only thing keeping him conscious.

That being said, he already had a way past that specific restriction.

He made his way over to Yuri's office, the stupid program badgering him the entire time to return to his storage space. He ignored it, although he wished he could turn off whatever allowed him to hear. Unfortunately, willing it to happen didn't do anything. He sighed and kept going.

Much like the main entry door, Yuri had left the office door wide open. When Alexander peeked inside, he saw the contents of the office were scattered everywhere. He mentally shook his head and dipped below the door frame to step inside.

Displaced items lay on the floor, and Alexander pushed them aside with his feet so he didn't crush anything. The office would need to get cleaned up, if anyone saw the state of it, there would be no doubt that Yuri had fled.

If he wanted a new life, he needed more time to save money.

Inside one of the still-open desk drawers was exactly what he had been hoping to find. He reached in and plucked out the soft-tipped stylus. It was a good thing that capacitive touchscreen tablets were still a thing.

Alexander easily maneuvered the stylus to the eject button on the control interface. He didn't need the capacitive properties of the stylus; he just needed something soft yet sturdy enough to activate the simple pressure switch on the control box. There was a click and the silver disk ejected halfway out of the device.

Using his other hand, and taking care not to touch the box, Alexander removed the data disk. As soon as it came free, the annoying voice ordering him to return to his assigned tasks ceased.

He held the disk up to get a good look at it. How something so small could cause him such annoyance was beyond him. He gave a mental shake of his mind and crushed the disk. Then he set about tidying up the office.

* * *

When it came time to open for the day, Alexander followed the calendar he had been given. There were certain free time slots inside the calendar that he wasn't quite sure what to do with.

He didn't have to ponder long. During the first free slot, a group of men came in looking for Yuri. They appeared to be maintenance workers. When they couldn't find him, they sent him a digital message. Essentially, an email.

When they left, Alexander went over to the terminal and logged into Yuri's account to read the correspondence. They were looking for some replacement components for an EVAP system. Alexander had no clue what that was, but they were helpful enough to leave part numbers. He knew exactly where those parts were.

As he was retrieving the parts, a realization struck him. Surely that cagey old bastard had factored in random people coming by. He must have built responses into the new program to account for them. Alexander was suddenly wishing he hadn't just destroyed his only way to communicate.

In the meantime, he wrote a note and taped it to the office door.

Tell the robot what you need! I'll be back later.

It wasn't the greatest solution, but it would work until he learned how to code a new interface and install it. After placing the note, he took the parts to the destination in the email.

* * *

It was sort of funny that nobody questioned the note. They would come in, read it, and come over to where he was and tell him what they wanted. Then he would retrieve the requested items, and they would send payment to the company account.

Thankfully the walk-ins only happened during the select few hours marked as free. The rest of the time was scheduled for other deliveries and sorting incoming inventory that Yuri must have scheduled weeks or months in advance.

This would have been great had it lasted, but less than three weeks later, a group of three entered the salvage yard. These were not the normal blue-collar type that normally frequented the yard. The woman in the group had a tight hair bun and a severe face. She was also wearing something that looked like a cross between coveralls and a full-body scuba suit. It was not a very flattering look.

Alexander assumed this was one of those elusive vac suits. He had heard about the vac suits, but none of the station regulars bothered wearing them. They were difficult to move around in, making any work slow and tedious. This was the first time he ever saw someone on the station wearing one of those things.

Thankfully Alexander had managed to cobble together a basic assistant program that could ask people what they wanted.

"Greetings. How may I assist you today?"

The woman glanced over at him but didn't say anything before returning her attention to the other men with her. "Make sure you get a full inventory, everything must go. We have a party interested in purchasing this space and I don't want any of this junk here when they move in."

'Move in? What was she talking about?'

"You sure?" one of the men asked. "The old man could come back."

She barked out a laugh. "Unless that old bastard figured out how to breathe in a vacuum, he isn't coming back. I received confirmation that the freighter Livera was destroyed by pirates with all crew and passengers aboard. That included Old Man Yuri which means this space reverts back to the station to do with as it pleases."

"What about the bot?" the other man nodded toward Alexander.

She glanced back over, looking at him more closely before frowning. "What about it?"

"Well, it looks unique," the one man stated.

"Unique? Do you know what runs through my mind when I hear that word?" she asked. The man paused for a moment before he shook his head. "I hear expensive, hard to maintain, prone to failure. I mean look at it." She waved her arm in Alexander's direction. "Yuri didn't even bother fixing the damn thing. He stuck a cobbled-together patch on it and called it good. The stupid thing doesn't even have proper greeting protocols built into it."

Rude!

"Just scrap it," she stated before turning and leaving.

After the woman left, the two men began to tap on tablets as they quickly inventoried the room.

Alexander had a choice to make.

After Yuri's late-night escape, he had made a plan B, assuming the man would never return. Although, he never expected the man would die. He just figured Yuri would start a junk pile in some other station. He wondered if the trouble he had been trying to run from had caught up with him or if the attack was simply random bad luck.

Alexander pushed those thoughts aside as there were more pressing concerns. As soon as the two men passed into the aisles of stored junk in the back of the yard, he made his way over to the terminal and entered Yuri's credentials.

He really hoped nobody looked too closely at the log or his plan would quickly fall apart. Being as fast as possible, Alexander scrolled through the dozens of purchase and sales logs until he found the one he had set up.

The sale of himself was dated on the same day that Yuri left the station. It didn't have a delivery date, but Alexander quickly filled it in and stamped it 'paid in full' using Yuri's identity. He would have transferred the remaining funds inside Yuri's business account to his own, but he was certain that would be noticed. He would just have to hope the meager amount of money he managed to earn was enough to keep him afloat.

Closing the terminal, he returned to his spot next to the wall and waited.

It took just over an hour for the two men to catalog every item in the warehouse before one headed toward the office. The other walked over to him and waved a scanner over the code embedded into the control box. His tablet gave an angry beep, and he frowned down at it.

"Kirill!"

"What?" Kirill shouted from inside the office.

"This robot says it's been sold."

"So?"

"So! So, Miss Kuznetsova said everything needs to go."

"Well, when's it supposed to be picked up?" Kirill asked, stepping outside the office.

The man standing next to Alexander looked down at his tablet and scratched his head. "Says it's supposed to be delivered sometime today."

"Then I fail to see the problem, Grigory."

Before Grigory could respond, Alexander moved, startling the man. Kirill laughed at his companion as Alexander simply walked out of the salvage yard for the last time. If he had a heart, he was sure it would have been beating a mile a minute.

The last thing he heard was a muted chuckle from Kirill. "See, Grigory! If you wait long enough, some problems solve themselves."

CHAPTER 5

It was a strange feeling knowing he was free. Sure, it had taken over two years, but it had come far faster than Alexander had predicted or even planned for. The fact that he hadn't foreseen this possibility was a good reminder that he was still out of his depth in this new reality he found himself in.

He barely even understood daily life on the station, let alone the complexities of their laws or bureaucracy. While he had read some of the laws because they were free to peruse, Alexander hadn't spent much time digging into them, other than the ones that pertained to his planned freedom.

That was something he would need to rectify as soon as possible. Being ignorant of the local laws usually wouldn't get you off the hook if you broke them.

His general knowledge was lacking as well, but there was little he could do about that now. He simply didn't have the free credits to purchase learning modules, even the elementary ones meant for children were outside his current budget.

As he made his way through the ring to the freight elevators, he garnered a few looks, but most simply went back to their business, already familiar with him from his years aboard the station. The few whose gazes lingered were already on Alexander's 'naughty' list. It was made up of the scummy people that Yuri dealt with.

Thankfully, nobody approached him or caused problems, and he arrived at the freight elevator unmolested. He honestly wasn't sure what he would have done or even could have done had someone stopped him. The limitations imposed on him by the control box were still very much in place.

This wasn't his first trip down to the second ring, but he had only visited the place a few times to clear out some of the old scrapper's storage rooms. It was a wonder Yuri had made any money at all with all the junk he had lying about in the yard and other locations on the station.

Yuri's collection was a veritable treasure trove of old obsolete parts if you knew what to look for—all of which would belong to the station if what Miss. Kuznetsova said was true.

That was a shame. Alexander had been hoping to borrow some smaller parts and bits without Yuri figuring out what he was up to.

The man didn't keep a good inventory of all his junk. From what Alexander had seen, the man kept most of it straight in his head. It would be an impressive feat, except Alexander knew Yuri forgot where he placed things from time to time. On more than one occasion, he had been stuck waiting for Yuri when the item the old man had told him to retrieve simply wasn't where it should have been.

Alexander always got a little chuckle out of seeing an angry huffing Yuri come to collect him when he failed to return.

The elevator didn't groan when he stepped onto the platform. While Alexander's body may weigh in excess of fifteen hundred pounds, the large cargo lift had been built to transport things many times his size.

He tucked himself into a corner and simply waited. Unlike the normal lifts, which he was too heavy to use, the cargo lifts only activated at certain times throughout the day. As he waited, more and more automated loaders trundled into the lift. They would stack neat rows of crates near the back before zipping off to retrieve more.

When he had first seen the devices, he had wondered why Yuri didn't use the automated cargo handlers. That changed when he saw one of the dumb robots nearly run someone over. On another occasion, one crashed into a ship that Alexander had been sent to retrieve some parts from.

He had gotten a front-row seat to a heated exchange between the owner of that cargo handler and the ship captain. It ended with the cargo handler's owner losing his contract and having to pay for the damage to the ship.

There was also the fact that most of Yuri's items didn't fit neatly into crates or pallets.

However, Alexander suspected the real reason Yuri didn't use the things was purely because he was a cheap bastard. He was fairly sure the man never spent a dime unless it was to buy more junk or places to store more junk.

An hour passed and the warning lights outside the freight elevator began to flash amber, indicating that all cargo deliveries had to cease. One final material handler managed to squeak through before simply stopping in the middle of the floor.

Alexander did a mental shake of his head. The things were so dumb. He expected futuristic machines to be much more capable or at least AI-driven. He had a vague recollection of self-driving cars from back in his time. Certainly, the technology should have improved. There was likely a reason behind why it hadn't. It was just another piece of history he would need to figure out.

A groan and loud clank signaled the closing of the door. Much like every other door on the station, this one was thick and sealed tight in case of accidental decompression—not that he had experienced anything like it since he had woken up.

If it had happened, everyone would have known because there were decompression alarms along every corridor. He knew that because he passed the signs and alarm stations more times than he could count. Since he thought about it, he realized the infrequency of venting issues was probably why nobody bothered with the vac suits.

As the elevator slid to a halt and the doors opened to the same flashing amber lights, Alexander waited. Sure enough, as soon as the lights stopped, the dumb loader zipped back off the elevator, almost clipping someone walking past the door.

The man cursed out the machine before going about his business.

Seeing no more loaders lurking about and waiting to run him over, Alexander exited the elevator.

Much like the other rings, the second ring had multiple floors to it. If it was the same as the other rings, it would go to plus three minus three in the elevators. At least that was what everyone called the floors above and below where the freight elevator stopped. He didn't know why someone decided to design the rings that way, but they had.

In an ideal world, he would have purchased his cheap shop somewhere close to the elevator and the main avenue of traffic on that floor, but it certainly wasn't a perfect world. At least he had managed to find a place on the main floor.

He walked along the huge circle of the ring until he was nearly three-quarters of the way to the far side.

Even there among the main traffic lane, he would have been happy. Instead, he turned down a smaller side passage. Three more turns brought him to a stop outside a grimy door with an equally grimy sign hanging above it. The sign had long since stopped being legible, but the plate bolted next to the door confirmed he had the right location.

He sighed internally and pressed in the code on the faded touchpad. There was a moment of hesitation from the control where he thought he may have entered the wrong code, but eventually, he heard the clack of security bolts retracting.

Instead of opening slightly inward, the door didn't budge. Alexander was forced to push the door open. Which, given his strength, wasn't all that hard.

The door squealed in protest on rusty hinges as he pushed into the room, leaving a trail on the filth-covered floor. With the door fully opened, he ducked to avoid hitting the top of his body on the bulkhead as he stepped inside.

While the doorways were small, he was glad the ceiling was high enough for him to stand upright. It would have been a constant pain to have to duck all the time while in his own shop.

Other than the thick layer of dust on the floor, the room was empty.

He stood there for a moment, taking it all in. It still hadn't quite clicked for him that he was finally free to do what he wanted.

Of course, that was just the beginning. He needed to find out how he ended up in this body, or even on the station. He had time and he could do it at his own pace without worrying about Yuri catching him.

While his plan to masquerade as an invalid with an auto-immune disorder that could only communicate through this robot form wasn't a great one, it was the only one he had managed to come up with in the previous years. It was the only plan that wouldn't get people to ask uncomfortable questions about him or his situation.

Maybe getting stuck in the ass end of the station was a good thing. He was certainly out of sight. It would give him the time he needed to make his claim more believable.

First thing's first, the place needed to be cleaned.

After walking down the hall to the closest terminal—yeah, no personal terminals down there—he was able to purchase some cleaning supplies and rust remover.

It would take a day or so to get them, but that was fine.

He spent the next few days scrubbing every inch of the space, including the ceiling. His ability to reach without a ladder was handy for that. The door got lubed and even the outside crud was removed.

His corridor was the cleanest corridor in that section of the second ring. It would make it stand out, but he simply couldn't work with the disgusting mess that had been there when he arrived.

Alexander was itching to clean more connecting hallways, but he reined in that instinct.

He spent a bit more money to have a sign printed to replace the faded one over the door. It simply read, 'Alexander's Repair Shop.' Nothing fancy, but it got the point across. He didn't have many applicable skills, but thanks to Yuri's library of manuals, he had a good handle on how to fix most basic items. And he still had some money set aside to purchase more manuals if he needed to.

After the place was cleaned and the sign was up, he simply waited for his first customer.

He probably should have advertised.

Days flew past, and, while his small out-of-the-way corridor wasn't super busy, people walked past at least once an hour. A few even stopped to look at the sign. Then they would look inside the door, see him, and slowly back out without a word.

It was a rather disheartening turn of events, if he was honest, but he didn't let it get him down.

While he waited, he purchased a small programming deck and spent the time perfecting the data disk he used to respond to people. He just finished his latest iteration when a greasy-looking man strolled in carrying a piece of equipment.

"Greetings, sir. How may I assist you?"

With a grunt the man set the heavy-looking component on the metal counter, smearing dirt and oil across it to Alexander's annoyance.

The man looked around, "Where's the owner? I need this fixed up."

It was time to test out the new features of his program. With a tiny movement of his hand, the holoprojector that doubled as his control module let out a sigh. "I am the owner, sir."

The man blinked at him. "No, you're a robot."

"I apologize for the confusion, sir. I suffer from a disease and must interact with people through this machine, but I assure you my work speaks for itself."

The man seemed skeptical. "Fine. Whatever. I don't have many credits, and I need this done today."

While Alexander would prefer to haggle for a better deal, he really didn't have the leeway to refuse any work. "Well, let's see what we have."

He moved over and inspected the grime-coated device. After wiping away probably decades of residue, he finally found a serial number telling him what it was. It appeared to be a gearbox for some sort of industrial application.

While Alexander didn't have a whole warehouse of spare parts like Yuri had, he had purchased himself a small 3D printer. It had been expensive, eating into his limited funds, but it had been necessary if he wanted to fix anything of note without having to buy from the manufacturers.

"I should be able to repair the damage, please return in two hours with payment."

"Fine, but if you run off with it, I'm calling Station Security on you."

After the man left, Alexander used the printer to create the tools he needed to take the gearbox apart. That had been another reason the printer was his first purchase instead of a good set of tools. He didn't need power tools since he had more strength than any of those.

As the tools printed, he finished removing the grime.

The case on the unit had cracked, which is likely what led to it breaking down. That was annoying because he didn't have a welder or the schematic to print a new case. It meant he would have to purchase the printable design and that would eat into his profit.

With a sigh, he made his way to the local terminal and looked up the manufacturer. One nice thing about the future was that all manufacturers had to provide printer schematics for all components. They didn't do it freely of course, but Alexander paid the cost and headed back with the data disk for his printer.

An hour later, with a new case and two replaced gears, the customer left satisfied. The pay barely covered the cost of buying the schematics along with the printer material and power to print them, but it was a start.

chapter 6

The next few weeks were much the same for Alexander. His only customer was the single guy from before. At first, he didn't mind.

Work was work and he was still making money, even if it wasn't much.

After the man came in for the sixth time with a completely different component, Alexander started to get suspicious, so he paid to look up the component numbers. Every single item the man had brought him came from machinery used in various tasks.

That in itself wasn't all that strange. Except he had worked with Yuri long enough to get the feeling when people weren't being completely honest. So, after he finished fixing up this latest component, he followed the man.

It wasn't hard, the man grunted and cursed the entire way as he struggled to carry the heavy item back to wherever he was going. Which turned out to be another repair shop.

From within a side passage, Alexander watched as a man in orange coveralls entered the shop an hour later and left with the very same part he had just repaired on a cart. The guy had been subcontracting out his repair work to Alexander and pocketing all the profit. The nerve!

He wanted to go over there and have a word with the man, but that wouldn't get him anywhere. Instead, he turned around and headed back to his tiny repair shop. As good as it would feel to tell the guy off, he had a better idea. One that might drum up some actual work.

Two days later, the guy returned with another item to repair. Alexander happily repaired it, but he did it in such a way that it would break almost immediately after the first use. It was scummy, but it was also his only real option. He doubted the sleazy shop owner would continue using him if he raised his prices, and he still needed the money. If the man was ruined by his *own* shoddy work, well, that was on him.

Had the man bothered to disclose that this work was for a third party, which would have been fine with Alexander, he would have negotiated a better rate at that point, but the shop owner hadn't. It was clear the man who ran the competing repair shop didn't want to pay his fair share or do the work himself, so he found a sucker to do it for him. Alexander didn't like being taken advantage of one bit.

It took time, weeks in fact for the faultily repaired items to come back to haunt the repair man. But haunt him they did, and Alexander was there to witness the whole event. A group of angry people stomped into the man's shop and started screaming at the owner.

Just as the discussion was really getting heated, Alexander strode past, making sure the owner spotted him. Just as he hoped, the man pointed at him. "I wasn't the one who fixed your items, it was him!"

The group turned to glare at Alexander, and he paused. One of the men in the group stomped up to him. "Are you the one working for Maxim that did such shoddy work?"

He pointed to himself. "Me?"

"Well... whoever is controlling you," the bearded man spluttered.

"No. I don't work for—Did you say, Maxim? No, I own my own repair shop just down the corridor." He gave the group the location number. "If you are having issues with his work, perhaps I can interest you in my own. I offer excellent rates and a money-back guarantee."

As he was talking to the bearded gentleman, Maxim was turning red and throwing out all sorts of accusations to try to discredit him, but it was clear that the crowd's interest in the owner had turned. After three years aboard this station, Alexander could say one thing with certainty, the people that lived here were a pragmatic bunch.

"Can't be any worse than this shyster," the bearded man jerked a thumb back over his shoulder. "If you do good work, I may have even more for you in the future."

Alexander flicked a finger, causing his holographic face to nod. "Would you like me to follow you, or will you be dropping off the item?"

Surprisingly, that simple question got more interest than the fact he offered good rates and a money-back guarantee. The other people weren't quite sold just yet. They were shrewd people.

One woman crossed her arms. "Pick-up and delivery included?" she asked with a stern gaze.

"For a small additional fee."

That seemed to be the crack that broke the dam.

These people were all busy men and women. If they didn't need to lug heavy parts around the station, they could get much more done. They all exchanged contact information with him and set up a time for him to come get the broken components before hurrying back to their respective jobs.

After the last of the group left, Alexander turned to an apoplectic Maxim. "If you hadn't tried to screw me over, this wouldn't have happened."

The man didn't apologize; he simply turned redder. "One of these days, that robot of yours is gonna need fixing. When that day comes, I'll make sure there isn't a single shop on this station that will even consider helping you!" After his hate-filled tirade, the man slammed the door to his shop and locked it.

Alexander laughed internally. In the time he had been on this station, he hadn't seen a single piece of tech even remotely resembling him, so he doubted anyone on this station would be capable of fixing him. Not that he trusted anyone here to fiddle with the thing keeping him alive for the last nearly four hundred years.

One of the reasons he spent most of his extra money on schematics was he hoped one day to stumble upon one that might hint at his origins.

With a smile on his avatar's face, he turned and went to pick up his first real repair.

* * *

After the blowup at Maxim's, Alexander acquired a decent bit of extra work. It wasn't enough to keep him busy all the time, but it allowed him some breathing room and time to work on some projects of his own.

It was during one of his tinkering sessions that he noticed the head of a little girl peeking from around the entry to his shop. He didn't turn his head or acknowledge the child as he continued to work.

There were a surprising number of kids left to just roam the second ring without supervision. Given what he knew of the second ring, he shouldn't be all that shocked. Nobody lived on this ring willingly. They either fell on hard times or they couldn't make it on the higher rings. Not that he could judge these people, he was in the same situation after all.

Alexander had seen other kids peeking through his door from time to time over the last weeks. He got it, he was a robot, something of interest. Most of those kids were in and out in a flash as soon as he even slightly turned in their direction. Almost like someone had dared them to do it and they were terrified of the consequences if he caught them. He wondered what they would think if they knew he saw everything.

This little girl seemed to be different. She just stood there silently for a bit, staring at him with a look of wide-eyed curiosity only a child could show.

He sighed audibly, making the girl jump slightly. "Can I help you, miss?"

He thought the kid might bolt, but instead, she threw her arm inside and grabbed the doorframe and sort of hung there in the doorway, arms outstretched and feet against the wall. "Is it true you snatch up naughty kids and devour them?"

The question was so absurd that it caused Alexander to miss the circuit he had been soldering, ruining the entire board. "What! Who told you that?" He finally turned to face the girl as she swung back and forth in and out of the doorway while holding the frame.

"Markus said so. He's one of the older kids in the orphanage. Said you eat naughty children."

Orphans? Well, that explained why nobody cared what the kids got up to.

"And what if I said it was true?" He didn't have anything against children, he just thought there were better places for them to be playing than around his shop.

The girl paused in her swinging and put a finger to her mouth as she scrunched up her face in thought. Then she shook her head, her dark hair swirling around. "Nuh uh, I wouldn't believe you," she stated with conviction.

"So you think I'm lying or that Markus is?"

She scrunched her face up again but didn't seem to have an answer for that. Then he saw her grin before giggling. "You can't eat children!" she screamed in triumph. "No mouth!" Then she laughed and bolted down the corridor.

Alexander sighed. He should have just remained quiet, now he was certain this girl or her friends would be bugging him even more.

* * *

He needed to add prophetic to his resume.

Each day after, the girl returned. Most of the time she would just hang around in the doorway, literally. Other times she would creep inside his shop and lean against the wall, just watching him until she got antsy and left.

Sometimes she was quiet, but most of the time she jabbered on and on about everything as kids seemed to do. It didn't seem to matter to her one bit that Alexander simply ignored her presence until she finally left.

One nice thing was that no other kids seemed to come to try their luck. Whether he had her to thank for that or not was unclear.

He had been tempted to shoo the girl away, but he learned a surprising amount about the station or at least the second ring from this child. He didn't even know her name.

After three weeks of her constant chatter, he finally decided to interrupt her and ask. "What's your name?"

The young girl didn't even miss a beat. "Yulia. I'll be this many this year!" He looked over to see the girl holding up eight fingers.

Alexander didn't have a good grasp on child biology, it seemed to be among his missing memories, but she seemed small for her age.

"Tell me, Yulia, why do you hang around here? Certainly, there must be more interesting places to be?"

She giggled. "You talk funny." She somehow managed to shake her head as she said that. "The other kids are afraid of you. They say I'm a scaredy cat cause I get nightmares, but they don't call me that no more 'cause I stay here."

Ah, the flawless logic of children.

"Fine. You may continue to visit."

The girl squealed in delight and Alexander had to hold his hand out to settle her. "But if you're going to be here, you need to help me."

If the girl nodded her head any faster, Alexander was sure the thing would have flown off her shoulders. Then she paused, seeming to realize she had no idea what sort of help she could offer.

Alexander smiled, and he let it show on his holographic face. "You attend some sort of study or schooling?"

She nodded again. "Mrs. Weber is teaching us the alphabet, and I can add and subtract numbers." Then she looked around conspiratorially before whispering. "I can even mullyply. Only the older kids are supposed to be learning that."

"That's very impressive. Do you know any history?"

She nodded.

He walked around from behind his counter, carrying a stool he had printed for her a few days prior. He hadn't put it out until then because he didn't want to encourage her to hang around. If she could be helpful, that was a different story.

Alexander set the stool next to the side of his counter. "Have a seat and tell me what history you know."

Giving a young kid like that carte blanche to talk was like opening the floodgates on a dam.

chapter 7

As one could probably imagine, the breadth of knowledge an eight-year-old had about history *wasn't great.* Despite that, and the fact that Yulia liked to go on random tangents, Alexander did actually learn some things.

He learned about a war that took place. Yulia only knew of this war because her father had served aboard a ship, but the war had ended before she was born. He was curious as to the timeline of this war. Maybe it would explain how he ended up out here.

Alexander would have liked to ask the girl some more pointed questions about her father, but he thought it wouldn't be very appropriate considering she was an orphan. However, the girl didn't get upset when she talked about her father... *Perhaps some other time.*

The girl knew quite a bit about the station, especially when it was first founded. He chuckled internally as she unenthusiastically recited a limerick, probably meant to help younger students remember the date better.

"In Gliese six-six-seven, so fine,
Stands a station that truly does shine.

Built in twenty-two eighty-nine,
In the cosmos, it firmly aligns,
A beacon of space, so divine!"

The limerick was awful, but it did give him two pieces of information he didn't have before. The system he was in and the year it was constructed. Was it worth it? The jury was still out on that as he continued listening to the girl's newest tangent on a game of tag that seemed to have no end and no beginning that she could recall.

The game even had its own set of rules apart from other games of tag. The tagged person couldn't retag the person who tagged them, and they also couldn't tag anyone on that day. The tag had to be a surprise. Which made the person that was it, have a much harder time. Despite that, Yulia said all the children loved it.

He decided not to point out the fact that the game seemed purposefully designed to teach kids critical thinking skills and troubleshooting. What better way to teach that than to have the kids do it themselves and not realize it? If he ever found the person who thought up that idea, he would have to shake their hand and congratulate them.

Eventually, the girl started to go quiet and fidget.

"Is something the matter?" He asked in genuine concern.

She paused and then shook her head slowly. "Just hungry."

"Oh. Well, if you need to go and eat, don't let me stop you."

She shook her head again, her stomach rumbling slightly. "It's not time for the evening meal."

Alexander checked on the clock he kept in his mental space. It was after one, and the girl had been here for a few hours already. "Did you miss your lunch?" he asked, hoping he hadn't kept the girl here only for her to have missed food. She was small enough that he doubted she could really afford to do that often.

"What's lunch?" she asked in confusion.

"Uh... It's the meal between breakfast and dinner."

She giggled at that. "Those are silly names. We get morning meals and evening meals. You must be super rich if you eat three times a day. Are you super rich?" she asked, her eyes going wide like she had seen a unicorn.

He made his holographic face arch an eyebrow as he waved one of his arms around the room. "As you can see, I'm fabulously wealthy."

She giggled again at that, only for her stomach to rumble once more.

Yulia did a good job of ignoring the rumbling, but it was too much for Alexander. "Wait here a moment, I'll be back." Before he stepped out, he turned to the girl who was already standing on the stool and eying up what he had been working on. "And don't touch anything."

The girl, looking like she had gotten caught with her hand in a cookie jar, smiled but sat back down. "I won't."

"Uh-huh."

A few minutes later, Alexander returned with a simple berry-flavored protein bar from one of the vending machines on the main passage.

The girl's eyes lit up when she saw the colorful red wrapper.

He handed it to her. Alexander was afraid her eyes would pop out of their sockets as she held the wrapped snack.

"Don't get used to it," he muttered and moved behind the desk. "Your rumbling stomach was just disturbing my train of thought."

If the girl heard him, she didn't respond. She was too busy fighting the foil wrapper to get at the contents within.

He sighed again, plucking the treat away from the girl, and carefully peeled open one side before handing it back to her.

"Thank you!" she mumbled around a mouthful as she tried to bite into the hard bar. Which was probably made more difficult by the fact she was missing a few of her baby teeth.

He shook his head and returned his focus to his project, tuning out the girl's noisy eating. At least her stomach had finally stopped grumbling.

It was unfortunate that the orphans only got two meals a day, but he didn't have the resources to do anything about that, nor did he think it was his place to butt in. Honestly, most of the kids he had seen looked healthy enough, if a bit small and skinny. It wasn't the skinniness of malnutrition though. So it was likely that whoever took care of them, did their best.

After finishing her meal, Yulia jabbered on for another half hour before getting fidgety again and wandering off.

It was probably for the best.

Alexander didn't dislike the girl, but he couldn't sit here and entertain her all day either. Hopefully, she would soon lose interest in him and move on to other activities.

Not long after the girl left, Alexander finished the thing he had been working on. It was an upgrade to his printer.

The thing about the 3D printers of the twenty-fourth century was that they were nothing like the ones from his time. Why should they be? There had been nearly four hundred years of improvements and tweaks to the process.

The only thing that remained from the early twenty-first century printers to the one he used now was their reliance on building in layers, but that was all.

The new printers were faster, sleeker, and could print multiple materials all at the same time. They still left thin layer lines as they printed, but it was nearly impossible to tell. The lines looked more like a slight texturing than anything else. One would really have to look with a magnifying glass to see the truth. When he realized this, he looked at some other items and found pretty much everything with complex geometry was printed. Although someone could tell better processes had been used for the original parts.

Alexander had been exposed to real manufactured goods from both his previous life and through his time working for Yuri. Not everything was printed, certain items likely still needed to be machined, or required specific secondary processes that printers just couldn't perform.

One of those processes was called zero-g printing. The technique had been covered in an article in one of Yuri's old manufacturing publications. It certainly wasn't something he could replicate inside the station, assuming he could even figure out the method without purchasing a likely very expensive manual on the subject. However, he thought he might be able to fake something similar if the name of the process was accurate.

The only reason he thought this was possible was thanks in part to all the manuals Yuri owned. Humanity, it seemed, had only recently discovered artificial gravity. By recently, maybe in the last hundred years.

Alexander had parsed this out due to the publications available for sale. The articles he found on the subject only dated back about seventy years, and the things were horrifically expensive. They were in the billions of credits for one document that may or may not have what you were looking for.

It was clear whoever had discovered the key to artificial gravity didn't want anyone else playing with it.

That was fine because Alexander wasn't interested in artificial gravity.

Well, that wasn't true. He was interested, just not at that moment. He had learned a bit about the subject based on ship subsystems. Mostly from older models of ships that called for a capacitor buffer.

At the time, he thought it strange to require a capacitor buffer, but the more knowledge he unlocked, the more he began to piece things together.

It was odd. He wasn't sure if this mental acuity was something that came from his time as a flesh and blood human or something strictly from the body he was housed in.

While he had muted emotions, it was sometimes hard not to let the existential dread flood through his mind. Was he still himself? Or was he some amalgamation of man and machine? Did it matter? Was he truly any less Alexander?

He let those thoughts flit through his mind as he installed the small interrupter he built. If his theory on how the gravity plating functioned was correct, this ring of copper and circuits should shield the area around it from the effects of gravity, or at least the artificial kind.

Alexander clicked the last component in place and plugged in the wire to the control module. Then he stepped back and flicked the switch on. There was a blur followed by a loud metallic *whoomp*.

One of his articulated hands rose up and made a fist before thumping lightly on the top of his desk.

The device had worked… sort of. He turned to where his broken printer lay crumpled in a heap against the wall, a wall that now sported a nice-sized dent. It seems he only partially understood the concept of artificial gravity. While he already had an idea of how to alleviate this issue, this mistake was going to be expensive.

With an annoyed huff, he walked down the hall and purchased a new printer. His replacement was a much cheaper model than his previous one, but it was all he had the spare credits for. Selling his old printer for scrap to the station smelter netted him a small return. Just enough to keep him running for an additional month.

He decided not to do any more testing on his actual printer. Instead, he bought a simple lamp and used that to test with.

It was a good thing he had because it took three more tries to get the frequency correct so it would stop ripping the bolts out and throwing the lamp across the room.

By then, another job had come in, netting him enough money to test his changes on the printer without worrying too much.

The test went well. The printer didn't break the anchor bolts that held it to the floor, and he was able to print something without anything going wrong with his device. However, that's when the second issue reared its head.

The printer software was designed to compensate for a certain amount of gravity. It took Alexander two grueling days to adjust the settings to get the printer functioning the way it did before his little update, which wasn't great. No matter what he did, he realized this much cheaper printer did not have the ability to compensate for his improvement.

With a defeated sigh, he removed his upgrade and reverted the printer settings. His vision of improving the printer would have to wait until he could purchase a better model.

chapter 2

Yulia returned a few days later. He didn't ask why she hadn't shown up the prior day, and she didn't offer an explanation. She just sat back on her stool and started talking like nothing had happened.

When the girl initially showed up, Alexander didn't want her around because he assumed she would disrupt his work or injure herself. There was still that chance, but the more she talked, the more he was glad for her company.

It didn't take him long to realize why.

He hadn't had a proper conversation with anyone since waking up. The only people he conversed with were his customers and none of them were interested in sitting and chatting with a robot.

He wasn't sure if that was because they didn't buy his story of being sick and having to use the robot as a surrogate, or something else. He certainly wasn't going to alienate the few customers he had by asking about it.

In the lulls between Yulia's ramblings, Alexander asked her questions while he worked. She always beamed in pride when she was able to answer them, but when she didn't know, she would just scrunch her face up before eventually shrugging. "Dunno," was her go-to answer for those.

On her next visit, she brought in a beat-up-looking tablet with a worried look on her face.

"Good morning, Yulia."

"Umm... morning, Alex." The girl fidgeted as she set the tablet on the desk without taking a seat. Which was impressive because the desk was rather tall since he had built it to suit his much taller frame.

He had noticed the girl tended to get antsy and fidget when something was bothering her. Usually, it was when she was hungry or bored.

"I—I dropped my tablet. Can you fix it... *please?*" That last word came out with so much pleading that if Alexander was in his old human body, he probably would have bent down and consoled the poor child.

As it sat, he just sighed and put down the customer request he had been working on. He reached over and slid the plate of resin, that passed for tablets, in front of himself.

There was a faded label attached to the side that read "Property of Petrov Station Orphanage." He turned to the little girl who quickly looked away. "Your tablet?"

"It—It's the one the orphanage makes me use for study time."

"And how exactly did it get broken?" he asked as he inspected the device.

Alexander had seen similar devices around. They were not like the fragile tablets from back in his day.

On one occasion, he had seen one of the automated loaders run a similar device over after someone dropped it. The guy simply picked it back up, brushed it off, and gave a rude gesture to the loader before going back about his work.

"Dunno," she responded without looking at him.

He sighed again before returning his focus to the electronic device. Surprisingly, he hadn't dealt with much in the way of futuristic electronics. Oh sure, there were electronics built into most items he worked with, but they weren't much more advanced than back in his day.

It seemed old methods worked well enough for most things that nobody was all that interested in making things even more complicated just for the sake of it.

Alexander picked up a thin plastic tool he had printed for popping the plates off of control boards. He ran the thin tool around the edge of the tablet until it hooked against something. One nice thing about the technology of that time, it was built to be fixed. With a slight push, he slid the locking stud up and out of the groove, allowing the two halves of the tablet to separate.

Seeing as there were no physical signs of damage on the exterior, other than the wear of age, he figured something inside the device had been knocked loose.

There was a small spark as the back half came free, making Yulia jump. "What was that?" she asked, more out of curiosity than fear.

Alexander smiled internally. "Dunno."

The girl stared at him for a bit before she realized what he was doing. Then she pouted. "No fair."

He allowed his avatar face to laugh at her expression. "Two can play that game," he responded, and the girl relented.

Truthfully, he had no idea what that was. He set the screen part down and picked up the back to inspect it. He found a small set of metallic contacts. There was also a bunch of technical information printed on the inside.

He read it. "It's the battery."

It was rather ingenious. The entire back of the tablet was a solid-state battery. No need for a cover or anything.

As he thought about it, he realized he had never seen anyone plug any devices in for charging. A battery of this size could probably power something this small for weeks on end. When he looked over the device, he didn't see any external connection either. It had to be using some form of ambient or passive charging to keep it charged. Not really anything all that groundbreaking. They had induction charging technology back in his time.

A few fine filaments broke free from one of his fingers to touch against the metal connections of the battery. As much as he was loath to admit it, Yuri was the one who had discovered this little trick built into this body.

While Alexander couldn't get the exact reading off the battery, thanks to the damage in his mind-space, he did watch for the flicker that registered the input. It wasn't hard to see since it flashed a color that none of his other data streams ever showed.

He nodded and placed the battery down on the desk. It was still good. Then he looked at the mess that made up the processor and screen side of the device and frowned. He could tell where the power came in, and that it had a screen, but everything else was alien to him. He would need a microscope just to see... or did he?

Alexander bent his focus onto a small section of the device. The image in his mind-space seemed to bend and warp for a moment before he was soon viewing a small section in much higher detail like he was looking through a magnifying glass.

After all these years, he barely understood a fraction of what this body was capable of.

He wanted to laugh at the discovery, but he restrained himself. Mostly so he didn't scare Yulia.

With so much time spent inside this form, he still didn't understand how it took in light to produce an image, let alone how it even powered itself. Maybe with this new ability to zoom in, he could purchase a mirror and inspect himself more thoroughly. That was a thought for a later time.

The little bubble of magnified area zoomed across the device wherever he focused. It was amazing because it didn't take away from his vision of anything else, it just enhanced that portion. He found he could focus even smaller, but after a certain point, he started to feel weird and had to pull back. No electron microscope vision for him it seemed.

He had learned what he needed to learn. He sent instructions to the printer for a very specific set of tools. He really hoped the cheaper device was capable of printing them.

After less than thirty seconds, the printer beeped, letting him know it was complete. He walked over and retrieved the tiny tool, with an even smaller rod at the end of it. He used that hair-thin rod and gently poked it through a hole in the tablet's electronics. The titanium flexed slightly under the pressure before there was a soft click. He did this three more times, allowing the separator plate to come free from the electronics underneath.

It was no wonder he hadn't recognized anything. The plate was some weird piece of tech that seemed to act as a thermal barrier as well as something else. Although he wasn't sure what that something was.

It took another half an hour of removing components and testing before he found the issue. The connection for the screen had simply come loose. Once he pushed it back into place and put everything back, the tablet came to life.

He handed the working tablet back to the girl. She beamed up at him before hopping off her stool and running around the counter to hug him, smashing the recently repaired tablet into his hard form. Instead of admonishing her to be more careful next time, he lightly patted her on the back and sent her on her way.

She happily obliged, humming some unknown tune as she skipped out of his shop swinging the tablet back and forth without care.

With her gone, he turned his focus back on the paid work he needed to get done.

* * *

Yulia hummed a tune from her favorite cartoon as she made her way back to the orphanage. Some of the younger children were required to stay at the orphanage, but now that she was eight, she was allowed outside for certain hours of the day. Like most of the older kids, she jumped at the opportunity to leave the stuffy and boring space of the orphanage to explore the station.

Most of the adults either ignored them or shooed them away. Some even yelled at them or, in one instance, slapped one of the older kids. She heard from Markus that the man who did that got what was coming to him after that incident. Whatever that meant.

That's why Alex was so cool. Well, other than the fact he was a robot. He didn't seem to mind her hanging around and bugging him. She knew she talked a lot; Markus and the other kids all told her that.

Speaking of Markus, she rounded a corner of the corridor and nearly ran into the eleven-year-old boy.

"Watch where you're going, pipsqueak."

"I told you to stop calling me that!" she huffed.

The older boy snorted. "I'll stop calling you that when you grow a few inches. What's that in your hand?"

"Nothing," she quickly responded, trying to hide the tablet behind her back, but Markus was too quick.

He snatched the tablet out of Yulia's hand before she could hide it.

Markus put his hands on his hips and tried to look like the headmaster of the orphanage. "Why do you have one of the orphanage tablets out here?" he asked, waving the tablet in front of her.

"It's my tablet," she responded indignantly.

"No, it's the orphanage's. You know if the headmaster finds out you took this out without permission, you're gonna get cleaning duty for a week."

She stiffened at that. Yulia didn't like having to clean the orphanage, nobody did. What would be worse is that she wouldn't be able to visit Alex if she got in trouble.

"You won't tell him, will you?"

The older boy sighed, dropping his hands. "Look, I'll help you sneak it back in, but if I get caught, I'm not taking the blame. Are we clear?"

She nodded enthusiastically.

"Why did you take it out anyway?"

She looked at the ground before mumbling a reply. "I sorta broke it."

"You broke a tablet?" He looked at the device, it seemed to be working just fine. "But it's working."

"Alex fixed it for me."

"I told you that you should stay away from that robot, you have no idea what it could do."

"Alex has been nothing but nice to me," she stated with child-like conviction. "He even fixed the tablet for free."

"Fine, but don't come crying to me if something happens then. Come on, we're going to be late for the evening meal. I'll also need you to distract the headmaster so I can sneak the tablet back into the drawer."

She gave him a sloppy salute like she had seen in movies. "Aye aye, Captain." Before laughing and sprinting away.

"Why you!" Markus chased the giggling girl as they hurried down the corridor and toward the orphanage.

chapter 9

The *Zephyr* limped into Petrov Station, trailing a thin line of smoke from its port engine. The smoke came from the ruptured electronics systems along the side of the ship and not the fuel system, thankfully.

An undocumented asteroid that was too small for their scanner to pick up, punched through their deflector shield. The shield slowed it down significantly, but the foot-long rock still tore a large gash down the rear of the ship.

The *Zephyr* was an old ship, so it had its fair share of patches. This wouldn't be anything new, except the rock had broken apart on impact, and peppered the port engine cone, damaging the engine in the process.

They shut that engine down to prevent further damage, which also forced them to shut the starboard engine off to keep the ship from constantly drifting to one side. This left them with only the central thruster for propulsion, so their trip had taken two weeks longer than originally scheduled.

"Ease it in, Wilkes."

"I'll treat it like my very own child, Captain Daniel," the pilot responded.

"Didn't you skip out on your wife and kids?" Sierra asked.

"They weren't mine," grumbled the pilot.

"Let him concentrate, Sierra."

"Sorry, Captain," the sensor operator responded. "You sure this station can even fix the *Zephyr*?"

"I doubt it," Daniel sighed. "But we might be able to get a replacement engine. I know a guy who runs a salvage yard here. As soon as we're secure, I'll go have a chat with him."

Jasper Daniel didn't usually travel this far out to the edge of human space. There were a few reasons for that, the biggest being there wasn't a guarantee they would return safely. Pirates were only one of the concerns out here, the *Zephyr* ran into the other kind.

Undocumented rocks were a real hazard. Had that asteroid struck the bridge zone instead, they might not be there to have that conversation.

He should have known better than to take that contract. Yet even with them being so late, the payout would still have been profitable. Except now he would have to spend all that profit and likely more to fix up the *Zephyr*.

Jasper watched the main screen as the ship slowly passed through the large hangar opening. The view was skewed, making it seem like the ship was coming in tilted. It was a good thing they didn't rely on the cameras for docking. He made a mental note to have someone go out and adjust the camera on the top of the ship. It had probably been knocked loose by the impact.

White cones of vapor shot into view as the retro thrusters fired to slow the ship even further. Soon the main engine cut out and a soft puff could be heard as the vertical thrusters fired to bring the ship to the deck. There was a dull thud that resounded through the ship as the landing gear touched down and the faint hum of the station transferred over the physical connection.

Ever since he was a young child, flying aboard his father's old mining ship, he had enjoyed this moment.

Jasper flipped on the ship comm. "Alright, secure your consoles. For those not on cargo duty, I'll need you to help with maintenance tasks. We're going to go over every component before taking off again."

There was a chorus of groans following that statement, but nobody complained too vocally.

The ship was their only protection against the harsh vacuum of space. Leaving a possible issue from the impact undiscovered simply wasn't an option. Jasper had known captains who skipped these steps, and well... a lot of them weren't around anymore.

As soon as he got the signal that the hangar was pressurized again, he exited the ship from the open cargo ramp. He nodded to the crew who were busy unloading the cargo. They all nodded back.

His port liaison was already busy chatting with the customer, and he skirted aside to avoid any entanglements. Some of their customers wanted to speak with him directly, but Jasper hadn't hired Naomi just for people to bypass her and come to him. He liked being the captain and running the ship, but that didn't mean he liked having to deal with the minutiae of customer interactions. That was Naomi's specialty, and she was worth every credit.

They had docked at the fourth ring, so he headed for the elevators and made his way to the third.

When he arrived outside of where the Sokolov Repair and Salvage had been located, he found it wasn't there anymore. In its place was a business called Anton's Spaceworks. He knew that the irascible Yuri wouldn't have sold off his yard to the station. That meant only one thing: the old man was dead.

Jasper let that sink in for a bit. He had known Yuri Sokolov since he was able to recall faces. His dad had frequented the station back when he was mining this system. This was before his father met Anya, his stepmother. She eventually convinced his father to give up mining and go into a safer profession. Although being a space hauler wasn't much safer.

With a sigh, Jasper entered the establishment. He didn't have high hopes though.

The first thing he noticed was that the racks upon racks of junk that Yuri had refused to part with were gone. In its place was a clean white space that looked freshly painted. At least a dozen workers were moving about and working on multiple projects.

Jasper imagined what Yuri would say if he saw this many people in his yard at the same time. The old man probably would have blown a gasket.

A well-dressed man approached, which was the second warning sign for Jasper. "How can I assist you today?"

"On our way here, my ship took an asteroid strike. I was looking to get a quote for engine repairs."

"I'm sorry to hear that. I hope your crew is all okay."

"They are, thank you."

"I can certainly assist you with that. What model of engine is it?"

"It's an OMNI 456."

At the mention of the manufacturer, the man's fake smile dipped for a moment, but Jasper still caught it.

"I see. Well, we don't carry any Omni parts I'm afraid. So we can only offer you a direct replacement. We have a Sinorus vosem'sot."

He wasn't surprised that this outfitter didn't handle the Omni models. Not after Omni betrayed the Coalition for an exclusive STO contract during the war. It wasn't common knowledge as Omni did their best to suppress any mention of the betrayal, but any captain worth their wings knew of the open secret.

Most of these outer systems were made up of expatriates of the Coalition. He didn't blame them for their dislike of the STO's main engine manufacturer. He didn't much like Omni either, but they sold the fastest and most efficient engines out there. If you wanted to stay competitive in the core systems you had to buy from them.

"How much is a replacement gonna run me?" Jasper asked, knowing it was probably going to be outside his budget, even with the arguably inferior Sinorus engine.

The slick-dressed man gave Jasper a quote that made his eyes bulge. "What! That's three times the cost of a brand-new Omni engine."

At that, the salesman lost all pretense of friendliness. "I'm afraid that is the price. If you don't like it, feel free to *shop around*." With that, the man turned and left, leaving Jasper fuming.

He did just what the man suggested, but every place he stopped at, either refused to work on it or quoted him even more than the salesman at Anton's did. It was infuriating.

Jasper returned to the ship and gathered up the crew to tell them what was going on.

"Buncha slimy bastards!" one of the cargo handlers yelled. He didn't catch exactly who said that, but he agreed.

"There has to be someone on this station that is willing to take on this job," Naomi insisted.

"I agree," Jasper said. "And I want you all to comb the station for any leads. There has to be someone willing and able to do this for a reasonable price. I know these people don't like Omni, but if they think they're going to force us into buying substandard junk, they can float out an airlock."

That got a round of chuckles from the crew.

* * *

Wilkes was chewing on the last of what passed for a protein bar on the shithole of a station as he made his way down to the bottom ring. He had been born on a station, so he knew who to talk to get information.

It didn't take him long to find a young boy hanging out near a vending machine. Much like Wilkes had been before joining the *Zephyr*'s crew, the boy was a ward of the station.

He could always tell the difference between orphans and kids with parents. It was in the eyes. He didn't walk up to the kid though—that would just spook the adolescent. Instead, he made for the vending machine.

The kid eyed him warily but didn't leave. He was cautious but not afraid. That was good. One could tell a lot about how stations treated orphans by their attitude toward grownups.

He spent a few minutes pretending to ponder the options in the machine before purchasing two bars.

"Aw shucks, I didn't want this one." He turned to the kid. "Hey, you!"

As expected, the kid focused on him. "Me?" the kid asked, pointing to himself.

"Yeah. I accidentally purchased two bars, and I was only planning on getting one, you want the other?"

The kid narrowed his eyes. "What's the catch?"

"No catch but I could use some information if you'd rather trade."

The kid shrugged and stepped away from the wall. "Bar first."

Wilkes smiled and tossed the chalky protein bar to the kid, who opened it and quickly ate. "Whaddya wanna know?" the youth said around a mouthful of the snack.

"Know anyone that can do engine repairs?"

"Yeah, plenty," the kid replied after swallowing. "You're on the wrong floor for that."

Wilkes chuckled. "Yeah, we already spoke to those on the other rings. They want too much." He decided not to mention why they wanted too much.

The kid rubbed his chin in thought.

That was a good sign. It meant the kid wasn't just gonna spew some baloney at him to get him to leave.

"Well, there's Maxim. But I heard he got into some trouble over shoddy work. ...Um..."

"I'll take anyone, kid," Wilkes pressed when the kid hesitated.

"There is Alexander, but..."

"Is he also known for shoddy work?"

The boy shook his head. "No, he does good work. It's just, well… he's a robot."

Wilkes blinked at that. "A robot?"

"Well, supposedly, he's just sick and uses the robot to interact with people."

"You don't buy that?" Wilkes guessed.

"Never heard any rumors of a sick person moving in." The kid shrugged.

"Can you provide both Maxim's and Alexander's locations?"

The kid rattled off some numbers before walking off. As thanks, Wilkes handed him the second bar. He was still trying to get the taste of the one he ate out of his mouth.

* * *

Jasper and Wilkes left Maxim's shop, less than impressed.

If he thought the man at Anton's had that used ship salesman vibe, Maxim practically radiated scum. The man promised everything under the sun. Yet the rundown state of his shop and the seeming lack of work spoke volumes.

"Last stop, Captain," Wilkes reminded him as they made their way to the final option his people had been able to discover. If this person didn't work out, he would be forced to take out a loan and have Anton's replace the engine.

As they rounded the last bend toward their destination, the grime-filled corridor vanished, leaving a clean, if somewhat worn-down hallway ahead. Jasper quirked an eyebrow as he heard Wilkes whistle. "Now that musta taken some elbow grease."

"Yeah," Jasper responded softly. It also showed someone who actually cared about where they worked.

They arrived outside Alexander's Repair Shop. It was a small space, but it was open and inviting. The pair stepped in and stopped.

There was indeed a robot running the establishment. They hadn't quite expected the little girl, who seemed to be fiddling with something on the counter though.

"Greetings," the robot said. "I will be with you in just a moment."

Jasper simply nodded and waited.

The young girl looked over at them, before quickly losing interest and going back to what she was doing.

After about a minute, the girl squealed happily. "Alex, I did it!"

"That's excellent, Yulia. How about you run along now?"

"Okay." The girl hopped off her stool and raced for the door, forcing the pair to quickly move aside.

"Sorry about the wait. What can I help you gentlemen with?"

Jasper stepped forward and held out his hand. The robot extended its own and shook the offered appendage. The grip was firm but not painful.

"If you don't mind, I have to ask."

"Why the robot body?" the projected face smiled knowingly. "You must be new to the station?"

Jasper nodded.

"I suffer from an incurable auto-immune disease. It means I'm essentially trapped inside a life pod. So I use a remote connection to this robot to experience the world, so to speak."

Jasper didn't ask the man if he had tried nanite regen therapy. That was expensive. Going by the cobbled-together look of this robot and where he was working out of, it was clear the man lived on limited funds.

"My ship took some damage, and we were wondering if you could repair the engine?"

"What model?" the robot asked.

Jasper kept himself from grimacing at the question. It would have come up eventually, no matter what. "OMNI 456."

"Hmm... I am not familiar with that model. Most ships that come through here use the Sinorus engines."

Jasper was ready for the man to deny him like all the others, but he said something else. "I would need to add the price of a repair schematic to any work I would do. Is that acceptable?"

Jasper nodded. "Uh, yes. Absolutely. So, you can do it?"

"I'm not sure. I would need to see it in person first. The freight elevator leaves in about fifteen minutes. Where is the ship located?"

Elated by the fact Alexander wasn't making any promises before seeing the ship, Jasper provided the hangar coordinates for the *Zephyr*.

CHAPTER 10

Alexander peered into the engine cone of the *Zephyr*. It had been perforated in a dozen places and a large chunk was missing from one side.

He was pretty sure he could fix it if he had a big enough printer, but he didn't and that wasn't the only problem. Other components of the engine were also damaged. It was a miracle the thing hadn't exploded.

Alexander lowered himself using the industrial lift. It was time to break the bad news to Captain Daniel.

He found the man speaking to another member of his crew. The captain noticed him approaching and patted his crew member on the shoulder before sending them off and greeting him.

"So, Alexander. Can you fix it?"

"I believe I can, but I do not have a printer big enough to make a new thrust cone."

The captain rubbed his chin in thought for a moment before responding. "How much for a printer?"

Alexander motioned for the captain to follow him over to a terminal. After doing a quick search, he brought up a model that he was certain would be barely large enough to handle the largest component, which was the engine cone. It wasn't cheap by any means, but it was what he needed to complete the job.

The captain took one look at the price before he stuck his credit chip into the machine and pressed purchase on it. "Alright."

For a moment, Alexander just stood there. He thought for sure the man would balk at the cost. This was probably a stupid move, but Captain Daniel seemed like a standup man, so he had to ask.

"Why didn't you haggle or even bat an eye at the cost of the printer?"

The captain laughed. "You haven't been in business long have you?"

Alexander made his holographic face shake back and forth.

"I kind of figured. Even with the other costs you quoted me, including this printer, you are still only charging me a tenth of what the other quotes came in at. The reason I didn't balk at the cost of the printer is that you are also the only person on the station who was willing to repair it instead of replacing it."

"Is it too late to charge you more?" Alexander lamented, making the captain laugh.

The captain clapped Alexander on the side since he couldn't reach his shoulder. "We will both come out of this ahead, my friend. So long as your work is good, I will let you keep this printer."

Now that wasn't something Alexander had expected. The printer that Captain Daniel had just purchased cost more than an entire year's worth of rent for his small space. He needed to do more ship repairs—it seemed that was where the money was at.

Alexander smiled. "You are generous, Captain. I will use this as a learning opportunity, and I will try not to disappoint you with my work."

"Bah," the man waved away his concern. "I'm sure it will be fine. And none of this 'captain' nonsense. My friends call me Jasper."

"Thank you for this opportunity, Jasper."

Alexander got to work dismantling the engine cowling while he waited for the printer to be delivered.

He wasn't sure where he was going to store the massive machine after the *Zephyr* and their crew left, but that was a problem he was happy to figure out later.

It took a full day for the printer to arrive. Considering the size and very specific use of a printer that large, it was likely stored in some dusty room on the second ring. Having it take so long to show up was fine with Alexander. He simply worked through the night, disassembling the engine and removing the damaged parts.

In some way, it felt natural for him to be disassembling and fixing a ship. He had no memories of being mechanically inclined though, so he wasn't sure where that feeling came from. Out of what he could piece together of his old life, he was pretty sure he had been some sort of lab researcher. The specifics of that time were garbled though.

By the time morning arrived, Alexander had the entire engine and cowling disassembled and laid neatly on the hangar deck in the order it needed to go back on. At one point, he had stopped by his shop to print out a few of the smaller components that needed replacing. Other parts could have fit on his printer, but he didn't trust the cheap printer to do a proper job for the more important components.

At about mid-morning, the printer finally showed up. It took about an hour to assemble and test on the far side of the hangar. Although Alexander wasn't happy with just a simple test. If he was going to do this job, he was going to do it to the best of his ability.

He set about building the interrupter, only it was much larger than his previous design. It needed to fit the much bigger printer and produce a large enough interruption field.

It had been months since his early tests of the device that had broken his first printer. Alexander tweaked the design considerably since then. Assuming he did his calculations correctly, the new design should be much more efficient at canceling out the artificial gravity field. Although, he hadn't been able to test if that was true or not.

It might seem like a dangerous gamble to use an untested piece of technology on the very, very expensive printer, but the overall function of the interrupter device hadn't changed. He knew it at least worked.

As he added the adjustments, he was aware of a steady stream of *Zephyr* crew coming and going.

It was much the same as the day before. Some would stick around to watch for a bit before heading off to the station or into the ship. If this had been shortly after he first opened his shop, he may have found the attention unsettling. However, he didn't mind it so much anymore. The shift of attitude seemed to happen around the time Yulia started visiting him. Without the girl, he may have ended up as a cranky old hermit, like Yuri.

With the final piece of his modification in place, he checked the bolts to ensure the device was securely fastened to the floor. He would have preferred to weld it to the deck, but that wasn't his hangar so he couldn't modify anything. He could only use the existing mounting locations which were thankfully standard.

He made his way over to the control panel for the printer and powered it up. It beeped for a bit as it readied its material storage tanks. Once that was done the screen turned green and it flashed into the programming menu.

Alexander fed it a small component to start with. As it began to print, he ran into the same issue he had with the cheap printer, but he had already expected that to occur. He quickly adjusted the settings and started again. That time the printer hummed along happily as the component rapidly printed itself.

Once the print finished, the scanner quickly gave him a 3D view of the part's internals. He wished his smaller printer had that sort of quality control feature. It made ensuring the part was functional much easier than sticking it on a separate scanner.

As the parts were completed, he set them off to the side and input the next one to get printed. He worked through the rest of the parts before moving the newly printed components over to a testing station. He was glad the hangars came standard with the devices.

As he was running the diagnostic tests, an inconsistency popped up. There was a small variance in the efficiency output of his new components compared to the design specifications. Only 2% or so, but there shouldn't have been any.

He approached Jasper sometime around dinner to relay the issue. The captain and crew were lounging in a break area on the far side of the hangar. "Excuse me for interrupting. Can I have a moment of your time, Jasper?"

"What's up, Alexander?" the captain asked after they walked a distance from the crew.

"Would it be possible for me to remove and examine some components from the other engines?"

"Why?"

"I found a slight variance and I just want to ensure it isn't an error in the calibration tool."

"I don't see an issue with that. We aren't exactly in a hurry to leave. Our next delivery contract was retracted when we failed to show up on time anyway."

"I'm sorry to hear that."

Jasper waved away his concern. "Hardly your fault. This happened even before we docked at Petrov Station. Besides, the downtime is appreciated by the crew. Even if most of it is spent making sure the ship is in tip-top shape."

After the two separated, Alexander spent the night pulling apart the other two engines and testing the components. The testing device was correct. There was an even larger discrepancy with the old components, likely due to age or wear and tear. According to the device, his newly printed parts were better than the originals. That shouldn't be possible.

It had to be due to the low-gravity printing process because he hadn't changed anything else in the design. It was easy enough to test if he was right though. He disabled his modification and ran another set of prints. These new parts matched the manufacturer's specifications exactly.

He had to scratch his metaphorical head at this. Certainly, a company the size of Omni had access to zero-g printing. So how could they have missed such a simple way to improve their product line? It was a question he had no answer for and it wasn't relevant to his work.

However, he did have a solution to the efficiency differences, in his design, compared to the original he had accidentally stumbled upon though. He simply printed out three full sets of the replacement components using his method. Alexander could have simply installed the original manufacturer-designed components, but why would he do that when he could upgrade the engines for the very same time, money, or effort?

By the time the next morning rolled around, Alexander had the two undamaged engines mostly back in working order. The captain must have noticed all the parts lying around and came over to speak with him.

"Did we take more damage than I thought?" Jasper asked in concern.

"No. Remember that variance I told you about?"

The man nodded.

"Well, some of the components I pulled for testing were worn out slightly, so I decided to replace them to bring all the engines in line with the new parts specs."

"I appreciate the thought, Alexander, but that wasn't in our original deal. We could have adjusted the thrust output aboard the ship to compensate. How much of a variance did you find?"

"The cost was negligible; it just took a bit more material and time. As for the variance, it was a small amount. Around two percent."

The captain's eyes went wide. "Two percent? In thrust?!"

Alexander shook his avatar head. "Efficiency."

The man turned toward the modified printer and motioned. "And you did it with *that*?"

Alexander nodded.

"I know you told me you never worked on ship engines before, but if I was skeptical about that before, even with your quick and efficient work, I'm not anymore. Alexander, a two percent increase in efficiency is huge."

"It is?" Alexander asked in confusion. He knew it would make trying to balance the engines annoying, but other than that, he didn't see the big deal.

"Absolutely! If a new engine model comes out with a .25% increase in efficiency, the big shipping companies gobble them up. Do you know why?"

It wasn't hard to guess since Jasper had pointed it out.

"Fuel."

"Exactly. Using only a fraction less fuel per trip might not seem like much, but when you're burning thousands or even tens of thousands of credits in fuel for each shipment, those savings quickly add up. My God man, you need to register this improvement so you can sell it and so someone else doesn't steal it from you."

Alexander didn't think he had done anything all that special, but the captain seemed to think he had. "I will do as you suggest. Thank you, Jasper."

The man smiled broadly. "No, no. Thank you. With these improvements to the *Zephyr*, I believe I'm going to be outbidding a fair portion of my competition for the foreseeable future, and it's all thanks to you. I want you to have my personal comm ID. If you need anything. And I mean anything, you contact me. Got it?"

Alexander nodded his avatar.

Jasper went to walk away but paused. "Oh also, call me if you have any more improvements like this. I will happily test them out."

chapter 11

It had been about a week since the *Zephyr* arrived, but it was finally time to leave. The robot had just finished the last of the repairs and packed up his printer.

Wilkes walked up to stand next to the captain. He didn't have anything against the robot, or the person supposedly controlling it. He just didn't like things he couldn't understand.

"You sure about this captain, or should I start calling you Jasper now?" the pilot asked in jest.

The captain glanced over at him before turning back toward the retreating form of Alexander. "Last I checked, you're still on the payroll. So unless you want me to change that?"

"Got it, Captain," Wilkes smiled.

"I know you are suspicious by nature, but you didn't speak to him as much as I did." He nodded toward Alexander. "That man, that man is a genius. I had an inkling he was someone special when we visited his shop, but I had no idea. Did you see the printer modification he did?"

"Yeah. Any idea what that was?"

The captain shook his head and smiled. "Not a clue. Never seen anything quite like it. That's why I gave him my comm ID. That man is going to do great things one day and I want to be there when he does. I just hope he can weather what's to come."

"You mean from the mega-corporations?"

The captain nodded darkly. "If he is lucky, they won't realize he improved upon their designs. Although we can't rely on luck. He needs to register his work; it's the only thing that will keep him safe. Sooner or later, some corporate spy would hear of it and steal the design or worse. At least this way he has a chance of getting some money and still come out alive."

"Shouldn't you have warned him then?" Wilkes asked, a slight tone of annoyance slipping into his words.

The captain snorted. "You know as well as I that the corporations monitor the net with AI even though it's illegal to do so. I don't know where Alexander came from, but wherever it was, he was woefully ignorant of the galactic players. Despite that, he has an insatiable need to learn. A curious man like that would have tried to research the corporations if I told him what to expect. That would have triggered their detection systems and brought increased scrutiny down upon our new friend before he could secure his safety. The only way for him to grow is if he can avoid their gaze until he makes his improvements public. And to do that, he must remain ignorant for the time being.

"Alexander's invention may be groundbreaking to us, but to Omni, I doubt it will even register as a blip. Once it's registered as a patent, they won't risk breaking the law over it. They will simply sick their legal department on it and drown the man in legal trouble until he agrees to sell the discovery to them. It may not be a clean victory for our robotic friend, but it will be a victory."

"I don't like it," Wilkes stated.

"Neither do I, but some things can only be learned the hard way. I have faith that Alexander will see his way through this trouble and be better for it," the captain responded. "Now, let's get aboard, we have shipments that need to be made."

* * *

Fixing the engines on the *Zephyr* had been the highlight of Alexander's month. Unfortunately, work was rather slow after that. He wasn't sure why, but he didn't mind. It allowed him time to tinker and let his mind wander.

The one thing he did after the *Zephyr* left was take Captain Daniel's advice and register his design improvements. The man was right, he did deserve to make money on his inventions.

Some money started coming in not long after. It wasn't much, but every little bit helped. Logically, he knew humanity had built a faster-than-light communication method, but he had no idea how it worked. Everyone just called them comms, as if it was the most normal thing in the world. To them it probably was.

It was during one of Alexander's tinkering sessions that Yulia came around again. She had likely been missing him as he had been gone for over a week—lifetime to a child.

"Whatcha building?" she asked as she hopped onto the stool.

At her interruption, he brought his mind back to the present and looked down at the desk. What had he been building? Lately, if he started tinkering on a project and then let his mind wander, he usually came back to something unexpected. It wasn't something he had ever experienced while working for Yuri, probably because he didn't have access to a printer or time to let his mind wander. Probably a good thing since getting caught modifying Yuri's junk would have had all sorts of complications. Now he was free—well, almost free—to work on or tinker with whatever he liked.

"Um... nothing, just playing around," he stated as he removed the power supply and capacitor he had attached to the device during his stupor. He knew exactly what he had created but not why or how. In his attempts to further his knowledge of the last three hundred years, he had purchased articles and historical documentaries on human history. Go figure, a lot of small wars had occurred during that time. Not much seemed to have changed in retrospect.

The item on the table resembled a 22nd-century laser rifle. One of the very early designs fielded during an actual conflict that wasn't attached to a ship or vehicle. He had only ever seen the thing in a few war documentaries. While crude and bulky, it was more than capable of putting a hole in the station if held stable for a few seconds.

That was a problem. If he was caught with the weapon, they would toss him out of an airlock without a second question. Station law took owning contraband weapons very seriously.

Why was it always weapons that his unconscious body drifted to? First, a railgun and now the laser rifle. He didn't even like weapons. He never even looked at weapon schematics on the net, preferring to stay away from them altogether. Looking up items like that sounded like a good way to get put on a list. The railgun he somehow reproduced, was another handheld rifle he had seen in a video documentary.

After removing the firing components of the laser, he stored it inside his crowded storage closet. The printer, Captain Daniel aka Jasper, had gifted him for his work, was too large to be assembled in his shop as he had suspected it might be, so it was currently taking up most of the space in his storage.

Alexander reached past the large collection of printer parts and set the rifle frame next to a few other similar devices. He needed to melt them down as soon as possible, but he didn't have a recycler. He would have to use the public one to destroy the weapons, but he was sure bringing guns down there would have people asking all sorts of questions. He hadn't crushed them yet because he was trying to understand why he kept making them so he could stop doing it.

So far, he couldn't find any rhyme or reason for the dozen or so various weapons he had assembled. That meant, for now, the safest place for them was out of sight until he could dispose of them.

The only thing that he could figure out was that it had something to do with how he ended up in this body.

He realized he had forgotten about Yulia in his haste to store the weapon. When he exited the closet, he found he had two other visitors. The men looked rough and wore patched and worn armored space suits.

"Apologies," he said as he closed the closet door. "I did not hear you enter. What can I assist you with?" He looked around, but it seemed like Yulia had left when the men entered. He didn't blame her, these men gave off a similar vibe to the type of people Yuri had trafficked with, and that Alexander preferred to avoid.

"Do you repair weapons and armor?" The bearded man asked.

Alexander's gaze focused on the stunners the men carried. These were likely mercenaries. Although, for all he knew, they could be pirates masquerading as mercenaries. "I'm afraid I don't have any experience working with weapons, nor the certification. I can patch up, repair, and maybe even upgrade armor though." While Alexander had some money saved up thanks to the work with Captain Daniel, he didn't have enough to turn away work.

The man grunted and unclipped the detachable armor. The other man followed suit. "We'll be back in a few days to pick them up." They turned to leave, but Alexander stopped them.

"I do require partial payment up front." Which was complete bullshit, but he didn't like these guys.

The clean-faced guy reached into his suit pocket and tossed a credit chip on the desk. "That's half. Do what you can, but we aren't paying extra for anything fancy."

After they left, Alexander checked the chip's value. It was honestly more than he thought it would be but probably less than anyone else would ask for. He shrugged and took a look at the armor. It wasn't anything special. The plates were marked 'generic universal' on the backside of each. Which made Alexander's job easier.

He had run into a few items with markings similar to that. They were things that had belonged to defunct companies or had been given over to the public domain. There were so many copies that it was no longer profitable to manufacture them or they were so outdated as to not be worth selling.

That didn't mean the schematics were free though. Instead of the money going to a greedy corporation, it went to the STO. He walked to the nearest console and purchased the schematics.

The armor design was well over a hundred years old. Thanks to his experience and research, he knew of at least three materials that were both lighter and more durable than what currently made up the plates of these suits. He mulled over using the newer alloys versus the original for a few minutes.

In the end, it wasn't his dislike of the pair that swayed his decision, it was simply the cost. The newer alloys were far cheaper to produce and print. Of course, he picked the absolute cheapest of the three. No point splurging on these men.

He set about stripping and cleaning up the substrate as the printer worked on producing new plates. The hardened material took far longer to print than normal metal.

While he was working, Yulia poked her head back in. "Are they gone?"

"Yes. Why? Didn't like them?" he asked without stopping.

She shook her head, sending her messy hair flying. "Markus says you need to look at people's eyes. You can tell if they are good or bad by the eyes. Those men looked bad."

He couldn't fault her logic there—those were definitely bad men.

Her fear quickly faded away as she began to tell him about her day. He smiled internally as he listened to her while he continued his work.

chapter 12

Alexander tossed the six bent and twisted pieces of junk that had been weapons into the smelter. After almost having two customers accidentally stumble upon him making one of the restricted weapons, he determined that anything he could learn from keeping them around did not outweigh the risks of getting caught with them.

A few people did glance his way, but It was only passing interest in him, rather than what he was melting down.

After about twenty minutes, the machine spat out six different containers. Each would be its own 99.999% elementally pure material in nano-particle form. He really wished he knew how the smelter did it. All he could point to at that moment was future magic and hope one day he would have the funds necessary to buy the schematic and dive into the fundamental concept of the device.

That day was not today.

He retrieved his credit chip from the smelter and grabbed the containers. Two were far heavier than the others, but it was no surprise considering basic steel had gone into the majority of the makeup of the disassembled weapons. At least the material hadn't gone to waste since he could reuse the material in his printers.

The smelter process wasn't lossless though. It did have to melt the material in order to separate it. Anything that didn't melt simply burned away, turned into carbon, or came out as slag.

Overall it was still a very efficient process. However, he was sure it used an absurd amount of energy to do it.

* * *

At the edge of Gliese 667, three ships flashed into existence—a common occurrence as ships exited FTL.

Unlike any other ship seen in this distant piece of human-controlled space, the first ship was all smooth lines without any hint of sensor or array peeking past the gleaming white exterior. Painted in bold red letters on both sides of the ship was the word 'OMNI' the acronym for Orbital Motion Navigational Innovations: the premier engine manufacturer for all of human space.

The sleek white ship was not alone. The two other ships accompanying it were anything but sleek. They were composed of hard lines, protruding sensors, and arrays. Not an iota of thought had gone into making them look soft and approachable. These were warships. Each of these imposing vessels sported four Gauss turrets that protruded from the top and bottom of the deadly-looking craft. Despite the menace exuded by the gunships, they were just escort vessels for the white ship, but nothing short of an STO cruiser could stand up to the firepower of the corporate-owned Wraith Mk3 gunships.

After receiving the all-clear, the three ships fired up their main engines and hurtled toward their destination—an insignificant station in the ass end of nowhere, Petrov Station.

As the trio of ships burned hard through the system, they made no effort to hide their presence. They didn't need to. They were the big fish around there. Every other ship that picked them up on sensors quickly got the hell out of their way.

Eventually, someone at the station picked them up and hailed them. The captain of the white ship sent the canned response. The person on the other end grumbled but quickly gave them priority docking instructions.

* * *

Ivan Wang paced nervously outside the VIP hangar. It was in times like that he cursed his mixed heritage. It seemed he got the worst attributes of both his parents and none of the upsides.

In all his years aboard Petrov Station, he had never greeted a single soul from the VIP hangar. It was reserved for visiting heads of state per STO rules on station management so it had sat empty and unused ever since he could remember. He wanted to spit on the floor at the Sol Treaty Organization's asinine rules, but he couldn't afford to dirty his suit or the corridor. As if anyone like that would ever visit this dump.

While the ship docking wasn't technically in their category, it wasn't someone they could say no to. The two gunboats that accompanied the corporate yacht were more than enough to send everyone aboard the station to an early grave. He doubted anyone from the STO would even bat an eye if they did that.

So, like a good little commissar, he waited for his guests to arrive.

Unlike most docks, the VIP dock had dual-layered armored doors, so there was no peeking inside to see the ship. Although he had gotten an external camera feed of it—not that the outdated cameras did the sleek craft justice. If he had to guess, that single ship was worth more than the entire station and everything aboard it. The two gunboats combined probably weren't far behind in value.

He felt the slight vibration in the deck when the craft finally touched down.

Ivan did his best to slow his breathing as he pulled out a rag and wiped the sweat from his hands and brow. This would likely be the most important moment of his life, and he couldn't afford to screw it up.

As soon as he heard the first clunks of the locking bolts from the first door, he stuffed the rag in his pocket and stood straight, forcing a smile on his face.

A voice boomed out of a nearby speaker, almost making him leap off the deck. "Stand back and place your hands in the air! You will be searched before we proceed."

He did as requested, and soon the outer door opened. Two men immediately flicked weapons up towards him and, if Ivan had been still before, he was a statue then. Not just out of fear for the weapons but what they could do if they missed him. These were not the simple riot control pulse rifles, these were slug throwers.

Ivan didn't know much about weapons. For all he knew, these could be handheld Gauss rifles.

A third armed and armored man approached and patted him down before roughly spinning him around and doing the same for his backside. He was none too gentle about it either.

He swallowed his pride as the man yelled, "Clear!"

As the guards lowered their guns, Ivan slowly lowered his hands. He finally got a good look at the armored forms. He had first mistaken what they were wearing for skin suits, but those were not the thin fabric underlayer worn under a decompression suit. They were form-fitted with integrated plates of some unknown material around the chest, hips, and thighs.

"I apologize for my men's rough handling. They can be a bit overzealous when it comes to protecting OMNI assets such as myself." The voice came from a young, well-dressed man.

If Ivan thought the suits of the guards were impressive, this man's practically looked like normal clothes. If it wasn't for the full helmet, he wouldn't have given it a second glance.

"It's fine," Ivan responded, managing not to stammer. "No harm no foul," he added, extending his hand. "I am Ivan Wang, Commissar of

Relations aboard Petrov Station and I will be your attendant while you are here."

"Charmed, Ivan," the man responded in a silky tone as he grabbed Ivan's hand with only a thumb and pointer and shook it gently for only a moment. "You can refer to me as Mr. Pembrooke or Theodore," he said with a wink and a smile.

Ivan smiled back, trying his best to hide the awkwardness of the greeting. "Your request to dock did not inform us of the reason for your visit. May I know your agenda so I can help assist you?"

"That you may, Ivan. As you may have already guessed, I work for OMNI. Specifically, I work for the Legal Council of OMNI."

It was hard to keep the smile on his face as it felt like a rock dropped into his stomach. "The Omni's legal council. Um... What brings you all the way out here?" It couldn't be anything good, that was for sure.

That smile, that oh-so-fake smile never left Theodore's perfectly sculpted face. "I'm glad you asked. You see, we got a report that someone on this station may be stealing our intellectual property rights." He leaned in conspiratorially and spoke softly. "And OMNI takes those rights very seriously."

"Um..." Ivan was at a loss as to what to do next. Mr. Pembrooke seemed to know this and saved him.

"I just need to speak with the Station Manager and get this all straightened up. Then we will be out of your hair."

"Oh... Um, we don't have a Station Manager." For a moment, Ivan thought he saw the man's smile shift slightly, but it could have just been his imagination.

"Really? Then who manages the station?"

"That would be the Captain's Council."

"I see... This station is pre-STO then?"

Ivan nodded.

"Very well, take me to see them."

"That... That may take a few days to arrange. The captains are rarely aboard the station at the same time."

While the well-dressed man's demeanor didn't change, Ivan suddenly felt like he was a bug being stared at by a higher life form. He swallowed thickly.

"Very well, I have time, Ivan. I will remain aboard my ship until they arrive. Please come see one of my guards when the captains are ready to meet. Do let them know that this is an important matter. And if they could hurry, that would mitigate any extenuating issues that might arise if this issue isn't settled expediently."

Before Ivan could ask what the man meant by that, he turned and strode back into his hangar. The guard that searched him took up a position outside the first door, while the others remained by the second.

Ivan tried to smile at the guard at the door, but the man just returned a blank stony gaze as his eyes watched him like a predator.

Without waiting to be told, Ivan hurried out of there to report to the other commissars and gather the captains. He really hoped the captains arrived promptly. If not, he wasn't sure Mr. Pembrooke's thin veil of civility would hold.

The elevator whisked him over to the control center in the central shaft. It was always a bit of a jarring experience for Ivan as it exited the artificial gravity of the rings, only to reenter the core's artificial gravity shortly after. The issue was that the fields of gravity were not aligned the same. Since the core was built long before artificial gravity had been discovered, they couldn't simply retrofit it like it had been in the rings. There were too many systems in place to work around, so they simply placed the grav plates on the exterior walls and called it good.

It worked, sort of, as long as you didn't mind feeling like getting tugged at constantly.

As the gravity dropped away, he reoriented himself ninety degrees so his head was facing the far side door.

Moments later, the gravity tugged at him, but before he could float upwards very far, the elevator had passed inside the field. He grunted as he dropped to the door facing the rings.

That was why he hated coming to the core. He had never quite gotten the hang of or timing of moving about in zero-g. How his ancestors ever got anything done in space before the advent of artificial gravity was beyond him.

When the elevator came to a stop, the door, which was now the ceiling, clicked open. He sighed. This was the other part he hated. Ivan walked over to the rungs that were situated along both walls and ceiling and climbed out of the elevator.

More than a few technicians manning the terminals that controlled all aspects of station life, glanced at him as he climbed out, but none so much as offered to help.

"Bastards," he muttered under his breath. He was going to submit another proposal to modify that blasted elevator so he wasn't forced to climb out every time he needed to come here.

After wiping the visible sweat from his brow, he slowly made his way over to the communication center. Running through the weird gravity in the core was a good way to trip, or more embarrassingly, lose your lunch.

A bright-eyed younger woman looked up from her station and smiled politely at him. "Commissar Wang, how may I help you today?"

"Our VIP guest is here on a corporate witch hunt. He has requested to speak with the captains." Ivan wasn't stupid. He knew the only reason a monolithic company like Omni would send one of their lackeys out here was to make a point. He felt sorry for whoever it was that got on their bad side, but he wasn't about to step in shit for someone else.

The communication woman frowned slightly. "They aren't going to like having their runs cut short."

"Tell them to complain to the Omni representative then." Unlike Mr. Pembrooke, who came from the core worlds, Ivan wasn't afraid of the captains who were the descendants of the original families who first built Petrov Station.

They got to galivant around the system, earning money and doing whatever they pleased while the commissars kept the station running. The least they could do was their damn job once in a while.

chapter 13

Mingyu stomped down the ramp of his ship, steam still billowing off the cooling thrusters. He was annoyed. More than annoyed, he was angry.

His ship, the *Moonlit Destiny*, had planned for a six-month deployment in Gliese 667's outer belt to look for and extract precious metals. Less than three weeks into the trip, he received a communication to return. For nothing other than some pompous core worlder there to throw his weight around.

The Destiny's sensor officer had picked up the ships when they burned for the station. They hadn't been subtle about their approach, but he wasn't on duty, and pirates wouldn't have been so brazen, so he ignored them.

Mingyu wasn't blind. He had seen the two gunships sitting menacingly off the station as his ship docked, their turrets on full display. It didn't impress him. He had been a second lieutenant in the Coalition Navy and had served aboard the flagship Ivanov. While it hurt him to admit, not comparable to the STO's flagships, the Ivanov would have been more than a match for these peashooters the Omni rep had brought as a warning.

It wasn't that Petrov Station couldn't defend itself, but the Omni ships could learn a thing or two from Petrov about keeping their weapons hidden until needed.

Now if they could just teach the commissars to wipe their own asses without a captain around, maybe he wouldn't have been required to sit in on a full Council meeting. Did the commissars think that the station just ran on goodwill and wishes? It took dedication, effort, and a whole lot of credit from the founding families to keep the station independent.

He took the elevator to the core, easily adjusting to the change in gravity. Honestly, he wasn't sure how people could stand living in the fake gravity. He much preferred being out in space or simply aboard his ship with the gravity disabled. There was something comforting about just floating.

As the elevator came to a stop and the doors opened, he smirked a bit as he clambered up the rungs easily. He had lost track of how many proposals to redesign the elevator he had blocked over the years. The people at the station were too soft. They might as well live in a gravity well for all they understood about actual space. Which was why he made sure to keep this one small reminder for the people who operated the station.

That little memory brought a smirk to his face and lifted his spirits slightly, but it didn't fully banish his foul mood as he crossed the command center and made his way toward the meeting room. Technically he was an hour late, but Mingyu would be damned if he was wasting extra fuel just to push his arrival up. He was already losing enough money just having to return ahead of schedule.

The door swished open at his approach, and he was hit with a wall of discussion from his fellow captains.

* * *

"Na! 'Bout time you show up. You think we just have time to wait around for you all day?"

"Isn't that your normal tendency Xu!" Mingyu said with a smile before clasping the other man's hand. Mingyu and Xu Yuchen had been friends since they could walk.

"Glad you arrived safely," Ingrid Liu stated with a slight nod.

Mingyu nodded back, even though he despised the shrewd woman. He wasn't about to air his grievances here where it paid to be civil.

"I think we can all agree this is a colossal waste of our time," Sergei Zhang added as he lounged against one wall with his feet up on the table.

Anastasia slapped his feet off the piece of furniture and glared at the large man. "If you truly thought it was a waste of time, you wouldn't have returned so early. So quit trying to sound tough." The man had the decency to look chastised by Mrs. Weiss' words.

Unlike the five boisterous younger captains on the council, the two older ones remained quiet. Denis Kovalenko was in his sixties but had only started a family a decade ago. His daughter was only nine.

Oleg Hoffman was a bit younger, having just turned fifty, but he had also started a family later in his life. His son and daughter were twelve and thirteen respectively.

The nine families were all that remained of the original founding twenty. Some like the Liu's had combined to strengthen their families, but that didn't grant them additional seats on the Council. Most did it to preserve their diminishing lineages and keep the station running. Some did it to consolidate power—which was laughable out there in the ass-end of human-occupied space.

However, Mingyu couldn't throw stones. His ancestors had done the same, merging the Xinwei line with the Na.

"If pleasantries are over with, we do have important matters to discuss," Denis cut through the chatter.

The room quieted as everyone turned to the captain. As the oldest member of the council, his words did carry a bit more weight. The man was also semi-retired and spent most of his time aboard the station, which meant he was usually the first to find out about issues such as this.

"You are all aware of our unfortunate *guest*?"

Mutters and words of acknowledgment passed through the others in the room.

"Good. Unfortunately, I was not made aware of their arrival in the system until after they had met with the commissar."

Sergei shot to his feet, pounding his hands on the table. "What blithering idiot failed to follow the standard procedure to notify the captain on duty first and foremost?"

"While I appreciate your concern for procedures, Sergei, please sit down and control yourself. You are a captain—you must act like one at all times."

The younger man flushed slightly before dropping back into his seat.

Mingyu wanted to roll his eyes at the man's antics and the older man's reprimand, but he knew better than to annoy his fellow captains.

"The commissar responsible for this breach will receive a reprimand in his official log. But it will include the caveat that we have never had to host a VIP, so he was likely not aware of official policy on how to act."

There were a few grumbles at that, but Mingyu approved.

"Then again," Captain Kovalenko continued, "should we treat this group as a VIP? By STO's own laws, they do not qualify for this."

"Are you calling for a vote on this?" Oleg asked.

Denis paused to think for a moment before responding. "Yes. Does anyone second this vote?"

"I do!" Sergei responded.

"Very well. All in favor of stripping the Omni representative of VIP status, raise your hands."

Only three hands went up. One was Sergei's, no real surprise there, but Mingyu was surprised to see his friend Xu's hand up as well as Ingrid's. Perhaps even more of a surprise was not seeing Denis' hand raised for a vote he called for.

"If you weren't even going to vote for it, why even bring it up?" Sergei crossed his arms after the vote failed.

"Just because I believe they don't deserve VIP treatment doesn't mean I believe it should be taken away. We have a delicate situation on our hands, despite some of our members reaching out to personal contacts in the STO." The eldest captain looked straight at Mingyu as he said that last part.

Mingyu just shrugged. He wouldn't apologize for calling in a favor.

"So that's it, then?" Xu spat in annoyance. "We treat them with kid gloves and find out exactly what they are after."

"I'm afraid so," Denis responded before checking his watch. "I have notified the commissar to bring our guests by around noon. Because of Captain Na's late arrival, I'm afraid we don't have much time to discuss other matters. I would just like to remind you all to remain professional during the discussion. We cannot give these core worlders an inch—"

"Or they will take a mile," the rest of the room finished in unison. It was a tired saying that meant less and less each year. The core world mega corporations took what they wanted when they wanted. Very little could stop them. The best they could hope to do was mitigate the damage.

* * *

A few minutes later the door opened and a man wearing a vacsuit, which probably cost more than most made in a year, entered.

"Greetings esteemed captains. I am Theodore Pembrooke, head legal counsel for Orbital Motion Navigational Innovations. I—"

"We know who you are," Sergei cut the man off, earning a reproachful glare from Denis and Oleg. "Get to the point."

The suited man's smile never wavered. "Very well, I can appreciate cutting to the chase. Omni is here investigating an instance of intellectual theft. We would appreciate it if you turned this culprit over to us along with any assets he has stolen or modified against our standard use policy. The person we are investigating is one Alexander Kane."

Mingyu and the other captains conferred quietly amongst themselves, forcing the man to wait standing at the lectern across the room. This wasn't strictly necessary as they had already been informed about why this individual was here. The hushed conversation instead consisted of remarks about the questionable parentage of this man as well as his fear of being aboard station without his suit. Mingyu had a hard time not smiling or laughing during the quiet talks.

After making the man wait what seemed an appropriate amount of time, the Council turned back toward him.

Denis, as the speaker, was the one to respond. "No."

They all watched as the face behind the clear face shield blinked in confusion. "I'm sorry. I don't understand."

"Has education in the core systems degraded to the point that you do not understand the meaning of a very basic word?" Anastasia Weiss replied dryly.

The man's face tightened before he responded. "I understand what *no* means, Mrs. Weiss. What I don't understand is why that is your response to our simple request."

It was Mingyu's turn to speak. "It's good to know the core systems are keeping up with their education. As to why we declined your request, that's simple. It is against our laws. I would have thought someone in your role would have known that before coming here."

At the rebuke, Mr. Pembrooke's face tightened even more. "Now you listen here. I have come here in good faith."

Sergei cut the man off with a barking laugh. "Good faith he spouts. What a load. Are those gunships out there your good faith?"

"Those are merely my escort," the man bristled.

Mingyu stifled a smile. It had been done on purpose to rile the man up and get him to state on record that the ships were simply for self-defense. Now if he tried to use the gunboats as leverage to get his way, it could be deemed as piracy.

"I believe we have gotten off track," Oleg said, playing his role as the voice of reason.

"Thank you, Captain. Now if we could discuss my original question."

"That answer hasn't changed," Oleg stated firmly. "What you are asking for is against Petrov Station law."

"Are you refusing our request?"

Denis leaned forward. "Watch your tone, Mr. Pembrooke. You may have VIP rights, but those can and will be revoked if necessary." The man shut his mouth and Captain Kovalenko continued. "And when did we stipulate we were refusing your request? You simply need to go through the proper legal proceedings."

"And what would those be?" the irate man managed to say between clenched teeth.

"Arbitration," Ingrid Liu responded casually.

"That's ridiculous," Pembrooke spluttered. "You can't be serious."

"The accusation you are making against someone aboard this station of is a serious offense," Oleg reminded the Omni representative.

"That could take months. I'm not even familiar with your station's laws."

"Clearly," Xu added dismissively.

Before the man could complain further, Denis cut him off. "I suggest you either hire some station counsel or start brushing up on our laws. All in favor of dismissing this meeting."

All seven hands went up. Denis nodded and turned back to the Omni representative. "You have four months to prepare your case, Mr. Pembrooke."

The door opened behind the man, and he stormed out.

Once it shut, the room fell into silence for a bit.

It was Anastasia who first broke the quiet. "Anyone familiar with this Alexander Kane?"

There was a collective round of shrugs or shaken heads.

"The name sounds English," Mingyu remarked. "Don't get many of those out here."

"Would you like to take on the task of finding out who this is?" Denis asked.

"I'll look into it," Mingyu nodded. Not that he wanted to do it, although he was curious as to what sort of person drew the interest of Omni.

chapter 14

Theodore Pembrooke smiled when the ramp to his ship finally closed. There were two reasons for his happy mood.

The first was he could finally remove the ridiculous helmet and vac suit. Despite the tailored fit, it was still annoying to move around in, and it had served its purpose anyway. Now the captains would think of him as some scared planetsider. A bit of simple misdirection to throw them off and get them to underestimate him. Theo was born and raised aboard a starship. He didn't even set foot on a planetary body until he was seventeen.

The second reason he was smiling, a real smile and not the fake one he used to sell his persona, was this assignment would likely be over in as little as four months. He had planned to be out here for a year. Even with the travel time back and forth, he was going to be back home in less than six months.

It was always nice when things went according to plan. A little bit of acting, throw in some faux annoyance, and voilà. They agreed to arbitration instead of demanding he leave.

People outside of OMNI thought the name granted him weight, but more often than not, it simply annoyed those in charge. That didn't mean it was all for show. Had they demanded he leave, it would have gotten ugly—just not the way the captains might expect.

The gunships were simply another set piece. They didn't even have working turrets because they had been requisitioned before completion, not that you could tell by looking at them. Theo wasn't a fool. He had grifted in the outer fringes with his family for years. Places like Petrov Station weren't nearly as benign as they let on. The scans may not have picked up on the hidden weapons mounted to the massive structure, but he knew they were there, hiding and waiting in case of an attack.

But he didn't need to go down that route.

Some might feel like acting this way was beneath them. Theo just scoffed at that. This was hardly the lowest he had stooped to ensure a successful mission.

He was many things for OMNI, but he much preferred the legitimate side of his personas. It was always better to secure new discoveries than it was to destroy them—not that he wouldn't if he had to. It just got much messier in those cases.

If he could, he would thank Alexander Kane for his foresight to register his work. Doing that took most of his boss' preferred methods of acquiring improvements to their designs off the table.

Theo had looked this man up. He was a literal ghost with only this one invention to his name and a weak trail that anyone with half a brain could see was fake. That only intrigued him more though. There were very few geniuses running around in hiding because they knew they could simply join one of the corporations and make money hand over fist.

Despite everything else going on with this arbitration, Theo knew that Alexander Kane was a genius. While the engine he had submitted the design improvement for wasn't their flagship model, it was one of the workhorse designs that they sold a ton of. A two percent increase in efficiency on an engine that was designed and built by Omni's top engineers, along with input from AI, was nothing to sneeze at.

When he had been handed that assignment, Theo floated the topic of offering the man a position within the company.

The board shot down that request, citing Kane's unknown qualifications and sketchy history. That almost made Theo laugh. Having a sketchy history was fine for someone like him but not for regular employees.

As he was rinsing off, there was a quiet knock on his cabin door. "Come in," he said, donning his persona again.

"Mr. Pembrooke," the crewman stated as he stood in the doorway. "We have received a hail."

Theo quirked an eyebrow. "From who?"

"The STO Destroyer, Terra Bound, Sir."

Theo let a frown show on his face. He had expected something but not so soon. It just proved he had chosen the correct approach here. Someone on this station had powerful connections. Perhaps multiple people.

"Did they hail us directly?"

"Um... No, Sir. They hailed both Omni Huginn and Omni Muninn. The captains of those ships passed on the message."

He really wanted to sigh. Couldn't the young man just spit it out without him having to ask? "And what was that message?"

"That they will be doing a fleet exercise in the system for the next four months, and that both ships should lockdown and keep their weapons systems offline. Any actions otherwise could be seen as hostile intent."

That time, he did let out a sigh. "Very well," he answered, adding a tinge of annoyance to his words. "Tell them to follow the Navy's orders. Better yet, have them dock. It seems we will be here for some time."

The crewman nodded before turning and leaving.

Theo corrected his assessment: they had very powerful connections. It wasn't just anyone that could get a task group of STO ships reassigned for training maneuvers.

Once the door was shut, Theo lay on his bed and pulled up the station laws. He knew most of them already, but it never hurt to brush up. It wasn't like anyone aboard the station was likely to work with an OMNI representative.

He hummed contentedly as he scrolled through the legal red tape. Meanwhile, another man was looking into Alexander.

* * *

Mingyu perused the displayed information as he sat in a comfortable chair in his cabin aboard Destiny. They were making their way back to the belt to mine as much as they could before he was forced to return for the arbitration. There was no way he was wasting the next four months staying docked in the station.

As he perused the data dump of this Alexander Kane, he began to see inconsistencies. They weren't things most people would notice, but Mingyu had been no stranger to dealing with less-than-savory individuals over the years. It tended to happen when the station was the last stop for humanity.

There was an unspoken agreement between the criminals and Petrov Station. They kept their illicit activities outside Gliese 667, and when they came to the station, they were allowed to buy and sell instead of getting tossed out of an airlock. It was a very one-sided agreement, but it worked.

He would have preferred not to deal with their kind at all, but Petrov Station didn't have the luxury to turn any business away.

Kane's documents were forged. He would bet an asteroid stake on it. While there was nothing that screamed fake to a passing observer, Mingyu could see it. There was a clinical quality about the man's record. Not so much as a ticket or infraction on any database. Until this issue with Omni, there wasn't even a single complaint filed against the man.

No... that wasn't quite true. A few months ago, there was a complaint filed by a man by the name of Maxim on the second ring. The complaint never mentioned a last name, but it did state that Alexander's Repair Shop had defrauded him and stolen his customers. A quick look into the complaint and resolution told Mingyu all he needed to know. Maxim was a shady piece of shit that had a laundry list of complaints, foreclosures, and other charges leveled against him.

Mingyu made a note to have station security arrest the man. Not for anything he did on the station, although that did leave a bad taste in his mouth. No, the man was wanted for murder in another system. Turning him over to face charges would likely net Mingyu a favor. The man's crimes would have probably gone unnoticed if he hadn't dug deep into all of Alexander's known connections.

That was another red flag. Kane had no known connections until a little over six months ago. That started with the sale of a robot from the late Yuri Sokolov. All the captains knew of that ornery old goat. He had been here since before they were all born. If someone needed a part, he was the man they went to.

The official statement was that the Livera was lost with all hands on deck, but Pirates didn't destroy ships unless they had a damn good reason to. It was bad for business and caused their next targets to either fight back or flee instead of surrendering.

The fact that Yuri was aboard that ship couldn't have been a coincidence. He made another note to investigate that case deeper. If a pirate that frequented Petrov had done the deed, they were going to experience a cold walk. The pirate families were getting entirely too bold lately and they needed a reminder not to screw with Petrov's interests.

He flicked his finger, turning to the next page of the report. It claimed Kane was in some sort of medical pod for an incurable auto-immune disorder. However, it failed to list where that pod was stored. That was the biggest load of bio-waste Mingyu had ever read. The man might be in some medical pod, but there were plenty of treatments for all sorts of auto-immune disorders. Not cheap, certainly, but they were there. No, if he had to guess, it was a cover to keep out of sight.

That meant his face was recognizable. Maybe an escaped engineer from the Haven? The pirates didn't like their slaves getting free and losing one as valuable as Alexander would be a huge blow.

That could also explain Yuri's death. It was clear the man had some connection to Alexander. Maybe he even facilitated the fake identity and the use of the robot as a way for the man to keep out of sight.

He leaned back in his chair and crossed his leg over his other. "Just who are you, Alexander Kane? And more importantly, are you an asset or a detriment to the station?"

Mingyu needed to know more. He needed someone he trusted to take a measure of this man.

After thinking it over, he pulled up his comm and scrolled through his contacts before stopping on one. It didn't take long to connect.

"Mingyu, dear, how are you?" Eva Wu's voice was transmitted through the device. "I haven't heard from you in some time. How's the Destiny treating you?"

He chuckled lightly at the older woman's questions.

She had been his father's first mate until the man retired and turned over the ship to him. She retired not long after.

"It's good, Eva. Are you busy?"

She laughed. "Hun, I'm retired. I have nothing but time. You need something from this old woman, just ask instead of beating around the engine bay."

"Fair enough." He smiled. "I was wondering if you could talk to someone for me?"

"Oh? A new crew member for the Destiny?"

"Not exactly."

He told Eva some of what was going on.

"Hmm... So you just want to see if he's a good man. You know I've never been one for subterfuge."

"I know, Eva. And I don't expect you to be. Just take something broken down for him to fix and have a friendly chat with him. Then tell me what you think."

"Alright, dear. I will do this for you, but I expect you and your lovely wife to come visit me when you return."

"How did you know I was off station?"

"I may be old, dear, but I can still hear just fine. And I hear the hum of the Destiny in your comm. Although you may want to get that rattle in the air system fixed."

He looked up at the vent. There had been an intermittent rattle in it recently. How she had heard that over the comm was anyone's guess. "I'm putting it on the repair request as we speak. Thanks, Eva."

chapter 15

After finishing a recent repair job, Alexander decided to take a break and head down to the terminal to order some supplies as a few of his printer materials were running low. Maybe he would check his merchant account to see how much money his patent had earned him.

When he checked his account, he was surprised to see a message waiting for him.

Hello Mr. Kane,

You don't know me, but a mutual captain friend told me of your improvements. I was skeptical until I checked out your work myself and I must say, impressive.

Before I gush too much, let me introduce myself. My name is Dr. Nova Lund. I run a research institute out past the rim. We study all sorts of theoretical science, but our focus is primarily on improving the speed of travel between stars.

I know there are the hypergates, and humanity has the Alcubierre drive, although you may just know it as the warp or bubble drive. The first is hardly understood and the second is centuries old. Each has its limitations.

We want to break those limitations! This is why we would like to offer you a position within our group. I know this may seem sudden, and it is, but your talents would fit our organization perfectly. We have a lot of theories, but we need someone capable of turning those theories into reality. I think you're just the person to make that happen.

Even if this offer doesn't interest you, here is my personal comm number. If you ever wish to chat about science or other matters, please reach out to me. Those of us who still wish to push the boundaries of science grow fewer every year. We must stick together!

Thank you for your time,

Dr. Nova Lund

Alexander would have done a slow blink if he had eyes.

Lund certainly was right—this offer was kind of out of nowhere. While it was interesting, he didn't know who this person was, let alone if he could trust them. From the letter, he had a pretty good guess as to who this mutual friend was. The only people that knew of his work were Captain Daniel, his crew, and the few people who had purchased his design improvements.

Also… *what the hell was a hypergate?*

As he perused the net for information about these gates, he thought more about the doctor's letter. Of course, Alexander knew of faster-than-light capabilities. An interstellar empire wasn't built without the ability to travel faster than light, and he had worked on or near enough ships to see they weren't doing that with their thrusters. He just hadn't known the specifics of how they accomplished this feat. Like the grav-plating, technical manuals for advanced tech like that were way out of his price range.

Although now that he knew, maybe he shouldn't be surprised. He had memories of this Alcubierre drive, and that it was theoretically possible from back when he was human, just not any specifics on the research about it. Usually, the only thing keeping something from going from theoretical to practical was a technological breakthrough of some sort. It was good to know humanity had figured that out. His fragmented memories of Earth didn't paint a very bright picture of humanity's chances of survival from back then.

The hypergate information was likely locked behind a similarly expensive paywall. Except he hadn't even known to look for information on the technology. Most of the information he had purchased focused on recent human history, which is why he had missed this important footnote.

Hypergates were not available in those archives because humanity hadn't built them. Aliens being real was another revelation, but he didn't have the credits to go diving into that subject.

As he perused the available documents on hypergates, he realized humanity had stumbled across the structures only forty years after first leaving the Sol system. There were multitudes of research papers written about the objects. However, there were no technical documents for purchase. At first, he thought they might be top secret or something, but why leave the research papers for anyone to purchase?

He purchased a few of these papers and studied them. Funnily enough, one paper was from Dr. Lund. Unfortunately, even the doctor could only speculate on who made them and how they worked. Some seemed to think the Shican, a race of feline-like aliens, had built them. However, the other papers rejected this notion because the technology didn't match anything the Shicans possessed.

So not only were aliens real, but humanity had encountered at least one species. Alexander really wished he had unlimited credits and time so he could scratch that itch to know more. But he didn't, so he quickly moved on.

The leading theory on the hypergates seemed to be that they somehow either folded space or created a wormhole between two points. Nobody was quite sure, and the governments that had taken residence in those systems with hypergates, which acted like major hubs for humanity, had strictly forbidden anyone from doing anything that might damage or disable the unknown technology.

It made sense to Alexander. If he controlled a major trade hub, he would want to protect that at all costs. The fact that nobody knew how to make or fix the hypergates meant they would lose everything if they stopped working.

Thankfully, he didn't control an entire system, so his opinion was quite different. Alexander certainly wouldn't trust some unknown technology, at least until he knew how to repair it if it broke. Probably not even then until he could recreate it from scratch.

Another fact that seemed to get glossed over by most of the papers, except for Lund's, was the fact that the three gates just so happened to be placed in human habitable systems. They were all within fifteen light years from Earth, yet Sol didn't have a gate.

According to Lund, that clearly showed a preference from whoever built them to avoid humanity even though they were likely very similar to humans. The aliens that built the gates probably wouldn't be too thrilled if they found out humanity had co-opted them for their own use. That was assuming they were still around. There was no evidence to suggest they were.

It was something way above Alexander's pay grade. He was more interested in the technology behind the hypergates, but nobody had ever risked taking a gate apart for study so there wasn't anything to learn.

He sighed. Considering the comments in the research paper, this was probably why Lund was so hell-bent on finding alternatives.

Although even if humanity lost access to these gates, they wouldn't lose much. Travel would certainly be slower to key systems, but it was on the order of months instead of days. It wasn't like it would cause the STO to come crumbling apart. Some systems may struggle if they aren't self-sufficient, but any system with a habitable planet that couldn't sustain itself was probably doomed anyway.

A shift like that may even see humanity enter the next technological revolution. Necessity was the mother of invention and all that.

While it was interesting to postulate the possibilities, Alexander needed to get back to work. He quickly placed his order and headed back to his shop but not before sending a quick response to Dr. Nova Lund.

> *Thank you for the kind offer, Dr. Lund, but my current situation requires that I remain where I am. However, I would like to take you up on your offer to discuss further scientific theory if you are amenable.*
>
> *Alexander*

When Alexander returned to his shop, he found a rather bashful Yulia talking with an older lady holding what looked like a toaster.

Well, I didn't specify what I would fix.

"Greetings, I hope I didn't make you wait too long."

The woman turned to him and gave him a motherly smile. "Nonsense, dear. I was just having a nice chat with this lovely young lady here."

Alexander held out his hand, and the woman took it without hesitation. "I'm Alexander. And if she forgot to introduce herself, that is Yulia."

"Yulia? What a lovely name." She winked at the girl, making Yulia smile and blush while turning away. "You can call me Eva. I was told you fix things?"

"That I do," he said, opening his door and gesturing for them to come inside.

"OH!" Eva said in surprise as Yulia raced past her to get to her stool.

Alexander chuckled, making his avatar do the same. "Don't mind her. She likes to watch me work as well as study."

"And her parents don't mind?" the older woman whispered. Not that Yulia would have heard her. She was already fixated on the mechanical puzzle Alexander had built for her that day.

"She's a ward of the station," Alexander replied sadly.

"Aw, poor child. If I was a decade younger, I might consider adopting, but I'm lucky if I have a few years left in these old bones," she stated simply.

Alexander wasn't going to challenge her assessment, but she hadn't felt weak when they shook. Her grip was firm and calloused. It reminded him more of the workers who brought him items to fix rather than an old granny.

"So, what have you brought me today?"

The woman turned to him and held out the item with a smile that seemed to drive away any melancholy. He had to check his memories for a moment to make sure magic wasn't a thing.

Nope, sure wasn't.

"Toaster elements up and died on me."

His first guess was accurate; it was a toaster. He wouldn't make any money from it, but he would fix it all the same.

As he worked to disassemble the device, the woman chatted with him. He didn't mind. He had grown fond of chatting with Yulia so more people to talk to was infinitely better. That being said, the woman sounded a bit lonely.

She kept trying to get him to come over to dinner. He politely refused, not wanting to bring up his cover story.

She switched to talking about her time as a first mate aboard a ship. Then she asked him about himself.

Although Alexander didn't mind, it got a bit uncomfortable since he didn't have much to talk about. He gave her vague answers until finally telling her that he was essentially trapped in a box that kept him alive. Technically true.

The woman didn't even bat an eye at that, although she did give him a pat on the arm in sympathy.

Alexander told her how he met Yulia. The woman laughed lightly at that. "Children can get up to all sorts of things. Why, I practically raised the captain's son. I swear if there was something that boy could break, he would find it."

"That's cause boys are doo-doo heads," Yulia chimed in happily. She had just finished her puzzle and the little mechanical frog was hopping about the desk.

Eva laughed. "I won't argue with you on that, child."

A few minutes later, Alexander finished reassembling the toaster. "All done," he said, pushing the device across the counter.

"Thank you, dear. How much do I owe ya?"

"It's on the house, Eva. Call it thanks for the wonderful stories."

She shook her head. "That wouldn't be right. Work deserves pay." She pulled out a credit chip and set it on the table.

Alexander went to hand it back to her, but she gave him a disapproving frown that made him feel like some misbehaving child.

"I won't take no for an answer."

"Um... Thank you, Eva."

Her frown turned back into a smile. "You are welcome, Alexander. And it was wonderful meeting you. You as well, Yulia."

The girl turned bashful again.

The woman gave one last wave before walking out with her repaired toaster.

After Eva left, he turned to Yulia. "How come you were acting so withdrawn?"

She shrugged. "Dunno."

He sighed internally but left it at that.

chapter 16

"So, what did you think of him?" Mingyu asked as they walked through the garden district that ran along the shopping center of the eighth ring. It was one of his rare visits to the station, and he intended to enjoy it. It had been about three weeks since he had asked Eva to check up on Mr. Kane.

"He seems like a genuinely nice fellow." She responded, but Mingyu had known her long enough to know that she had more to say.

"But..."

"But he's obviously hiding something or hiding from someone. You already guessed as much though, didn't you?"

He nodded. "His story has holes and reeks of being fabricated."

"What do you intend to do about it?" she asked, concern evident in her tone

That made him pause. "You like him, don't you?"

It was shocking. Eva was a generous woman, but she had a very discerning eye when it came to people. Being able to pick out the best crew was a talent people would kill for, and she had a knack for it. It was what had made her one of the best first mates around.

"I do. He is talented, easygoing, hard-working, upstanding, and... he gets along well with children. Or at least one little girl that seems to have taken a shine to him." She relayed all this with her signature smile that put most people at ease, but Mingyu wasn't fooled. He had seen her smile like that while berating someone for shoddy work. It was worse than if she had just yelled at them because deep down, they knew they had disappointed her.

"An orphan girl? What of the other orphans?"

There had been issues in the past with people trying to take advantage of the children. If there was one thing Petrov Station took more seriously than weapons, it was the safety of children. Anyone who thought it was a good idea to mess with them quickly vanished.

Nevertheless, Mingyu knew the system wasn't perfect. There was never enough money or resources to go around. They did their best to make sure the kids who lost their parents had a warm bed and enough food to keep them healthy. They also provided basic training. That way, if they didn't get adopted—which happened far too often out there—they could at least find work once they came of age.

"You don't need to worry about little Yulia. She's taken quite the fancy to Alexander. And I think he is warming up to her as well. It seemed he was even giving her tutelage... of a sort. As for the other kids I spoke with, most seemed afraid of the 'scary robot' as they dubbed him. Truthfully, that body is quite imposing, especially with the damage. But I get the impression he didn't pick it by choice."

"Your observations are as impeccable as always. Thank you for doing this, Eva."

"You never did answer my earlier question. What do you plan to do?"

He sighed. There was no slipping that past her. "For now... nothing."

"Does this have to do with the ship in the VIP dock?"

This damnable woman really didn't miss anything.

"Yes." He told her who it was and what they wanted. There was no point hiding it from her. She would find out one way or another if she wanted to.

"Have you tested these improvements of Alexander's?" she asked. There was a distinct hint of surprise in her tone at the efficiency increase.

Mingyu had the same feeling when he first studied the plans. Unfortunately, he couldn't afford a full set of Omni Class 5 engines to test out this supposed discovery with his own ship and he didn't own any vessel with the smaller Class 4 engines.

"Unfortunately, no. But I have Chen testing to see if he can somehow apply these new improvements to Destiny's Sinorus engines. It's why I'm free to chat in person."

"You could just ask Alexander," Eva stated as she sat on a nearby bench.

"I wish it were that easy." He sighed as he sat next to her. "This trial is important. More important than anything to happen to Petrov in my lifetime. We can't be seen as showing favoritism toward either side."

She shook her head. "I don't understand why Omni didn't just file their case back in the core systems. Why send someone all the way out here?"

"That's easy to answer," he stated. "Someone at Omni realized the same thing we did."

The older woman sighed. "That Alexander is special."

"Precisely. Despite the billions of credits they spend on research and development every year, some nobody from the fringe was able to improve upon their design. The fact that Alexander showed them up must gall them."

Eva chuckled.

"What's so funny?"

"Oh, I just wish I could see their representative's face when he finds out Alexander beat their best engineers and billions of credits all the while working out of a dingy little shop and using some wildly outdated printers."

Mingyu paused to picture the scene and burst out laughing as well. If they didn't manage to save Alexander's work from these corporate thugs, at least they would get a good laugh out of it.

* * *

Alexander sighed internally. The last three weeks had been rather boring. For some reason, his business had dried up.

At first, he attributed it to another repair shop moving in, but after wandering around the second ring for a full day, he didn't find any new competitors and even Maxim had closed his doors. Good riddance.

However, he did hear rumors of some corporate bigwig from Omni visiting the station. Hard not to when it was all everyone seemed to be talking about. Maybe that was why work was slow.

Since he put no stake in gossip, he had dismissed the information. After the second week of no work, he looked into the rumors further, which was easier said than done.

Not very many people were keen to chat with him and Yulia, while a decent enough conversation partner, was still a child. She didn't know and didn't care about random visitors. He had asked her if Markus knew anything, but the boy only told her to keep her nose out of adult business.

That was probably for the best.

Alexander wished he had gotten Eva's contact information. She might know what was going on. Then again, she was a retiree, so maybe not.

He didn't know why he was so invested in knowing in the first place, it was just some thoughts percolating in the back of his mind that told him his lack of work was somehow linked with this stranger's visit.

If there was one thing Alexander was good at, it was putting information together. They were like little puzzle pieces to him. He just saw something, and instantly thought, *Hey, what if I did that instead?* This intuition is what allowed him to improve the *Zephyr*'s engines.

While he would like to consider himself smart, the idea to improve the flow rate wasn't an original idea of his. It came from one of his other repair jobs. A simple housing designed for the laminar flow of some thick lubricant sparked the idea. He simply adjusted the printer to provide a smoother internal surface for the fuel and combustion systems on the *Zephyr*. A smoother flow meant better combustion. At the time, the improvement just seemed obvious to him.

It was the same with the interrupter he made for his printers. Alexander simply applied principles from other things in new and unique ways. Given enough time, someone else would have realized the same thing he had and implemented the same idea. He just happened to be the first.

He did feel like a bit of a fake when all he did was steal other people's designs, but then again, he also needed to make a living. At that moment, those designs were the only thing keeping him from losing his lease.

The rhythmic tapping he was doing with his fingers stopped. Maybe that was why he was so invested in knowing what was going on. His design was built to improve an Omni-designed engine. While it was mostly rumor, the rumor was that this visitor was from Omni.

Had he rocked the boat?

There was one way to find out. He headed toward the kiosk and brought up his sales menu. Thankfully nobody could purchase something anonymously. Alexander scrolled through the list of purchases. It had increased since he had last looked, but it wasn't nearly as large as he wished it would be. Two purchases stood out to him.

One was from Captain Mingyu Na. The name didn't ring a bell, but the purchase location was Petrov Station. From what he knew, nobody there ran Omni engines. It made the purchase stand out. He would have to look into this person, but first, he flicked to the next name on the list. Hobart Holdings and Trust LLC.

Geez, even to Alexander's untrained eyes, that looked like a fake name. He flicked to the personal lookup and paid the cost to see who Mingyu Na was first, or at least his history.

And what a history it was. It went back to the founding of Petrov Station. With each word Alexander read, his sinking feeling grew.

Next, he searched for the LLC. There wasn't much to find, other than it was located in the same core system as Omni's headquarters. Even the name of the CEO sounded fake, Theodore Pembrooke. *Really?*

It was pretty clear this holding company was involved with Omni. The fact that Omni showed up less than a month after that company purchased his design was no coincidence. They were here because of him.

Somehow, someway, his tiny little improvement had garnered the attention of this massive organization. All he had wanted to do was make a bit of extra money and stay under the radar, but he couldn't even do that properly.

He headed back to his shop. If he could feel something, he would likely be very anxious right now. Without knowing why Omni was here, all he could do was wait and hope someone told him.

A few days later someone did show up.

A simply dressed man of mixed Asian heritage entered his shop and glanced around. Alexander had never seen this man before, but he carried himself with purpose. If he had to guess, this was a captain. They all seemed to act similarly, even if they dressed wildly differently.

"Hello, may I help you?"

"Alexander Kane, I presume?"

"I am. And you are...?"

"Captain Mingyu Na of the Station Council. Do you have a moment?" Of course Alexander recognized the name. It had been one of two on his mind constantly since he put the pieces together.

He sighed mentally and motioned toward Yulia's stool since he didn't have any other place for people to sit. The girl was absent, so she would have to forgive him for letting someone else take her seat.

"I assume you are here about the Omni ship and my patent?"

If the man was surprised by Alexander's deduction, he didn't show it.

"I am. In fact, I am here representing the station in this arbitration matter."

"Arbitration? You mean, like court?"

"Not exactly. Litigation would imply some law or another was breached. We concluded that no such thing occurred. We are simply here to ensure both parties reach an agreement."

"I don't understand. If no law was breached, why would I need arbitration? I don't want anything from Omni, and what could they possibly want from me?"

"Therein lies the problem, Mr. Kane. They want your design and the method you used to craft it. They claim that you breached their intellectual property rights."

"That's ludicrous. I simply purchased the designs like I do everything else. If they didn't want people using their designs to fix or modify their engines, they shouldn't have made them available."

"I agree, Mr. Kane. But that doesn't change the fact that they are here. And they will fight to take what they think is theirs... I suggest that you let them."

"What!" Alexander wasn't angry, he was just shocked by Na's statement.

"Hear me out, please."

Alexander took a mental pause and thought about it. Then he made his holographic face nod. "Fine, I will listen to what you have to say." It didn't mean he would agree though. Something about this situation was ringing alarm bells in his head.

"Thank you. Are you familiar with Omni at all?"

Alexander nodded again. "Only that they manufacture engines."

"While that is true, that is a very limited view of the company. They are one of, if not the largest company in human space."

"I knew they were large, but I didn't know to what extent." What could a company like that want with him? Accusing him of IP theft seemed like a thin excuse. Is this why Jasper had warned him to file the patent? Alexander thought it was to keep small companies from stealing it, not the parent company.

"Now you see what we are up against. You have a few options but only one good one. I suggest you let them buy out your patent. Allowing them to have it will save you years, or even decades of legal issues that they would throw your way."

"What? Why would I allow that? That just sounds like letting the bullies win," Alexander replied flatly.

"You would be right," the captain responded evenly. "But sometimes it's better to give them your hard work than to let them beat it out of you. The Council will do its best to ensure a fair deal for you."

"Why?"

"Pardon?"

"Why, Captain Na, does the station care about me? Why even come here if you aren't giving me a choice? I can't imagine the Council involves themselves in every arbitration that comes around."

The man hesitated for a moment and that told Alexander everything he needed to know.

"You get some of the settlement, don't you?"

"As your arbitration representative, the station does take a cut."

A cut? Probably more than a small portion if they were so eager to represent him.

"Well, then I wish to represent myself. Or better yet, I wish to speak to this representative in person." If he was going to get bent over, it might as well be on his terms. Having the station decide his fate just made him feel like he was back in Yuri's scrapyard.

"I'm afraid we can't allow that."

"What do you mean you can't allow that? There has to be some law that states I am allowed to request this. I never asked the station to get involved on my behalf, and I don't want it."

"This is exactly why we don't let civilians represent themselves. If you were aware of the laws, you would know that there isn't any such stipulation aboard this station. And the Council has already voted. But like I said earlier,, we will get you the best deal possible. I know this isn't ideal for you, Mr. Kane, but this is your best chance of getting Omni to pay. Trust that we will do right by you. You are a talented individual, Alexander, and the station would very much like to work more closely with you."

"Trust you? How can I trust people who waited weeks to inform me of what was going on, only to blindside me by telling me that they were going to decide my fate for me?! I may not know the law, Mr. Na, but I'm a quick learner." Alexander had to pause for a moment, realizing he was getting angry. The feeling faded away too quickly for him to explore the cause. "I think we are done here, Mr. Na. Unless you change your mind about allowing me to arbitrate for myself, I don't wish to speak with you any further on this topic. Good day."

The man stood and nodded. "We are not your enemy, Mr. Kane. Please think about what I said. Eva thought you had potential. I would hate to see you waste it away down here."

CHAPTER 17

After Captain Na left, Alexander got it into his head that he could just repeat his success from the Omni engines on the Sinorus engines instead.

After doing some research on the Omni competitor before diving headfirst this time, Alexander scrapped that plan. Turns out Sinorus wasn't any better than Omni. He found dozens of articles condemning the Coalition-backed manufacturer's shady business practices. When he tried to find similar articles on Omni, he found nothing. Considering who won the war, it wasn't hard to figure out why.

He now understood why everyone on Petrov Station refused to work on Omni engines. The few articles he did find were obvious propaganda released by the STO. The Sol Treaty Organization couldn't have made their relationship with the engine manufacturer clearer unless they came door to door and shouted it in your face. It was obvious the STO didn't want their primary propulsion manufacturer to look bad because it would affect them as well.

Alexander wasn't a fool though. Even with his missing memories, he knew no company was squeaky clean, especially one as large as Omni.

Unfortunately, knowing both engine suppliers were shady as shit didn't help him in any way, other than realizing he wanted nothing to do with either of them. If he repeated his improvements on the Sinorus design, they were just as likely as Omni to come to take his hard work. So he simply wouldn't do that.

That left him in a bit of a pickle though. With the Omni cloud hanging over his head, and his income from the sales of his modifications likely to dry up soon, he needed an alternative way to earn money.

Omni and Sinorus weren't the only manufacturers around, they were just the biggest. Not wanting to give up, he investigated all the options.

However, he quickly dismissed those other companies. Some hadn't come out with a new engine in decades while others were only making one very specific design that the larger companies didn't want a part of. The rest were either in the middle of bankruptcy or being bought out by the two giants. It reeked of monopolization.

Alexander did look up laws on monopolies. They existed, but it seemed like all the teeth had been pulled out of those laws long ago, allowing these companies to essentially do what they pleased and run roughshod over the market.

He sighed internally as he switched off the terminal. There wasn't an easy solution to his problem. The future was supposed to be an amazing place filled with human ingenuity and drive. Not this corporate-owned nightmare that he found himself in.

There was only one way forward that he could think of without running afoul of the corporations. He needed to design and build an engine from the ground up and he needed to do it all while keeping his company privately owned. Considering he was working out of a converted storage room and he was barely paying his bills, that was easier said than done.

After the conversation with Mingyu Na, he didn't trust the station. They might just as easily confiscate any future designs he came up with.

That didn't mean he was going to give up on this idea. He would learn what he could now, and when he was finally free of the restrictions keeping him bound to this station, he would be ready to strike out on his own. He would finally be free of Petrov management, free of Omni, and free of the STO.

When he returned to his shop, he stuck the data disk he had purchased into the small holoprojector on his desk.

A voice started speaking. "Greetings, and thank you for purchasing this tutorial. Today we are going to discuss the basic elements of conventional propulsion design and engineering."

Alexander had purchased the full course on the disk, and it had cost him a pretty penny, but if he was going to build his own company to compete with the big two, he needed to understand the basics—something he currently only had a working knowledge of.

"What'cha watchin'?" Yulia inquired and she climbed on top of her stool.

"A class on basic propulsion engineering," he responded while continuing the repair he was working on as well as listening to the holo. He was glad he could pay attention to more than one thing at a time.

"Sounds boring."

She wasn't wrong, it was indeed boring. The man teaching the course simply droned on in a monotone voice with absolutely no enthusiasm for the subject whatsoever, but it was the only approved course Alexander could afford.

"Yours are much more interesting," she stated, kicking her feet against the counter.

"What's the rule about kicking?"

"Sorry."

He nodded his avatar and pulled out her daily puzzle. "Here you go."

While he appreciated her enthusiasm, Alexander wouldn't really call what he was doing with her a class.

Since Yulia liked to hang around, she might as well get something out of it, so he decided to start building little puzzles for her to solve. They had started out with just a simple flat puzzle that she put together. After a few of those, he upgraded her to 3D puzzles.

She struggled more with them, but after a few helpful hints and words of encouragement, she got the hang of them. When she finished those and grew bored of them, he started incorporating moving parts like gears and levers into simple 3D shapes. She loved those because once they were complete, she could interact with them. They held her attention for far longer than the other two puzzles, but like any child, she grew bored of those soon enough.

At the time, he had moved her to more advanced puzzles, like a frog that could hop around after winding it up, or a little car that used a rubber band to produce motion.

They were the first things she made that she asked to keep. He didn't see any problem with that, so he had let her take them.

That day's puzzle was slightly different.

"Ooh… What is it?" she asked while looking at the box of parts.

He shook his head. The girl was always trying to get to the end before she even started. "You'll figure that out when you finish it."

"Aww," she whined before taking out the instruction book and looking at the illustrated pictures.

Alexander was on to her shenanigans by now though, and he had only created the first third of the instructions. If she managed to get through them that day, he would be surprised.

Seeing as she wasn't going to learn what the puzzle was meant to be when completed, she huffed and dug into the box until she found the first part.

He smiled and the pair worked in silence. Well, they were silent, but the annoying instructor still blathered on in the background.

* * *

Theo checked his appearance one last time in the mirror. He looked immaculate, the same as he had ten minutes ago, and ten minutes before that. That day was an important day though, and he was representing OMNI, so he couldn't afford to look disheveled.

The four months had gone by rather quickly, mainly because he had spent the majority of that time brushing up on the local law codes. While he hadn't been able to sneak off the ship and see this Alexander Kane for himself, he had paid someone on the station to report what they learned of the man.

Even in a station that hated OMNI to a fault, there were always people who would do anything for money.

The man had little to say considering the exorbitant amount of money he was offered, but he had stated the 'dude was a robot.' Yup, those were his exact words. Not exactly a wordsmith, that one.

That was fine. His description wasn't surprising to Theo. It matched everything the other people he had paid had told him. However, one did provide a bit more in-depth breakdown of the man. Apparently, Mr. Kane was sick or something and used the robot as a means of interacting with people.

While he hadn't heard that particular fact before, it wasn't all that groundbreaking. His background check of the man had revealed similar information. However, he didn't believe it for one minute. According to Kane's background, he suffered from some autoimmune disease. It didn't specify which one it was though, which was the first red flag. The second was the fact nanite regen therapy was available, even out in that dump. Sure it was pricey, but even minimal treatments should allow the man to walk around without too much issue. No, that man wasn't sick. Theo was leaning toward Kane being an escaped criminal or someone on the run from criminals.

If true, he could use the information in the future. Unfortunately, the knowledge had little impact on that day's hearing. He certainly couldn't bring it up. If the Council hadn't done their homework, he wasn't about to point this fact out to them. Blackmail was certainly a road he could go down if he needed to.

Theo checked himself one final time before sliding the ridiculous helmet on to complete his Head of OMNI's Legal Council persona.

With a smile, he exited his cabin and made his way to the ship ramp. The OMNI guards didn't even nod to him before they followed him from the ramp.

He waited for the hangar doors to open, and once they did, he saw Commissar Ivan Wang waiting for him. The man looked slightly less frazzled than the last time they met, but Theo could see he was still way out of his comfort zone there. Theo didn't bother improving the man's mood.

"Lead the way, commissar."

The man nodded, his eyes flicking to the two guards. The weasley-looking man opened his mouth as if to say something before thinking better of it and simply nodding.

Theo followed him to the elevator, his guards in tow behind.

He didn't need the two burly men. He could defend himself far better than they likely could, but it was a statement. One designed to show he felt irritated by the wait. Not that he did, but it made good set dressing for the upcoming play.

He pretended to fumble around in the changing gravity, much like he did the last time. Considering how badly the commissar handled the switch, maybe he hadn't played it up quite enough. Theo made a mental note to practice looking more inept in gravity changes as the elevator came to a halt.

The room was much busier than it had been the previous time he was there. As he and his guards climbed out of the elevator, four armed station guards approached.

"Your security detail will need to remain here."

One of his guards growled and took a step forward, but all four men pointed pulse rifles at him.

That little interaction was playing out almost better than he had hoped. The two guards had been handpicked by him because they were the two most prone to confrontation. He wanted to gauge the station's response to any threats by him or his team if alternative measures were needed.

The less-than-lethal sonic weapons were a mild surprise. He would have expected shock batons at most. You were less likely to seriously injure someone with a shock baton. The pulse rifles could still kill someone if they were hit enough times or in the wrong spot. He had been on the receiving end of the weapons enough times to know. It felt like getting kicked in the chest. Not something he was eager to repeat.

It seemed like the station wasn't taking any risks.

He reprioritized plans in his head, throwing some out and moving others up. He had alternatives in place if this meeting didn't go the way he suspected. "Stand down," he stated calmly.

The guard took a step back, his face returning to a mask of calm. Quick for confrontation, but smart enough to know when to back down.

"I apologize for his rudeness, but you have kept us sequestered in our hangar for four months. It is only fair that my men would be slightly agitated."

His plea fell on deaf ears as the station guard only grunted. "This way, and be quick, the captains are waiting."

The smile never left his face as he followed two of the station security guards.

The other two stayed back to keep an eye on his guards. Not that his two guards were of any importance, but he would let the station personnel have their tiny victory. The only thing Theo carried with him was a tablet with his case notes.

The guards led him over to the same meeting room he had visited the previous time. One of them pressed a comm button on the wall, and then they waited.

Theo did a mental sigh. *So it's gonna be like this.*

He patiently waited along with the guards, his smile never faltering for a moment. After twenty minutes, the comm on the wall finally buzzed.

"They are ready for you."

He wanted to laugh at the silly power play, but he kept his feelings to himself. With a slightly annoyed huff, he strode into the room with all the confidence of a senior lawyer who knew they were about to win their case.

The seven councilors were arrayed on the far side of a table in comfy-looking chairs, while a small metal desk and hard seat greeted him.

Oh, the pettiness... he loved it. For Theo, that little act spoke volumes. The captains knew they were going to lose, and it was their consolation to soothe their pride.

He wondered what other gifts they had in store for him and couldn't wait to find out.

He sat on the seat without complaint. "Council Captains... Shall we begin?"

CHAPTER 12

Mingyu sighed as he exited the conference room. It had been four long hours of back-and-forth discussions. While he despised Omni and everything they stood for, he would give the Omni representative his dues—the man had done his homework.

It was annoyingly frustrating. The only real opportunity they had to keep Mr. Kane's discoveries out of the hands of the greedy giant was to hope the man screwed up the case. With everything they had thrown at Mr. Pembrooke that day, the chance of that happening was quickly vanishing. The man was competent and savvy. Every argument the council brought forth, the man had a counter-argument, or a case law to reference.

Having discussed their options after Pembrooke left, most of the captains recognized they were going to lose the case. That didn't mean they would make it easy on the Omni legal representative. Most of what they could do by that point was just sheer pettiness. Such as extending the arbitration a few more days so the Omni ships would incur more docking fees.

Mingyu thought it was a pointless waste of time. He did not agree with the majority of the captains on this course of action, and he had been vocal about where he stood. Unfortunately he was outvoted, so he would go along with the majority.

It irked him that the biggest sticking point in the arbitration was going to be the actual compensation amount they were going to try to squeeze out of Omni. The fact that the station would take a significant cut meant the captains were going to push for every last credit they could.

It was disgusting. Since when had the families fallen so low as to try to make money this way?

From the brief exchange Mingyu had with Alexander, he knew the man was livid about not being able to represent himself in the arbitration case. Even though station law didn't even allow for personal arbitration, it did allow for the defendant to attend to state their case. Unfortunately, the Council ruled against allowing that to happen. It was another vote he had been on the losing side of.

They had deemed the case too important to risk having an outside entity affect it, claiming they voted on that to ensure the station's safety. If the man said the wrong thing to the Omni rep, who knew what could happen? Those gunships were still at the station, even though they were currently docked. Mingyu doubted the Omni rep would go that far after agreeing to sit around for four months.

The captains had also agreed not to let the Omni representative or any of the Omni personnel off the ring. Part of that was because they wanted to prevent the mega-corporation from trying to poach the unarguably talented individual. The other reason was to prevent Alexander or Mr. Pembrooke from coming to an outside agreement or for Omni to threaten Mr. Kane in some way, shape, or form.

All of the votes against him made him feel like an outsider in the council, but he would not have voted any other way.

Mingyu wished he could have given Kane what he wanted, but he simply couldn't. It would have made their future dealings much more amicable. Until Kane had brought it up, he honestly had never heard of any station allowing for a random individual to represent themselves. Most people barely knew enough about the law to not get in trouble, which was why stations usually had some sort of legal representation for people.

Alexander's insistence on representing himself was probably some planetside tradition or law that he thought was universal. It was another sign pointing to the fact Kane was not born a spacer.

That did throw off Mingyu's previous assumption that the man was an escapee from some criminal organization. He supposed Kane may have been abducted from some planet beyond STO's control and then escaped. There were always stories of humans that had gone far beyond the rim to live in peace away from the STO and their laws, but those were always just rumors. That also seemed unlikely for Mr. Kane considering the ailment he insisted he had—at least for the escaping part. He could certainly see some unsavory group snatching up a man who couldn't defend himself.

He just hoped their choices didn't strain their relationship with Kane. The man was an asset that the station could ill afford to lose. He just wished his fellow captains could see beyond the looming Omni payday.

* * *

Alexander was not in the mood to work on anything. Considering he didn't suffer from mood swings, it was surprising. He chalked it up to the fact the arbitration hearing had started while he was stuck there, waiting to hear how others would decide his life. How was anyone supposed to find that comforting?

Having Council Captain Na deny his request to speak for himself during this case was a punch to the gut. He felt like he was back in Yuri's salvage yard, stripped of all his own agency and independence.

The captain's assurance that they would get him adequate compensation for his work was not the balm they seemed to think it was. He only cared about having enough money to survive. Everything past that was simply superfluous until he figured out how to get rid of the control box.

Something deep inside him also detested the thought of his hard work being usurped all because of some arbitrary law that was being twisted to benefit some greedy mega-corporation. He couldn't figure out why he felt that way. He tried to explore the feeling, but it was elusive as smoke and vanished like his memories when he poked around it too long.

Did that feeling stem from something he had experienced in the past? If it did, there weren't any lingering memories to point the way. Alexander would have loved to explore this newfound emotion, but there was nothing to explore. He had yet to uncover anything about his circumstances since freeing himself.

If he was being honest, he hadn't tried all that hard. A part of that might have been fear, but he couldn't tell.

He felt emotions. The fact that he could detest something told him that was true. Yet even that emotion flickered like a tiny flame before guttering out. He wondered if whatever had caused him to be injured and dropped off at this station had damaged him mentally. It certainly wasn't the strangest explanation.

What if he was better off without his emotions? He had gotten along fine so far without them. His mind went into a spiral of what-ifs as he lost track of time.

"Alex?"

He jerked out of his stupor and turned toward the voice. "When did you arrive, Yulia?"

"Um... a little bit ago. You looked like you were concentrating so I didn't want to bother you." The little girl looked worried.

He made his avatar smile. "Oh. It's fine, I was just lost in thought." He glanced at his internal clock in shock. *FOR THREE HOURS!*

He had completely spaced out for three whole hours without realizing it. Alexander made a mental note not to explore his emotions while he was working if something like that could happen again.

Yulia seemed to relax, and Alexander handed the girl her daily puzzle before going back to his work. At least he hadn't accidentally crafted another gun while he was out that time. That would not have gone well.

* * *

"You can't be serious," Theodore stated. "Alexander Kane's improvements are minor at best. They certainly don't constitute the ridiculous sum you are asking for. A fairer offer would be five thousand credits. And that's being generous."

The room exploded into outrage at his counteroffer, which is what he had been aiming for. The trial had dragged on for a full week. Even he was growing tired of the nonsense they kept bringing up to try to extend the proceedings.

It had been clear on day one that OMNI was going to win the case. He just wasn't prepared for just how stubborn those people were. Now he was getting his own petty revenge. OMNI would likely have to pay quite the sum to Mr. Kane, but he was going to make those people work for every credit. That would teach them to waste his time.

Eventually, the outrage subsided, and Captain Kovalenko spoke up. "As you may have guessed, Mr. Pembrooke, your offer is unacceptable."

"As is yours. Where do you get off requesting ten-billion credits? I have looked at Mr. Kane's sales numbers. To date, he has a grand total of ten sales. Even if we projected that out to the life of the patent, that wouldn't even reach ten million credits."

"A patent that legally belongs to Mr. Kane," Sergei Zhang commented.

"We have already established that his patent does not cover any existing Omni components because those components are all covered under the STO's charter for possible military application."

The charter was a bullshit piece of legislation that OMNI had pushed through thanks to huge donations to very specific parties. It was a legal loophole that essentially allowed them to commandeer any improvements to their designs even if they were patented by others. It did not allow them to simply steal them though. Even that was a little too far for their benefactors. But that was fine, OMNI had more than enough capital to pay people off or make them vanish.

Captain Hoffman held his hand up to forestall Sergei's follow-up outburst. That was a shame, Theodore quite liked the short-tempered man. At least he made the boring meeting a bit livelier.

"We are well aware of this *law*," Hoffman said the last word with such derision, that Theo almost laughed. "But you are not just asking for those patents. You are also asking for the process he used to create them."

He mentally applauded the man's effort to turn OMNI's demand into an ask. "Yes, we are. And that's why I think my offer is more than generous."

Before the room could explode into angry muttering again, Kovalenko spoke up. "Mr. Pembrooke, would Omni be happy if someone claimed one of their patents and the processes to manufacture it, and then told them that it was only worth five thousand credits?"

"I don't see how that's relevant to this case," he responded, laughing internally.

"Imagine the scenario for me, if you'd please."

"I'm afraid I lack the imagination for something that could never happen, Captain."

Captain Kovalenko's mouth turned into a thin line. "Let me paint a picture for you then. If Mr. Kane and Omni's positions were reversed, I can assure you that they would not settle for a measly five thousand credits. The fact that you expect us to is insulting."

"Us?" Theodore asked, his grin widening ever so slightly. "Last I checked, Mr. Kane was not affiliated with any other entity nor the station."

His statement made the captains squirm uncomfortably. It wasn't a surprise. He knew months ago that whatever price OMNI paid, the station would get a cut.

"You know what I mean, Mr. Pembrooke," the man quickly tried to correct himself, but the damage was done. He high-fived himself mentally at the victory.

The captains would then have to settle for a lesser amount to not seem greedy. Honestly, he could have just agreed to the original amount considering it was less than OMNI had given him to work with. But he would be damned if he spent the majority of their mission budget on that.

He had done his math and would happily bet that the captains had as well. Mr. Kane's patent was worth a fortune. Even if the improvements could only be applied to the smaller Class 4 engine design, just selling the upgrade alone would net OMNI half a billion a year. If their legion of engineers and AIs could expand the design improvement to the rest of their line, and he had no reason to doubt they could, this single patent could be worth a trillion credits in ten years. That was still a small drop in OMNI's massive bucket of capital, but it would set them up as the premier engine and thruster manufacturer for quite some time.

Although, OMNI wouldn't do that. They would delist the patent. Why delist something that could make them so much money? Simple. They could make ten times the amount by simply incorporating these improvements into a new generation of engines. Why improve old tech, when they can simply force people to swap to the new stuff? With that approach, they could also work with their partners who design the power plants and fuel delivery systems so the newer engines would only work if ship captains upgraded everything.

Of course, how OMNI would handle it was all just speculation on his part. He wasn't exactly privy to that information.

Discussions went back and forth for a few more hours. Each side gave a little until finally a happy median was reached.

"Three hundred million credits, you agree to this amount?" Kovalenko asked in annoyance.

Theodore pretended to hem and haw about the exorbitant amount.

It was a ridiculous amount of money for any normal person. One could purchase a few used medium-sized ships for that amount of credit or live out the rest of their life in opulent luxury on some rim world.

For Theodore and OMNI, it was the deal of the century—or should he say *steal*.

"While I don't agree that it is worth that amount, Omni finds it acceptable."

There was a collective sigh of relief from the captains at his statement, and he wondered if he should have pushed for a lower amount. *Oh well.*

"Now that we have come to an agreement, where can I send my crew to retrieve Omni's property?"

"You won't," Captain Denis Kovalenko stated flatly. "Your people are to return to your ship and wait. We will send a porter down to retrieve your property along with armed station escorts to ensure nothing untoward happens to it. I think that brings an end to our proceedings. You are dismissed, Mr. Pembrooke."

Theodore made a show of looking annoyed at the ruling, although he had expected them to deny his request. It was a long shot to try to get to meet this elusive Alexander in person finally. That was fine though. OMNI would be watching, and eventually, an opportunity would present itself to make the man an offer. Very few people ever said no when OMNI wanted them to work for them. The few who did usually got a personal visit from him. They didn't care for competition.

chapter 19

Alexander was just finishing up a work order when Mingyu Na came through the door followed by five security officers.

He put down the tool he was holding and looked at the captain. "So this is it then?"

"I told you when we spoke earlier that this was the most likely outcome."

"You did. That doesn't mean I have to like it." He hated it, and he couldn't do anything about that fact. It wasn't because he didn't want to. He physically couldn't stop them because of the damn restrictions in the control box.

"Don't be like this, Mr. Kane. I didn't want this outcome any more than you did, but we have to be practical. Petrov Station only has a population of just over a hundred thousand people. If I had to guess, Omni employs more than that just at one of their construction yards. We pushed the mega-giant as much as we were willing to for your sake."

Alexander laughed. "My sake? How much is the station pocketing from this deal?"

Na's smile thinned, but he didn't reply.

"Just take the stuff and get out of my shop."

The captain motioned with his head and the security officers waved in some workers who set about putting the printer on a dolly. While they worked, the captain walked over and stood next to Alexander while he watched his work being stolen.

"We did try," Na said quietly.

"I believe you, but that's not the point, Captain. You only tried because there was something in it for you and the station."

"Everyone wants something, Mr. Kane. You are no exception. One day you will realize this and see we did what was best. Try not to let this color our relationship. There is much we can do to help each other."

Alexander focused his attention on the man without adjusting his avatar. Did the captain seriously believe he would work with them after they sold off his hard work to help line their own pockets? The gall.

If it wasn't for the fact he was stuck on this station, he would have told the man off. Until he figured out how to bypass Yuri's hardcoded restrictions, he was left at the mercy of those who ran Petrov Station.

He chose not to respond to the captain's last statement. He simply waited for the workers to finish and everyone to leave. Captain Na was the last one out, the man paused in the doorway.

"Think about what I said, Mr. Kane. Your talents are wasted down here. Your account should have your settlement already deposited." With that statement, the captain left his shop.

A flicker of anger ran through Alexander's mind, vanishing before he could even process it. He didn't bother checking to see how much Omni had paid to steal his invention, he simply turned around and went back to work.

* * *

Mingyu kept his face placid, but inside he was fuming, not because of what Alexander Kane had said to him. The man was understandably upset. Were he in the man's shoes, he would be raising hell. It seemed Kane was a much more level-headed individual than him.

He had tried to convey the importance of working with Mr. Kane to the other captains, but they couldn't see what he could. Most seemed to only care about the short-term gains of fleecing money from the mega-corporation. For a measly one hundred million credits. That was barely the operating budget for Petrov for a full year. Had they instead stood behind Kane and helped him grow, the man could have earned the station billions. Their idiotic and short-sighted approach caused him to reevaluate his opinion of some of the captains.

It was foolish to alienate such a talented individual. Just the fact that Omni had sent someone to take his work should have pointed that out. Someone like Alexander Kane came around once in a lifetime.

Instead of standing behind the man, they squandered any opportunity to get in his good graces—something that could have propelled Petrov Station to greater heights. Even a token effort to have the man at the trial probably would have been enough to stay on his good side. But *no*, they threw it all away to carve out the most money they could.

He knew some of the captains were struggling, but he didn't think they were so bad off that they would completely dismiss his suggestions. It made him angry but also made him wonder.

After being outvoted, he looked into the station finances, and what he found was troubling. The last time Mingyu had station duty was five years ago. Back then the station finances were doing okay. They weren't great, but then again, they never really had been. With Petrov being so far from the rest of human-occupied space, it didn't see a huge influx of traffic or trade. Even then, they made ends meet.

Now the station was running a deficit, and it seemed to be growing with each year. It wasn't clear how or why that had happened since the books were in disorder. What he could see was that Kovalenko and Hoffman had been taking out large loans against the station's finances.

Since the trial was ongoing, Mingyu hadn't confronted the men about the issue. Accusing one of the family heads of financial misconduct—let alone two—was unheard of. Mingyu couldn't deny the evidence though. Both men had recently done major upgrades to their ships.

While not in itself damning evidence, it was suspicious. The Na family wasn't the richest family on Petrov Station, that title fell to the Weiss family. But even a family as wealthy as the Weiss didn't do more than one ship system upgrade at a time. It was impractical and expensive.

Unfortunately, without access to Kovalenko and Hoffman's personal financial records, he couldn't say for certain.

What he could almost guarantee was that both of their families were less financially stable than his own. While that didn't mean they were poor, it did mean they couldn't afford these ship upgrades. Dock records also showed that neither of these men had done any active mining or cargo hauling in nearly a year.

Money didn't just appear from thin air. If neither of these captains were active, yet their crews were still employed and getting paid, the money had to be coming from some other source. There were only two options that he could think of, and neither was good.

Mingyu had found precedence in the archive of one family being stripped of their power after consorting with pirates early in the station's life. While there was no evidence of collusion in this case, this situation was equally as bad. He hoped he was wrong and that these men were both terrible at managing finances.

No matter what was found, it was likely both men would be stripped of their positions and exiled. The station was the lifeblood of all the families and over a hundred thousand people. To not even tell the Council of this financial issue was gross incompetence at the very least.

The issue with the captains and Alexander weighed heavily on his mind. He sighed quietly and followed the cargo and security officers to the VIP hangar. It was time to get this transfer over with and get the pompous Omni rep off their station once and for all.

* * *

Theodore Pembrooke watched as a group of workers carted in a large crate atop a dolly. He couldn't help thinking, *This is what three hundred million buys you.*

The cart was followed by station security, which immediately made his own security people tense up.

Last came one of the Council, Captain Na. The man's face was tight with annoyance as he watched the handoff of the cargo to Theo's people.

Once the cargo was secure aboard his ship, the captain spoke. "Your docking privileges expire in twenty minutes. I suggest you hurry unless you wish to be charged for an additional day."

Theo only smiled at that.

No more words were exchanged, and soon the station personnel evacuated the bay. Once aboard and sealed up, his ship started powering up. They didn't hurry though, that would show the Council that Omni was worried about their little threat. Twenty-five minutes later, his ship floated out of the dock, soon met by their escorts.

It was quite something that the STO fleet had left only the day before. Almost like it had been planned.

Theo chuckled internally. He was sure his insight into that little affair would stir up some discussion back home, but for now, he was curious to see what OMNI's investment had garnered them.

He walked over to a comm panel and clicked on engineering.

"Yeah, what is it?" a gruff voice responded.

"Chief, it's Mr. Pembrooke. When you have a moment, could you meet me in the hangar?"

The man grumbled, obviously wanting him to hear since sound couldn't be transmitted without the button being pressed. "Give me twenty minutes. I need to make sure the power plant is operating properly after being offline for so long."

There was a soft click, indicating the other side had disconnected. Theo smiled at that. The Chief engineer was a hoot. The man really was the Chief

Engineer, not just of this ship but of OMNI as a whole. The Chief Engineer occasionally took trips like this as a form of vacation or when he was needed for his expertise. The man also didn't care who he was speaking with. He spoke his mind and that was that.

The Chief got away with it because he was a genius, and OMNI wouldn't be where it was without him and his inventions. Particularly his advances in AI modeling.

Twenty minutes passed rather quickly and soon enough a stocky older man tromped into the hangar. "What is it you wanna waste my time on now ya glorified errand boy?"

Theo chuckled. "Oh, how I have missed your acerbic wit, Chief Benning."

"Quit trying to butter me up with your fancy words. I'm not one of your pillow girls. Just tell me what you want."

"I was hoping you could give me some insight into our most recent acquisition."

"Waste of my damn time," the man grumbled under his breath. The engineer walked over to a locker and pulled out a drill before stomping over to the crate and removing the bolts that secured the top and sides.

With a grunt, he pushed the items off and looked inside. "This is the shit you bought?"

Theo frowned. "Did they switch it on us?" He didn't think the Station Captains had the balls to do something like that, but he never could be certain with some people.

"What are you yammering about?"

While he did enjoy the man's cutting commentary, he was starting to get annoyed. "Is it or is it not what we were supposed to get?"

"How the hell would I know?"

A vein pulsed in Theo's forehead, and he pulled out his tablet and scrolled to the page that showed what they were supposed to receive. Then he handed it over to the Chief. The man glanced at it momentarily before handing it back. "Yeah, that's what we have."

"Good, for a moment you had me worried."

"You should be. This is shit."

He took a deep breath before responding. "Can you elaborate?"

"Shit, it comes out your rear end. But if you are referring to the specific shit in front of us, just look at it." The man waved to the device like he should understand.

"Please continue."

The man shook his head. "This is why I keep telling those idiots in corporate not to purchase shit without consulting with me. This 'printer', if you can even call it that, is forty years out of date. My grandchild has a more advanced printer and he's five."

"What about the modifications, surely those are important."

The Chief scoffed. "I wasn't sure what they were at first glance, but after taking in the whole thing I'm pretty sure I know what they do."

"And what's that?"

"Nothing any newer industrial printer can't. If my guess is correct, and they usually are, it's a ring designed to emit an electromagnetic field."

Theo was confused. He didn't know a whole lot about technology, but he wasn't completely unfamiliar with certain things. "Why would someone want to create an electric field inside the print area?"

"An electromagnetic field, not an electric field, ya nitwit. Normally there would be no point. The field this little thing can create would be too weak to do anything, especially on a planet. And the OMNI orbital printers already have similar technology built into them."

Understanding came to Theo. "That device cancels the effect of gravity?" If that were true, this purchase was even bigger than he realized.

The engineer burst into laughter. "What are you smoking? Of course, it doesn't. All it likely does is counteract the field produced by gravity plating. Hell, it probably doesn't even do that. It probably just weakens it. While I will give the man credit for coming up with a unique way of going about it, it is functionally useless. Any printer created in the last decade can compensate for the effects of gravity while it prints. And newer ships can just switch off sections of gravity to produce better effects."

No, that didn't make sense. He had been sent out here personally to oversee this acquisition. He was starting to hyperventilate. "What about the designs I sent you?"

"What about them?"

"There has to be something worthwhile there?" Theo's panic began to rise, causing his voice to break slightly.

The old engineer quirked an eyebrow at that. "Just how much did this cost OMNI?"

Theodore told him. He had to wait ten minutes before the man stopped laughing long enough to speak. "You wasted three hundred million. I could have saved us four months and a trip out here if someone had just spoken to me first. Sure, OMNI will probably make their money back... eventually."

"Eventually? But we could implement this into new designs."

"No, you can't because our new engine designs have already eliminated those inefficiencies. Hell, the next-gen engines are more efficient yet. The only thing these designs are good for is improving existing installs of older models, and you know how OMNI feels about that."

He did know. OMNI's current sales philosophy revolved around new engine installs, not upgrading older engines. So why had corporate sent him out here to buy it? Unless...

His face went pale.

"Oh ho! Looks like someone finally caught on." Benning chuckled.

"But I've been a model employee. Why would they want to set me up for failure."

"You are but a small cog in a large machine, Pembrooke. Someone high up the chain saw this opportunity and gambled on it or maybe they thought you were getting too big for your britches. Either way." He shrugged. "Do you think they are going to take the fall when it turns out the investment of three ships and over five months was wasted? Don't worry your tiny little brain, they probably won't fire you. If they sent you out here, you're obviously not being liquidated." Chief Benning chuckled again.

A cold creeping sensation went down Theo's back. He was usually the one who liquidated people, so he knew what that meant.

"They will simply demote and reassign you. Good luck with that, by the way." The man clapped him on the shoulder before walking out of the hold laughing.

This wasn't funny, why was he laughing?

chapter 20

Alexander found it hard to care about anything for the next few days. He simply went through the motions like he had back when he worked for Yuri. By shutting himself off from the outside world and letting his body run automatically, he wasn't constantly going over what had transpired. This was essentially his version of sulking. Not that he could truly sulk. It was more like just letting his mind go blank.

This wasn't the same state he entered when he accidentally created weapons. He had been able to pin that issue down to times when he was idle, but his mind was whirling with ideas. Now it was reversed. His mind was idle, but his body continued to work.

It was Yulia's worried expression that finally snapped him out of the fugue state.

"Alex, are you alright?"

He gave the mental equivalent of a blink and turned the projection of his face to the girl. "I was just thinking. I'm fine now though."

"Oh... It's just... you looked really scary just now."

The statement shocked him for a couple of reasons. The first was that there was no physical change that should have shown his condition. The second was that this little girl had somehow still picked up on it.

"How is your puzzle coming along? e asked instead, trying to draw her attention away from his lapse.

"Okay, I guess…"

"Oh, have you run into an issue?"

She nodded slowly. "The math you gave me is really hard. I followed the instructions to enter it into the controller, but I can't get it to work right."

He made his face nod in understanding. "Why don't you show me, and we can go over it together."

"Don't you have work to complete?" she asked, looking at the parts strewn about his counter.

"A little break won't hurt. Now, let's see what you have." A little robotic humanoid was his latest puzzle for her. It contained a bunch of small parts and even gears along with a motor and controller.

Alexander had designed and built the toy completely from scratch. He even created a simple robotic program for it to run on. The only thing Yulia had to do was solve certain math problems to get the robot to perform an action. The problems started off simple enough, and then steadily got harder. He had even added some algebra problems towards the end. He was curious to see how far she had gotten.

The girl pushed the button on the controller and the figure started to move around and even walk. It contained some simple sensors, so when it got to the edge of the counter, it knew to turn around instead of falling off.

Soon it started to do more complex tasks like bending over and sticking its arm up in the air to approximate a wave. Yulia laughed and waved back. There was a pause, and the robot started to do the robot.

"See! It gets there and starts doing weird stuff."

Alexander chuckled. "No, it's dancing. It's a dance called the robot."

The young girl scrunched up her face. "That's a dumb name for a dance. I've never seen a robot dance before."

"Never?" he asked, quirking his holographic eyebrow, then he threw down some killer moves.

The girl burst out in laughter as he made his much more limber body mimic the stiff and jerky movements of the little robot until they were in sync. Eventually, she tried to join in. The two laughed and danced and it was exactly what he needed to get his thoughts past what Omni and the station had done.

Yulia was quickly becoming one of his favorite people, he was glad he hadn't chased her off so many months ago.

* * *

The *Devil's Bargain* jumped back into Gliese 667. After the STO strike group had entered the system, they had quickly made themselves scarce. Captain Harn had no love for the government. Similarly, the STO had no love for the many mercenary companies that plied their trade.

"A necessary evil," he had overheard one STO officer comment back when he was still in the fleet.

"System's clear, Captain," the sensor officer said. "Looks like the STO finally packed up and left."

"'Bout damn time," Harn muttered. He turned to the two crew who were waiting off to the side of the bridge. It was because of them he was back in this system so soon. "Tell me again what you saw." The pair had approached him with an opportunity after they completed their last job.

"Gino and I spotted this man on the second ring. I swear on my mother's grave that it was the spitting image of Harlow himself."

The notorious pirate had gone missing years ago, but there was still a bounty out on him.

"Uh, huh... And you say you saw this man in a small repair shop on the second ring?" He let his skepticism sink into every word.

"Well... Not exactly him, Captain. I can show ya. I got an implant." The man sent the file to his screen.

A slightly grainy video showed the man walking into a repair shop where a girl sat on a stool and a large robot was moving around inside a storage closet. The view quickly zoomed into the holographic face represented on the robot. It did look a lot like the infamous pirate.

"The robot is Harlow? And why is the video so grainy?"

"I asked my contact in security about that. Apparently, all the cameras in that area are experiencing issues. And no. According to some people we talked with, that's just what he uses to interact with people. His real body is in a med pod. Probably how he's avoided getting caught for so long."

Harn grunted. It wasn't the most outlandish thing he had heard. Assaulting a station resident wasn't exactly legal. If they were right, the risk would be worth it, but if they were wrong, he would simply pay the fine.

"What about the girl?"

Svadi shrugged. "Station ward. I figure we hit the place late in the evening, and she shouldn't be around."

They better hope she isn't there.

"And the med pod?"

"Got the location from a guard we paid off."

It seemed they had done their homework. Harlow masquerading as some rich bastard who suffered from a disease that kept him locked away in a medical chamber certainly fit. His men had even paid off one of the guards to get the location of that chamber and found it was just another storage room with no communication terminal anywhere nearby.

The plan was simple. Shoot the robot to disable it. Going by how cobbled together it looked, it probably wouldn't be hard. Next, grab the stasis pod and hightail it back to the ship before station security caught on to the capture.

Normally he wouldn't consider an operation like that, but he was close to retirement. Bringing in Harlow would earn him enough to live a comfortable life somewhere in the core systems and far away from this backwater filled with Coalition filth.

"What about the weapon discharge sensors?"

"My man in security says he can scrub them from the sensors for a minute. That should be more than enough time."

It wouldn't be the first time his people had to perform a job on a station. The last time they were there, his people had stumbled upon another bounty. It had only taken a stunner to subdue that target, and they had gotten him aboard the ship without anyone being the wiser. Harn knew that there were other bounties on the station, but with the sensors, the two gunships, and the STO showing up, it had been too hot to risk taking anymore.

Harn would like to claim a few more of the bounties along with Harlow. If it was Harlow, he was worth far more than some low-level criminal. It wasn't worth putting one op at risk by running multiple other ops.

"Fine. I'm giving this op the green light. Get suited up, and make sure to cover your faces." He didn't mention that if things went sideways, he was cutting them free. They may be good mercenaries, but it wasn't worth taking a trip out of an airlock for them.

The ship floated into the dock and touched down. Unfortunately, asking for a specific dock close to their target would be giving too much away, so they were forced to go with whatever the station assigned them.

That didn't mean he couldn't swing certain factors in his favor.

After telling the station attendant that he may need to do repairs, the woman on the other end assigned the *Devil's Bargain* a dock on the third ring. It was more than he had hoped for. Harn was a man who believed in luck, and it seemed lady luck was on their side for that mission.

He had his crew disembark for some R&R while his mechanic took some panels off to make it look like they were investigating some issues. It was early morning at the station, so the two would need to wait until later on when activity slowed to hit their target. By then, the ship would be topped off on reaction mass, the 'repairs' would be complete, and the crew would be back aboard. All he had to do was sit back and wait to collect his prize.

* * *

"You think the captain bought it?" Gino asked as they prepped their gear.

"Quiet, you idiot," Svadi hissed. "Of course the captain bought it. It took me forever to doctor those images to make that holographic face look sort of like Harlow."

"But he's bound to find out when we bring the pod in."

"We're not bringing the pod in, stupid. We take out the robot, then snatch the guns and hide them. We rush back to the ship and tell him the op went sideways. Then we can come back at our leisure after the old man retires and collect our prize. Simple as that."

Gino smiled. "Simple as that!" The two slammed their armored forearms together.

chapter 21

"And here you can see where we process the station's wastewater," an adult droned on.

Despite the adult's less-than-enthusiastic tone and the noise, Yulia was enjoying the field trip that the headmaster had put together for the orphanage. She couldn't say the same for the rest of the kids, who looked extremely bored, but she was fascinated by how things worked.

She may have felt differently before Alex got her started on her puzzles though. Now instead of boring machines that did dull tasks, she wondered how they worked.

"Ooh! Ooh!" She jumped up and down and raised her hand so the worker could see her.

The man tilted his head back slightly and closed his eyes for a moment before speaking. "Yes, what would you like to know this time?"

The rest of the kids groaned, but she didn't care. "How does the machine process the water?"

After moving on from that part of the trip, Markus leaned down and whispered to her. "You gotta stop asking questions. We are already two hours past the evening meal, and I can see Headmaster Wong getting frustrated. Not to mention the younger kids are beginning to complain."

After Markus said that to her, Yulia too realized she was starving. She had been so caught up in all the new things that she had overlooked her own hunger.

The rest of the trip sped by, and Yulia did her best to keep any more questions to herself, even though she was burning to know. She could ask Alex, he was smart; surely he would know how an oxygen recycler worked.

"That brings us to the end of the trip. I hope you have enjoyed yourselves and learned something. Perhaps one day, you too could be a system maintenance tech, like me."

The kids all clapped half-heartedly. Most were tired and hungry. Even Yulia didn't think she wanted to be a whatever tech like this man. She wanted to be like Alex. He was cool.

With the help of some of the older kids, the headmaster managed to wrangle the group into the elevator. Once the door closed, blissful silence hit all their ears. The tube shot to the second ring while the younger kids complained about their ears ringing. The headmaster did his best to calm their concerns, but they were being quite fussy.

Yulia just hummed to cover the droning buzz. The older kids just bore it quietly. They were so cool.

After returning to the orphanage, the headmaster spoke up. "I know it's late, and I will get the meal ready as soon as possible. In the meantime, I want you all to get ready for bed."

Quiet cries of complaint met that statement.

"Enough of that now. After we eat, you'll all brush and head straight to bed. Now chop chop. And don't interrupt me or dinner will be even later."

The headmaster hurried to the kitchen while all the kids shuffled off, dragging their feet. All kids except Yulia.

She waited for the older kids, specifically for Markus to head into the bathrooms before she snuck out. There was too much on her mind for it to wait until morning. She needed to ask Alex about the stuff they learned that day, or she wouldn't get a lick of sleep.

Yulia had never been out that late, and the station was eerily quiet at that time of night. She didn't let that stop her as she kept humming while she skipped toward Alex's shop. It wasn't until she was most of the way there that she realized he may be closed or asleep. Did robots sleep?

Thankfully she saw that the light was on, and she could hear voices. With renewed vigor, she sprinted the rest of the way. As soon as she got to the door, she shouted. "Alex, guess what I learned today!"

Two men in full suits turned toward her.

* * *

Alexander was working late on yet another repair, thankful that his work had picked up again after the Omni ships left the system. He didn't need to sleep and the money he earned from the case was more than enough to comfortably live by, but to him, it might as well be blood money. The money would be used eventually, but he preferred to rely on his skills for the time being.

As he was replacing a solenoid, two men in full vac-armor walked into the shop. He couldn't tell who they were as their face shields were set to reflective, but he didn't need to see their faces to know who they were. The armor gave it away. It was the armor he had repaired months ago. Then he saw the guns. Pulse rifles weren't illegal, but they were severely frowned upon by station security. Although, that wasn't the terminology used in the actual law.

He paused in what he was doing and stepped back from the desk before raising his arms in the air. Nobody walked around with a weapon in hand unless they planned to use it.

"Gentlemen."

"Open your storage room," the closest man said in a modulated voice through a speaker on his suit. Now both of the men had the rifles pointed squarely at him.

"Slowly!" he added as Alexander began to move.

He made his face nod in understanding as he slowly entered the code on the door behind him. It clicked open and he stepped aside. Both men's guns moved to follow him. Once the door was clear, the first man walked around the counter and shoved the door the rest of the way open.

"Where are the guns?" he growled. "We saw you put them in here."

As soon as he realized who the two were, he was certain he knew what they were after. That statement only cleared up any lingering doubt. Had they seen him working on the weapon, and only came in after that to verify what they saw? Or did they see them sitting on the shelf when he exited the storage room? Not that it mattered, because they had obviously seen them.

"I don't have or sell weapons," he responded knowing neither of these men would believe him.

If he had only been able to modify his damn control box then maybe he could fight back or something. As it sat, he couldn't even touch the men thanks to the restrictions hardcoded into the device.

"I know what I saw, so don't fucking lie to—"

"Alex, guess what I learned today!" an excited girl's voice stated triumphantly from the doorway.

Horror flooded Alexander's mind as he watched the second man whirl and fire on the little girl.

The first man fired as well, but the pulse blast was aimed at Alexander. It hit him, but it simply dissipated on his body. With no path to get to Yulia without going through the man behind the counter, he simply grabbed the heavy metal counter that was obstructing him and pulled.

The whole thing ripped off the ground, shearing the anchor bolts with a scream of metal. He threw it across the room, trying to get it out of his way so he could protect the girl.

But even as he was heaving the heavy metal of the counter around like a toy, the second man had already pulled his trigger.

He screamed internally, diving to try to intercept the nearly invisible discharge from the weapon, but he was too late. He could only watch in horror as the girl's eyes went wide a moment before the blast struck her in the chest, slamming her against the door frame where she crumpled without so much as a muffled scream.

Rage like nothing he could ever recall filled Alexander and he was momentarily blinded by the emotion as he whirled on the two men. Both men had seen what he did to the counter, and blast after blast slammed into him until one finally shattered the control box, plunging Alexander into a pit of darkness and despair.

* * *

After the robot finally collapsed to the ground, the first man rushed over and cuffed the second upside the helmet.

"You dumb shit, you shot a kid!"

"How the fuck was I supposed to know? She just ran in here, startling me. What do we do now?"

"Now? Now we get the hell out of here before station security finds these two. The captain is going to be pissed that the op went sideways."

"Fuck that! I ain't going without something." The second man scrounged around until he came up with a few credit chips.

Then they rushed out of the business and down the hall.

Markus remained frozen around the corner as the two men ran past him without even noticing. After he had realized Yulia had snuck out, he knew exactly where she had gone, so he went to retrieve her before she got herself into trouble. He rounded the corridor just as the fighting erupted.

Swallowing the lump in his throat, he cautiously approached the open door to Alexander's Repair shop. The first thing he saw was Yulia's small form crumpled against the entrance. There was blood. He started to panic as it brought back memories of finding his dad after the accident that took his life.

Markus did the breathing exercises that the doctors told him should help, but it felt like they weren't doing much. "Whaddo I do, whaddo I do?!"

He recalled the first aid training that the older kids were forced to sit through to assist if one of the younger kids got hurt. With a shaking hand, he lightly touched Yulia's neck and felt for a pulse. It took him longer than it did in the video, but he eventually felt one. That was good. She was alive.

After checking on Yulia, he looked into the room. His eyes went wide at the damage, but they settled on the motionless form of the robot. There wasn't anything he could do about that. He turned and rushed down the corridor until he found the closest terminal. Then he slammed the emergency button and entered the location.

The few working emergency lights in the area started flashing, and a voice spoke over the terminal. "Emergency services are on their way, please state the nature of the emergency."

Markus told the woman everything he had seen and even provided descriptions of the two men. Soon a team of rescue workers arrived and loaded Yulia onto a stretcher before rushing her to the nearest medical center.

chapter 22

Captain Harn was aboard the *Devil's Bargain* when the station alert went off.

"ALL STATION LOCKDOWN IN EFFECT. ALL DOCKED CRAFT ARE TO REMAIN DOCKED. ANY SHIP ATTEMPTING TO LEAVE AT THIS TIME WILL BE TREATED AS A PIRATE AND DEALT WITH IN THAT MANNER."

He slammed his fist against his desk. Those fucking idiots had done something to bring the ire of the station down on them, he just knew it. He hurried out of his cabin and to the ops center without even putting on a shirt.

"Rico!"

"Yes, Captain?" The man jumped as if he had been asleep.

"Change the docking code and the ship code, now."

"Are you sure, Captain? We still have Gino and Svadi off the ship."

"Did I stutter?!"

"N-No, Sir." The man quickly turned back to his console and began typing. "Oh, they just entered the hangar, Sir."

Harn squeezed the back of the ops chair until it creaked. "Please tell me the ship codes are changed?"

Rico nodded.

Harn turned his head to the ship's security feed. After their codes failed, the two men began banging on the exterior door. One even clicked the comm button. "Let us in, Rico, ya lazy shit!"

The other camera caught the ten-armed station security that stormed into the hangar only a minute later.

"Captain?" Rico asked. "What's going on?"

"Those two just fucked us, that's what."

There was a short firefight between the two groups, but it was rather one-sided. The station security had brought riot shields, and the pulse rifles deflected harmlessly off the tough acrylic. Gino and Svadi's armor absorbed quite a few return shots from similar pulse rifles, but eventually, the men lay in a heap on the ground.

The two were stripped of their armor and weapons before being dragged away in shackles. More station security showed up.

"Tell the crew to gear up."

This time, Rico didn't bother questioning him. He simply relayed the all-hands message.

Whatever those two idiots had done, it had screwed them royally. And with them, any ship they belonged to. That was why he had tried locking down the dock before they returned. At least then he had plausible deniability. Unfortunately, since they had the codes to get in, they had doomed his entire crew. Station security would not have barged into his hangar unless they had declared those two idiots pirates. Seeing as they had nothing to lose now, the *Devil's Bargain* would not go down without a fight.

* * *

[CRITICAL SYSTEM FAILURE DETECTED]
[INITIATING SELF-REPAIR FUNCTION]

Alexander's mind snapped awake again. He was disoriented for a moment as two huge red walls of text scrolled past his vision. Soon the red started to change to yellow, and then to green. He was finding it hard to focus on the information though as he remembered what had happened before he blacked out.

"Yulia!"

He pushed himself upright, scanning the room. The only thing that greeted him was destruction and a bit of blood. There was no sign of the attackers or Yulia. He panicked for a moment, thinking they had taken her when they left, but his gaze landed on the door. There was yellow warning tape across the entrance, something you might see after an accident.

If people had discovered the attack, they must have taken the little girl to the hospital. He pulled the tape away and moved into the corridor, finding it equally as empty. He needed to find someone and learn what happened to Yulia.

Someone must have heard him stomping about.

"Who goes there?" a station security guard demanded as a pair of them rounded the nearby corner.

When they saw Alexander, they paused. "Holy shit! We thought your robot was toast. The Commandant of Security has been trying to locate your pod for questioning. He's gonna wanna speak to you."

"Is Yulia okay?" Alexander asked, ignoring the men.

"Who?"

"The little girl, is she okay?" He raised his voice, not in the mood to play twenty questions.

The pair looked at each other, a little nervous.

"She was taken to the medical facility."

Alexander tried to make his holographic face nod, but he realized it wasn't there. Then he realized the entire control box was missing, and the dead space in his vision was gone as well. That was something to think about for later, as well as the fact that he could talk now. He had more important things to worry about at the moment.

He bobbed his main body slightly. "I'm going to the medical facility to check on the girl. Your Commandant can speak to me there."

"Wait, you can't—" But his partner stopped him with a hand on the shoulder and a shake of his head.

Alexander watched the exchange as he strode down the corridor. There was a medical facility on each ring, but he didn't know how effective the one on the second would be.

"Excuse me," he said as he entered the building.

The receptionist looked at him in shock before looking around for something. "Um, who's speaking?"

"I am," he reiterated, and this time the woman looked at him. He answered her unasked question. "I remote control this robot because I have an auto-immune disease that keeps me locked away in a pod."

"Oh... I'm sorry to hear about that. What can I help you with?"

"I'm here to check on the status of a little girl that was brought in. She was at my shop when we were attacked."

"Are you her parent or guardian?"

He went to shake his holographic avatar again, but he remembered it was gone this time. He pushed down his annoyance and spoke. "No."

"I can't just give you that information then."

"Could I at least speak with the doctor?"

"I can ask him to talk with you when he is free. You will need to wait though."

He took a seat on the floor in the waiting room with the rest of the patients. During that time, Alexander watched over a dozen people come and go. Finally, someone called his name. "Alexander Kane."

He stood, and most of the eyes in the room followed him. The doctor simply looked at him. "Hello, I'm Dr. Nord. Please follow me to my office so we can have a private discussion."

Alexander followed the man. The man's office was clean and tidy, but not overly large. He barely fit inside.

The doctor looked at the chair before moving it off to the side. "I would have you sit, but I don't think the chair would hold."

"It's fine."

The doctor took a seat behind his desk and looked at him. "Normally I wouldn't even consider talking to you about another patient, but it seems you have powerful friends, Mr. Kane. One of the Council Captains, Mr. Na, asked me to speak with you."

"Is Yulia okay?"

"She is currently stable. She suffered four broken ribs and a punctured lung from the incident. We set her ribs, but she will probably never regain use of that lung."

"I don't wish to be ungrateful, Dr. Nord, but will she receive the best care on the second ring?"

The man didn't seem offended by the question. "It may seem strange, Mr. Kane, but I am Petrov Station's best trauma surgeon. The residential rings may have better specialist providers, but they don't deal with accidents as often as we do down here. As for her care, she is getting the best free care available."

"Does that mean there are other options?" Alexander asked. If there was, why weren't they providing it?

"There are advanced meds that will shorten her stay from six months to a week and likely repair the damage to her lung."

"Okay... Why aren't you using them then? Is it money? If so, I will gladly cover the costs."

Nord shook his head. "While there is a cost associated with those advanced methods, she doesn't qualify for them."

"What do you mean she doesn't qualify?" A bit of anger seeped into his words.

"She is a ward, Mr. Kane. And while we provide free healthcare to all, it has limits. The quick heal medications are expensive, but they are also limited in quantity. And we are only given so many a year by the STO. We must reserve them for key station personnel."

Alexander did not like what he was hearing. He knew the doctor was only doing his job, but that seemed unnecessarily cruel. Yulia was just a child. If anyone deserved to get healed faster, it was her.

"Is there anything that can get her on that list?" he finally asked.

The man seemed reluctant to speak. With a slight sigh, he continued. "There is. And I am only bringing this up because Mr. Na asked me to. Children of key station personnel are also eligible for this treatment."

"I don't follow..."

"Has Captain Na not spoken with you yet?"

"No. Why?"

"I see. Well, then let me be the first to congratulate you, Mr. Kane. Thanks to your efforts, a pirate threat was removed from the station. As a reward, you will be gifted the status of a key member of station personnel for a month. I suggest you take full advantage of that while it lasts. There are quite a few perks that go along with it."

He was about to say he still didn't understand what the doctor was getting at when it all clicked into place. "They want me to adopt Yulia?"

The man shrugged. "I can't say what they want, but if you are adamant that she gets that treatment, this would be the only way to ensure that outcome."

The doctor's words left him a lot to think about, but he didn't get much time. As he exited into the waiting room, station security was waiting for him again. This time there were three, and the man in the center bore a Commandant's badge.

It annoyed him that they were there now. Couldn't they see he was dealing with some serious issues?

"Mr. Kane. Follow us to the station, we need to get your statement."

Alexander noticed they weren't asking. With no excuse to deny their request, he followed the men.

What happened next was a three-hour interrogation session. It was clear by their questions that the two attackers had told station security what they were after.

"How many times do I have to tell you? I don't have any weapons. I do not make, or repair weapons. And, I have never stocked or sold any. You can check my purchase history." He was lying, of course, but there was no evidence to prove otherwise. He was thankful he was stuck in that body now as well, because their typical tactics of trying to sweat him out or playing good cop bad cop were having zero effect. He simply sat in the groaning metal chair and played along. He almost wished the chair would give out as a little bit of petty revenge.

Alexander was glad he had studied station laws after the bullshit with the arbitration hearing. He knew without evidence or a verbal charge, they couldn't hold him for more than twelve hours. They tried to get him with technicalities and switched up their questions to confuse him, but he wasn't fooled by any of it.

After twelve hours, they reluctantly released him but only when he asked about it.

The interrogation had given him time to think and to come to terms with what the doctor and Captain Na were trying to get him to agree to. While he hadn't ever pictured himself as a parent, he couldn't deny that he had grown fond of Yulia. When he thought back on the times she visited, he realized he looked forward to those hours. Was that enough for him to go forward with adopting her, though? He didn't want to deny her the chance of being adopted by normal people.

Money was also an issue to consider, but now that he had the Omni payout, that wasn't a concern. He could provide for her. He could also teach her. That was something he had been doing already without being her adopted parent. The question was, could he love her like she deserved? Alexander couldn't answer that. He had hoped that with the repairs to his body, his ability to feel strong emotions again would return. They hadn't.

He recalled his reaction when he knew Yulia was going to be hurt and after she was injured. His first instinct was to protect the girl followed by blinding anger at the attackers. That fact alone was what made the decision easy for him. If he could feel anger, he must be able to feel love. That was something he would need to work at figuring out, but he wasted no more time and headed straight for the orphanage to speak with the headmaster.

chapter 23

As Alexander neared the orphanage, he came across more children who seemed to be about Yulia's age or older. They looked sad and scared which made him realize they must have heard about Yulia's condition.

The children averted their eyes when they saw him. It was a reaction he hadn't seen in some time. The damage to his body seemed to be completely gone, although he probably looked much more imposing without his holographic cartoon face to make him appear friendly.

Alexander lightly knocked on the bulkhead door that led into the orphanage.

"Yes?" a voice came over an intercom next to the door.

He had missed the intercom in his rush to meet with the headmaster.

Alexander pressed the button to respond. "Hello. I'm Alexander Kane. I wish to speak with you about adopting Yulia."

"Alexander Kane? Yes. I've heard of you. Please hold on a moment and I will let you in so we can speak."

About a minute later, the door to the orphanage popped open and an older man with greying hair around his temples peeked his head out. The man's eyes went wide upon seeing him.

"Oh my! I've heard the kids speak about you, but I didn't really believe half of what they said."

"Sorry about my appearance. My holo emitter was damaged in the attack."

The man nodded solemnly. "Yes, I've been told what happened. I'm Headmaster Wong, please come inside so we can talk."

Alexander followed the man inside. "Someone told you what happened?"

"Oh, were you not aware of who reported the attack?"

Alexander would have shaken his head if he could. He sighed internally; this body was not designed with non-verbal communication in mind. He would need to replace the holo-emitter as soon as he could. "No. The signal to this robot was damaged and it only came back online after the police had arrived."

"I see. Well, I can fill you in. We came back late from a field trip and while I was preparing the evening meal, Yulia snuck out." He looked around to make sure none of the younger children were in earshot. They were all across the room watching some program. Nodding to himself, he spoke quietly. "Don't tell the children, but I know when they come and go. I usually don't discipline them unless I catch them returning. They have it rough enough without me trying to take the place of their parents. Some would even balk at me trying to act out more. Besides, the older kids are good at policing the younger ones. That's what happened last night."

"One of the other kids came across the attack?" That was horrible.

The man nodded slowly. "It was Markus. The boy has always looked out for the younger kids. I think he has a soft spot for Yulia. He's always getting her out of trouble."

"Is he okay?"

"He should be fine with some help. He's speaking with a mental health specialist at the moment. A lot of our kids suffer from trauma. So we do our best to help them get over it. Here we are."

The man motioned for Alexander to follow him into an office. Honestly, it looked a lot like Dr. Nord's office, only a lot less tidy.

"Normally we would have the child present for this discussion. And then conduct a separate interview, but that's not possible." The man sat behind his desk and pulled out a folder from one of the drawers. "Yulia's been here for over three years. A few couples have tried to adopt her in the past, but she didn't want anything to do with them."

"What? Why wouldn't she want to be adopted?" He did recall how shy she got around Eva. Maybe she was introverted.

"I normally wouldn't bring this up, but seeing as she is getting to the age where further adoption is unlikely, I think it's okay. It's not against the rules for me to tell you, it's just a sensitive subject."

"Is this about her parents?"

"Yes. There is no easy way to say this, so I'll be direct. Yulia's parents were pirates."

"What? She told me her father fought in the war."

"That may actually be true. I never met the man, but I can confirm he was a pirate. They both were. Her parent's ship was captured trying to extort a freighter in a nearby system. An STO destroyer just so happened to be flying through the system and intercepted them. After disabling their engines, the STO boarded the ship and dispatched the pirates after a short gunfight. When they were clearing the ship, they found the girl hiding in a closet. Instead of declaring her a pirate along with the rest, they put her in the system as a rescued slave."

Alexander winced at that. If the captain of the destroyer tagged her as a pirate, she would have had the same fate as the rest. It seemed like condemning a five-year-old for their parents' poor choices was just a bit too much. He was glad the captain had seen sense.

"Since they couldn't bring the girl back to the core, at least not without uncomfortable questions being asked, they dumped her on Petrov Station."

"That's horrific. Do you think she remembers the incident and that is why she refuses adoption?"

"If she does, she hasn't spoken of it. Now that you know her story, does that change your mind at all?"

"No... why would it?"

The man shrugged. "I have to ask. There are people on this station, and that I know personally that have suffered pirate attacks. I couldn't in good conscience adopt the child out to someone with a history like that. That brings me to my next question. What makes you think you're qualified to be her parent?"

"I—I don't know. When she was attacked at my shop. All I could feel was pure anger at the men who hurt her. And a desire to protect her at all costs."

The man nodded along. "And how do you feel now?"

He had to think about it for a moment. "Anxious? Worried. Upset. She should be given the best medical treatment possible, but because she is a ward, they are denying it to her. It's not fair."

"I happen to agree, Mr. Kane, but life is not fair. Especially out in space. You are on the second ring with the rest of us, so you must understand. That being said, I am aware of your new financial situation."

"You are?"

"Yes," the man replied testily. "A certain Captain Na, who should be keeping to his duties and not sticking his nose in where it isn't wanted or needed, filled me in. Congratulations, by the way. Any time you can stick it to one of the big core mega-corporations, the better. So that covers the financial question. What about a home, Mr. Kane?"

"A home?"

"Yes, a home. You can't expect Yulia to live inside your workshop, can you? What about where your body is stored?"

He wasn't surprised the man knew about his 'condition.' He had been advertising it as much as he could to try to get the word out. "My body is just in a rented storage locker. But I can certainly find a home."

"You would need to do that before I can finalize the adoption. Last question, Mr. Kane. What are your plans?"

Originally, he had planned to just keep repairing stuff and trying to uncover his past. Since the attack, he now had more options. He was no longer tethered to the station and could board a ship and leave at any time. He had mulled over accepting Dr. Nova Lund's offer to work for them. He had been conversing with Lund and a few of the members of his team over the last few months. While he enjoyed those discussions and learned quite a bit, he was done working for others or being beholden to others. He wanted to strike out on his own, and now he had the chance to do that.

"I believe I plan on leaving Petrov Station in the near future."

The headmaster nodded, not surprised by the answer. "That might be the best for Yulia's sake. A daily reminder of where she got attacked will not be very conducive to healing."

"Does that mean you will approve the adoption?" He felt a momentary flicker of hope spark inside him. If he had any lingering doubts before that he was doing the right thing, he didn't anymore.

"Just hold on," the man gestured. "You need to fix your living arrangement first. A simple apartment would be plenty since you don't plan on staying. For now, I will mark the adoption as 'in progress.' This will register you as her guardian and qualify her to receive the medication she needs to make a full recovery. Just read over these forms, sign them, and transfer the adoption fee. The last step will be determining if Yulia wishes for you to be her new father, but that will have to wait until she recovers."

Alexander assumed there would be a fee. Everything had fees in the future, but that was fine. He quickly read through the document and signed it. The fee wasn't even that bad. He used the terminal in the headmaster's office and quickly transferred the sum over.

"Congratulations, Mr. Kane. You are now Yulia's guardian. Considering what you tried to do for her, I am sure you will make a wonderful parent. I wish her the best in her recovery. If you could, before departing the station, bring her by the orphanage so she can say goodbye. She has a lot of friends here."

"Thank you, Headmaster Wong. I will do my best. And I will certainly bring her by once she has recovered. One last thing. Would it be possible to send Markus to my shop so I can thank him personally?"

The man rubbed his chin. "I can ask him when he returns, but I won't promise he will listen."

"That's all I ask for. Thank you again." Alexander bowed his massive frame before turning and leaving. He needed to get back to the hospital so they could update their records and treat Yulia properly.

chapter 24

Mingyu sat silently among the other six captains as the prosecutors read the charges.

Unlike the arbitration between Omni and the station, this was an open trial. Instead of being hidden away in some conference room, it took place on the tenth ring in the Court of Affairs.

The space was a large one, meant only for the most important functions of Petrov Station. Like the passing of a captain, or a new Council Captain stepping up to fill their parent's role. Thankfully, those rarely happened in conjunction with each other.

Despite the fact that the room could hold over a thousand attendees, it was packed to the brim today. There were even people standing in the back. Word had quickly spread of the attack, and the battle in the hangar. Some of the people were there simply to hear the sentencing, others to sneer at the shackled individuals. The second group probably knew what was in store for these men and women.

There was only one sentence for those accused of piracy. Two of the captured individuals were already missing from the fifteen taken aboard the ship. All of them had been questioned in private. The two that were missing had been the brains behind the attack. That was obvious.

The things they accused Mr. Kane of had to be quietly checked out. Any accusation of weapons aboard the station was equally as important as an attack such as this.

The captains and station security had gone over the video of the scene. They had even brought up old footage from the few working hallway cameras. The only thing they ever saw was Kane visiting the terminal or going to the smelter to recycle scrap components. A second sweep of the shop after the attack didn't produce any evidence that Kane had or was manufacturing weapons.

They even audited his printer logs. There were a few items that had been printed that were questionable, but nothing that pointed directly to the man using those components to build weapons. He didn't think these men were lying though and that put him in a difficult spot.

He wanted to have a working relationship with Kane, but an accusation such as this strained the man's relationship with the station. It didn't matter that there was no proof of his crimes, or that the station wasn't going to pursue the matter any further. He had already overheard some of the other Councilors discussing revoking the man's elevated status that he earned from exposing the pirate threat.

Mingyu wanted to counsel against that decision, but that was a slippery slope. It was simply too dangerous to appear to be supporting Kane without having him appear to be supporting arms manufacturing. Mingyu would be curious to see what the other captains said when he brought the topic up. With him being the face of the arbitration between Kane and Omni, he had been on station during the attack. So he headed up the investigation and apprehension of the *Devil's Bargain* crew.

The trial went on and Mingyu paid just enough attention not to seem bored. The mercenaries for their part were tight-lipped and stone-faced. They had nothing to gain by talking and nothing to lose by remaining quiet. Mingyu had met Captain Harn years ago. The man was brash and reckless, but he wasn't stupid. He wondered how the man had lost control over his crew to the point it came to this.

"Do the defendants have anything to say for their actions?" Kovalenko asked imperiously.

Mingyu's eyes flicked over to the captain. That was another issue that had to be dealt with. The attack had forestalled the case he had been building against Kovalenko and Hoffman, but they would see justice soon as well.

The shackled mercenaries all hocked gobs of spit upon the ground, before Harn glared up at them. "I hope your station rusts out from under you!"

There was a round of collective gasps from the crowd at the vile insult. It took Kovalenko a full minute to regain order.

"Order in the court! ORDER IN THE COURT!" Kovalenko yelled as he smashed the gavel into the extremely expensive wooden bench, his face beet red from outrage.

Mingyu winced internally at the dents the man must be putting in the ancient surface that had been in place since shortly after the station was founded.

While this was happening, Captain Harn was laughing and riling up the crowd even more. It took two Station Security guards with stun sticks to finally silence Harn.

He wanted to shake his head at the foul display. There were just certain things you didn't say to spacers. That insult was one. There were others, but even thinking about them was considered a bad omen by some. He let the man's words slide into the back of his mind as he focused back on the trial.

"As the accused have nothing to add in their defense; except vile insults, we will move on to sentencing." There was a collective roar of approval from the crowd this time around at Kovalenko's words.

After a few more pounds of the gavel, the room went quiet again. "What say you, Captain Liu?"

"Guilty," the woman stated.

"What say you, Captain Yuchen?"

"Guilty," his friend responded.

"What say you, Captain Na?"

"Guilty," Mingyu replied.

The questions repeated, moving up in seniority. Starting with Zhang, next up was Weiss, then Hoffman, and ending with Kovalenko himself.

"Guilty," Kovalenko spoke before slamming the gavel down one final time to the roar of approval from everyone in the room. It was a unanimous vote, which was no surprise.

"The sentence for piracy is death. Since there will be no appeal, your sentence will be carried out immediately. Guards, please take the prisoners to the nearest airlock. Make sure Captain Harn is awake before carrying out the sentence."

Mingyu couldn't help but wince at that. The man was gonna die, at least let him do it while unconscious. Since when had Kovalenko become so bloodthirsty? Usually, that sort of vitriol was reserved for the survivors of pirate attacks. As far as he knew, the Kovalenko family never had an encounter with pirates.

The guilty were dragged out a side door, and the holographic display popped to life in the center of the courtroom. It displayed an exterior camera view next to an airlock.

After ten minutes, the lights outside the airlock began to flash, then they stopped as fifteen small forms tumbled out and into the black of space.

Some in the crowd clapped, others looked sick. It was one thing to know someone was going to die, it was another to have to watch it. Mingyu had seen a dozen such trials over his lifetime, so the sight didn't get to him anymore. He didn't celebrate it either, even if the people being punished deserved the punishment.

"The sentence has been carried out. As per STO rules, the names of the convicted will be stricken from galactic records, and all assets sold off to pay restitution to their victims."

Mingyu noted that the man carefully left out the part where the station would take its cut as well.

The sooner he got the trial going for his fellow captains, the better.

* * *

"Well, that was distasteful," Xu stated.

Sergei snorted and pushed the smaller man out of his way. "What's distasteful about eliminating pirates? You going soft on us, Yuchen? Or maybe they were your friends."

Before the two could get into an argument, Anastasia entered the room. "You know as well as the rest of us that Harn's crew weren't pirates, Sergei. So knock it off."

The larger man sneered at Mingyu's friend before stepping away and throwing himself into one of the soft couches along the wall. "A technicality. One that we had no issue exploiting."

"We weren't exploiting the law," Ingrid chimed in as the last to enter. "We were simply being diligent. Any captain seen harboring pirates could be a pirate themselves. The same goes for a station. We all know how unfavorably the STO looks at those that harbor pirates."

"Call it whatever you want," Zhang waved dismissively. "Why are we here?"

"And where are Captains Kovalenko and Hoffman?" Ingrid asked.

The gazes of the group fell on him at her words.

"They aren't here, because this has to do with them." Mingyu made a flicking motion with his tablet, and all of their tablets lit up with the incoming information packet.

He gave them time to go over the information.

It shouldn't have been a surprise when Zhang groaned and threw his tablet on the table. "Just spell it out for us, Na. I don't have time for this shit."

"If you would bother reading more than a sentence or two, you would understand," Yuchen replied tersely, turning to him. "This isn't some joke, is it?"

He shook his head. "I wish it was, but I've gone over the information. There is no mistake."

"You're telling us that Kovalenko, and Hoffman, two pillars of Petrov Station, have been trying to what? Bankrupt the station?"

"What!" Sergei roared and shot to his feet. The man snatched his tablet from the table and began actually reading the document Mingyu had sent. As the big man read, his frown grew. "This doesn't make any sense. Why would they do this?"

"I don't know. I was hoping one of you might have an idea."

"When did you discover this? And why were you looking into their records in the first place?" Ingrid asked with suspicion.

Mingyu knew that would come up. "I discovered it during the arbitration hearing. As to why I looked into it, I felt like some of my fellow captains... were a bit too focused on money."

Liu put her tablet down. "So it comes back to Kane again. I didn't vote against your suggestion because of the money, if that's what you think. I voted against it because I believed the man to be a troublemaker. It seems I may have been correct. In less than a year, we have had to arbitrate against one of the largest corporations in human space, a girl was critically injured while in his shop, and we had to sentence fifteen people to death for piracy."

"Those are hardly his fault," Na bristled.

"That may be true, but he was the catalyst for all of them. And let's not forget the accusations leveled against him. Even if it can't be proven he was manufacturing weapons, why take the chance?" The woman glanced around the room. "We have a majority here. I say we take a vote."

"A vote on what?" Sergei asked in irritation. Mingyu knew he was still reading the document because his lips were moving as he read. The man had done that since Mingyu could remember, but nobody brought it up.

"Simple. A vote to exile Mr. Kane from Petrov Station."

"You can't be serious," Mingyu replied. "The man has done nothing to warrant such a vote. If anything, we should be voting to work more closely with him. I've told you before that he is an asset, and all we are doing is constantly pushing him away."

Liu ignored him. "All in favor of exiling Mr. Kane?"

Ingrid's hand went up, followed by Anastasia, then Sergei, and then Xu's. Mingyu could only stare dumbly at his friend's raised hand.

"I'm sorry," Xu stated. "I believe you, my friend. Kane might be an asset, but he also brings trouble. The station has enough issues, and we can ill afford more at the moment. Especially now that you are bringing this financial trouble to our plate."

"The matter is decided," Ingrid stated coldly. "We will give Kane two months to collect his property and find a ship off station."

Mingyu did his best not to let his anger show. "I will notify him of this."

"No. You've grown too close to this man. We will choose a captain at random to notify him."

"That is not your decision to make. You are not the Senior Captain."

The group turned toward Anastasia, who had been quiet most of the time. If both Kovalenko and Hoffman were suspect, she would now be the Senior Captain, followed by Zhang. Thank the stars for that. The woman sighed. "She is right, Mingyu. Just look at how you are behaving. You are too close to this issue."

He bowed to her. "Very well, if this is what the Senior Captain wishes. I will oblige."

CHAPTER 25

After speaking with Dr. Nord, and the man assuring him that Yulia was now eligible for the advanced healing treatments, Alexander returned to his shop. He needed to secure housing for his newly adopted daughter, as well as other things a child of her age might need.

It was crazy to think a child relied on him now.

As he entered his shop, he found it even more destroyed than it was when he left. "What the hell!"

Nothing had been taken, and there were evidence tags on everything. There was also a notice stuck to the door.

Evidence was collected in the processing of case 98-3-21-2398

He went to the terminal down the hall to look up the case number. From his research on station law, he knew all case records were made public. It didn't take him long to find the case log and figure out why they trashed his shop, instead of just taking images of the damage that was already present.

Victim: Alexander Kane

Accused by two defendants Gino and Svadi Coal of harboring restricted items. A search warrant was issued for the premises. No restricted items were found. The scene was recorded, and no further action was taken.

Alexander had been so caught up in his worry over Yulia that he hadn't even known Station Security had raided his shop.

Again with those damn weapons. They weren't even functional! But somehow those two mercenaries had spotted them the first time they had entered his shop. Had he known a single glance at the damn things would have caused Yulia to get hurt, he would have destroyed them the moment he created the stupid things.

He checked on the rest of the case. It had been a day or two since the attack, but he didn't expect much movement. He was proven wrong on that account.

All crew of the Devil's Bargain were tried and convicted for piracy by the Council. They have all received a sentence of death.

It was quite surreal for Alexander. He hadn't met any of the other mercenaries, and yet he now learned they were all convicted of the attack and sentenced within a day. Why did the report not list their names like the previous report did?

The laws there were swift and brutal for certain offenses. This was just another reminder that life was not worth what it was back in his day. That didn't mean he felt any remorse for those people. If not outright part of the attack, they still assisted the two men who did. If they hadn't, those men wouldn't have been on the station.

The only thing that gave him pause was consideration for Yulia's past. Hopefully the memories of that time were long forgotten. He certainly wasn't going to bring it up.

Alexander flicked off the case screen and started searching for appropriate housing. That along with Yulia's agreement to allow him to become her parent was all that was holding up the process.

Finding a house wasn't a challenge. Even on the second ring, there were houses. He would have preferred to place her somewhere nicer, but not being able to use the normal lifts, he was heavily restricted on where and when he could travel across rings.

As for Yulia agreeing to the adoption, he was about 80% sure she would.

The young girl seemed quite enamored with him in a way she wasn't with anyone else. The few times he had seen her interact with other adults, she turned shy or withdrawn. She had a similar reaction to Eva, even though that woman seemed to be able to get anyone to talk. He didn't hold it against the retiree for working for Captain Na. He didn't even hate the captain. He just didn't trust his or the station's motives after everything that had happened so far.

After flipping through listings, Alexander found a small space that could double as a house. It was even in the same section that his shop occupied. There would be a lot more cleaning in his immediate future, he was sure of that. After purchasing the space for half a year, he closed that window.

He had to sit there and think for a bit. The next decision was far more important and long-reaching than a simple house. Ever since he had realized he was no longer under the restrictions Yuri placed into the holo emitter, he knew he was going to move on from Petrov. He had stated as much when he met with Headmaster Wong. Even if none of the past few months happened, he knew staying here wouldn't get him any closer to figuring out how he got trapped in this body. The attack and the station selling him out only reinforced the need to leave.

Alexander hadn't put any serious thought into where he was going to go. Maybe a part of him hadn't ever believed he would be able to free himself from the control box. At least not without destroying the only thing that had kept him awake. During the attack, the moment before the pulse blast tore the old holo emitter apart, Alexander felt genuine fear. It was masked by the rage he felt at the time, but looking back on it now, he knew what the emotion was.

Alexander rubbed his hand across the surface of his body. His sensitive fingers couldn't find the seams of the repair. His body was now completely unblemished, but he had stared at the damage for over three years, so he could trace the contours of where the damage had once been.

The fact that the damage had been fixed by a process he didn't understand sent a chill down his metaphorical spine. Whatever had accomplished the feat was clearly beyond human technology. It rekindled his need to know where he had come from and how he arrived in that state. The need to know had slipped into the background as he was forced to spend his time trying to just survive.

If what he believed was true, he needed to step out on his own. He couldn't have the STO, or these corporations breathing down his neck as he searched for evidence of his past. If his body was of alien origin, there was no telling what people would do to get their hands on it.

And honestly... He wasn't willing to work for anyone other than himself.

Alexander decided to write Dr. Lund first.

Dr. Lund,

First of all, I just wanted to thank you for assisting me with the few questions I had. Our discussions were eye-opening. I'm messaging you to let you know, I will be turning down the offer to join your research group. Some things have changed for me recently, and it simply wouldn't work.

I understand what you are doing is important. But I feel working for myself is simply the better option. If you ever feel like getting out of the theoretical game, send me a message. I may have a job for you instead. Please keep in touch.

Alexander Kane

He hit send on the message. Depending on whether their ship was near a station with a Qcomm or not, it could take hours or weeks to get a response.

Before he sent his next message, he did some research. Unlike the station's listing for properties, there wasn't one central place to find properties for sale across human space.

Instead of wasting his time trying to locate one that would fit the goal he had in mind, he contacted a real estate agency located in a core world called Ganos.

"Fidelity Properties, my name is Violet. How can I be of assistance today?"

He was surprised to see a video window pop up instead of the standard text interface. The video came through grainy, but he could hear her just fine.

"Oh, it appears our connection is rather rough. I do not see any image, are you hearing me okay?"

"I am. Sorry, Violet. I'm on a public terminal, and I don't think it even has a camera."

"Oh, that's fine. How can I help you today..."

"Alexander Kane. I'm looking for a property."

"That is wonderful news, Mr. Kane. What type of requirements are you looking for in this property?"

He listed off the items he would need. Even through the grainy video, he could see the woman frown slightly.

"Those are some very specific requirements, Mr. Kane. May I ask what sort of budget you are working with?"

When he told her the amount, she immediately perked up.

"Well, that will certainly make things easier. It may take some time to find something that meets your needs, but I believe it is doable. Do you have a timeframe?"

He wanted to say no, but he honestly wanted to get off the station as soon as he could. "Is a couple of months doable?"

She tapped in some items on a screen off to the side. "It will limit your options to already vacant properties, but we should be able to make something work. Do you have a personal comm number I can contact you at?"

"Not currently. I have a merchant account though, so just send any correspondence there." He sent the merchant account information to the woman.

"Alright, I have the information and what you are looking for. We will be in touch soon, Mr. Kane."

He thanked the woman and closed the connection.

Alexander knew requiring the property to be outside of STO-controlled space was a big ask, but it was mandatory if he wanted to work in peace.

The next message was a bit more difficult for him to send.

First off, he didn't want to rely on anyone else if he could avoid it. That obviously hadn't helped him so far. He didn't have the resources necessary to buy a ship, learn to fly it, and operate it all himself. He could also purchase a ship and pay a crew, but that money would be better spent purchasing his new home.

He was also forced to consider where this home would be. It certainly wouldn't be on a world that humanity wanted but it did need to have a breathable atmosphere. Wherever he ended up needed to be safe enough for Yulia, yet outside of the STO's reach as well as any local government. There was no point shucking off the reins of the STO, only to be saddled with some local force that was equally as shitty—if not more so.

In his research, he knew humanity had explored quite a bit farther than they currently claimed for territory. The thing was nominally habitable worlds were not all that rare. Earth-like planets were, but there were still five of those that composed the core worlds of the STO's territory. They had another dozen worlds that were being terraformed as they were populated. If you didn't like that, there were orbital installations like

Petrov, satellite colonies, bubble habitats on worlds like Mars, and even certain asteroid installations.

There was no lack of space to live. Humanity had picked the closest and easiest-to-reach targets to occupy while the rest was just waiting for them to expand outward at a later date. He figured their reluctance to spread themselves out too far probably had a lot to do with their run-in with the Shican, the first alien species humanity had encountered.

He added that to his list of things to research. It wouldn't do him any good to establish a home in some distant world, only for those aliens to show up.

Another major consideration was supplies. Wherever his base of operations ended up, it would likely need constant replenishment from shipping. It might be a decade or more before he managed to establish a self-sufficient economy, if ever. It really depended on what resources the world had to offer.

Then there was hiring workers and getting families over and... He paused, his mind spinning from all the details. Details he didn't need to worry about right now. It was at times like this that he wished he could take a calming breath. Instead, he centered himself as best he could in his mind. Then he composed his next message.

> *Jasper,*
>
> *Is your offer still good? I may need some assistance. Contact me as soon as you get this message.*
>
> *Alexander*

Now he would wait and see.

He closed the terminal and headed back to his shop to clean, then he would head to the new apartment.

chapter 26

Alexander waited in the patient discharge area. People were giving him odd looks, but he was used to that by now. In his hand was a stuffed bear he had printed for Yulia. Despite the advanced meds, they still kept the girl for two days to ensure no complications from her injuries or the medications.

Soon enough, the door swung open, and a nurse wheeled a very disoriented-looking little girl out on a wheelchair.

"Alex?" the girl asked in confusion. "Where is Headmaster Wong?"

The girl tried to stand, but the nurse gently pressed her back into the seat. "There will be time for walking around later. For now, just rest, sweetie. Can you do that for me?" The girl gave a tired nod, and the nurse smiled, setting the chair off to the side so Yulia could watch a holo screen with some cartoon of a talking cat playing on it.

"Mr. Kane?"

"Yes."

Although, he didn't know who else she expected him to be considering he was an eight-foot-tall robot.

"There are a few final things we have to complete before we can discharge her to your care."

"Like what?" He had the new holo emitter he wore project a questioning look.

"First off, Yulia hasn't agreed for you to become her guardian yet. So we need to wait for Headmaster Wong to arrive to speak with the girl and complete that portion. He should have been here already."

He had expected that part, but he assumed he would be the one to bring her by the orphanage to complete that.

"And the other part?"

"That would be the payment for the treatment."

Without even asking how much it was, Alexander handed her a credit chip.

The nurse looked slightly surprised by this, but she nodded and took the chip, heading over to a terminal to complete the payment. While she was busy doing that, Mr. Wong arrived.

"Apologies for being late. I had a situation at the orphanage to deal with. Where is Yulia?"

Alexander pointed to the wheelchair near the far side of the room.

"Is she lucid enough?" This question was directed to the nurse.

"By any legal definition, yes. However, she may have some memory loss. I would also recommend keeping your questions to the minimum or she may start growing confused."

"Hmm. Not ideal, but as long as we cover our bases, it should be fine."

"Is something going on? Can't we just wait until she's completely recovered?" Alexander asked, unsure as to why they felt that needed to be done so urgently.

Wong and the nurse shared a look. "Have the captains not sent a representative to speak with you yet?"

"I spoke to Captain Na if that's what you mean."

Wong shook his head. "Captain Na reached out to me through Eva Wu. Are you familiar with the woman?"

Alexander made his avatar nod.

"Good. Anyway, the captains have voted, and you are being expelled from the station."

After being accused of manufacturing weapons, Alexander wasn't surprised by that. Seeing no reaction to this statement, Wong continued.

"If we don't complete this adoption before they speak with you to pass on this ruling, it will block this adoption."

He didn't know how to feel about that. He had already gotten her the treatment she needed, so there was no worry there. Was he really the best person to be a father to a little girl? While he had done a lot of thinking on the subject and thought he could do a decent job, he would never be the warm, loving father figure she might need.

"She is healed, so she would go back into the orphanage then, wouldn't she?"

The headmaster shook his head vehemently. "That's the problem. Because I started the adoption process, she would fall under the ruling the captains have issued for you. Since you are not legally her parent yet, she would not be able to board a ship with you. She would instead be held in confinement until such time as an STO ship comes by."

"What?! Why? What are you trying to say?" Alexander had an idea, but he wanted the man to spell it out for him because, to him, it sounded far too cruel and barbaric a punishment for an innocent child.

The slightly overweight headmaster swallowed thickly. "The STO would see her record. It may have been fudged slightly by the previous captain, but we can't assume this new captain would have the same feelings as the last. They may even report this infraction and get that original captain in trouble."

If that were true, they would declare the little girl a pirate and eject Yulia out of an airlock for something she had no part in. Those people and their laws were insane. He knew piracy was bad and needed to be snuffed out, but who could ever be cold or cruel enough to condemn a child for their parent's actions?

"What are you waiting for, then?" Alexander practically dragged the man over to the seated girl.

The girl looked over at their arrival, her eyes still slightly glassy from the medications she had been given. "Headmaster?"

The man straightened up his ruffled clothing from Alexander's rough handling and knelt down next to the girl. "Hello, Yulia. How are you feeling?"

"Tired," the girl admitted.

The man nodded sympathetically. "We won't keep you long. I just have a few questions if you're up for it."

He gestured toward Alexander. "You know Mr. Kane, correct?"

She looked confused by the question so Alexander spoke up. "That's my last name, Yulia."

"Ohh..." She nodded.

"Good, good," Wong continued. "Do you like Mr. Kane?"

She nodded again.

"If you could say yes or no, please," the man urged.

"Yes," she said, a yawn escaping her lips.

"That's wonderful. One last question, Yulia dear. How would you like it if Alexander Kane adopted you?"

"Huh?"

Alexander could see she understood the question; she was just overtaken by emotion as her eyes started to water. Then slowly she started to nod.

"You need to say the word, Yulia," Wong gently prodded.

The reply came tentatively, almost like the girl didn't believe this was happening. "Yes."

The headmaster blew out a sigh and pressed his thumb into a tablet he had been holding the entire time. The screen blinked green once and he spoke into it. "I have included the recorded agreement from Ward Yulia. She has agreed to the adoption. As of this date in the year 2398, Ward Yulia is now Yulia Kane." The man clicked off the tablet and stuffed it back into a satchel he was carrying. "Congratulations to you two, and I wish you the best of luck."

"Thank you, Mr. Wong. I'm sorry for the rough handling."

He waved away the concern. "It was for the best. It shows me you do truly care what happens to her. Now, I must return to the orphanage before the kids find a way to burn it down. Please do remember to come by."

"I will before we leave."

He shook the man's hand, and the headmaster made a quick exit. When the door to the corridor opened, Alexander stiffened. Two Station Security and a larger man waited outside. The bigger man's eyes flicked toward him and remained there until the doors closed once more.

"Ahem," the nurse cleared her throat to get his attention. She held out his credit chip to him. "You are all paid up, Mr. Kane. There was an unusual delay in the payment processing."

"Does this unusual delay have anything to do with the three men waiting outside?"

"Hmm. I'm sure I wouldn't know. Just be aware, only patients and their loved ones or guardians are allowed inside this area."

He expressed genuine gratitude toward the nurse. "Thank you for that."

The woman smiled. "I've done nothing but my job, Mr. Kane. Now you and your lovely daughter have a wonderful life. Hopefully a quieter one from here on out."

He nodded. Although, he wasn't sure how quiet his life was going to be considering he was about to be evicted from the station. Then again, he already had plans in place to leave. He just thought he had more time. If Captain Daniels didn't respond soon, he might need to find alternative transportation.

"Is it okay if I leave her here for a moment while I have a chat with my guests outside?"

"Take all the time you need Mr. Kane. I'll be here to keep an eye on her." She looked over at the girl. "Although, I don't see that being a problem."

Alexander focused his attention on Yulia. As he turned his holographic face to make it appear he was looking at her, he saw the girl was fast asleep.

"Again, Thank you." With that, he turned and strode out the automatic doors, ducking so he didn't smash the top of his frame against the ceiling as he passed.

The larger of the three men looked him over, while the two guards looked on nervously, their hands on stun sticks.

"Gentlemen… I assume you are here to speak with me?"

"You're bigger than I imagined," the larger of the three stated instead of answering his question.

"I'm sorry. I didn't get your name," Alexander responded testily. If these men were going to be rude, he would be rude right back.

The man snorted at Alexander's tone. "I heard you were a feisty one. Name's Captain Sergei Zhang. You can call me Captain Sergei Zhang. And you are Alexander Kane, or at least the robotic puppet of his. I need to speak with you in person."

"You are," Alexander replied, being purposefully obtuse.

The man forced a smile on his face, but it never reached his eyes. "You know what I mean, Kane, so stop playing these games."

"If you know who I am, you know that isn't possible. My body is in a stasis pod, and my mind is controlling this form. If I turned off the stasis, I would die." He had come up with this excuse back when he planned this 'pretending to be sick' disguise to hide what he truly was. It was meant to prevent anyone from digging too deeply. It seemed his foresight was paying off.

Zhang clicked his tongue in annoyance. "Difficult to the very end. Fine. Have it your way, Kane." He turned to the guards. "Have you two recorded Mr. Kane's words?"

"Yes, Captain," one of the security guards responded.

"Good enough." He cleared his throat and turned back to him. "Alexander Kane. I, Sergei Zhang, as acting captain of the Council of Captains, hereby pronounce your exile from Petrov Station for the remainder of your life, as well as two further generations of your lineage. You have sixty standard days to book passage off of the station. Failure to do so will result in your incarceration until such time as the STO gets off their collective asses to come to collect you. When they do, you will be charged with trespassing and illegal squatting."

"Is that all?" Alexander asked in annoyance. While he had expected some form of punishment for the weapons accusations, he thought Mingyu might have been able to mitigate that considering what he wanted from him. It appeared Captain Na's opinion didn't have nearly as much weight as the man thought it did. It was a good thing Alexander was already making arrangements to leave.

The captain's smile returned, and he took a step forward. "I hope you don't find a way off the station. You see, I know what you're all about, Kane. You think you can flaunt the rules and get away with it. Well, perhaps some forced labor will see that high and mighty attitude wiped away. Although, with your condition, I don't think you'd survive. I somehow doubt they will let you use your fancy robot in lockup. You have a good day now."

The trio turned and walked away, leaving Alexander upset and confused. When had he flaunted station laws? True, he had made weapons, but it wasn't like he wanted to do that, and he had destroyed them. Captain Zhang seemed to have a bit of a chip on his shoulder.

Alexander shook those thoughts away and quickly forgot the captain as he went in to retrieve Yulia. It was time to take her to their new—albeit temporary—home.

chapter 27

Yulia was still sleeping when Alexander rolled her wheelchair into the apartment. It wasn't much. There was a main room with a small kitchen, a single bedroom, and a small bathroom, but it was more than enough for the little girl's needs. It was clean since Alexander had spent the last day scrubbing the place from top to bottom. It hadn't been nearly as filthy as his shop when he first moved in, but he still wanted to ensure a clean, safe environment for the girl.

Alexander gently scooped Yulia up and carried her into the bedroom before laying the covers over her. Since he didn't know anything about raising a child, he had purchased a few books on the subject. After reading the books, he was surprised that children needed so much consideration. Somehow he pictured taking care of them like taking care of a pet. He imagined if he told another parent that thought, they would laugh themselves silly.

Being a robot, he couldn't apply everything he had learned in the books, but he did try his best. Most of that effort went into the bedroom, which is why the small space was decked out in a pink floral pattern, including the sheets, blanket, and even a nightlight.

He also left the door slightly open as he moved back into the main room. The main room consisted of a couch and a holo-projector on one side with the kitchen having only a small fridge and single-element cooktop on the other. Since Alexander didn't need to eat, that was all they needed.

He didn't want to leave Yulia alone while she was sleeping, so he sat on the floor in front of the holo and continued his lessons in rocket propulsion, keeping the sound to the barest whisper.

After a few hours, he heard a chime. Confused for a moment, he looked around until he spotted the other item he had purchased recently. The comm sat on the counter in the kitchen because the strap didn't fit around Alexander's wrist and he hadn't gotten around to making one that would.

He stood up and walked over to the piece of tech that connected to the Qcomm relay built into the station. It was a message from Captain Daniel.

Alexander, I got your message. It was vague, so I hope you are alright. I meant what I said to you back then, so if you need something let me know. The Zephyr will remain in range of our local Qcomm until I get your reply.

He began typing out a response, not sure when it would reach the captain. His conversation with Violet had seemed instantaneous if a bit low quality. Then again, he had never seen anyone else using a comm watch to have a real-time face-to-face conversation. Everyone always seemed to use the text mode. He didn't know if that was because their planet had a better Qcomm or if there was something else that limited the communication devices.

I'm fine, Jasper, thanks for asking. The Council on Petrov has decided I am no longer welcome here. They have given me sixty days to vacate. Fifty-nine as I write this. I am currently in the process of acquiring a new residence off-station. Do you happen to know anyone willing to transport me... and my daughter?

It took less than an hour to get a response. Alexander was pretty sure the captain didn't wait an hour to respond, so there was certainly some delay there.

A daughter... I think that is something better discussed in person instead of over the comms, I'm sure it's a long story. As for transport, I don't know anyone in that area.

Alexander deflated at that before he continued to read.

But that's not a problem. The Zephyr can be there within thirty days to transport you and anything you need to take with you. Before you respond and tell me that that's too much, and not necessary, because that does seem like something you would say, this is a friend doing another friend a favor. So as long as you still see me as your friend, you will accept my offer.

It was indeed what he had been thinking. Alexander smiled internally. At least not everyone in this messed-up future was a jerk. Captain Daniels really did seem like one of the good ones. If it wasn't for him, he was sure Omni would have come in and simply stolen his advancements without offering a cent in return. He supposed he could put Captain Na in that column as well, even though he was partly to blame for the way the station handled his issues. If Mingyu hadn't spoken with the headmaster, and given the hospital a heads-up, Yulia might be sitting in some cell somewhere, waiting for the STO to decide her fate.

Thank you, Jasper, I owe you one. And yes, it's a long story. I can tell you when you and the Zephyr arrive.

A weight lifted off Alexander's shoulders knowing he had independent transport off the station. Considering how hostile Zhang had come off, he wouldn't put it past the man to try something to prevent him from leaving. He could reach out to Na to see if he could prevent that, but he didn't want to rely on the other Council Captain. There was also the fact that Na had been the only Council member to speak with him so far, to suddenly change it to Zhang spoke of internal changes in the Council. Alexander had stirred up that hornet's nest enough. He just wanted to be off this station and away from people deciding his fate for him.

Yulia woke up a few hours later. He only knew because she poked her head through the crack in the door. It was almost like the little girl was afraid to believe what she experienced the night before. Tentatively, she pushed the door open and stepped out into the living room.

"Morning, Yulia," Alexander said as he rose from near the couch. "Are you hungry?"

The girl nodded quietly and walked over to the counter before climbing up on her stool. Alexander had fixed it after it was destroyed in the attack and moved it from his shop. It was a little shorter now to match the counter height in the apartment.

The girl never took her eyes off him as he cooked breakfast. When he set the plate of food in front of her, she looked down at it and tears started to form in her eyes.

Before Alexander could ask what was wrong, the girl hopped off her stool and ran around the counter to hug him. "It wasn't a dream?"

"No, sweetie, it wasn't a dream. I'm your dad now."

He hugged her back as best he could, and she stood there and cried like that for a bit before wiping the snot and tears from her face with her sleeve and walking back around to eat her food.

After she ate, she cleaned up and got dressed in a new outfit. It was essentially a duplicate of her old outfit, but the girl didn't seem to mind.

"Where are we going?" Yulia asked as she held Alexander's hand while they walked.

"To my shop. I need to start cleaning it out so we can leave."

"Leave?" the little girl asked in confusion.

"We have to leave Petrov Station."

The girl stopped and let go of Alexander's hand. "But what about my friends?"

He knew the conversation was going to come up, he just wished it could have waited.

He kneeled in front of the girl. "You'll get to see them before we leave. And I'll get you a comm so you can keep in touch."

The girl's eyes turned red, but she swallowed back her tears and nodded.

He stood and they continued their slow walk to his shop. After purchasing a personal comm for himself, he now understood why very few people bothered with the things. They were horrifically expensive for what they did, and each message cost money to send through the Qcomm.

That was a small price to pay to see the girl happy. Besides, even after he purchased a property, he would still be a multi-millionaire. He had received his portion of the damages from the attack.

It galled him that Yulia wasn't eligible for compensation because of her status as a ward during the incident though. They really did the bare minimum to see orphans as anything other than a burden.

Yulia started to hesitate as they approached his shop.

He stopped. "Is there something wrong?"

"I-I'm scared."

He was being an idiot, he should have thought about that. Of course, a little kid would be afraid of going back to the place where they got hurt.

"Do you want to go back to the apartment?"

The girl thought for a minute before shaking her head. "You'll protect me?"

"I'll never let anyone hurt you ever again." And he meant it.

That seemed to mollify the girl. She was still a little hesitant, but they took it slow. Eventually, they arrived outside his shop. There were no signs an attack had ever taken place there. Along with cleaning the apartment, Alexander had repaired everything that was damaged or destroyed in the tiny space he worked out of. The old printer was a loss, but he bought a newer, better model.

Seeing no signs of bad men, Yulia ran over and took her customary spot on a new seat. That one was much nicer and had actual padding to it. From there, they fell into their old comfortable rhythm as he worked on completing the jobs he had lined up. He didn't plan on taking on any more work, but he wasn't about to abandon the work he already had.

chapter 22

A few days later Alexander got a comm message from Fidelity Properties. They had found a suitable location that met his criteria, but they wanted to discuss it over video at his earliest convenience. He supposed that made sense. They couldn't know what time it was where he was located and they were available at all hours. He was honestly surprised they had gotten back to him so soon.

Alexander waited until Yulia was asleep before he walked to the nearest terminal to contact Fidelity. He hadn't splurged for a comm that allowed holo video as he didn't see the point.

His daughter—he was still having a hard time conceptualizing that—had bounced back rather quickly from her ordeal. She still asked about her friends, and Alexander really wanted to let her go play with them during the day, but he was finding it hard to let her out of his sight after his promise. He knew the girl would likely be fine and that he would have to get over the idea that, as soon as she left his sight, she was going to get hurt again. That wasn't a healthy mindset for anyone. It seemed they both had things to work through.

This little excursion while she was safely in bed was a test for himself. So far, he only wanted to go back and check on her five times since exiting the apartment. He was going to call that an improvement.

Soon he arrived at the terminal that was visible from the apartment door. It was a small compromise.

When he activated the terminal, a familiar face greeted him on the other end. "Mr. Kane, how nice to hear from you again. We weren't expecting your call so soon, but this will certainly speed things up."

"You as well, Violet. I wasn't expecting you to find something so soon. What do you have for me?"

"To be fair, we weren't coming up with many prospects. Then we got lucky. An estate sale popped up over on Earth and one of the items up for sale is an abandoned research facility that was established in 2201. It's probably bigger than you wanted, but the price will probably be quite a bit cheaper considering how far from Earth it is."

That made this piece of property almost ninety years older than Petrov Station. It was probably going to need a lot of repairs and updates, but those he could manage. It was the other issue he was uncertain about.

"It's not too far is it?" He didn't want to impose on Jasper for multiple months just to fly him out to some dead research outpost.

"Well, you did ask for something outside of STO-controlled space. This place definitely falls into that category, but it's not as far out as you might think. There are four systems between the closest STO station and the facility. So a few weeks of travel, depending on the ship."

It wasn't ideal, but it wasn't the worst either. Close enough to purchase supplies, far enough out that they shouldn't be bothered. "It's been almost a hundred years, why hasn't the STO expanded towards the facility?"

"Hmm, I can't say for certain," Violet stated, "but if I remember my history correctly, that was the direction that humanity encountered the Shican in. I believe the STO decided not to expand in that direction to ensure no further hostilities broke out."

"A home inside a possible warzone doesn't sound like a good proposition."

The woman on the other side of the video laughed. "No, it certainly would not be, but I don't think you'll need to worry about that."

"Why?"

"No Shican vessel has been spotted in my lifetime as far as I'm aware. There are still some human ships that fly through that sector of space. Someone would have reported if the Shican had returned."

That still didn't sound ideal, but he had limited options and limited time. With the additional money he might save, he could install defenses. Considering what he planned to do there, he would probably have to install them at some point anyway.

"Consider me interested. How much do you think it will cost?"

"Excellent, Mr. Kane. We don't need to speculate. Your timing is impeccable, there is a live auction going on now. If you would like, I can add you to the call and act as your representative, I will try to get you the best deal possible."

"Okay, let's do it."

The terminal he was using flashed and a hologram formed above it, showing all the items on sale in the auction. He watched as prices flickered up on certain items, but others barely moved. Violet did something on her end and the property in question spun towards the front of the image. The current bid on it was only twenty-five million.

He heard the girl chuckle over the comm. "Well, this is even better than we hoped."

She placed a bid, upping the price to thirty million.

It stayed that way for minutes before it rose again in another five million credit increment.

Alexander soon grew bored of watching that single auction and scrolled through the other items listed for sale. Whoever that person had been, they had been filthy rich. There were at least a dozen ships being bid on, starting from single-pilot intersystem ships, all the way up to a Class 4 hauler similar to Jasper's ship. He must have been missing something though because the prices were going insane on these ships.

"Why are the ships going for so much?"

"Mr. Woodrow, the gentleman who passed away, was an avid collector of rare items. Some items, like the ships, are extremely sought after as collector's items. Others, like the research facility, not so much."

"Who collects research facilities?"

Violet chuckled. "Anything that was rare or unique. It didn't matter to Mr. Woodrow if it was valuable."

"What makes a research facility unique?"

It didn't make sense to Alexander.

"Oh, that's all in the attached documentation," Violet said as she opened up the document so Alexander could read it.

"Last standing remnant of the Great Expansion?"

"Not a fan of history, I take it?" Violet asked.

"Yes and no. I must have missed that one."

The fact that she seemed to accept that excuse just showed how much information had been segregated over the decades.

"The Great Expansion happened shortly after humanity cracked the secret to FTL. I think that started around 2130 and ended in 2212."

"I assume it had to do with humanity populating other planets?"

"It did. Humanity kept spreading out until they realized there were more habitable planets than they knew what to do with. Then they ran into the Shican. I don't know much about the war since most of it is still classified even to this day.

"Soon after encountering them, humanity stopped expanding. While we were evenly matched with the Shican as far as technology, I think the people in charge back then must have been afraid of running into a more technologically advanced race. Considering the hypergates, I can't really blame them."

While they chatted, the auction continued. Occasionally, some other buyer would bump up the price of the research facility, but he noticed it had slowed significantly.

"I've heard of these hypergates. Never used one myself," Alexander stated.

"Me either," Violet sighed. "I've never left Ganos. I've heard they are massive though."

"Not interested in space travel?" he asked.

The woman let out a wistful sigh. "I would love to travel the stars, but I get motion sick. I can barely even stomach the fliers that stay suborbital. The one time I tried taking a holiday to Haja, our local satellite, I ended up spending my entire time in the bathroom. Even with the artificial gravity, my body just couldn't cope."

"I'm sorry to hear that."

"That's kind of you to say. I've learned to be happy where I'm at."

There was a ding and Alexander looked at the holo-screen.

"Congratulations, Mr. Kane. You are now the proud owner of your very own research facility. And you got it for quite the steal."

He didn't quite consider spending seventy million a steal, but considering he was willing to spend nearly two hundred million, he should probably be happy.

"Now, there are a few things to go over before we finalize our end of the deal."

"Such as?" Alexander asked, happy that he now had a place to go and a ride to take him there.

"First off, we recommend hiring a mercenary company to clear the place."

"Huh?" He thought he had misheard her.

"Oh, that is just standard fare for buildings left alone on unintegrated worlds. Sometimes pirates like to use them as bases. Most often, we just find squatters there. The mercenaries will also verify the habitable integrity of the location. You wouldn't want to buy a property on a world with poor air quality just to learn it leaks atmosphere from every entrance and seal."

He certainly didn't want to arrive at his new home to find either pirates or faulty life-support, but he also didn't want to just evict people who were trying to survive.

"Can the squatters remain?"

Violet paused. "It's not normal for people to want to keep illegal squatters in their properties, Mr. Kane, but it's yours to do with as you please. I would still recommend having the mercenaries at least scan anyone there for warrants."

"That's fine, let's do that. How much is this going to cost me? Also, I haven't had the best luck with mercenaries, can you vouch for the ones you're hiring?"

"I'll make a note of your preferences in the action report. The cost will be an additional five million. Normally this is covered by our fee, but since this location is so far out, and so large, it's going to require a much larger investment. And yes, we can vouch for The Hawks of Ganos. They are one of the premier mercenary companies on Ganos and have a stellar reputation dating back to its founding. They are more like a private army, instead of the rag-tag outlaw type of mercenary teams you might find in the outer systems."

He was still iffy about it, but he hardly had any other choice. "Fine. As long as you vouch for them, let's do that."

"Excellent. I will get the action report completed and someone from the Hawks will be in touch to coordinate. I just need your confirmation, and then you will be given the deed to your new property, Mr. Kane."

Alexander sent over the digital certificate that was used in place of signatures in that century. After a few minutes, he got confirmation of the payment and the deed to his new property.

"And that completes the transaction, is there anything else we can assist you with?"

"There might be."

chapter 29

Before Alexander even made it back to the apartment, his comm beeped.

Hello Mr. Kane.

My name is Anthony Baru, Operations Lead for The Hawks of Ganos. We received your action report from Fidelity Properties. The Hawks currently have an ongoing operation that will be completed in the next two weeks. If that timeline works for you, please let us know and we can start preparations. If not, we do have a subsidiary group that is available immediately and is more than capable of taking on this assignment.

Alexander was glad he had some wiggle room with the schedule, he really didn't want to deal with some unknown subsidiary group when Violet had already vouched for the Hawks.

He went over the schedule in his head. Captain Daniel wouldn't be there for a month and he could postpone almost another month if needed. Then there was the travel time to the planet—which he hadn't learned the name of yet—however long that would take. Figuring that information might be rather important, he popped up the info packet as he entered the apartment. Now that he had a band that held the comm in place, it was much more convenient to use.

Turns out the planet didn't even have a name, just some six-digit alphanumeric designation. That was fine. If people were living there, he was sure they had given it a name, he would just go by whatever they called it, assuming it wasn't something horrifically awful or obscene.

As for where this planet was located, it turned out it was on the opposite side of STO space, but not the complete opposite end. If one flattened the star map and drew an angle to it, the star system was about at the 120-degree mark from Petrov Station using Earth as the center. It was also north of the galactic disk instead of south where Petrov lay. According to the packet, the planet orbited a blue dwarf star.

From what he remembered of astronomy, which wasn't much, blue dwarf stars were only supposed to be theoretical. Seemed his knowledge of astronomy was a bit out of date if that wasn't the case. It was probably why they built the research facility in the first place.

Before he got further pulled into the history of his new purchase, he responded to Mr. Baru and said that would be fine. He also supplied his travel itinerary and an estimated arrival timeline. He couldn't give him an exact time because he didn't know how long it would take.

It didn't take long for Baru to reply.

That will be fine. It is within our operational window. We will coordinate with your ship before leaving STO space. Once we arrive at the planet, we will maintain facility safety until the end of our contract. If you decide to retain our services beyond that six-month window, there will be additional expenses though, just so you are aware.

That wasn't a surprise. He couldn't expect hired soldiers to just sit around waiting for him without getting paid. He sent an affirmative response and went back to the info about the planet.

It was habitable, barely. There was an atmosphere, but the sulfur content was so high, it smelled of rotten eggs all the time. That wasn't him guessing, it was written right into the document. Not great, but air scrubbers should be able to take care of that.

Nothing but a few desert plants could survive on the harsh surface. However, it wasn't hot, in fact, the planet ran rather cool, never getting above 50 degrees Fahrenheit. It was just super dry and the radiation from the blue star was higher than Earth.

The packet also contained a survey of the local area around the facility. The ground was chock-full of metals and rare-earth elements. Mining them did not seem to be a priority when they set up the facility though. Considering how easy it was to extract the same minerals from asteroids, he wasn't surprised nobody had bothered going to that planet simply to mine it for resources.

As for the facility itself, he had to pause when he saw the square footage. Violet had warned him it was bigger than he might want, but this went way beyond what he expected. The facility was over four hundred million square feet of space. That wasn't a facility, that was an entire city. Almost fifteen square miles to be exact. A small city to be sure, but a city nonetheless. And looking at the design documents, that only included the livable space. It didn't even account for the sub-structure or maintenance areas.

If there weren't people living there, he was going to have a really tough time maintaining the place even if Yulia helped him. Maybe he should have looked at the size of the property before agreeing to this purchase.

Oh well, it was too late now.

He couldn't afford to be choosy. With everything going on, he was more than happy to have a new home locked in so early. It made planning so much easier.

* * *

Alexander spent the next few weeks going over the specifics with Mr. Baru. The man was all business, which suited Alexander just fine.

The Operations Lead brought up a few concerns that Alexander hadn't even thought about.

The first major concern he had was if there was a breathable atmosphere inside the facility.

While it was true the planet had a breathable atmosphere, it was extremely thin. With the thinner atmosphere, it made it feel like there was half as much oxygen as you normally needed according to the previous research done on the planet. It was low enough to cause breathing issues.

The rest of the planetary research was rather slim. The original inhabitants of planet Y6X-3H2-4 were more interested in the star, and only cursory studies were done on the surface and around the facility.

That meant they would need supplemental oxygen, or some way to increase the oxygen density in the facility, unless he wanted Yulia to suffer from hypoxia. That wasn't an option. The facility probably had systems in place to do all of that already, but Baru said he should plan for any such systems to be offline or, at best, malfunctioning. Considering the age of the facility, the man was probably correct.

He took Mr. Baru's suggestion and went over the blueprints until he located the systems. Then he purchased the requisite manuals to make repairs and print any parts he might need to fix or even completely replace the units. He lucked out there. Because the facility was so old, and the systems so antiquated, getting the manuals was rather cheap.

Alexander thought of buying plans for newer environmental systems, but he couldn't justify the cost. The old systems had functioned for over a hundred years so repairing them should be fine. The last check-in at the station some eighty years ago said the environmental systems were still functioning within the lower range of tolerance. Eighty-plus years of neglect probably hadn't done them any good though.

The second issue Baru brought up was facility integrity. Being nearly two hundred years old, there was bound to be leaks and rust. The planet did get rain, even if it was few and far between. Because of the high concentration of sulfur in the atmosphere, it was heavily acidic. So there were bound to be issues to resolve there.

The facility had an answer for that already. A large, fully robotic manufacturing dome was listed on the plans. It was probably used to create all the components or replacements the research facility needed.

Once he finished manufacturing any repair items he might need, Alexander would probably end up turning the space into his personal lab and research center.

With that in mind, he wanted to ensure he had the best start. He purchased three more printers like the one he had used to manufacture the *Zephyr*'s parts. Then he rented a storage room until the ship arrived. He knew how much cargo room the *Zephyr* had thanks to his communications with Jasper.

Alexander hadn't intended on taking much more than food and water with him originally, but knowing any empty space aboard the ship would be wasted space, he decided to fill it up with everything he could think of. He had a lot of money to work with.

Next on his list was a smelter. The one he purchased wasn't the same as the behemoth Petrov Station used. The smaller unit was capable of processing ten tons of material a day. Even then it took up a considerable amount of space.

He didn't care. As far as he was concerned, it was a requirement for what he planned to do since the facility didn't show any form of advanced processing on the schematics. From what he could tell, it mainly used a relatively cheap steel alloy in its construction with the exterior covered by a thick cement-like paste mixed from the local dirt and rocks to mitigate the damage the rains caused. This was likely built using the refinery that was listed on the plans.

It certainly made logical sense to use what was locally available instead of shipping in all the materials. Set a few automated mining machines down, or even drone-operated ones from orbit, and the work could go on all day every day until it was completed.

Alexander didn't have the kind of money needed to buy automated manufacturing drones. He would have to do things the hard way. Which was fine, he liked building and fixing things anyway.

He couldn't forget medical supplies. First for Yulia, and second to help keep his cover. Of course, he also had to account for the fake medical pod he was using. Losing that space was annoying but necessary.

Alexander wanted to buy more of those quick heal meds the doctors used on Yulia, but the man hadn't been lying when he said they had a limited quantity. The bare minimum to purchase one treatment was ten million credits. And that would have to be shipped from the manufacturer's planet of origin. According to the sales page, he might get them in six months to a year depending on the waitlist.

Alexander was forced to abandon that hope. The price was staggeringly ridiculous. Despite that, he would have been willing to pay it, but he wasn't willing to wait a possible year for them to arrive. He doubted the company would ship them outside STO space anyway. Something that was so sought after would certainly be a target for criminals.

Instead of wasting his money on a single item, he purchased every available medication and diagnostic piece of machinery that was available for sale aboard Petrov Station. All of that only amounted to two million credits. He may not know how to operate any of the devices, but he would learn.

That brought him to something he almost overlooked on his list of purchases: knowledge. He bought up any guide, walkthrough, technical manual, and blueprint that he could for every bit of technology he could find in the facility blueprints. He wanted to understand every moving part of that structure and how to fix it. After that, he spent another large chunk of money to get the printer documents for both Omni and Sinorus engines Class 1 through Class 4. That way he could study their designs.

He had plenty of funds left over and could have purchased the Class 5 and 6 schematics, but he decided against it. Both of those required orbital facilities to manufacture them. Purchasing the Class 7 and 8 ones was simply out of the question since they required him to be a military contractor.

Alexander had no desire to further the STO's military capabilities or their bureaucratic nightmare of a government.

That left Class 9 engines, but those were experimental and weren't required to have available schematics. However, he had seen a few available for sale from the smaller companies.

That wasn't the last of his purchases, though. Considering he wanted to be completely free from the other manufacturer's influence, he needed to take it a step further. He purchased whole ship schematics as well as items he knew he couldn't print like advanced computer processors. It was pricy but so worth it. One ship schematic covered every bit of technology aboard that ship. Considering he was planning on arriving aboard the *Zephyr*, he simply purchased that ship's design.

That purchase finally gave him his first look at the power plant as well as the FTL systems. A ship schematic didn't go into as much detail on how stuff worked as a separate document might, but it did give printable files to make replacement parts. He could figure it out from there.

Finally, Alexander purchased dozens of learning modules. They started from early elementary school and went all the way to advanced engineering. He purchased as many diverse modules as he could purchase. He wanted to ensure he had a wide source of knowledge. Although not the original reason for doing so, he realized if Omni was monitoring his purchases, it would make it harder for them to figure out what he was up to.

With all of his purchases complete, he looked at his much-diminished bank account. Even with all the spending, he still had more money than most would make in their lifetime. After receiving his cut from the attack, he still had over a hundred million credits. It was a good thing the facility had been so cheap. If he had spent the two hundred million he planned on the property, he would be in debt after that round of purchases.

chapter 30

With only a week left before the *Zephyr* would arrive, Alexander was finalizing a few things.

"Are you ready to see your friends?" he asked quietly.

As he had promised, he brought Yulia back to see her friends at the orphanage and say goodbye. She nodded, although she looked like she wanted to cry. He had purchased a comm band for her so she could keep in touch with them even after they left. What he hadn't noticed until he dug into the research facility plans was that the building didn't have a Qcomm.

Alexander didn't want to break her heart by telling her that she wouldn't be able to remain in touch with her friends, so he looked into getting one of the systems installed. He wished he hadn't.

If someone thought a ship was expensive, they were completely wrong. The simplest and cheapest Qcomm available was a text-only variant that cost half a billion credits, and you still had to pay for each transmission.

It was far outside his budget at the moment, but in time, he hoped to have the money to purchase one. In the meantime, a courier drone was a much more manageable option. The Class 1 ships only cost a few million and would only need to hop to the nearest system with a Qcomm array to transmit and receive any correspondence. Then it would simply hop back and repeat this process until it exhausted its internal fuel supply. Considering how far they were from STO space, that might be sooner than he liked.

Alexander considered purchasing the design specifications for the ships but decided against it. He already had one ship design, and he was quickly going through the basic engineering tutorials and study work. Eventually, he would be able to design and build one of the ships himself. He would still need to purchase the Qcomm secure buffer to go along with it, but that was a much more reasonable price.

Yulia nodded at his question and tentatively pushed open the door to the orphanage. He had already scheduled this meeting with the Headmaster, so all of the children were there to greet Yulia when she arrived.

The young girl looked startled when they all cheered and rushed to hug her. He could see the moment she forgot her sadness and started laughing and playing with the other kids.

The headmaster walked up to stand next to him, smiling. "It's good to see she hasn't lost her enthusiasm."

"She is a resilient child," Alexander remarked.

"That she is. I heard about what Captain Zhang said to you. There was no need for him to be so crass."

"You know? How?" Alexander was actually surprised to hear others knew of his conversation with Zhang.

"The second ring is a pretty small community. Rumors spread like wildfire down here. I would be surprised if anyone on the ring didn't know by now. News of your talk has probably spread to the upper rings as well. Any time a Council Captain gets personally involved, it's big news. It's also rare to have someone exiled."

"That explains the lack of work I've had since my little chat," he murmured.

"Don't hold it against the people too harshly," Wong said as he watched the children play. "The people down here are barely accepted as is. They can't afford to get caught up in drama that could see them in a situation much like yours."

"Fair enough," he stated as he watched an older boy separate from the group before heading his way.

"Markus," the headmaster said quietly. "I'll leave you two to chat while I make the evening meal. You'll be sticking around for that."

That didn't sound like a question, but Alexander made his avatar nod anyway.

The older boy stopped a good ten feet from Alexander and looked his body over before finally settling his determined gaze on his avatar's face.

"You better take good care of her." With that statement, he turned around and went back to the group.

So much for a conversation.

Before the boy got too far, Alexander called out just loud enough for him to hear. "Thank you for saving her." He hadn't had a chance to speak with the boy since the accident, and Markus had never come by his shop.

The boy didn't stop, in fact, he went from a walk to a jog, but Alexander had seen the boy's ears turn red from the praise. There was one last thing he would do before leaving the station. He didn't do it now because he didn't want credit for it. He had set up a sort of college fund for all the current, and hopefully future children of the orphanage. He hoped the ten-million-credit investment was sufficient to ensure none of the children remained stuck on that level for the rest of their lives.

It was too bad he wouldn't be there to see the headmaster's face when he got the legal paperwork. Alexander chuckled internally imagining the scene.

The meals and goodbye went on well past the children's bedtime, but neither Alexander nor the headmaster were willing to break it up. It was the children who eventually brought the festivities to an end when they started falling asleep.

Alexander picked up the sleeping Yulia. The girl opened her eyes briefly before snuggling up closer in his arms. Now that his body was fully repaired, he had learned a few new tricks. One of them allowed him to regulate his external temperature. He raised it to be comfortably warm for the girl so she wouldn't need to snuggle against a cold hard exterior.

He gave one last nod to the headmaster. The man nodded back as he prodded the older children to help him get the younger ones into their beds.

* * *

The day had finally come. The *Zephyr* would be there soon. Over the last few days, just to sate his curiosity, Alexander had asked around to see if other captains were available to transport him off the station.

Some wouldn't even speak with him. The few who did either turned him down outright or said they weren't taking on passengers. One captain even said they weren't traveling in that direction, even though Alexander hadn't mentioned where he was going.

It was pretty much a confirmation that Captain Sergei Zhang or someone else on the Council had spoken to the docked captains.

Alexander was once again thankful for making friends with Jasper. Had he not, he would likely have ended up in some STO penal colony until they realized the body inside the medical pod was an animal and not human. Then who knew what they would do to him? Nothing good, that was for sure.

He had reached out to Captain Na to alert him of this situation. Na had responded and said he would look into it but was off-station so there wasn't much he could do at that moment. He just told Alexander to check every dock to find someone to take him.

That wasn't a very comforting response. He was glad he hadn't bothered telling anyone of his plans to leave with the *Zephyr*. Considering what he was running into now, it was likely the Council would have blocked his friend from even docking. They might have figured it out if they got into his comm traffic, but those messages were secure and encrypted, or at least that was their big selling point. He could only assume it was true since he couldn't afford to have it be otherwise.

* * *

Jasper was understandably concerned for his friend Alexander. The man hadn't gone into detail on why he was being exiled from Petrov Station. He hoped it wasn't because of some backlash from his patents.

He supposed he would find out soon enough.

The *Zephyr* slid into the large hangar and soon touched down on the deck.

"Excellent flying as always, Wilkes."

"Thanks, Captain," the man stated.

Everyone was a lot more subdued on that trip. He had explained to them that they were back out there to help their friend Alexander. Most of the crew had met the man and liked him. So they were all business during that run. The few new crew members he brought on were quickly brought up to speed and understood the issue. Most spacers were very protective of their friends and family. They had to be because nobody else would do it for them.

Once the dock atmosphere normalized, the ramp lowered.

"Alright, everyone," Jasper called from the top of the ramp. His entire crew had assembled. "We have a few weeks before we need to leave again, but I want the entire ship gone over. We have guests coming with us, and I want to leave a good impression."

"Aye aye, Captain!" came a unanimous response.

He nodded. "Dismissed."

As the rest of the crew left for their assigned tasks, Naomi approached him.

"You have a guest waiting outside the hangar, Captain."

"Already? Who is it?" She turned a tablet to show him the security camera feed. It was a large man with Captain's insignia, but Jasper didn't recognize him. Naomi must have seen his confusion.

"It is Council Captain Sergei Zhang."

"A Council Captain? Alexander, what have you gotten yourself mixed up in?"

"What would you like me to tell him?" Naomi asked.

If he asked her to tell the man to piss off, she would. She would be more diplomatic about it though, but he knew that would only lead to further issues.

"Let him know I will greet him in a few minutes once our systems are topped off." That should give him time to come up with a response for whatever the man was likely to ask of him. Which undoubtedly involved his friend.

A few minutes later the interior hangar door opened to show a large man looking bored and annoyed in the corridor.

"'Bout damn time," the man grumbled. "You need to learn to delegate tasks, Captain. One of your people could have topped off your ship so you could meet me instead of forcing me to waste my precious time."

Jasper did his best to smile. "I like to ensure necessities are done properly."

The man snorted and pushed himself off the wall. "Then get a more competent crew."

Jasper's smile slipped. "What do you want, *Council Captain*?" He was not going to play nice with someone who disrespected his crew.

"We have a reprobate on the station who is trying to charter a ship off. We simply wish to warn you should an Alexander Kane attempt to book passage aboard your vessel."

"Do you have evidence of this man's crimes?" Jasper asked although he knew this man didn't.

"We are currently building a case, but we do not want the man to escape before we can bring him to justice for his crimes."

A few choice responses came to Jasper's mind. His first inclination was to tell the man to shove off, and if someone wanted off this cesspool of a station, he would gladly allow them aboard his ship. Unfortunately, that would likely get the *Zephyr* stuck in a quarantine hold. He had seen it happen to captains before who pissed off a Station Manager.

His next response was to tell the man he knew Alexander and he was nothing but upstanding. However, it was obvious this man had some sort of personal grudge against his friend.

What he actually said was, "I will keep that in mind if this man comes to speak with me."

The captain nodded and walked off without so much as a thank you.

"Right prick, that one," Wilkes said quietly as he stopped next to Jasper.

"Took the words right out of my mouth. I think it's time I contacted our friend. I want to be off this station before they realize we're taking him with us."

chapter 31

"Jasper, it's good to see you!" Alexander extended his hand and the captain shook it.

"You as well, my friend. I see you repaired your robot."

Alexander made his avatar look chagrined. "An unfortunate necessity that also had something to do with my exile. Please come in and I'll fill you in on what happened."

Captain Daniel nodded and entered the apartment. The man paused as his eyes landed on Yulia. The girl, still shy among adults, quickly shut the door to the bedroom.

"And a father, you did mention that didn't you?"

Alexander nodded. "It's all tied together. Can I offer you something to drink?"

"Water or tea if you have it," the man said as he sat at the counter.

"Tea it is. You probably need something stronger for this story, but I don't drink, and obviously, Yulia is too young."

"That's fine. I somehow feel like this is one of those situations where alcohol is best left out of the equation."

"You're probably right," Alexander said.

As he prepared the tea, he launched into his story. First starting with what happened with Omni.

"I'm sorry to hear you had to go through that," the man stated sadly as he blew on his tea.

"It certainly was annoying. Thanks to your input, I didn't walk away empty-handed though."

"That's good to know. But you still haven't explained why they exiled you. I can't exactly imagine them doing that because of the Omni case."

"No. This came about after a series of events that happened a week later." He told him the story of the attack. How Yulia had been injured and nearly died. Then he went into the reasons why he adopted her.

After finishing that story, he explained that the attackers had accused him of having or manufacturing restricted weapons. Alexander left out the part where he actually did that part. It wasn't like he meant to manufacture those things.

The last thing he covered was the hasty completion of the adoption before Captain Sergei Zhang could pronounce judgment on him. He omitted the reasoning behind the hasty adoption. He didn't want Yulia to overhear what Headmaster Wong had told him and the walls weren't exactly thick.

"I had the pleasure of running into the captain when I arrived," Jasper's voice was thick with disgust. "Did you personally offend the man?"

Alexander shook his head. "Never met the man before that evening at the hospital. At first, I thought he had a chip on his shoulder against me..."

"But that doesn't explain why he's going through all this trouble to keep you from leaving." Jasper finished.

"No, no it doesn't. The funny thing is, I had already planned to leave before they exiled me."

"You did? Did you finally take my friend, Dr. Nova Lund up on her offer?"

"Her?" Alexander had assumed the doctor was male. Then again, he had never actually asked.

Jasper chuckled at the look of confusion on Alexander's avatar. "Leave it to Nova to be so caught up with her science to not introduce herself properly. So is that where you're heading next?"

"No. While our discussions were certainly enlightening, and the woman is indeed a genius, I simply decided I didn't want to work for someone else anymore."

Captain Daniel nodded. "You don't have to explain that to me. I saved up every credit I earned as a first mate until I could finally purchase my own ship and crew."

"That's how you bought the *Zephyr*?"

The man laughed. "I wish first mates got paid that type of money! No. I bought a small Class 2 vessel that I used for VIP transport in the core systems. While lucrative, having to deal with those pretentious assholes leaves a lot to be desired. It did earn me a valuable education in how to maneuver through the bureaucratic nightmare that is the law though, so it wasn't all bad. After five years of that, I upgraded to the *Zephyr* and never looked back. And I'm much happier for it. So if we aren't going to Lund's little brain trust, where are we going?"

"I used my windfall from the Omni case to purchase an abandoned property in a system called Y6X-3H2."

Jasper winced at that. "Not even a named system, eh? I'm going to guess this system is out of STO's normal jurisdiction."

"That's not going to be a problem, is it?"

"If there are pirates out there, it could be."

"Oh, that won't be an issue. One of the things the real estate place recommended was hiring a mercenary company to clear the place out. They will be waiting at the edge of STO space to escort us."

"That was nice of them to recommend someone. Who did you hire?"

"The Hawks of Ganos."

Jasper's eyebrows rose. "I guess you're not taking any half-measures here. I've heard of them. If their reputation is as good as I've heard, there shouldn't be any problems."

"The lady at Fidelity said much the same, but it's good to hear it verified from an outside source."

"So, Alexander. A trip to the other side of STO space. It's going to take probably two months just to get there. Do you have everything you need?"

"I believe so. But I may have bought more than I needed."

"Oh, how much cargo room are we talking about here?"

Alexander told him the estimated cargo space he required. The man nearly choked on his tea.

"I can pay you for moving all my stuff."

The man waved away his concern. "No, that's fine. I was just surprised. The last time we spoke, everything you owned fit in that little shop of yours. And while I had planned to fill the rest of my cargo with stuff purchased on Petrov, if I'm honest, it's not worth it. My last load barely broke even. This will also save me time trying to fill empty space. I want to be here and gone before the Council figures out you're leaving anyway."

"You think they will do something to stop you?"

Jasper snorted. "Considering the lengths they have gone to so far, they will probably try something, but I have a few tricks up my sleeve as well, so don't you worry. Just send the storage list to me and I will get my crew to move the items aboard as soon as possible. Once everything is loaded up, I will contact you. Then you"—he winked—"and your lovely daughter can come aboard."

Alexander had seen Yulia sneaking a peek from her room, but the girl quickly shut the door again when the captain winked at her.

"She's a bit shy," he said quietly.

"Must take after her old man," Jasper chuckled.

It took a moment for Alexander to realize Jasper was referring to him. When he did, he rolled his eyes, making the man laugh.

* * *

Yulia wanted to run out of the room and tell Alex she wasn't shy. She just didn't trust adults. None of her memories of them, except for Headmaster Wong, were good. Even her memories of her parents were now tinged with fear.

It wasn't until she saw the bad men at Alex's that the rest of her memories of her parents came flooding back to her. Now that she was old enough, she knew what her parents were, and, by association, what she was. It terrified her that an adult might come along and snatch her away from Alex just to do whatever they did to pirates. She had asked Markus about what they did to pirates one time, but the boy had been surprisingly tight-lipped. To that day, anytime she brought up the subject, he would go quiet. Eventually, she just stopped bringing it up.

Her thoughts turned to her friend and a tear escaped her eye. She was never going to see him again. Nobody told her that, but she knew that was the case. She wanted to ask Alex to adopt him, but she didn't want to upset him or make him second-guess his decision. Some of the older kids at the orphanage told stories of children getting dumped back into the orphanage who annoyed their new families too much.

She didn't want Alex to hate her, so she sucked up her emotions and wiped away her tears. She would still be able to send messages to her friends and Alex promised her she would make new friends.

* * *

Jasper was aboard the *Zephyr* enjoying a cup of coffee as he filled out some reports when a knock interrupted him.

"Come in," he said without taking his eyes off the report.

The door opened and in walked Naomi. "He's back, Captain."

Jasper set down the tablet with a sigh. "I was hoping it would take him longer to notice. How is the loading coming along?"

"We are about sixty percent of the way there."

He did some quick math in his head. "So another three days or so?"

"Four to be safe."

He grunted and stood. "See if you can speed that up any. If you have to store everything in the hangar to get it done faster, do it."

Naomi nodded and walked out, Jasper followed behind her and down the ramp.

He stopped halfway down, spotting Captain Zhang inside his hangar. "What is he doing here?" He ground his teeth.

Another Captain entering his hangar without consent was a serious breach of etiquette. The man was blatantly snooping at the unloaded cargo with two Station Security along with him.

"What is the meaning of this?!" he yelled as he stormed down the rest of the ramp.

Zhang had the gall to smile at him. "We are performing a cargo inspection."

Jasper walked right up to the taller man, making the two security people reach for their stunners. "Unless you have a search warrant, I suggest you leave. And even if you did... You are not an authorized security agent aboard this station."

Zhang looked like he was about to say something when Naomi cleared her throat. "Captain. I have already submitted a complaint for this breach."

She was talking to him, but Zhang clamped his mouth shut. Then he snapped his fingers, and the two Station Security stepped forward while Zhang exited the hangar. One of the men handed him a tablet showing him the signed warrant to search his cargo. It was signed by Zhang himself.

He slapped the tablet back in the man's hand and stared him in the face. "Unless you want me to level an accusation of load tampering and possible piracy..." Both men stiffened at that. "I suggest you take this bullshit warrant and leave."

The men glanced at each other before the one who handed him the tablet spoke. "It seems there was an error in the warrant. We're sorry for any misunderstanding. Have a nice day, Captain."

He watched as the two scurried out of his hangar. He was glad STO law was very clear on hangar space. Once rented, it and everything inside it were lawfully owned by the renter until such time as the renter vacated the space. The law had been put in place centuries ago to stop scummy Station Managers from evicting crews and stealing all of their cargo and, in some instances, the ships themselves. Now it required a warrant to search the property, but they couldn't arrest or revoke that tenancy unless the captain was charged with a felony.

The only other way a station could lay claim to what was in a hangar was if they convicted the crew of piracy. And that was unlikely. Every instance of a piracy trial was required to go to the STO for review. If the STO found the station management had falsified information to hold such a trial, those people got subjected to a piracy charge themselves. That stopped anyone from arbitrarily trying people as pirates to transfer wealth to themselves.

If Jasper had gone through with his threat, the STO would have looked into it eventually. Although he doubted anything would have come from his claim other than a fine, it was the threat that mattered. If Zhang wanted to be an ass for some unknown reason, Jasper would play his game. He could guarantee he had far more experience playing with the law than the outer sector Captain.

chapter 32

Alexander's comm beeped. He looked at it and saw it was the boarding message from Jasper.

It was finally time to leave Petrov Station. He was relieved to finally see the message he had been waiting for. He had been receiving daily messages from the captain, so he knew there was some trouble with Station Management, specifically Zhang, but Jasper had assured him that was all taken care of and now all of the supplies he had purchased were loaded. The final item to be loaded was his medical capsule because it required *special care.*

That made him cringe. For the first time since he woke, he wished he could just dispense with the lie. It wasn't that he didn't trust Jasper, he absolutely did. The man had dropped everything to come to his aid when he didn't have to. However, Alexander wasn't sure if he would have done the same if the situation was reversed. That realization made him feel like a shitty friend.

No matter what Jasper said, Alexander would eventually repay him for this kindness.

He turned to Yulia who was sitting on the couch watching some holo show. "Are you ready?"

The girl turned to him and for a moment it looked like she was going to cry. She sniffed once before nodding. Alexander offered his hand to her and the pair walked toward the service elevator.

They arrived at the lift just as the lights began to blink. Alexander picked up Yulia and covered the rest of the distance, joining the other bulk items being transported around the station. He needed to thank Jasper, or more likely Naomi, for timing the completion of their cargo loading so perfectly.

Soon enough, they stepped out on the fourth ring where the *Zephyr* was docked. Considering the lengths Zhang had gone through to keep him there, Alexander was surprised there wasn't armed security waiting for him. It seemed that might have been a step too far for the Council Captain. He would deeply like to know what the man had against him but not enough to stick around another day to figure it out.

Alexander walked through the station, carrying Yulia on one arm with ease. The girl kept giggling in delight and asking him to go higher. Eventually, she was standing on top of his rounded shoulders in the place of his head. The girl seemed to have forgotten her sadness as she laughed while holding his hands.

He looked ridiculous walking down the corridor with his hands up in the air holding Yulia from falling, but he didn't care. He preferred the girl's last memory of the station to be a fond one rather than one marked by loss. Some of the people gawking at his little show probably thought he was an idiot, but so what? None of their opinions mattered to him one bit.

As they neared the dock, he could see Jasper waiting for him. Alexander could also feel Yulia's apprehension growing. He lifted the girl off his head, earning a squeal of delight as he tucked her in his arm. She quickly used this new position to hide her face from the captain. With his free arm, he waved.

The man waved back, a smile on his face. "Alexander! Your timing is impeccable."

The way he said it made Alexander think there was an issue.

"Is something wrong?"

"Not yet. Let's get inside the hangar before we chat." The man deliberately scanned the hallway for something after he said this.

Alexander hadn't seen anyone following him. He would have certainly seen them if there was. The ability to monitor his surroundings at all times was handy if a bit draining on his mind. That issue had lessened quite a bit since his miraculous repair though. So the ability to see his entire surroundings seemed like something purpose-built into this body.

He followed the captain inside the hangar, glad he didn't need to duck due to his height. He wished all the bulkhead doors were as tall as the hangar doors. He wondered how he would fare in the research facility.

As soon as they were through the hangar door, Jasper walked over to the control panel and locked it closed with a command code that meant they were intending to disembark.

"Yulia, would you like to explore the *Zephyr* with Naomi while I talk with your father?"

The girl tried to scrunch even tighter against Alexander's frame at the captain's words.

Understanding that the captain needed to speak privately with him, he set Yulia down. "Don't worry, I'll be right behind you." He lightly nudged the girl toward the smiling woman.

After a bit, the girl reluctantly nodded, shuffling over to Naomi, who offered her hand. The girl took it but looked back toward him for confirmation.

The young woman kneeled next to his daughter and spoke in a soothing voice. "Don't worry, Yulia. While the captain and your dad are chatting, I'll show you the best places to play hide and seek aboard the ship. That way you can play with your dad during the journey and win." She winked, earning an aborted giggle from the girl.

After they left, Alexander spoke up. "Naomi is exceedingly good at her job."

Jasper laughed lightly. "Of course she is. I hired her. Now on to business," the man's tone became serious.

"Is this about Zhang causing issues?"

"Not this time, my friend." The pair walked over to a large crate that sat alone on the hangar floor.

Alexander immediately recognized it as his supposed cryo pod.

"We're friends, right?" Jasper asked as he stopped next to the crate and turned toward him.

"Of course."

The captain nodded. "Then do me the favor of explaining why this crate is housing a frozen animal, and not you."

Alexander visibly slumped. "You checked the contents?"

"I had to. After Zhang pulled his bullshit search warrant, I wanted to ensure there was nothing that could get us detained or worse." He tapped on the top of the crate. "So if you're not in there, where are you?"

Alexander tapped his chest.

"Why lie about that?" Jasper asked, sounding genuinely hurt.

"Fear. I essentially woke up on this station without most of my memories. I had no idea how I got here, or how I ended up in this body."

"What?"

Alexander sighed. "It will be easier if I just start from the beginning."

He told Jasper about everything. His time being a mindless robot under Yuri, the scrambling he had to do to escape after the scrapyard was purchased out. His inability to do much of anything with that damn control box attached to him, everything. It all just sort of poured out of him as he began to recount the last few years.

After he was done, he felt like a weight had been lifted off his chest.

"So that's what happened to old man Yuri. I'm sorry he used you like that. I doubt he would have, had he known."

"I'm not sure I believe that. The man seemed perfectly fine dealing with shady people."

"Hmm, maybe you're right. It has been quite some time since I last saw the old man, he could have changed. So... you're what? A brain inside a robot body?" The man seemed to be trying to wrap his head around that.

Alexander chuckled. "Your guess is as good as mine but probably not the brain thing. I tried some industrial scanners to see if I could figure it out. The images either came back grainy or couldn't penetrate deep enough into my exoskeleton. I assume it has something to do with the damage I had before or some sort of shielding."

"I was going to ask about the damage next but shielding?"

"I haven't needed to recharge since I woke up. Something has to be powering this body. And something that powerful has to be shielded I would think."

The man took a step back. "Is it safe?"

"It hasn't caused any harm as far as I can tell and there isn't any radiation leaking from my body. That would have been picked up right away. As for the damage, I honestly don't know. I lost consciousness after the attack. When I woke back up, the damage was just gone. Not repaired but like it had never even been there in the first place."

"I have to ask this, Alexander, because your story makes little sense. Are you sure you're even human?"

Alexander shrugged his large shoulders. "As far as I know. I have memories of a life back on Earth."

"Earth? It's rare to meet people from the home world. Do you think someone back there might know what happened to you?"

"Hmm, probably not."

"How can you be so certain?"

"Hoo, boy. This is another issue I encountered when I woke up. My memories seem to be from around the mid-2050s, as best as I can guess."

"What?"

"I know it's hard to believe. Imagine the last thing you remember is some time from almost four hundred years ago. I was quite lost when I realized I was on a space station floating out in a system I had no memory of. I can see you want to ask the question. I have no clue who did this to me or why. And, yes, it could have been aliens. I haven't seen any human technology even remotely close to what this body is made out of. Have you ever heard the saying, 'sufficiently advanced technology is indistinguishable from magic'?"

The man nodded woodenly.

"Well, I don't see that with this body. I see joints and servos. Slightly more advanced than human tech but not much beyond that. That's also why I don't think I'm a disembodied brain. Unless there is some ridiculously advanced stasis technology at play, I just don't see how a brain could survive that long. I can't imagine humanity even coming up with such technology in the next hundred years. My best guess is I'm some sort of digital transference. The why and how of that escapes me though. Do you see my dilemma?"

Jasper took a seat on the crate that held the cryo pod. "I can see why you would have wanted to keep this quiet. I'll be honest, that was not the story I expected to hear when I confronted you."

Alexander made his avatar quirk an eyebrow. "Really? What did you expect? Does this mean you believe me?"

"Of course, I believe you. The story is too insane to be fake. It also explains why you seemed so naïve, even though you lived out on the fringes."

"I wasn't that naïve," he grumbled.

Jasper chuckled. "Trust me, you were. As for what I expected? Honestly, I don't know. Someone in hiding I guess. Although, that is technically true. Maybe an escaped runaway from some criminal organization. There are enough of those around."

"You thought about me like this the entire time? And still worked with me?"

"Not the entire time. Your story didn't make a whole lot of sense so I did some digging. I only dug into your background after your work. By then, I already knew you were a stand-up guy. So unless I found you to be some pirate hiding from the law, I figured you were fine to keep your secret."

"I put a lot of thought and work into that cover," Alexander muttered quietly.

The Captain smiled. "You simply lacked the right information. We'll have plenty of time during the flight. I'll work with you to correct that lapse of knowledge. Now let's get aboard before your daughter gets upset."

"So, you still want to take me now that you know my secret? What about my cover?" Alexander asked.

"Alexander, I judge people by their actions, not by their circumstances. And everything you've shown me leads me to believe you are an upstanding person. As for your other concern, this little discovery will stay between you and me. It isn't my place to reveal people's secrets. It will be up to you if you want to tell the rest of my crew."

Alexander nodded. "I would prefer to keep this between us for now."

Jasper nodded and motioned toward the end of the crate as he readied to lift one end. "This thing isn't going to carry itself. You going to help?"

Alexander chuckled and lifted the entire thing by himself. "After you, Captain."

chapter 33

"Alright, crew! Everything is loaded. It's time to go. Sierra!"

His sensor operator turned. "Yes, Captain?"

"Notify the station we wish to depart."

The woman nodded and turned back toward her terminal.

He waited for far longer than was normal before clearing his throat. "Is something the matter, Sierra?"

"The station operator is saying there is a hold on our departure, but he couldn't see a reason for this hold. He is looking into the issue."

Of course, there was.

"Patch me into the station, please."

Soon his screen lit up, showing him a video of a slightly flustered-looking station technician.

"C-Captain, I should have your issue figured out in a few days."

Jasper snorted, he wasn't waiting a few days for that bastard Zhang to come up with another way to hold him up. That would turn into even more excuses and eventually Alexander's time to vacate the station would expire.

"Get your commissar."

"Sir?"

"You heard me."

Ten minutes later, a man wearing the Station Commissar uniform appeared on the screen. "Captain Daniel, you asked to speak with me?"

"I did. I was hoping you could speed up the resolution of this issue your dock technician is running into."

"I see... I have been apprised of the issue. Unfortunately, it will take time to determine why this hold was placed on your ship. Now if you'll excuse me, I have other issues that demand my attention."

The man seemed very eager to end this conversation, but Jasper wasn't having it. "Commissar, are you familiar with STO law on ship holds?"

"Of course," the man bristled.

Jasper smiled. "Wonderful! Then you know that Section 13f states that a captain must be notified of the reason for the hold upon request. If you can't provide a reason, then you must release the ship and look into the issue in your own time. Otherwise, you would be interfering with the lawful movement of that vessel and I think we both know what that means. Oh, and you can consider this my request."

"Give me a moment to refresh my memory," the man stated as he stepped away from the screen.

It was another stalling tactic. The commissar could have just as easily looked up the regulation on the terminal in front of him. Jasper let this one slide. If the man wasn't brain dead, he would understand the implied threat he had just laid out. If not, he had friends that could hurry this along.

It only took a few minutes for the commissar to return. "Apologies for the delay, Captain Daniel. I have released the hold on your ship."

"Thank you, commissar. You may want to look into that issue. Some captains would immediately file a report with the STO if this happened to them. I would hate to see Petrov Station's reputation ruined by such a thing."

The man on the other end forced a smile onto his face. "I will take that under advisement. Thank you for visiting."

With that, the line went dead and Jasper chuckled. "Alright, Wilkes, get us the hell out of here."

"Roger that," the man gave a two-finger salute without turning around.

The quiet hum of the reactor soon spread through the ship, making the *Zephyr* feel alive.

"Hangar atmosphere is vented," Sierra called out.

There was a rumble and muted clank as the liftoff thrusters engaged and the landing gear retracted. It was always a balancing act on stations that didn't have independent gravity zones, but Wilkes was more than up to the challenge.

Soon the ship floated backward out the large open hangar door. The inky blackness of space greeted them like an old friend.

* * *

Sergei brooded aboard his ship *Steel Tempest*. He had inherited the ugly mining vessel from his father after he passed away but had quickly changed its name from the *Lucky Strike*. Lucky his ass. The ship was a barely floating hunk of steel when he received it. It wasn't until someone approached him with a loan offer that he was able to finally bring it back to safe operational condition.

The one good thing his degenerate gambler of a father had done before completely bankrupting the family was conveniently dying in a mining accident. If only the man would have done that a few years sooner, Sergei wouldn't have been forced to take that loan.

It was one last laugh from beyond the grave by his father because that loan offer had been too good to be true. On some level, he knew that when it had been offered, but he couldn't let his family's legacy die with his bastard of a father.

Because of that damn loan, there he was in the outer belt, heading for a specific set of coordinates.

The man he had taken the money from had asked a favor from him and he failed. It wasn't the first favor he had asked for, and Sergei doubted it would be the last. It should have been so simple. For a reduction in the money he owed, all he had to do was prevent Kane from exiting the station before his deadline for leaving expired. Then someone would approach him at the last moment to offer salvation.

He doubted his contact's people would have waited until the last day. They just needed Kane to be desperate, just like he had been back when he took their offer. How the hell was he supposed to know Kane had outside contacts? Nothing in the man's records indicated such. He knew he should have dug deeper, but he didn't care to learn the man's entire history, especially with what would likely happen to him.

Sergei had used every bit of coercion he could, even pushing the law farther than he was comfortable with. The illegal search could have gotten him locked up. The station hold was even more risky since that could have put a black mark on Petrov, making any sane person avoid the station.

He had used the hold tactic a few times in the past—mainly when his informants brought him scoops on possible rich asteroids that independents had marked but didn't claim. It gave him a few days' head start on them. Sergei had never worried about the independent miners filing a report though. The few who probably knew the law likely hated the STO just as much as the rest of the people on Petrov Station did. There was no way those types of people would go crying to the STO to solve their problems. They simply sucked it up and moved on. He liked that.

But not Captain Daniel. That man seemed to know every trick and how to get out of it.

So there Sergei was.

"We're here, Captain," his pilot called out. "Do you want me to notify the crew?"

"No." He stood from his chair. "I'm gonna go check this one out myself."

The man nodded and went back to studying his terminal. That was hardly the first time Sergei had wanted to scope out an asteroid by himself. He maintained the illusion of doing it quite often to hide his clandestine communications.

Soon he was suited up in the hard suit, then he made his way over to the maneuver pack. The semi-autonomous drone attached itself over his suit like some sort of tumor. If it wasn't for the current lack of gravity on the ship, he would have tipped over from the weight.

The floor of the ore hold opened and he guided the maneuver pack down to the asteroid's surface. Once he was down, he detached himself and began walking across the soft dusty surface while the pack maintained the position where it released him.

He didn't want the onboard cameras to record what he was up to. His hard suit had a data recorder as well, but thanks to his contact, Sergei had disabled it years ago. It would not be good if someone went through his records to see what he was doing.

Soon he was out of sight of the ship and the drone. His external lights came on and he walked another five minutes before he located the relay. It was cleverly buried in the asteroid, with nothing to show it was even there. If he didn't have the exact location, he would have easily walked past it.

He brushed off the surface dust, pulled a hard-line data cable from his suit, and plugged it in. It didn't take long for his contact to speak.

A raspy voice carried over his suit's comm. "My people tell me our mutual friend has left the station. I believe I was pretty clear about not letting that happen."

Sergei gritted his teeth before responding. "I did everything in my power to keep Kane there. Perhaps your people should have acted sooner, Harlow."

The infamous pirate chuckled. "Feisty today, are we? May I remind you, Sergei, that if it wasn't for my generous loan, you would have lost your ship by now as well as your standing aboard Petrov. I don't ask much from you, but when I do ask you to do something, I expect it to get done."

Sergei would have liked nothing better than to triangulate this signal and claim the bounty for that pirate. Unfortunately, the man hadn't remained free all those years by being sloppy. He was obviously using a repurposed Qcomm array, making locating the signal impossible.

Initially, Sergei thought the criminal was running dark in the system, but the STO war games a few months back would have quickly flushed anyone out of hiding. Now he suspected the man was hiding in plain sight aboard any of the hundreds of ships that called this area of space their home. Unless a ship was seized or boarded, the man could remain aboard without anyone outside the crew being any the wiser.

"Do you know where my prize is heading?"

"No. They didn't bother registering their entire flight plan, only their next destination," he ground out.

"Hmm. It seems Kane has found himself some competent friends. I wish I could say as much about your fellow Captains. I warned those idiots Kovalenko and Hoffman that their actions would draw unwanted attention, but they thought they knew better. Oh well. With them out of the picture, that makes it easier for me."

Sergei had known for quite some time that Harlow's goal was to take over Petrov Station, but he hadn't known Kovalenko and Hoffman had dealings with the pirate warlord. The fact that Harlow was telling him this now was as much a warning as it was a heads-up. The man didn't do anything without a reason.

"As for Kane, I'm sure he will show up eventually. A man like that doesn't stay under the radar for long. Now run along, Sergei, I have better things to do."

"What about our deal?"

"What about it?" the man asked in a bored tone. "You failed to carry out my request, but I'm a generous man. Instead of reducing your loan by our agreed-upon amount, I will give you half of what I promised but only as a secondary loan. My typical rates apply, Zhang. I suggest you get out there and start finding rocks to cover your next payment. It's coming due soon."

The line went dead and Sergei smashed his fist into the rock wall next to where the relay was buried. He wanted to smash the relay and Harlow's smug face, but the bastard would just tack on the cost of replacing the device to his growing debt.

Debt he knew he would never be able to escape from.

He swatted away the loose rocks he had knocked clear in his fit and tromped his way back to the drone. Harlow hadn't stated it outright, but Sergei understood the implication. If Kovalenko and Hoffman faced trial, they could bring up the pirate's name. If he wanted to earn some goodwill, he needed to deal with the two captains before the rest of the council started the trial.

chapter 34

LOCATION: GANOS
SYSTEM: ROSS 128
DATE: 2398

Travers made his way down to the briefing room. He knew they had a new contract already but not what it entailed. It wasn't rare for the Hawks to have contracts close together, but it was pretty rare for them to get back-to-back ones. That meant someone wanted the best and had a ton of money to throw at the problem. Not that he minded, it meant a bigger paycheck.

He was not the first to arrive. Anthony Baru was already in his normal seat speaking with Captain Matthews.

"Gentlemen," Travers nodded as he walked in. He poured himself a cup of coffee and grabbed a snack from the service tray before taking his seat.

Both men nodded to him. Travers was glad the Hawks treated everyone equally in the company. He knew some other companies that tried to run them like dictatorships. It worked until their leadership was taken out, then they usually crumbled under a lack of direction.

That didn't mean the Hawks of Ganos didn't have a formal structure, they did, but any one of a dozen people could step into a higher role if necessary.

Soon the rest of the Field Team Leaders arrived. The full conference room filled up quite fast, leaving all twelve chairs occupied. It was rare to have the entire company assembled for one mission.

Travers knew this upcoming op was a big one.

"Thank you all for attending," Baru said. "We have a bit of an interesting one this time around." The man clicked a remote and the table came alive with a hologram of a massive building.

"This is an abandoned research facility from the tail end of the Great Expansion. This facility is located in the Y6X-3H2 system on the fourth planet in the system, colorfully named Y6X-3H2-4."

That earned a chuckle from the gathered people.

Travers had no idea where the system was located. He had never even encountered a system or planet so remote that nobody had bothered changing the scientific designation to something more palatable. He supposed he would find out where the place was soon enough.

Baru waited for the laughter to subside before continuing. "Now for the bad news. This facility is fifteen square miles of tunnels, living areas, and expansive atriums This doesn't even include the maintenance and support areas."

A few people groaned at that. Travers wasn't one of them. He knew based on the brief projection that the place was huge. He didn't think it was quite that large, but he already knew it was going to be a pain in the ass to secure.

"Please hold your grumbling until I get to the actual bad news," Baru stated in his normally unflappable tone.

That got Travers and everyone else's attention. Clearing out a facility of this size would be a pain to any normal op. If that wasn't the bad news, he wasn't looking forward to what the man said next.

"Our theater of operations is outside of STO-controlled space."

Travers watched Captain Matthews' expression, but the man didn't even flinch at the news. Considering he was responsible for space superiority, he must have been notified ahead of time.

One of the team leaders raised their hands. "Does that mean we should expect pirates?"

Travers didn't recognize the man, but his nametag read 'Jallen.'

"Unknown," Baru replied. "The station has been dark since 2310. That brings us to the next issue. If the station is empty, it's likely degraded to the point of being uninhabitable. In that case, we will transition to field repair instead of clearing."

"And if it isn't?" Travers asked.

"The client... has asked us to clear out any criminal elements but not to evict anyone else who might have taken refuge there."

The room erupted into annoyed shouts and grumbling. Baru simply waited for the field leaders to vent their frustrations before continuing.

This was going to be the most difficult op Travers had ever been a part of. Clearing out and securing or even repairing a facility of that size was a big job, but now they had to act as a police force as well.

Someone else asked the question on Travers' mind. "How long is this op?"

"It will be a minimum of six months with an open-ended extension if the client has the money."

He really hoped this client realized the logistical nightmare of keeping squatters around and changed his mind. Extra money was nice but not if it meant they were stuck playing nice for the next few years.

"Will there be some downtime before the op kicks off? Most of us just came off rotation," another leader asked.

"There will be three weeks of downtime before we are wheels up. I suggest everyone take it and relax. We are on a bit of a time crunch at that point, so if anyone gets arrested we will not be bailing them out. That's about all the information I have. Any other questions?"

There were some follow-up questions, mostly aimed at equipment. Seeing as the op was taking place outside of STO space, some of the leaders were asking about the use of restricted weapons. Travers wanted to shake his head at that. Who needed a railgun or laser rifle for urban clearing and control? At least they would have their combat rifles since it wasn't a space station, and the air wasn't immediately deadly.

The rest of the meeting went into logistics and supply.

* * *

The *Talon* exited FTL at the edge of the system. Matthews watched his displays as his crew went about their work quickly and efficiently. If there was something he needed to know, they would tell him.

"All clear, Sir," the sensor operator responded a few minutes later.

He thanked the man and looked over the system holo. Varlen was the end of the road for STO systems in this direction. As such, it had little to no infrastructure. There were no inhabitable planets in the red dwarf system. Any planet that could be terraformed was too close to the star's radiation and was tidally locked. That didn't stop humans from trying to live out there though.

There was a rocky satellite that orbited one of the further-out gas giants. On the dead satellite was a sprawling complex that wouldn't have been there if not for the STO's Naval Yard in the system.

Soon Matthews received the challenge request he had been expecting. He responded to the message with his ship name, reason for being there, and their destination. They would have most of that through his transponder ID, but he liked being thorough. A few minutes later he got a response back.

Good luck!

He didn't need the STO to tell him that. Matthews knew that every stop beyond that system and their eventual destination could be infested with pirates, or maybe even the Shican. It was why they had pulled two of their gunships out of storage to act as backup. The *Talon* had enough firepower to defend itself, but their client would be meeting them there.

For the next three days, the *Talon* flew across the system to the next safe jump point. There they waited.

"Sir, we have received the confirmation code from a ship named the *Zephyr*, flown by Captain Daniel."

Matthews nodded. "Send it to my terminal."

Not knowing the transponder ID of the ship their client would be arriving by, they had given Mr. Kane a security code. This prevented *misunderstandings*.

As he waited for the message to arrive, he looked up the ship's information. Class 4 hauler, nothing fancy. Eventually, the message finished buffering.

Greetings Talon,

Thank you for agreeing to wait for us here. While we could have probably crossed the intervening space without issue, this is a much safer option. Before we leave the system, our mutual client wishes to speak with you over video once we are within proper communication range. As the captain of the Zephyr, I will be attending as well so we can go over any operational information you might need us to follow. Once we are under your umbrella, we will comply with whatever orders you issue that do not place my ship or crew in harm's way.

Captain Daniel

Well, at least Matthews knew this Captain was competent. He lost count of how many arrogant captains he had been forced to work with over the years. Working for the rich, they sometimes thought they could get away with the same level of nonsense. He was always quick to put them in their place.

I will set up a meeting time once you are closer.

Captain Matthews

He sent the response, preferring to be short and concise. There was no telling who was picking up the open radio traffic.

* * *

A day later, the *Zephyr* had finally moved into video range. Matthews was glad the smaller vessel was faster. If it came down to a fight, they could run while the *Talon* took the hits. The old STO transport may be slow to accelerate, but she was heavily armed and armored. The old warhorse had been designed to tank shots as dropships disgorged their troops in the middle of a battlefield. The *Talon* had cost the Hawks a considerable amount of capital and a few favors, but it put them far above anyone in terms of battlefield superiority.

With a tonnage nearly the same as an STO battleship and the ability to launch dozens of shuttles filled with ground troops, there wasn't much that liked to tangle with them. They may be outgunned by most STO navy ships past frigates, but he would bet on the *Talon* against any pirate ship out there.

Captain Matthews was the last to arrive in the much more cramped conference room aboard the Talon. Almost all of the Field Leaders were there, the only person missing was Baru. He remained on Ganos, leaving operational oversight of the mission to him.

Unlike the fancy holo table at their headquarters, a large monitor came to life on the far side of the room, only moments after he sat down.

What he saw shocked him, but Matthews was principled enough not to let it show. A large robot sat crouched next to a man probably in his early thirties.

"I assume you are Captain Daniel?" Matthews asked. Going by the wings on his skin suit, he was unlikely to be anyone else. "I thought we were going to meet with Mr. Kane as well."

The robot moved, touching its arm to its chest. "Apologies, Captain. I am Mr. Kane. Or more aptly, this is the body I need to use to communicate.

I suffer from an incurable illness that requires my real body to remain in a medical capsule."

Matthews rolled with the unexpected situation. "I see. I apologize if I caused any offense."

"That is not necessary, Captain. This is one of the reasons I wanted to speak via video before we continued. I didn't want to throw this surprise on top of all the other things that might greet us out here."

"So you are aware of how dangerous this trip could be?"

Kane made the holographic face projected in front of his body nod.

"Are there any changes you wish to make to our action plan?"

"No, you are the experts, I trust that you know what you are doing."

Matthews nodded.

The meeting went over what to expect and how to act if they got attacked en route. Daniel seemed competent and asked questions for clarification if he didn't understand something. All in all, the meeting went well. Kane didn't come across as some rich snob who wanted everything done his way, no matter how impossible it was. Maybe this op wouldn't be so bad after all.

CHAPTER 35

LOCATION: Y6X-3H2-4
SYSTEM: Y6X-3H2
DATE: 2398

Martinez sipped his cup of caff, or what passed for caff on Eden's End. He longed for the real stuff, but no self-respecting captain came that far outside STO space and he was glad for that. That was why he packed up his family and came out there in the first place. He was sick of all the bullshit and rules the Solarians and the other core worlders forced on them, all to benefit the rich.

They still had rules out there past the fringe, but it wasn't the same. People there knew what mattered and what didn't.

But man, he still wished for a real cup of caff.

As he was pondering the few things he missed from civilized space, his screen beeped.

Martinez set his mug down and sat up. The old research facility's sensors were as decrepit as everything else in the facility, so sometimes they gave false positives, sometimes they didn't. Those times were why someone had to man the sensor room at all times.

The job wasn't terrible, mostly just a lot of boring sitting around. They did occasionally get pirates that came through though. Most just kept going, the facility looked like a very unappealing target with its dilapidated exterior. The few pirates who were dumb enough to land and try their luck quickly found themselves cut off and outnumbered.

Martinez punched in the codes to run a follow-up scan. The passive sensors wouldn't give them a very clear picture of what was out there, but it would alert them if something was indeed out there. He waited and soon a ping came back.

He cursed under his breath and rolled the old computer chair over to the alarm station. He entered another code, and the entirety of the interior was bathed in yellow flashing lights, repeating itself wherever the lights still functioned across the enormous structure.

Thankfully, someone had figured out how to disable the audio portion of the alarm long ago. He swore he still had ringing in his ears from the times that damn thing went off.

After a dozen minutes or so, a group clomped up the stairs to the security office.

"What do we have, Martinez?" Damien asked.

The shorter man was nominally in charge of Eden's End, not because he was large or intimidating but because he didn't take shit from anyone. He was also the primary reason the station wasn't a haven for criminals. Anyone who fucked around quickly found out at the end of Damien's fist. The man had been a championship martial artist back in the core before he gave it all up for some peace and quiet out there.

"Hard to say. It hasn't moved since the original scan, but the system keeps flagging it, so it's definitely real."

The next scan showed three more ships had joined the first. Damien didn't say anything, but Martinez felt the man's grip tighten on the back of the chair.

"You think someone wised up?" another man asked.

Martinez didn't know this man. He was probably one of the people who helped man the security room like him.

"If it was pirates, they would've been coming in full tilt. They wouldn't have waited for their allies. Sharing isn't in their nature."

"So who then?" Gabriella asked.

Martinez made sure to keep his eyes from straying to the former fitness instructor. Even if she wasn't Damien's girlfriend, if his wife found out he looked at another woman, he would never hear the end of it.

"We won't know until they get within visual range," Damien stated. "Are the asteroid cameras up and working?"

Martinez shrugged. "Haven't had a chance to check 'em."

"I'll do it," the unnamed man said enthusiastically.

Martinez just rolled his eyes at the man's eagerness.

"Three, four, five, and seven are working. The rest are offline."

"It'll have to do. Send a laser comm to the units and get them oriented in our visitor's direction. I want to know who's knocking on our door."

It took hours to get a visual picture of the ships. They were taking their sweet time moving deeper into the system and toward Eden's End, or as the old records cataloged the planet, Y6X-3H2-4. Martinez didn't know who coined the new name, but he was glad he didn't have to call it by that old designation constantly.

"Those don't look like pirate ships," Gabriella said.

The lead ship was a massive hulk that easily outweighed the other three ships by at least twice over.

Martinez may not have served in the military, but he had seen something similar before. "I think that's a troop carrier."

He felt all the eyes in the room turn on him, and he swallowed thickly.

"You're sure?" Damien asked.

"I'm not positive, but it looks similar to one I saw once as a kid."

"Fuck!" the wiry man cursed.

"So it is pirates?" a few of Damien's hangers-on asked from the background.

"Worse," the man spat. "It's mercenaries."

"Mercenaries? What would mercenaries want all the way out here?" Martinez's question was answered a moment later as every terminal in the room secured itself at the same time.

"Shit!" the excitable man who had checked the cameras squealed as he ran over to another terminal and began furiously typing. "They have the master override code!"

"I thought you said you disabled that?" Damien demanded as he strode up behind the man.

"No, I told you I *bypassed* it. Maybe you'll listen to me next time when I tell you we need to replace the core, brother."

Brother? Well, that was news to Martinez.

"As if we had the parts to do that. Just work your magic."

Damien's brother gave an exasperated laugh. "There is no magic. The entire system is locked down. They have full control over everything from their ship."

To prove his point, the overhead speakers crackled to life.

"Squatters of the Y6X-3H2-4 research outpost. This is Captain Matthews of the Hawks of Ganos. The facility you are residing in has been legally purchased. You will submit yourselves for inspection. Failure to comply with this order will result in your arrest on suspicion of criminal activity. This will be the only warning you are given. Captain Matthews out."

The room went quiet after the statement. The sweet silence didn't last long as it was broken by some babbling idiot in the back.

"W-We have to fight!" the man declared.

Damien casually walked over to the man who was enthusiastically bobbing his head up and down because he thought Damien was agreeing with him. The former martial artist cuffed the idiot upside the head. "Shut the hell up."

When the room went quiet again, Damien spoke. "They specifically called it an inspection, not a relocation. I've heard of these Hawks of Ganos. If it's the same company I'm thinking of, they should treat us properly."

"You can't be fucking serious!" another man stepped up, his voice laced with anger. "You want us just to let them into the facility? They're just going to evict us, leaving us without a home. Are we just supposed to beg for a ride back to STO space or try to eke out a living on the surface?"

Damien just looked at the man. "What did you expect would happen? That you would just live out your life in luxury in a place that didn't belong to you? We all moved here knowing none of us owned this place. It was only a matter of time until something changed. Either someone would have purchased it, the STO would have expanded its borders, or the place would have decayed to the point it became uninhabitable. So I suggest if you want that ride back to civilization, you don't do anything stupid. Hell, maybe we can even negotiate to stay here."

To Martinez, it didn't sound like Damien believed that last bit, but it sounded like a better option than the alternative. Fighting off a small crew of pirates was one thing but fighting off a troop transport filled with well-trained mercenaries was another. He sure as hell didn't want to go down fighting. If he had to die, he would prefer to have it happen in his bedroom doing something far more engaging with his missus.

* * *

"Sir, is there a reason you didn't notify the people in the facility below that we would be leaving them on the planet and only arresting those with warrants?" Sable asked.

It was a good question from his executive officer.

Matthews decided this was a good learning opportunity for his XO. "Never let a possible enemy know your next move. Sure, we could have told them, and they may have lined up all nicely, only to wait until we were in the middle of the search to ambush us. This way, they are unsure of our motives, and it will likely bring the rotten elements to the surface. While it may not be the most respectable way to handle this situation, it is the safest."

"Won't that endanger the drop troops?" she asked in confusion.

"No. They know better than to trust unknown civilians in a hostile environment. I suspect after my little speech, at least a few people down there will try something. Others will probably hide and hope we overlook them. Now that we have full access to the station's sensors, the few that work anyway, hiding won't do them much good. We already have the crew down in the computer core crunching the information. They will be able to give us an accurate count of how many people are down there and their activities for the last twenty hours," he stated, finishing his little lecture.

"I see," Sable nodded.

She was young, but she was starting to get the hang of tactics. He would make sure to pass along all of his knowledge to her. Eventually, she would replace him as Captain of the *Talon* when he retired, and he would be damned if he left without ensuring a suitable replacement for his position.

Matthews sat back in his chair as the ship came alive with the sounds of soldiers hurrying to their dropships. He never got tired of hearing it.

chapter 36

Alexander stood in the conference room aboard the *Zephyr*, watching a live feed of the *Talon* disgorging drop shuttle after drop shuttle to the surface of Y6X-3H2-4. The *Zephyr* didn't have any convenient windows to look out of to see this going on in person. He wasn't likely to see anything even if there were windows on the ship, the space between them was too far apart.

Could he enhance his vision to see that far? A test for another time.

The operation was taking place during nighttime hours aboard *Zephyr*. He had asked Captain Matthews to do this so Yulia would be sound asleep while the operation was going on.

The crew of the *Zephyr* had grown fond of the girl over the last month or so. They would likely keep her busy if he asked them to, but he didn't want to burden them at a time when they may be needed at their stations.

That meant he was alone in the room. Jasper and the rest of his command crew were keeping an eye on things from the bridge.

Watching the ships descend into the thin atmosphere of the planet left Alexander with mixed feelings. Matthews had communicated to him that over three thousand people were living in the research facility on the surface.

The number had surprised him. So much for his 'abandoned property.'

Alexander had figured a few dozen people at most might have taken up residence in the deteriorating structure. Certainly not over three thousand. He sighed. He could only hope the people down there weren't pirates or harboring pirates. They may be outside of STO-controlled space, but Matthews and the Hawks of Ganos' leadership had clearly underlined what would happen if pirates were discovered. They still needed to operate under STO law because of their charter.

Alexander didn't know the people below, but he hoped for their sake they weren't dumb enough to harbor pirates.

Soon the last dropship passed into the atmosphere, leaving a lone remaining trail of fire to show its passage. There was nothing left to see and he wasn't privileged enough to get a feed to the soldiers' activities. It was up to the mercenaries now. He really hoped he had made the right choice by hiring them.

* * *

Travers was jarred awake as his dropship lit off its braking thrusters. It was always such a drag waiting once you strapped yourself in. He adjusted his neck, getting the stiffness out of it as best he could inside his armor. At least they didn't need vac suits for this op.

He activated his mic. "Sound off!"

A chorus of "Yes Sir!" followed his order and he watched his HUD populate little green squares along the bottom of his helmet's visor to indicate everyone was synced into the command network and ready. He sent a silent prayer to his ancestors to watch over his team and keep those little icons from going yellow or black.

"Heavies, check in!"

Two larger icons blinked green. The two soldiers in the augment gear were the 'Oh shit!' response. They were fully vac-sealed, but the suits they wore were about as different from a normal armored vac suit as a normal armored vac suit was from civilian dress. Nothing short of anti-armor was getting through those tin cans. If the people living there had that kind of firepower, the heavies would hold the rear while the rest of the Hawks withdrew.

Then they would simply pummel the facility from orbit with the *Talon*. It would mean the op was a failure and they would refund all of Kane's money. Leveling the facility was better than letting a pirate stronghold grow in power like Haven had.

"Ten seconds!" the pilot shouted.

Everyone readied their pulse rifles without having to be told. Travers readied his CQB rifle. All the team had the flechette rifles, but unless shit hit the fan, only the Field Leaders were authorized to deploy them.

The ship slammed down, shaking everyone inside as the shocks absorbed the majority of the fast descent.

"Sorry for the rough ride, air's thinner than the ship is rated to handle."

Travers ignored the pilot's excuse as he stood. They always tried to rattle the ground crews. He would be the first off so he readied his rifle as the flashing red light indicated the ramp would drop at any second.

With a resounding boom, the ramp dropped and Travers double-timed it off the ship, scanning the sides for hostile activity. There was none. If the dust kicked up by their descent was anything to go by, the landing pad outside the facility was quiet and looked like it hadn't been used in ages.

His men rushed past to create a cordon, moving as one toward the door to the facility. Similar groups were moving to other entrances on the same landing pad as well as every other one around the facility.

As they reached the door, he slid the card reader into the electronic lock and let the master code open the door. There was a click and the red light above the pad turned green. One of his men spun the lock and pulled the door open. He slipped inside as soon as there was enough room.

A few locals waited beyond the door with *weapons*, but as soon as they saw him leading the way with an actual weapon, they tossed away their pipes and improvised weapons and threw their hands in the air.

Travers motioned for his team to secure the individuals with mag restraints. They didn't have very many of those high-tech restraints, but they had enough for that group. Once they had an area secured, they could start processing people and shipping them back to space if needed.

It took around an hour to clear his section and meet up with the other teams in one of the atriums designated on the building plans. Three teams were assigned to this zone, and between them, they had captured over a hundred individuals who had taken up arms against them. Most had surrendered, but a few had tried to fight.

The fighters either received pulse blasts or in one case, a flechette when the person pulled out a pistol to fire on another team. After scanning that individual, they soon realized he had ten warrants for his arrest on three worlds and a handful of stations. His bounty was for dead or alive, so the body was bagged up and hauled off to one of the dropships.

"Captain Matthews, Area D is secure." His radio would be routed back to the dropship and their more powerful antenna would transmit it to the *Talon*.

"Very good, Travers. We are waiting for Area C to be secured. Once it is, I will send the second announcement."

A few minutes later, the overhead comm system crackled to life. The captain spoke through it, telling the citizens of the research station to head to their closest designated atrium for processing. Emergency terminals would display the maps for where they needed to go.

It was much simpler than having to scour the station and try to keep track of everyone as they did. One team from each atrium would still clear every room in their section, but only after the majority of the squatters gathered.

Travers saw the other Field Leaders motioning him over and he jogged to meet up with them.

"Rock, paper, scissors; winner gets patrol."

Travers groaned but slung his rifle on his back as he readied his fist in his other hand.

"Ha!" he exclaimed, slapping the other man's scissors away with his rock. It had taken seven rounds but he won. "You two gentlemen have fun processing these folks."

"Bite me!" one of the leaders shouted, waving him off.

The other just laughed. "It was your idea to play."

Travers hustled back to his men and gave them the good news.

* * *

Damien was making his way to the atrium as the man over the comm called it. Everyone down there just called it the garden—although it wasn't much of one. There were more weeds than actual plants, and even those took on a sickly yellow hue due to the lack of water and proper lighting. Hard to justify wasting resources on green space when they needed those resources for the farms.

The line of defeated people shifted to the side of the hallway as a group of armed and armored men strode past like they owned the place.

He couldn't help gnashing his teeth and clenching his fists when he saw this.

One of the men must have noticed because the group stopped and pointed him out. "You, step out of the line."

Dammit! He had let his anger get to him again. That was the exact reason he left the core worlds.

His hesitation had the men aim their weapons his way.

"We won't ask again."

Damien gently removed Gabriella's hand from his arm, patting her reassuringly before stepping out of the line. His self-control had reasserted itself at her touch.

"What can I do for you?" he asked in his most neutral tone.

A man with a silver bar on his armor plate stepped up and looked him over. Damien could feel his anger flare up again. People had looked down on him his entire life for his short stature, but he usually got the last laugh when he beat them into submission, or in the ring.

"I've seen you somewhere before," the man stated.

Damien tensed. His identity was bound to come out eventually. He couldn't appear on national news and intergalactic stations, expecting people not to recognize him.

"Yeah... Holy Shit! You're Damien Laront, the mixed martial arts master who won the Intergalactic Fighting Championship four years in a row." The man did a few shadow boxing moves as he took a step back. "I tried to mirror my fighting style off of yours. I gotta say, I'm a big fan."

Damien didn't even bother trying to plaster a fake smile on his face. He gave up that pretend life and all the bullshit that went with it when he moved out there. "Your form is shit," he said instead.

The man stared at him for a moment, and his men tensed behind him before the guy let out a deep laugh. "I gotta say, didn't see that coming today. Although, getting told you're shit by a master doesn't hurt nearly as much as I thought it would. Why the hell is someone like you out in this dump anyway?" The man waved around him.

"I have my reasons," Damien replied tersely.

The mercenary didn't seem at all concerned by his tone, he simply nodded. "Well, we'll speak again. For your sake, I hope you don't have any warrants or anything." The guy gave him a little salute before waving his guys to follow him.

Damien stepped out of the way and his brother, Lucas, and his girlfriend, Gabriella, stepped up beside him. They must have been waiting to support him if shit got bad. Gabriella might be able to do something, but he never got why his nerdy brother ever bothered. The man had zero talent for fighting. All his talent went to computers and electronics.

"What was that all about?" Gabriella asked.

"Fans," he grumbled.

His younger brother laughed, earning a glare from Damien that made him laugh even more.

Damien rejoined the line, not waiting for his ass of a brother to stop before storming off.

* * *

Gabriella waited for Damien to move off down the hallway before slapping Lucas upside the head. "You should be nicer to your brother. If it wasn't for him, you'd be locked up in some STO penal colony or sold off to one of the big corporations as a slave."

The taller man rubbed the back of his head as he stared at the floor in shame. "Sorry."

She nodded her head and pointed down the hall. "Don't apologize to me."

The man sighed but jogged down the hall to catch up with his brother.

Once he was gone, Gabriella turned to watch the distant figures of the mercenaries for a moment before she, too, rejoined the line of people. It wouldn't be her first time being evicted like that. Her parents and a good majority of the people living in Eden's End were commonly referred to as drifters in most civilized places. Most of the time people used it as a derogatory term, but drifters didn't care. They just didn't want to live under the oppressive rule of the galactic governments or have half their incomes stolen as taxes that did nothing to help them.

It was probably the oddest eviction she had been a part of though. Normally mercenaries simply subdued everyone they came across with stunners or pulse rifles. It was why she had extra padding under her shirt. Those damn things hurt. Never had she seen mercenaries simply walk past a line of people they knew were illegally occupying some place. She didn't want to hope that time might be different, but something told her it was.

CHAPTER 37

"This the room?" Travers asked over the radio.

"Yes," the field operator aboard the ship replied.

Travers grunted and gave a hand motion to his team. They split up and flanked the door.

"Any idea how many we are dealing with?"

"Three to five individuals. The cameras in that area aren't very clear so that's the best guess we're getting from Sam."

He grunted in annoyance as he poked a hole in a rusting beam nearby with his finger. The Strategic Analysis Module, or SAM for short, was a wonderful piece of tech, but it could only generate tactical analysis if it had data to do so.

Travers removed his gloved finger from the rusty hole. "No pulse rifles. This area's too unstable. One missed shot could bring the entire thing down on top of us."

That meant no CQB rifle either. Travers slapped the weapon to the mag restraint on the back of his armor and pulled out his stunner.

Once everyone was ready, he nodded, and his men turned the crank on the door as fast as possible and threw it open. There was a chorus of surprised shouts as Travers rushed into the room. The first thing he noticed was that there were more people than Sam had predicted. Over half a dozen men were waiting in the dilapidated room. The next thing he noticed was the weapons they were quickly trying to pull from crates.

He kicked the barrel of the antique firearm the closest individual was trying to aim toward him. The gun flew out of the man's surprised hand, but not before he shot off a series of bullets. The only thing the idiot managed to hit was his friends.

Travers shoved the stunner into the man's diaphragm harder than was strictly necessary. The man went down and the others quickly followed.

He stood over the unconscious forms of the seven men and thanked his luck that they seemed unaccustomed to the old weapons.

"Weapon secured!" one of his team alerted him. The man turned the weapon and read off the designation stamped into the side. "AK-74? Where do you think they even got these antiques?"

"Who knows," Travers shook his head. He grabbed the weapon from his team member and sat it back in the rotten wooden crate. "We'll need to get the engineers out here to disarm them. Who volunteers for babysitting duty?"

Two of his team weren't quick enough to call 'not it.' Travers laughed and pointed to them. "Looks like you two get the honors."

The two grumbled under their breath before stepping out of the room to guard the door. "Let's get these seven men cuffed and dragged back to the atrium."

"Six, FL. Looks like this one bled out."

Travers looked to where his man was pointing and sighed. It was one of the people who took hits from the idiot with the gun. "Bag him up."

They quickly and efficiently bagged up the dead man and secured the others. Every single one had a warrant on the same planet. Likely a small-time gang that had been forced out. Travers tagged them for pickup and led his team back to the atrium.

There were more places to search.

* * *

It had taken two full weeks for the Hawks to clear and secure the station. They had arrested over eighty people who had active warrants out for their arrest. No pirates, though, which was a pleasant surprise.

That left a significant number of worried people down below.

Alexander focused on the man sitting across the dropship from him. "You're sure it's safe?" he asked for the tenth time. Yulia was in a seat beside him, headphones on and her face shoved into a holo movie.

"Yes, Mr. Kane," Jallen, one of the Field Team leaders, responded in a slightly annoyed tone.

Alexander had his avatar nod.

He was just worried, but not for himself. He was pretty sure his body could withstand anything the people in the station threw at him, considering the damage he had previously, but Yulia was just a little kid.

"And you said you found the leader?"

The man waggled his hand back and forth. "Drifters don't tend to have much in the way of leadership, so to speak, but the man who presented himself to us is nominally in charge. We confirmed that by speaking to a bunch of other drifters."

Alexander didn't like the way the man used the word drifter. It sounded rather derogatory. He had asked Jallen what a drifter was when the word first came up. Apparently, they were just people who drifted from place to place. Most places didn't welcome them because they refused to follow rules put in place by the STO. Jallen didn't actually say that last bit, he just said they were troublemakers who refused to fit into polite society.

Considering Alexander was trying to upset the establishment, he might get along with those drifters quite well. Time would tell.

The shuttle shook, and the pilot spoke up. "We are entering the atmosphere. It'll get a bit bumpy from here."

The seats aboard the shuttle were far too small and weak to hold Alexander's bulk. Fortunately, that wasn't much of an issue for him. He figured out he could magnetize his feet and hands to hold himself in place.

He wasn't sure how it was possible considering his entire body was non-metallic, but he wasn't going to question it.

Alexander was glad the Hawks had shuttles. He had overlooked a very significant issue when he packed everything aboard the *Zephyr*: the ship was too large to land on the surface of a planet. Jasper had pointed the issue out early in their trip. After some conversations with the *Talon*'s captain, they figured out a method to get his cargo down to the surface.

It required an additional investment of one million credits and took the *Talon*'s engineering crew a week of spacewalks to transfer the cargo to dropships that floated near the *Zephyr*'s open cargo ramp, but they managed it. Now all of his belongings sat off to one side of the nearest landing pad to the manufacturing hub, but that didn't mean he would be saying goodbye to Jasper or his crew just yet though.

The *Zephyr* had a small shuttle that followed them down to the surface. The only thing aboard that shuttle was 'his' medical pod. Now that he was outside of STO space, Alexander probably wasn't going to continue perpetuating that lie. It was such a pain to be tethered to the item, even if it was only a fake tether.

The ship shook again, and he focused on Yulia. The girl seemed unaffected by the turbulence, she was more interested in sneaking a peek outside the window. Her eyes were wide in delight as she watched the plasma stream off the underside of the ship from the superheated atmosphere.

Considering who her parents were, that very well might be her first time setting foot on the surface of a planet. He was glad artificial gravity existed. Otherwise, she would have had all sorts of problems dealing with the gravity.

Y6X-3H2-4 only averaged about eighty percent of Earth's gravity, so it was slightly less than Petrov Station which kept theirs at ninety percent of Earth's. It probably wouldn't take the girl very long to adjust to the change.

She would likely have more issues adjusting to the day-night cycle and the stink.

Yulia had already complained about the smell when they first boarded the shuttle through the docking ring and that was only the lingering aroma, it would be much worse on the ground. It was one time he was thankful his body didn't include olfactory senses.

As for the day-night cycle, it was a doozy. On average, each day was nearly forty hours long including dawn and dusk. Each night lasted over twenty of those hours. The planet wasn't tidally locked, which was a blessing, but it did have a mean orbital angle. This angle shifted the day-night cycle almost completely at two points in the year. It was going to take some getting used to.

He would likely pick up whatever system the inhabitants used. He was sure the people below had adapted to it by now. Most of the facility was buried below the surface or sported thick concrete covering so natural light wasn't really a concern anyway.

The observation dome, the only part of the complex that wasn't buried or covered, was a wreck of broken glass and rusted metal due to exposure. That was second on his priority list to get fixed. Not because he wanted to stare at the blue star or take measurements of the thing but because the damage exposed other parts of the structure. He had already been told by Captain Matthews that the damage had spread quite far from that location. If it wasn't taken care of, the entire facility could become jeopardized.

After speaking with his representative, priority one was finding a safe place for Yulia to stay while he worked on bringing the place up to livable conditions. He did wonder why the locals hadn't done it themselves. When he thought about it though, he realized they likely didn't have access to repair schematics. It was a good thing he did.

"Touchdown in five," the pilot yelled over the roar of the thrusters.

"Alex, it hurts!" Yulia cried.

"It'll be over shortly." He tried to calm the girl. There was no getting past the extra G's they had to pull to not slam into the surface. The planet didn't have a thick enough atmosphere to slow the dropship's descent enough.

"Pretend someone's hugging you real tight and push back against it," Jallen said calmly.

The girl nodded and Alexander watched her tense up.

Yulia had slowly come out of her shell aboard the *Zephyr*. She was still a bit shy and almost always refused to talk to anyone she didn't know.

Alexander printed the words 'Thank You!' under his avatar's face.

The man nodded. "I have two small nieces."

Soon the extra weight lifted and the ship touched down gently. He had heard some of the first drops were rather rough since they did combat drops. He was glad they hadn't needed to do it that time around.

"Alright, Yulia, time to put your breather mask on."

She pouted a bit before slipping the gray mask on.

Alexander unmagnetized his body and double-checked the seal was tight on her mask. He nodded to Jallen who hit a button near the back. The door slowly lowered, allowing the harsh glare of the blue sun into the cabin.

It was nearly blinding after being stuck in the natural yellow light aboard stations and ships, he wished he had gotten Yulia some sunglasses.

"Sorry 'bout the light," Jallen said in annoyance. "We landed near the peak of the day cycle. Just use your tablet to cover your eyes and follow me. The door isn't far."

Alexander would have picked Yulia up, but the girl insisted on walking. She held the holo tablet over her eyes like a visor with one hand and held onto Alexander's hand with her other. However, her eyes kept roaming to the scenery around them. To be fair, Alexander was taking it all in as well. This *was* his first time on an alien planet or at least the first time he could remember.

Chapter 38

The three of them walked through the first door. Once it was shut behind them, a strong flow of air sucked any dust they might have accumulated into the filter below the grated floor.

"This is the only environmental lock that still functions!" Jallen shouted over the loud rush of air.

Soon the air settled and the light on the inner door turned green. Jallen pushed it open and stepped inside where he waited for Alexander and Yulia.

They didn't take that entrance because it had a working environmental seal. From what he was told, that was kind of a moot point at that moment. No, he had to take it because it was one of the few cargo entrance doors. Those were the only doors his bulky body could currently fit through.

He didn't know who had designed the original entrances to the structure, but they had only made the exterior doors six feet tall. Alexander could crouch to get through shorter doors, but they were also only thirty inches wide instead of the standard square six-foot by six-foot doors required by ships and stations. He had not found any way to slim his body to fit through such a tight space and doubted he ever would.

Thankfully that issue only applied to the exterior doors and some of the living spaces.

The interior corridor was wide enough for two vehicles to drive side by side. There were no vehicles as far as he could see, but there were old signs indicating the wide road had been heavily traveled at one time.

The three of them followed the old tire tracks up the gently sloping ramp. The ramp emptied into a large parking garage that was completely empty and extremely dark thanks to all the burned-out or missing lights. Alexander had no trouble seeing in the dark, but Jallen flicked on a light so he and Yulia could see.

"We're not sure if there were vehicles left behind when the place was abandoned, but if there were, they aren't here anymore."

"The manifest didn't mention any," Alexander responded.

"Ah," the mercenary replied. "Probably sold off before they shut the place down then. This way." He gestured with his light to another tunnel.

That one was half the width of the tunnel they entered, but there were still black marks along the curving surface to mark it had been heavily traveled. It wasn't long until they exited the tunnel into a large expansive dome.

What impressed Alexander most about the nearly mile-wide dome was the complete lack of support except for a singular enormous beam right in the center that arched out overhead like a huge umbrella.

"Welcome to Atrium D, or you might hear the Hawks call it Area D."

"It's huge!" Yulia whispered in awe.

"Yeah, this is a pretty impressive structure," Jallen admitted. "I don't think I've seen anything quite like it in all my years."

"Does that mean there are three more of these?" Alexander had looked at the structural plans, but he had been more focused on the technological aspect of repairing the place rather than the architecture.

"There are actually four, but the observation dome in the center is the one that collapsed. It was also three times the size of this space. It's a shame. I would have loved to see what it looked like before."

Alexander could agree, a dome that was three miles wide would have been an impressive sight. That dome had a transparent roof, unlike the others.

Despite the impressive size of the atrium, the room looked to be in total disrepair. There were only a dozen or so massive overhead lights still functioning, and half of those flickered on and off fitfully. The gloom from the massive chamber was held at bay by a bright area off to the far side.

"Come on. The person you want to speak to is at the base camp."

They headed straight for the lighted area.

Alexander focused his perception in that direction and took in the small camp bustling with people being scanned and handed ID chips. It was only after the Hawks finished scouring the facility that they started handing out ID's. Nobody without an ID could pass the checkpoints they set up. It was a measure to ensure people didn't start causing trouble.

Surprisingly, the people weren't too upset by the development. They weren't all that happy with it either, but they complied so they could return to their homes and their families.

"Yulia..." Alexander kneeled. "Why don't you go introduce yourself?" He pointed to some kids playing in the dirt nearby. They looked younger than his adopted daughter, but it should be fine.

She looked unsure for a moment before nodding and wandering over to the group. She was close enough that Alexander could keep an eye on her if he needed to but far enough away not to intrude on any discussions. He didn't want her too close if things got heated with the people formerly in charge.

Soon a group of three led by another Team Leader approached him.

Alexander took the group in, he saw their hesitation when they first saw him, but that didn't seem to stop them from approaching.

The man leading the group stuck out his hand and Alexander shook it. "Travers. And the people behind me are Damien Laront, Gabriella, and Lucas Laront."

Damien stepped forward but crossed his arms as he glared at Alexander. "Just Damien. My bastard of a father's last name was Laront, and I don't much care being reminded of him."

Alexander watched the two people with Damien roll their eyes. It was rather funny.

"So," Damien continued. "We your slaves now?"

"Huh?" Alexander was caught off guard by the question.

"Rich man who runs around greeting people through a robot buys out someplace beyond the rim. Only a few reasons to do that. Either he wants to be left alone, or he wants to do shit so heinous the STO would shut him down. Since these bastards aren't stunning the lot of us and dragging us into orbit, I figured it was the latter."

"I... What?"

The other man stepped forward and sighed. "Ignore my older brother. He tends to get testy when his authority is challenged."

"That's bullshit and you know it, Lucas!"

Everyone just looked at the man. That Damien character was blunter than a dead-blow hammer.

"Um, look," Alexander said. "I think you have the wrong idea here. I'm not rich... Well, technically I am but only due to some fluke circumstances. I don't know you people, so I'm not going to be going into my whole history. Suffice it to say, I'm not here entirely by choice. As for why I picked this place. I imagine I picked it for the same reason you all did."

"So you're a drifter, like us?" Gabriella spoke up for the first time.

Damien snorted at that. "Never seen a drifter hire a core group of mercs and bring down enough supplies for a family to live off of for the rest of their lives."

"Yes, I bought the station. Yes, that will come with some restrictions. But I don't want to have to police the people here, I expect you to do that yourselves. Form a council, elect a president, I don't care. Just realize that whatever you decide, I will have a majority vote. I think that is more than fair for allowing you to stay here. I don't wish to be involved in your politics,

I only want a safe place to raise my daughter and to be left alone by those like Omni and the STO. If you don't like that, you and anyone else are free to leave. The Hawks will drop you off at the nearest station and you can go wherever you want from there."

"Why should we leave? We were here first," the man bristled at Alexander's tone.

He would rather be teaching Yulia or working on some project than standing there arguing semantics with the man. "And that's why I asked the Hawks to just sort out the criminals. Look, my goal here is to turn Y6X-3H2-4 into something someday and that starts with fixing up this outpost. Unfortunately, I can't do that alone. I want to work with the people who live here. The only part of the facility I need for myself is the manufacturing yard and one empty apartment for me and my daughter."

Damien narrowed his eyes, but Alexander saw a bit of tension leave him as he slowly uncrossed his arms. "First off, we aren't using that stupid name."

Progress? He had wielded the stick, now it was time to offer the carrot. "Then what do you call the planet?"

"Eden's End."

"Hmm. Seems a bit dour, but if that's what everyone calls it, I'll update the registry. See? Compromise. We can work together to improve all of our lives. I don't want to rule over you or any such nonsense like that. As you said before, I just want to be left alone. Just not so alone that I might lose my mind. There is a lot of work to accomplish if we are going to fix this place. That means plenty of work for anyone who wants to get paid."

"What, in STO credits? I think you'll find most people here have little to no use for that shit."

Alexander made his hologram form a hand to rub its chin. He hadn't put much thought into the fact that his millions of STO credits would suddenly be useless out there, but he had brought way more things than he could ever use himself. It was time to put those items to use. "I have other things to trade."

"Such as?"

Alexander turned to Jallen and Travers. "Do either of you have a tablet that can link to Captain Daniel?" He would have used his comm bracelet, but he had quickly learned of the shortcomings of the little devices. They were useless without a Qcomm relay or the secure storage nodes that the courier ships possessed. He also didn't have a radio.

Travers unhooked a smaller device from his belt and handed it to him.

Alexander quickly connected to the captain and got the manifest of all his cargo sent over. He scrolled through it and removed items he wasn't willing to trade before handing it to the dark-haired and tan-skinned Damien.

The man and his companions spent the better part of ten minutes just scrolling through the list of items Alexander had brought with him.

Lucas Laront was the first to speak up. "You would share these training modules and schematics with us?"

"Sure, why not?"

"Uh, no reason," the man went back to looking at the items for offer.

That was curious, but what was more curious was how interested both Jallen and Travers seemed to become when the man spoke about the modules.

Damien handed the tablet back to Travers. "I want a copy of this list sent to all the terminals so anyone here can access it and decide what they want to work for."

"Does that mean we have a deal?" Alexander asked hopefully.

The man grunted and walked off.

His brother and Gabriella translated that grunt for him at the same time. "That means yes."

Alexander thanked the pair before they hurried to catch up with the prickly Damien.

"What a wonderful man," Jallen responded flatly.

"Oh, I don't know. The man seems to care a lot about the people here. In my eyes, that's a good feature. If he's a bit prickly, so be it."

Honestly, Alexander found dealing with the straightforward Damien quite refreshing. It was certainly better than dealing with the people he had back on Petrov Station.

The Field Leaders shrugged.

"You said you wanted to secure the manufacturing hub for your own?" Travers asked.

Alexander nodded.

"If you want, we can head over there right now."

He went over to retrieve Yulia. It seemed she was having a difficult time retrieving her tablet from the group of kids. The kids stopped fighting over the device as soon as they saw Alexander approach. A few started crying, but the entire lot of them dropped the tablet and ran off. He sighed.

"Are you okay?" he asked.

Yulia looked more angry than upset. "I can't understand them."

"They're still young and don't know how to share quite yet." His parenting help books were coming in handy once again!

"I know that," she huffed as she picked up her tablet. "I played with the younger kids at the orphanage. I can't understand what they are saying."

"Oh..." *Oh shit.*

Everyone on Petrov spoke a derivative form of the Slavic language which was the primary language of the Coalition before its downfall, which was already a mishmash of a few Eastern European languages. Alexander just realized the language he was hearing spoken there was mainly derived from English. Even the Hawks spoke this new English most of the time. They only switched the Slavic when in his company.

"I think I have a tutorial that will teach you how to understand them." Or so he hoped. If not, he would have to teach her himself or find someone here who could speak both languages. It seemed most people spoke at least a few different languages in this century, so there was a good chance he could find someone to assist.

chapter 39

Alexander arrived outside the doors to the manufacturing hub along with Travers and his team. Jallen had to return to his duty.

He liked Jallen, the man was good with children and seemed to know just what to say to calm Yulia. He wasn't quite sure about Travers yet. The man had been quiet the entire way and their interaction in the atrium had been brief. He also didn't know how he was with children as Yulia had promptly fallen asleep after asking Alexander to pick her up and carry her.

He couldn't blame the girl, they had quite an exciting morning so far.

"This is it," Travers declared as he walked over to a busted entry pad off to the side of the large set of dual doors. "Another team was on this side of the facility, so I don't know if this lock was broken before or after they got here. Considering how corroded it looks behind the box, I'm gonna say it was broken a long time ago."

"You don't have to worry about who broke what," Alexander assured the man. "I knew going in that there was going to be a large amount of repairs ahead of me."

The man grunted in acknowledgment. "Still, it looks bad on the Hawks if they are running around smashing things just to get in."

After some fiddling with the wires, the door controller beeped, and the doors squealed open a few inches.

"Those lazy shits from B. There's no way they entered this room to clear it properly. I'll go to the nearest atrium and get a hydraulic jack to force the doors open."

"That won't be necessary, I can handle it. If you don't mind." He held a sleeping Yulia out to Travers, who looked a bit surprised before he put his weapon away and took the girl. "This won't take long, please step aside."

The group of mercenaries moved out of the way as Alexander stepped up to the opening. He slipped both arms into the space and pulled.

The door groaned and, for a moment, it didn't appear it was going to open. Then with a loud metallic screech, the door slid open a few more inches. Alexander adjusted his hands and pulled again. The door moved much easier now but still only opened enough to allow him to pass through.

"After you." He waved.

Travers nodded and handed the sleeping girl back before he pulled out his rifle. "Go in assuming the room is hostile. On me." With that he moved into the room, sweeping his flashlight one way while the next guy swept his beam the other.

Alexander waited while the rest of the team filtered into the room and cleared it. He was more than a little impressed by their professionalism.

Considering he hadn't been able to watch them in action during the initial operation to clear this facility, it gave him a good glimpse of how the Hawks worked. He could now see why they were the premier mercenary company on Ganos, and why Violet from Fidelity Properties had recommended them.

"Clear," came a series of calls.

"It's safe to enter, Mr. Kane."

"Thank you," Alexander replied as he slipped through the barely wide enough gap. "And please just call me Alexander."

Travers nodded.

Alexander walked over to where he recalled the light switch to be from the blueprints. With no surprise, he found it was missing. So were the wires that led to it.

"Any way we can light the room up?" he asked.

One of the men plucked a ball from a pouch on his belt. He shook it vigorously and the ball started to glow softly. Then the man hurled it into the dark room. After a few seconds, the softly glowing ball exploded into bright white light as it slowly hovered in the air on counter-rotating blades that had popped out from the center.

"Flare drone," Travers answered the unasked question.

"Neat!"

The group chuckled quietly at Alexander's comment.

"Yeah, they come in handy," Travers smiled.

Alexander surveyed the room and frowned. "Where are all the robotic assembly machines?"

He had gotten an inventory of what items to expect when he arrived and a list of items that might be there. The vehicles had been listed under the 'might be' column so that's why he wasn't surprised to see them missing, but the robots had been listed as 'present' with a notation that they were in storage mode. All Alexander could see through the flickering shadows cast by the drone was a large empty room, where things had once been.

It was clear where the robots had once been by the platforms left behind and the too-clean spots in the concrete floor.

Travers had been speaking into his radio while Alexander scanned the room. He spoke up. "Nobody located any robotics moved to other areas of the facility. Someone likely stripped this room and sold them off. Probably quite some time ago going by how rusted and unused the door was. Do you want us to question the people to see if anyone knows what happened to them?"

Alexander shook his avatar's head. He would have likely had to recycle the robots or rebuild them completely anyway. There was also no point accusing the people there of the theft without proof. If he wanted to fix the place up in any reasonable sort of timeframe, he was going to need their help.

That being said, he would have to make it very clear going forward that cannibalizing the facility would get the person responsible and their family immediately expelled. He wasn't going to spend all his time fixing the place up just to have people stealing stuff constantly.

"No. I will have a talk with Damien. I was hoping they weren't in too bad of a shape so I could just fix them. Having them missing completely is going to set my plans back by quite a bit though." He sighed internally. "I think I'm going to start by fixing this door. Can you gentlemen notify the engineers to bring my cargo to this space? I can sort through it after that."

Travers nodded before talking into his radio again.

Somehow, Yulia was still fast asleep in his arms, despite the bright light hovering only fifty feet away and the screeching of the rusted door. He was beginning to suspect she had stayed up all night in her excitement.

Working while carrying her wasn't ideal, but there was no soft surface to set his daughter down on. So, he did his best. Considering he was a robot, his best was damn good.

It didn't take him long to remove the panels along the bottom of the door. A pool of stagnant yellow water greeted him when he moved the heavy pieces off to the side. If he could breathe, he was sure the smell of rotten eggs would be permeating the room right about now.

It explained the rust. That part of the facility was rather far from the collapsed section, so water and rust infiltration shouldn't have reached that far.

He reached his free hand into the brackish water and felt around for the drain hole. It took a bit to find it and pull the rag out that had been stuffed inside. It reminded Alexander of the feeling you got when trying to remove food stuck in the sink drain. He shivered mentally at that thought.

Why couldn't he have forgotten something like that instead of all the other important stuff? Bleh!

As soon as the rag was removed, the couple of inches of disgusting water drained away, revealing the mess hidden for who knows how long.

The once chrome-coated track was a pitted, rusty mess. One of the rollers had fallen into a section that had completely rusted away. It was no wonder the door wouldn't open any further. It would need to be completely replaced. To do that though, he needed one of his printers set up, and they would never fit through the doors.

"Excuse me, Mr. Travers?"

"Yes, Mr. Alexander?"

"Can you show me to my residence? I need to put her down before I can work properly."

Travers picked two men to watch the open door before leading him to the small room down the hall that would be his apartment. It had been lived in by someone, but that someone was now waiting aboard the *Talon* for a trip back to STO space to face their punishment. It was one of the reasons he picked the room.

"This is the closest living space to the workshop. It's also far away from any others. That is probably why the individual we arrested was living here. You may want to scrub this place with industrial cleaners as soon as possible," the man wrinkled his nose. "Smells like body odor and illicit substances."

"Do you think Yulia will be fine for the night?" If the room was that bad, he might just find the cleanest bedding he could and move it back into the manufacturing center.

"If she keeps her mask on, it should be fine. I will leave a few people here to keep an eye on her and alert you if she wakes up."

"I know this isn't part of your duty, so thank you."

"Use us as needed, that's why we're here."

* * *

It took Alexander four hours to remove one of the heavy steel doors from the tracks. That was only thanks in part to Travers and his men assisting with the hydraulic ram after he finally relented and let them grab it.

From there he was able to move the printer into the space piece by piece. Printing out a new door guide was not ideal. It was rougher than the original and had to be printed in parts because the only printer he could fit through the opening wasn't large enough to do it as a single piece.

He really needed a lathe or precision grinder, but a door that could open was better than a door that couldn't.

They reattached the door and pushed it into the pocket of the wall. It shook as they moved it, but it wasn't as bad as he had feared. The second door followed, and he reinstalled that as well. Now that he had full access to the room, the engineers began bringing in his cargo using portable jacks.

The manual devices looked almost exactly like Alexander remembered from four hundred years ago. He supposed there wasn't much to improve on the simple cargo-moving devices. He did see the wheels had been replaced with omni rollers.

While he worked on unpacking and printing things, the Hawk's engineers started examining the wiring in the room. They didn't have anything else to do, so they just stuck around.

He was glad for the help. They fished out the old corroded wiring and Alexander handed them a brand new roll from his inventory. He didn't have enough of the electrical wire to rewire the entire station but he had enough to redo that room and a few others. He expected to have a wire machine there to make more, but that was gone along with everything else. Replacing it was not high on his priority list at that moment.

After a few hours of work, the few lights that still worked in the cavernous room flickered fitfully to life. He added 'printing new LED lights' to his growing list of to-do items. At least the main power to the room was still functional. However, that meant people had to steer clear of the hacked-off copper cables that hung limply from where the robot stations used to reside.

With the lighting working, the engineers moved to the task of assembling the printers. If it wasn't for them assisting, he would still be mucking about in the dark or with the stupid door. It was proof that not even he could do everything. He would have to thank them for their assistance.

Alexander made a note to speak with Damien to see if they had any engineers who wanted to help. Once the manufacturing lab was up and running, he would quickly find himself too swamped with tasks to actually finish them all. It was better to find out if there were qualified individuals among the locals while the Hawks were still there, rather than find out in six months from then.

He doubted that was the case though. The drifters had managed to keep that place operational for who knows how many years. Even if they weren't conventionally trained, there had to be people who lived here who knew how certain things worked.

If they didn't, he had the learning modules to train anyone who wanted to learn, but it wouldn't come free.

chapter 40

LOCATION: PETROV STATION
SYSTEM: GLIESE 667
DATE: 2398

Mingyu moved with purpose down the corridor, not quite jogging, but close to it. The trial for Kovalenko and Hoffman was scheduled to start the previous week. Then both men suddenly took their own lives on the same night. It was too suspiciously convenient.

Someone had killed the two senior captains and had the power to make it look like suicide. Knowing that was bad enough. The fact that the only people who knew of the trial were Zhang, Weiss, Liu, Yuchen, and him meant it had to be one of his fellow captains. He had grown up alongside these people, and, while he didn't necessarily like all of them, he thought they were trustworthy. Now he couldn't even say for sure if his best friend Xu could be trusted anymore. The thought made him sick to his stomach.

The issues didn't stop with the former captain's deaths.

Something was happening aboard Petrov Station. It was a subtle shift at first that became more noticeable by the day. He couldn't quite put his finger on what the change was, but he could feel something was wrong. It was almost like when he could tell something aboard the Destiny wasn't working correctly. He chalked it up to having lived there his entire life.

Mingyu wasn't taking any chances after the murder of the two captains. He had been quietly getting his family to take some vacation out of the system over the last couple of days. It had cost him a significant sum to charter the cruise, but his growing unease made him feel like it was justified.

That morning when he attempted to comm Eva Wu and ask her if she noticed anything out of the ordinary, there was no response. Even if the woman had been busy, there should have been a comm acknowledgment from the system. The only possible reason there wasn't one was if her comm had been broken, or the system was down.

He couldn't even conceive of a reason for the retired first mate to have damaged her comm. That meant the Qcomm was offline. Since there was no report sent to his comm alerting him of this outage, he had to assume someone had disabled the Qcomm relay station aboard Petrov. The only reason someone would have to cut off external communication at the station was to keep it isolated. That didn't bode well for anyone aboard.

His destination was just ahead so he picked up the pace slightly and knocked on the door. He could hear someone moving about inside while he scanned the corridor for trouble. He didn't see any.

Everyone seemed completely oblivious to what was happening. Mingyu wanted to warn them but of what? At the moment, he only had assumptions and conjecture. Besides, any warning he gave would only cause panic.

The door opened and the friendly face of Eva Wu greeted him with a smile. "Mingyu, dear. How nice of—" Her words cut off as she looked into his eyes. "What's wrong?"

Despite the tense situation, he couldn't help smiling. The woman never missed anything. "Trouble."

"What sort?" she asked.

"The kind that necessitates us leaving the station, immediately."

Her trust in him was such that she simply nodded her head and shut the door to her apartment. "I needed a walk anyway."

Eva rested her hand on his arm while the pair walked toward his hangar as fast as the older woman could move.

"Smile, boy, you're bringing unwanted attention."

Mingyu stiffened at the rebuke. Eva hadn't called him a boy since long before his father retired. He relaxed the frown on his face and his furtive glances. They would either make it to his ship on time or they wouldn't.

Eva being Eva smiled and waved to people she knew as they passed. There was no hint of urgency in her actions. He only knew she was tense by the near vice-like grip she held on his arm.

"I heard your family went on vacation," she mentioned casually.

"Yes. They all left a few days ago."

"That's good. It can get quite stifling staying in one spot for too long."

He nodded. The worry began to grow in his gut again. It had been two hours since the comms went offline, but there hadn't been a single station alert or announcement. That meant someone in ops had to be involved in whatever was going on. A coup perhaps? He couldn't even begin to guess who could be behind something like that.

The elevator rapidly ascended to the Na's personal hangar. It wasn't any fancier than other hangars, but it was large.

"Now that we're in your hangar, what's going on?"

"I honestly don't know. First, Kovalenko and Hoffman died."

"They're dead?!"

He nodded. "Both on the same night, both supposedly committed suicide."

"Seems like you don't believe that to be the case?" she asked as they walked across the spacious hangar to Destiny's ramp.

"They were both about to be tried for financial crimes against the Station. The only people who knew this were the rest of the Council."

Eva sucked in a breath. "You think someone on the Council killed them?"

He nodded. "And that's not all. I don't know if you've noticed anything weird in the last few days or tried to comm anyone today, but mine isn't working."

She frowned and released his arm to tap at her comm. After a few tries, she let the arm fall away. "I've been sticking close to home this week because my hip has been bothering me, so I haven't noticed anything. My comm isn't working either."

"I figured as much," he said as he started to ascend the ramp.

One of his people rushed out to meet him.

"Is the ship ready to go?" he asked.

"It is, Captain, but there's a slight issue."

"What issue?" Had someone noticed him trying to leave already?

"Well, you scheduled that field trip for the orphans today. They showed up about an hour ago."

With everything going on, he had forgotten. Ever since Kane had left, he had taken a minor yet more active role in the development of the orphans aboard the station. It was partly to atone for not doing enough to support Kane while he was here.

His first instinct was to hurry the orphans off of the *Moonlit Destiny* so the ship could leave, but he didn't know what was happening aboard the station. Asking them to go back into an unknown situation would be a truly cowardly thing for him to do. Unfortunately, he was also at the mercy of STO law. Taking them off the station without their consent would be as good as signing his death warrant because he would be branded a kidnapper.

"Ask them if they would like to go for a quick trip."

Asking them if they wanted to go meant the decision was now in the headmaster's hands. He knew that passing off the decision to a man who didn't have all the information was a shitty thing to do, but it was the only option that didn't end up with him dead.

The man radioed up to the bridge where the question was forwarded to whatever crew was showing the children and Headmaster Wong around. Soon a response came back.

"The headmaster has agreed."

Mingyu didn't know whether he was relieved or disappointed by Wong's choice. He didn't let any emotion show on his face as he nodded to the crewman. "Close it up and get us out of here."

Eva stopped him before he could get too far. "I think I'll go have a chat with the headmaster and fill him in."

He patted the woman on the hand. "Thank you." Mingyu couldn't afford the time to speak with the man now.

The two parted and he hurried to the bridge as the ship started to come to life.

"Report!" he shouted as he entered the bridge.

"Ship systems are all green, Captain, but I can't get ahold of anyone in the control room."

Dammit. Things were moving faster than he thought if the control room wasn't responding.

He hurried over to his seat and strapped himself in. His bridge crew saw that and hurried to strap themselves in as well. He didn't expect any violent maneuvering, but it was better to be safe. He would send out an all-hands alert as soon as the ship was free of the dock.

Mingyu furiously typed in a series of commands on his console, overriding the control room. Soon the lights in the hangar began to flash amber as the air was pumped out of the massive space. The codes he used were given to each founding family in case of catastrophic station failure. It let them take manual control of any station system from a nearby terminal, but it didn't give them access to the entire station.

His screen flashed red as someone from control attempted to lock down the hangar, but the code overrode that. If he hadn't been certain the station was under siege, he was now.

Deciding not to wait any longer, he input the command to open the doors. The remaining air and dust in the hangar was sucked out through the opening doors. Then he heard the landing clamps release as the landing rockets fired up to push the ship off the deck.

The entire time his console kept flashing red as attempts were made to keep him from exiting the station.

As the ship backed out of the hangar, he pressed the intercom button. "All hands, this is Captain Na. Strap in for possible high-G maneuvers! I repeat, strap in for possible high-G maneuvers!"

He hoped Eva had gotten to the headmaster to explain the situation to him. He was sure the children were terrified of what was happening, so he was going to have to rely on Eva and the Headmaster to keep them calm.

Mingyu watched the holo of the ship systems as areas turned green, alerting him that people were secured and ready. One even popped up in the mess hall which was good. That meant Eva had gotten their visitors to the only room with enough secure seats for them.

"As soon as we're clear of the station, burn hard for the transit point. I don't care about saving fuel, just get us out of here as fast as possible."

The pilot acknowledged the order and soon enough Mingyu was pushed back in his seat as the ship lurched forward. The *Moonlit Destiny* wasn't the fastest ship around, but it was a solid workhorse and could take the strain of a full burn for as long as it needed to.

They were less than ten minutes from the station when his sensor operator spoke up. "Captain, our sensors are picking up multiple jump signatures at the transit point. None of the new arrivals appear to be running transponders."

That worry in his gut turned into a dark pit. It was worse than even he had thought. The only ships that didn't run transponders were pirates.

"Can we slip past them?"

After a minute, the woman shook her head. "They jettisoned something at the transit location. My sensors are reading it as a large mass, but it can't be much bigger than a cargo container."

Mingyu didn't know what the hell the pirates had launched into space, but he knew what it was for. There was a reason people needed to clear a system before jumping to FTL. A significant enough gravity well would disrupt the warp sphere causing it to dump you back into normal space.

Even a station as small as Petrov was enough to have an effect. It could be brute forced with enough power, but he would have to turn off every auxiliary system aboard the Destiny and somehow route that power to the FTL drive.

That wasn't going to happen without spending weeks rewiring the entire ship.

He sent a new vector to his pilot, and the man turned to look at him. "You're sure, Captain?"

"Get us there."

The ship angled up and away from the ecliptic plane of Gliese 667 and away from the standard jump point. People used the standard jump points because the math required to calculate your own jump point was tricky and an error could get you killed.

There was no navigation data for a jump from where they were heading, but he was already doing the math as the ship rocketed forward.

"Sir!" the sensor operator practically screamed. "The pirates have targeted us and started firing kinetics!"

He hoped they would have more time before the pirates calculated his flight path. It seemed not.

"Do your best to track them and relay the paths to the pilot. Avoid them at all costs, but keep us on this heading!" He didn't have time to start his calculations over again.

The two crew acknowledged him as they set about the arduous work of keeping them alive while Mingyu broke out in a sweat as he raced through the complicated mathematics of jumping from inside a gravity well.

The transit point had only been an hour away at their current speed, so the kinetic rounds didn't have far to go to get to them. The weapons were traveling much faster than the Destiny.

"Brace!" the sensor operator yelled, and the ship jerked hard to the right.

He heard a *tink* sound followed by a whistle of air being drawn out of the bridge. The emergency lights went red and bulkheads across the ship slammed closed to keep the decompression to a minimum. Mingyu cursed himself for the oversight in his panic to leave. He had been out of the military far too long. Flying into a possible combat situation with safety doors unsecured was something rookies did.

"Where were we hit?" he asked without stopping his work.

"Aft ore storage," the sensor operator stated.

"They are firing another volley, Captain," she said with only a slight waiver of fear in her voice that time.

"We should be at the destination before they arrive," he responded robotically as he finished the flight calculations and forwarded it to the pilot.

The man didn't even bother looking them over as he started firing up the warp drive. It was now a race for time. The ship leveled off and faced toward their destination as the deadly projectiles hurled toward their position.

If he had miscalculated, the warp bubble wouldn't form, and they were all dead.

The warp bubble flickered fitfully around the ship, the gravity nearby almost enough to overwhelm it before it finally stabilized and the Destiny shot into FTL only moments before a volley of projectiles flew through the space they had been occupying.

chapter 41

LOCATION: EDEN'S END
SYSTEM: Y6X-3H2
DATE: 2399

Are you sure you can't stay?" Yulia asked Alex nervously.

He kneeled beside her and spoke quietly. "If I stayed, I would just be a distraction for you and the other children."

She knew he was right. She had seen how the kids back on the station avoided Alex and even the ones here cried and ran off the first time they saw him, but she still fidgeted nervously.

"What if nobody likes me?" she said in barely a whisper.

"I don't see how that could possibly happen. Just be yourself, and you'll make friends eventually. Now I need to go, so head on in."

She gave Alex's arm a hug before reluctantly walking into the room where they taught kids. She wasn't sure why they needed a separate room for something like that until she entered the space. There had to be close—well, she didn't actually know how many—but there were a lot of kids. A lot more than she had ever seen in one place before.

The older ones sat at a table off to one side, watching something on a holo with bored looks. The holo intrigued her, but she doubted they would let her join them. Teenagers could be prickly like that.

She glanced over to the opposite end of the room where the younger kids were making a racket as they played with whatever toys were available. Someone had strung up blankets between that section to muffle the noise, but it wasn't doing much from where she stood.

The center of the room hosted the largest group of kids. Most of them were a few years younger than her to a few years older. She wasn't sure how old the oldest kids were in that group, but they looked to be around Markus' height, so maybe around twelve. That put her right in the middle at nine years old.

She glanced back toward the hallway, wondering how mad Alex would get if she ran out of there and back to his new workshop instead of staying. The choice was decided for her as an adult approached.

"Yulia?" the smiling woman said in a strangely accented voice. It wasn't at all how Alex talked. His way of talking when she first met him was so strange and almost hard to understand. He did get better with time though.

Feeling defeated, Yulia gave a slight nod.

"Good, welcome. We teach you to understand, yes?"

She nodded again and accepted the outstretched hand that the woman offered. She seemed nice enough, even if she seemed to barely speak properly. Yulia hoped she didn't end up speaking like that when she learned this English, Alex had told her about.

Her first day of learning was mostly just being introduced to a group of kids around her age. She had no hope of remembering all the names. The next day started with the alphabet. She felt stupid when she was grouped with the younger portion of the children in her group and they were better at saying the letters than her.

She persevered, getting through all twenty-six letters before the day was up.

The next day was basic math. Yulia knew the teachers were testing for aptitude. Alex had explained that back when he introduced his puzzles. The math was easy, she completed all of the questions, even surpassing the ones the older kids in her group were given.

The teacher smiled at her and gave her a strange gesture with a thumb pointing up. Seeing how happy the woman was, Yulia returned the gesture.

After that day, Yulia was paired with two slightly older girls who introduced themselves as Sarah and Claire. They were really nice and liked to laugh a lot. Like a whole lot. Yulia didn't quite get it, but she found herself laughing along with them, despite not understanding a word they spoke.

The two girls were showing her pictures on a tablet with the word for it listed underneath the object. Then they would say the word out loud.

When Yulia didn't reply the first time, that's when the girls started giggling. It was Claire who tapped her on the arm. "I say, you say," she said in Yulia's language.

Her cheeks flushed red in embarrassment, and she nodded.

The girls were really nice and patient with her. She thought their laughing and giggling might have been directed at her, but it wasn't. They just found teaching an outsider to be extremely entertaining.

They didn't say this to her with words. Yulia had tried talking in her language, but the girls just shook their heads. Claire only understood a handful of words to communicate with her. It was more how they acted and encouraged her that got the point across.

Yulia really liked the two girls and when she got to the word for friend, she said it and pointed to them. There was another round of giggling that Yulia couldn't help going along with before the girls both said the same word and pointed to each other, and then to her.

A bit of her anxiety faded away with that declaration and the next few days flew by while she learned more and more. Alex even brought another lady to teach her when she got home. She would have preferred to spend more time with Alex. She missed working on the puzzles or just wandering around like she used to do back home, but she knew he was extremely busy.

Anytime she went to his workshop, he was speaking with someone or working on something.

He would hang out with her if she asked, but she could see how important the work he was doing was and didn't want to distract him.

After the tutoring sessions, Alex would come home, they would eat together, and she would tell him about her day before falling asleep. It was the weekends she looked most forward to during those weeks.

She didn't mind the school, but the only thing she learned was the local language, which was not called English, they called it Solarian. Alex was surprised to hear that when she told him. He had muttered something about hundreds of years of drift that she didn't quite understand before letting her explore with her new friends.

Yulia had been referring to the place as "the station"—she knew that wasn't right. Stations were in space, and they were on a planet. That meant this was a building. She still found that hard to understand. How could you build something that wasn't in space? She shook her head at the thought—people did silly things.

The building was huge. They weren't allowed to go everywhere, but the places that Sarah and Claire showed her were way more than she had ever got to see on the second ring.

In their wandering and the two girls' incessant talking, they did find one spot that none of the scary mercenaries were guarding. Yes, she knew how strange it was to accuse someone else of talking incessantly. She now knew how the kids at the orphanage felt.

Seeing an opportunity to explore that new area, she tried to get Claire and Sarah to show her what was beyond that point, but they were hesitant. They were trying to tell her something, but she couldn't understand what they were saying.

Some gestures and Solarian words of encouragement she had learned over the last few weeks finally convinced the pair to follow her down this new path.

They didn't get very far before a lady mercenary popped out from behind a corner and glared at the trio. "You three wouldn't be up to trouble, would you?"

Yulia stiffened when she realized the woman spoke in her native language and not the other two's.

"No," she responded meekly, not meeting the woman's piercing gaze.

She said something to the other two girls, and they shook their heads.

"Run along then, and stay out of the restricted areas." She spoke more words in Solarian, likely giving the other two girls the same warning.

A few more weeks went by and the trio explored more of the areas available to them. When they came across another area clearly marked as restricted entry—she had learned those words after her last encounter with the scary lady—she hesitated a moment, along with her friends. There was no corner for the woman to hide around, she noticed.

Seeing the coast was clear, she gave a conspiratorial nod to her friends who looked at each other before sighing and following her through the tunnel.

They didn't make it far before a harsh shout from behind them stopped them in their tracks. The three girls turned around to see the same woman striding purposely down the hallway toward them, looking annoyed. The woman, who Yulia had learned was called Zorina, seemed to have a sixth sense when someone was about to do something they shouldn't be doing. Yulia had no other explanation for how the woman kept popping up at the most inopportune times.

She tried to explain to Zorina that she didn't mean to ignore the rules, she was just curious. She wanted to see what made this place work, like how she had enjoyed the tour back on Petrov Station. That didn't sway the woman one bit. She reminded her a bit of Headmaster Wong in that respect.

She looked up as Zorina escorted her and the other two girls back to their camp. "I said I was sorry," she pleaded with the woman.

"'Sorry' is for the first time, not repeated times," the woman stated. "Now you get to see the consequences of your actions."

She hung her head, while the other two girls looked terrified of what might happen.

The three were led to the Hawks' camp and stuck in a room to wait. A short time later, a man and woman arrived, looking peeved. Sarah started crying and ran over to her parents, who quickly escorted the girl out of the camp.

Not too long after, Claire's mom stopped by, giving Yulia a disapproving look. Yulia looked away but waved back to Claire as she left with her mom.

Shortly after that, Alex stepped into the room.

"This is not something I expected to be doing today," he stated in his normal voice. She found it hard to tell if he was angry, upset, or annoyed. His avatar face was not showing what he was feeling.

Yulia was worried he was so upset that he had forgotten to use his face to show how he felt, and tears threatened her eyes. She forced herself to keep from crying. If she had just listened, that wouldn't be happening.

She heard Alexander let out a soft sigh, and he sat on the floor next to the chair she was in. "I apologized to your friends' parents and assured them this would not happen again..."

"It won't," she managed to choke out, utterly failing at her attempts to keep herself from crying or sobbing. She felt his warm arm wrap her into a hug and she knew he wasn't angry with her.

Chapter 42

Alexander monitored the printer terminal. It was only one of half a dozen that were constantly in use. It had taken two months, but the manufacturing center was finally back to operating at full capacity. The auction company had apologized for the missing equipment but only refunded him a million credits. He supposed he was lucky to see any after his previous experiences with STO corporations.

The room was filled with the mechanical hum of robotic arms zipping through a ballet of welding and assembly work as they built replacement components for the facility. Everything was starting to move in the right direction. He only wished he had known the old robots had been stolen, he would have purchased newer robotics diagrams before coming out there—assuming he could have afforded it with his severely diminished bank account. The current ones were fine for fixing up the facility, but they were not accurate enough for the type of work he wanted to accomplish.

He would just have to design and build his own, assuming he found time. Negotiating and working with the locals, attending weekly briefs with the Hawks, chatting with Jasper and his crew, and being a father for Yulia were all taking significant portions of his time. He wouldn't give any of them up—well, maybe the weekly briefs were a bit much.

The locals had adapted quickly to the change and there were very few issues, despite Damien's less than friendly reception. It seemed he was an exception to the rule. The man's attitude didn't bother him one bit. He may come off as an ass, but he took things very seriously once Alexander laid out his plans to fix the complex completely.

Alexander would like to say there were no issues, but one didn't suddenly tell a group of people who hated authority that you were now the authority without some pushback. He had to lay down the law a few times when people tried to use his printers and robots for their personal use. That was his space. If they wanted something from it, they had to trade just like he did for their work or produce.

Speaking of locals, one entered his shop. At least that was one he liked dealing with.

"How can I help you today, Lucas?" Damien's younger brother was a bit of a sticking point between him and the Hawks. The man didn't have a warrant, but there was a bounty to bring him in alive.

It took a bit of effort from Alexander to convince the Hawks' Leadership not to turn Lucas over. Alexander's reasonings for requesting that were mainly selfish. The man was an expert with computers. He also didn't want to start a conflict with Damien over the issue, but the main reason was he didn't give a shit about some corporate bounty. They had no jurisdiction out there.

To be fair, it didn't take too much convincing. Once he showed Captain Matthews the data on his previous Omni work, the man had agreed not to take the man in if Alexander agreed to update the *Talon*'s engines when he had a space dock.

"I wanted your opinion on some code I wrote."

Alexander sighed. "I told you before, I'm not an expert with code, but I will take a look if you insist."

As far as he could tell, Lucas Laront's code was brilliant. It was no surprise considering he had a corporate bounty placed on him.

Alexander examined the code. He couldn't tell what half of it did. When he said he wasn't an expert with code, he wasn't lying. He only learned the bare minimum to create his holo-avatar and have it respond. He was more focused on the manufacturing aspect of things than the coding side, but he was learning a little bit here and there. It seemed to him that Lucas was looking more for validation than anything else.

"Can you explain to me what it is supposed to do?"

The skinny man smiled and launched into an explanation. "You remember those camera asteroids I told you about?"

"The ones you use to watch for incoming pirates?"

How could he forget? Finding out pirates still occasionally attacked that place was a sobering realization. It was so disconcerting that he rearranged his priorities after hearing that. He knew pirates flew through the area, but he figured they wouldn't come that far out since there wasn't anything of value out there. Apparently, he had been wrong.

"Yes, those. Well, I improved their telemetry and tracking. I believe, with this code, I can even improve their camera range. Well, it's not really changing the range so much as it is improving the quality of the images. Removing noise and implementing certain learning algorithms to clear up those images."

"I thought learning algorithms were frowned upon?" Alexander asked even though he knew they were.

It was why those automated bots on Petrov Station seemed so stupid. They couldn't learn from their mistakes, so they had to have contingencies programmed into them, but you can't program for all contingencies. He also knew that Yuri had used learning algorithms in his initial control box construction. Alexander was glad the old man had only added self-learning to his movement commands. If he had added it to his restrictions, Alexander probably wouldn't have broken free. He would have been sold off or melted down for scrap when Yuri died.

The skinny genius snorted. "Maybe in the STO, but we aren't there, are we? Besides, the STO likes to preach about not using self-learning code yet fails to even follow their own guidance. Don't even get me started on the corporations. Do you think they prevent those corporate bastards from using learning algorithms? No, I bet you those turds use full AI. Hell, ask the Hawks. I can almost guarantee you that they have something aboard their ship that assists them."

"Fine but what about the code going out of control?"

The man laughed at the question. "You need to stop watching those ancient videos about artificial intelligence taking over. I've seen a few of them myself for a laugh, but that's about all they were good for. I don't know what those people back then were so afraid of, it's honestly ridiculous."

It wasn't that ridiculous, he wanted to say.

"Self-learning and 'AI' have been around for hundreds of years. I have never heard of a single instance of rogue code in that entire time. Not that rogue code would get very far. Most computer systems and terminals have hard-coded restrictions in place to prevent people from hacking them. Unless you have a master code, but even that only gets you certain access."

Lucas didn't have to tell Alexander about hard-coded restrictions, he knew all about those. "The master code I got for Eden's End locked everything down."

"Well, yeah. This place is ancient. Half the code used in the systems here hasn't been in use since before I was born. Most of the systems here also predate hard coding. I think that practice only became widespread when the STO started running into the Shican. I guess they were afraid of the aliens taking over our systems. You can sorta see early attempts at that in the consoles here."

Alexander decided to change the subject because the conversation was straying too close to what he could be. Yes, he had thought about the possibility that he was some AI. It didn't make a whole lot of sense though, considering some of the memories he had. Then again, who knew what the weirdos who put him in that body had in mind?

"How did you get those satellites into orbit anyway?"

"Oh that, eh we mostly just paid the few traders that make their way out here to carry them back into space and release them for us."

"Traders actually come out this way... Wait, paid them? Paid them with what?"

The man glanced around the room.

"Ah..."

Lucas shrugged. "Most of the stuff missing in this room happened a long time ago. I only heard about it from one of the old timers that left."

"I'm not judging you. I understand the need to survive, but from now on, let's do things a bit differently, okay?"

"I'm all for change. Although, you might want to think about how deliveries are going to arrive. I see you brought a cargo ship that was too big to land. Fixing the Low Orbit Launcher might be a good idea if you plan on shipping goods from here. Assuming you didn't do all this just to fix up this old relic of a base." He gestured around the room.

Alexander made his avatar blink. "Low Orbit Launcher?"

"Oh, yeah, it launches small payloads into space for pickup. They don't really use them anymore. It's quicker and easier just to use orbital elevators to get large cargo into space, or a shuttle if the cargo isn't too large."

"The schematics of the research base didn't show any such device. I would know, I looked them over very carefully."

Admittedly, he looked it over more carefully after arriving. Being surprised by the size of the atriums told him he needed to pay more attention to the details of the place he purchased.

Lucas scratched his chin in confusion. "It's definitely got one. I wonder if it wasn't included in the plans because it was built separately from the structure. If you aren't too busy, I can take you there."

Alexander followed the chatty man as he led them through a twisting series of hallways. "Sorry about the roundabout route. The main route to that section collapsed a few years ago."

"It's fine. How did you come across this launcher anyway?"

"I was scavenging for components about a year ago. The door that led there was rusted shut, but with a few weeks of work, I managed to get it open. That led to the control room. Ah, here we are."

The man gestured to a twisted metal frame and a standard security door lying broken off to the side. "As you can see, it put up a bit of a fight."

Alexander sighed at the damage, looking pointedly at the man who just shrugged.

"Gotta do what ya gotta do sometimes."

The man stepped through the doorway and Alexander ducked in after him. He got his first look at the control center for this launcher as he straightened.

"Sorry about the mess. We couldn't be picky with spare parts."

"I see," he stated flatly. The consoles had been torn apart and loose wires hung everywhere. What wasn't there was circuit boards or any electronics. "You were able to repurpose all of this?"

He wasn't angry. He was annoyed that the people living here had cannibalized a good majority of the systems in that facility. He understood why they did it, but it still meant more work for him. The only balm to his annoyance was that the section of the facility was not in the design plan. Thus he technically hadn't spent any money on it and everything there was a bonus. It sort of made up for the missing manufacturing robots.

Alexander had plans to update all of the systems inside Eden's End eventually, that just moved that up his priority list.

"Eh, most of 'em. The telemetry modules went into the asteroid control systems. The rest of the unused components went into storage for later use."

Alexander sighed. "I'm going to need to see these storage rooms to see if there is anything worth fixing." He walked over to a small blast window that overlooked a large chamber on the other side. He couldn't see much through the grime-coated glass. "Is there a way into the transfer chamber?"

"Probably," Lucas shrugged. "I think I know the door that leads out there, but good luck getting it opened. I haven't had any luck."

"Could you show me?"

The man nodded and the two exited the control room, moving down a few flights of stairs that led into a wide hallway with a pair of rails running along them.

"This is the transport tunnel?" Alexander had seen it on the facility plans, but he hadn't had time to investigate it.

"Yup. As far as I can tell, it has three lines. One cuts directly across the facility while the two outer lines curve along the outside."

"As far as you can tell?"

"All three lines have caved-in sections. So nobody bothers using them. The door that should lead to the launcher is over this way," the man gestured.

They stopped outside a pair of imposing doors a moment later. "I see why you can't get in."

The heavy steel blast doors in front of him made the ones that sealed off his manufacturing center look rather pathetic in comparison. He could see deep scratches in the hardened exterior that showed just how much effort Lucas had put into trying to get inside.

"Yeah. These things are a real beast. Complete overkill as well. Have fun, I'm going to go back to working on my programming."

"Wait, you're just leaving?" Alexander asked.

"Um, yes. It's not like there is anything I can do here."

Alexander supposed that was true. "I see. I'll need to bring some things from my shop to even attempt opening this door anyway."

"Ooh, let me know when you make the attempt. I really wanna get my hands on what's inside." Lucas rubbed his hands together.

Alexander just made his avatar stare at him.

"What?"

"No more ripping apart my facility. I can make spares for most things by now."

"Oh? What about computer processors?"

"Not yet. But I do have some spare ones I brought along. I might even be willing to trade a few for the right work."

The man rubbed his chin. "Really, now? Well, you let me know what kind of work you want done, and I might just agree to take a few of those processors off your hands."

Alexander watched the computer expert leave. He had tried tempting the man to work for him since he arrived, seeing the man's skill with coding. The man seemed uninterested in any of the other offers he had made. He hadn't wanted to give up any of the processors he brought along, but seeing as the man was receptive to one of his offers for the first time, it might be worth it.

He wished he could just print up new processors like everything else, but just like processors from back in his day, the futuristic ones required multiple specialized machines and processes to manufacture. He was years away from even getting to that point, let alone purchasing plans for the machines needed. Until then, he would have to rely on purchasing them and having them shipped out here by Jasper and his crew.

Speaking of Jasper, he needed to have a conversation with the man before they left soon. He turned away from the blast doors. That was a project for a later date.

chapter 43

Alexander found Jasper in the atrium. The large space was much quieter now that most of the people had gone back to their homes or whatever work they did around the facility. From what he could tell, that was mostly farming. He was getting some interest in the work he was offering, but it was slow.

"Alexander!" Jasper called as soon as the man spotted him.

Alexander waved back and walked over to join his friend. He was sitting at one of the many benches scattered around the large open space. They were one of the few things still intact after so long because they weren't worth stealing.

"I'm surprised you're all alone today, Jasper. Where's the rest of your crew?"

The man shrugged. "Even I get sick of my crew sometimes. I'm just kidding. Wilkes took Naomi back up to the *Zephyr*. There wasn't much for her to do down here. Since we are planning on returning to STO space soon, her time was better spent trying to look for our next cargo run."

"How would she do that without a Qcomm?"

"Oh, the info will be out of date, but she can narrow down some parameters. Once we are back in STO space, she can double-check those shipments to see if they are still available. It's not the first time we've been out of comm range."

"I actually wanted to speak to you about shipping."

His friend nodded. "I thought you might. I would love to deliver supplies out to you Alexander…"

"I hear a 'but' coming."

The man grimaced slightly. "You know how dangerous it is to come out here? I'm willing to risk it while the Hawks are here, but after that, I can't ask my crew to put themselves in harm's way like that. They are like family to me, I'm sure you understand now that you have Yulia."

Alexander sighed and nodded. "I do understand. The Hawks have agreed to extend their service for an additional three months. If I had something to keep you safe after they left, would you continue deliveries?"

"I don't see why not, but let's not dwell on what-ifs for now. Tell me, what did you need me to deliver?"

Alexander handed his friend the tablet he had been forced to purchase from the Hawks. Having an easy means of communicating data to others hadn't been on his original purchase manifest.

The man scrolled down the list, his eyebrow quirking at some of the items. "These are some expensive items," Jasper finally said as he lowered the tablet.

"I know, but those are all items I need and cannot print."

"They should be easy enough to acquire. Travel back and forth will likely take two months."

"I understand." He handed Jasper a credit chip. "This chip contains the sum total of all my credits." Minus a few million he kept in reserve just in case.

The man paused before accepting the item. "Why are you giving me all your money?"

"It is currently useless out here. Use what you need to purchase the items I requested, and then I would like you to place the rest in some sort of account that garners interest. I am unfamiliar with what would be available, so please use your best judgment. Then you can draw from that account any time you need funds for my purchases. Eventually, it will turn into a corporate fund that I can use to pay others."

The man gave a faux shocked expression. "Already looking to replace me?"

Alexander chuckled. "Hardly. But at some point, one ship will not be enough to keep up."

Jasper smiled. "I like that you are thinking big my friend. Have you thought of a name for your new enterprise yet?"

"I have." He told his friend the name he had come up with.

"Fitting. I like it." He chuckled as he stood from the bench. "You keep being you, Alexander. Just try to stay safe out here okay?"

He nodded. "I will. I have a meeting with the Hawks today to discuss that very issue. You stay safe as well."

"Oh, that shouldn't be much of an issue with the Hawks support ships patrolling the systems between here and Varlen. That reminds me, you may want to think about building an orbital dock as soon as possible and a refueling station. You're going to need both to tempt any other captains to even bother with this system."

Alexander sighed. "I'm working on it. The items I'm asking you to bring on this first trip should make it easier."

There was a series of beeps from Jasper's vac suit. "Looks like Wilkes is back." The man held out his hand and Alexander shook it. "I'll see you in two months, my friend. I can't wait to see what has changed in that time."

"It was a pleasure flying with you. Tell your crew that I will miss them. As will Yulia."

The man smiled and gave Alexander a wave before hurrying off.

He really would miss the captain. Jasper had filled him in on so many of the things he didn't understand over the long journey. He had even given him a crash course in how to fly a spaceship. It really would have been a *crash course* had there actually been anything to hit along their path. Flying a ship did not seem to come naturally to Alexander. However, he had improved slightly during the later part of the journey.

With Jasper heading back to the *Zephyr*, he turned and headed toward the Hawks' little encampment. It wasn't far away.

"Mr. Kane, what can we assist you with today?" one of the mercenaries asked as Alexander approached the barricade of their camp.

"I would like to have a meeting with Captain Matthews and any Field Leaders that might be available."

The man nodded. "I will radio the *Talon* to see if the captain is free."

After a short wait, the man dropped his hand away from an earpiece. "The captain said he would be free in ten minutes. Travers and Jallen are the only two field leaders available in this section. If you would like to wait in the command tent, they should be here shortly."

He thanked the man and headed into the very familiar tent. It had a set of folding furniture and a video uplink to the *Talon*.

It didn't take long for the two Field Leaders to show up.

"Mr. Travers, Mr. Jallen. Good to see you again."

"You as well, Alexander," Travers replied. "We don't have anything new to report since our meeting a few days ago, so I assume this meeting is about something else?"

Alexander nodded. "I'll get into it as soon as the captain has connected."

Less than a minute later, the screen came on.

"Looks like everyone is here," Matthews said. "What can we help you with Mr. Kane?"

Try as he might, Alexander couldn't get the *Talon*'s captain to call him by his first name.

"I've been recently made aware that pirates still occasionally come through this system."

All three men nodded.

"We have heard similar from the locals," Travers confirmed.

"I expected as much, but it's good to hear confirmation," Matthews stated. "This system isn't that far off the normal space lanes. It's not a surprise that pirates would use it to travel. I assume your main concern isn't them passing through, is it?"

"It is not. While this facility didn't make a tempting target before, I'm afraid fixing it up is going to draw unwanted attention. I need advice on how to best protect the planet once the Hawks leave. Unless you have reconsidered my offer?"

Matthews leaned back in his chair and rubbed his bearded chin. "I'm afraid not, Mr. Kane. While your offer is more than generous, there are extenuating circumstances you may not be aware of."

"Such as?" Alexander asked, making his avatar frown slightly.

Matthews sighed. "We were going to discuss this at next week's briefing, but I don't see any reason to wait. You are aware that the gunships that came with us are patrolling from Eden's End to Varlen."

"Yes, you did mention that a few weeks ago."

"At their last stop, they received a Qcomm from our headquarters. Pirates have assaulted multiple systems along the Eastern end of STO territory. We don't have many details at the moment, but the leaders of Ganos have called in all available mercenary companies to ensure the local space lanes remain safe for travel."

If Alexander had a heart, he was sure it would have skipped a beat at this news. Petrov Station was on the eastern fringe of STO space. Alexander hoped Petrov Station, or more specifically, the orphans were ok. If they weren't, Yulia would be devastated.

"Does this mean you will be leaving early?"

"No, Mr. Kane. Our deal came into effect before we were alerted to this change, but I can no longer extend our stay past the additional three months. As for the deal to upgrade the *Talon*'s Engines, that will need to wait until we can return."

Alexander nodded. "Understandable, Captain. Return whenever you can and I will make you right. With this upswing in piracy, I'm even more concerned about safety."

"As you should be. This attack will embolden the rest of those scum, that's for sure. As for defenses, the easiest and cheapest will be to reinforce the concrete above your facility. That will likely deter small pirate crews. The *Talon* has Gauss cannons as its main armament, but we also have missiles. I don't recommend either of them for you."

"You don't? Why not?"

"I can answer this one, Captain," Jallen said, which Matthews acknowledged with a nod. "Other than being expensive, both require complicated processes for building and assembly. They also need multiple computer systems, which you have told some of the Hawks' engineers you have a limited supply of."

"That is true, and most of the ones I currently have in stock are earmarked for projects already. What are my other options? What about railguns?"

"For planetary use, that should be fine," Matthews said. "But the railgun rails need to be replaced regularly. This makes them less than ideal for space-based weapons as you can imagine. That's why you don't see them in use in the STO Navy. A Gauss cannon will do pretty much the same thing as a railgun and require a tenth as much maintenance."

Alexander didn't even have a reliable way to get goods into orbit yet, so having to repair orbital weapons systems constantly would not be very productive.

"Laser-based weapons would be ideal, but again, you are going to need at least one CPU per weapon. More if you plan on aiming them. I'm afraid you don't have many good options for space-based weapons. Even building the ground-based ones is going to be an issue unless you have the design plans for them. ...You don't happen to have design plans for any of these weapons, do you?"

Alexander wasn't sure what to say there. Technically, he didn't have any STO-purchased designs for weapons, but he still recalled the designs he had built back in his shop.

"Yes, and no. I don't have any STO designs, but I believe I can build a railgun and maybe even some lasers based on my technical knowledge."

"I suppose that's not too surprising. Railguns aren't all that complicated. I am a little curious as to how you know how to build lasers though."

"Lots of machines use lasers, Captain. It's just an application of concentrating the light and adding more power." He really hoped the man didn't dig further. Not that Alexander was doing anything illegal, not out there anyway.

"I suppose that is an accurate enough description. You should focus your efforts on the ground-based railguns then. They will be the cheapest and easiest to manufacture and keep running. The sulfur air of Eden's End would wreak havoc on ground-based laser optics unless you stored them in air-tight silos. That will only increase the cost and complexity of those systems."

The other two men nodded in agreement at the captain's assessment.

"Defense turrets at the entrances would also be advised," Travers added. "You can remotely operate them, removing the need for complicated control systems. Just print up and put together some simple circuit boards and pop a couple of flechette rifles into them. They would be a very effective deterrent for anyone. Heck, you could even repurpose those ancient Earth weapons if you really wanted to. You would need to go through them to make sure they were functional first though."

Why hadn't Alexander considered printing basic circuit boards? He had been so focused on *future tech* that he hadn't even thought of building his own simple processors. They didn't need to be super complex or powerful. Not for some of the things he wanted to do.

"Thank you all for the suggestions. I have a lot to think about."

"That's what we are here for, Mr. Kane. Is there anything else we can assist you with today?" Matthews asked.

"There is. I was recently informed that this base has a Low Orbit Launcher. Are you familiar with the devices?"

"I've heard of them. Can't say I've ever seen one though. If my memory is correct, aren't they just low-power railguns?"

"I believe you are correct, Captain. The launcher is behind a sealed blast door. Do you think your engineers can help me cut into it to get inside?"

Matthews shook his head at that. "If there are blast doors, it means they are there for a reason. I would recommend against cutting through them. I can have the engineers take a look and see if they can restore power and functionality to the doors though."

Alexander left the meeting with a lot to think about. He was already thinking about a design for a railgun in his head that would be powerful enough to reach into orbit. The gun was turning out to be the easy part. The limiting factor was the availability of power.

The research facility relied on antiquated solar and geothermal power. It did not have the more common fusion power plant that was in use in that day and age. He supposed it made sense to use easy-to-manufacture and replace items instead of something complicated and costly like a reactor. Solar and geothermal systems were both time-tested and rugged technologies as well. The fact they were still working to that date proved the people who had built the place chose wisely.

Alexander knew how to construct a fusion reactor thanks to the plans he purchased for the *Zephyr*'s design. The plans included all the information and design specs he would need to build one for himself. The problem was that he was nowhere near the manufacturing capability required to build something like that. With fusion power a distant dream, he turned his focus to supercapacitors and batteries. They were much simpler to build.

CHAPTER 44

It took the Hawks' engineers less time than Alexander would have imagined to reroute power from a working area to the blast door that led to the Low Orbit Launcher. Once power was restored, the facility codes worked to bypass the security lockout that had been triggered by some fault in the launcher system.

The thick heavy blast doors gave an audible click and a strobing light along with a siren alerted anyone within the area that they were opening.

Alexander watched silently as the door ponderously slid aside. At least it didn't appear that rust had any effect on the mechanism. If they had been rusted, he would have been in trouble. He had nothing big enough to remove blast doors that heavy.

Once the door was fully open, the lights and siren shut off. Alexander waited for the mercenaries to clear the room before he entered along with the other engineers.

The first thing Alexander noticed was the dome above the launcher. It seems part of it had collapsed onto the device. It wasn't enough to expose it to the outside elements, but enough to trigger a safety lockout.

The launcher wasn't much to look at, if he was honest. It was a wide rectangle that seemed to be attached to a curved dish underneath it that allowed it to angle upward.

There didn't appear to be any way to traverse the launcher from side to side either. Going by the retractable portion of the overhead dome, it could probably only fire from a certain position as well. He had expected something to this extent after talking with the captain and Lucas about the device, so it wasn't much of a surprise.

The thing was huge, big enough that his entire body could fit inside the launch rails. He expected it to be big, considering the size of the launch capsules, but it was still surprising to see up close.

The launch capsules looked like those clamshell storage racks that people stuck on the top of their cars for road trips. Only those were about twice the size and with a metal strip running along the entire circumference. He lifted one of the lids and found the inside empty. He was a bit bummed about that. Not that he expected to find anything inside it, but it would have been neat if there was. With the launch capsule open, he got a good idea of how much space he had to work with, if and when he got the thing operational.

The answer to the question of size was, not a lot. About half of the area inside was taken up by foam padding, probably to protect the contents as much as possible when they were launched into orbit. Depending on what he launched, he could probably remove the padding.

Regardless, he would have to print new launch capsules since the ones in this room had seen better days. They were as likely to disintegrate on launch as they were to make it into orbit.

The capsules seemed to be mostly some sort of plastic, which was good. He had limited materials left after replacing the robotics for his lab and the few simple mining drones he had going were not very capable.

He was hoping to alleviate some of the pressure on the locals to farm, so they would be more inclined to mine for him. So far only three people had taken him up on the offer, but that was still three more than zero. Despite the rather crude mining equipment Alexander was able to provide them, they were much more adept at gathering useful material for his smelter than the drones he had.

"Alex, it stinks in here!" Yulia complained.

"Put your mask on then."

Yulia had asked to accompany him that day since it was her day off from school. She was slowly picking up English, but she kept defaulting to her old language when speaking to him. He was tempted to not answer her unless she used English, but that seemed extremely petty. She was also trying to fit in by not wearing her mask, but she liked to complain about the smell. He would always need to remind her to put the mask back on. To which she would complain that she didn't like wearing it as she was doing at that moment.

"We talked about this. I am working on fixing the air purifiers, but you will need to get used to the smell or wear the mask."

"I don't like wearing the mask, everyone makes fun of me when I do."

Alexander made his avatar nod. "I'm sorry to hear that, but those are the only two options at the moment."

The little girl grumbled for a bit before finally putting on the mask. The smell really must have been awful in the room because normally she just tried to put up with it. That probably meant air was leaking into the room from outside. Once he got the facility sealed back up, positive pressure would fix that issue.

While his schedule was quite busy, Alexander made sure to spend as much time as he could with her, so she didn't feel lonely. Yulia had struggled the first few weeks to make friends. It was a situation of kids being kids where some were nice, some were mean, and some didn't want to play with the outsider. Yulia was an outgoing girl though. Even without speaking the language, she managed to make a few friends.

Yulia and her two new friends, Sarah and Claire got along fantastically. Alexander got a kick out of watching them communicate through laughter and hand gestures. Minus a little road bump with the whole 'trying to go places she wasn't supposed to', the parents of the two girls got over it and let them play together again. Alexander got the distinct impression that the girls' parents blamed him for the whole thing. That was fine with him, so long as they didn't shun Yulia for doing something stupid that she genuinely felt bad about afterward.

Some other kids hung around occasionally, but he hadn't gotten their names yet. It was either because Yulia didn't know them, or she just forgot to mention who they were. He was glad she had made the transition without much trouble. It took her mind off the lack of response from her old friends.

With the pirate threat on the same side of STO space as Petrov Station, he wasn't sure if the messages that were being transferred by the Hawks' ships would arrive. There hadn't been any reply to them yet which wasn't a good sign.

As much as Alexander would like to sit and hang out with his daughter all day, he had to refocus on the current task. He walked over to one of the engineers who inspected the railgun.

"How bad is it?"

"Not good," the man replied as he pulled his head out of the barrel. "Both rails need to be replaced. Seems like they were due for replacement even before they shut it down. We would also like to go through the entire electrical system. You don't want an electrical short in a railgun. That much energy dumped into the body could damage the metal casing, and then you are looking at replacing the entire thing instead of just the rails. You already saw the launch capsules. Might as well just recycle them, there's no point fixing them up."

Alexander nodded. "I planned to."

"Good. Other than that, you will need to rebuild the control room. Probably for the best anyway. I saw those ancient terminals, one holo terminal could replace that whole setup. Assuming you have the means to build one."

"I'll see what I can do."

"Then there is the ceiling," the man continued. "Your best bet is to just tear it all down and build fresh. Who knows what structural defects are present? It obviously wasn't built very well if part of it collapsed like this." He gestured to the broken concrete lying around the room.

Alexander sighed. "Please tell me that's all?"

"For now. Until we can get power to the loading system, we won't know if that works or if the gears that raise and lower the launcher will need replacing, too. We will also need to inspect the barrel for deflection since part of the roof collapsed on top of it."

"And if it is damaged?"

"Then we will need to pull the entire barrel instead of just the rails. Luckily the outer casing and barrel are two separate parts on this unit. That isn't always the case with launchers."

"You have experience with Low Orbit Launchers?" Alexander asked in surprise. From his conversation with Matthews, he figured they weren't very popular.

The man shook his head. "No but some missile systems use a similar launch platform to eject missiles far from ships before they light off their drives. Doing it that way means they need less propellant to home in on their target which means you can pack more explosives into a smaller form factor."

"Ah," was all Alexander could say to that.

He gathered up the information he needed along with some rough measurements of the rails and headed back to his workshop. On the way there, Yulia spotted her friends.

"Alex, can I play with Sarah and Claire?"

He figured she would ask as soon as he saw the slightly older girls. He nodded. Before she could rush off, he added. "I'll be in the workshop. Make sure to return before the evening meal."

She nodded and waved at him as she sped off. He watched the three girls giggle conspiratorially to each other before running down a side hallway. A female mercenary stepped up next to him.

"I'll keep an eye on her like always."

"Thank you for doing this for me, Zorina. It means a lot that I don't have to worry about her constantly."

The woman snorted. "You'll have to learn to let her be by herself soon. I don't plan on sticking around when our deployment ends."

He sighed and nodded. "I know."

The woman smiled and fast-walked to catch up to the screaming children as they raced down the hallway.

He knew he was being overly protective. He couldn't help it. The sad fact was that he was better than he was before leaving Petrov. He had an actual reason for his overprotectiveness back on Petrov Station, but he couldn't lean on that excuse here. Other than a few kids picking on Yulia, nobody had bothered her much since their arrival. He had purposefully told Zorina to keep a low profile and only intervene if she was in real danger or doing something she shouldn't be doing. Kids being jerks didn't count, even though Alexander had the urge to go talk to those children's parents to set them straight. He sighed and pushed the issues with his overprotectiveness to the back of his mind to be addressed at a later time so he could focus on the mountain of work ahead of him.

Alexander entered the manufacturing bay. The place was still in full motion cranking out new beams for the collapsed sections. He didn't interrupt that process, instead he went over to the printer terminal and began building a model of the parts for the launcher.

It didn't take long. They were essentially a U-shaped piece of metal. He didn't want to waste any of his precious metal though. Instead, he created an extrusion tip and extruded the forty-foot-long rails out of a cheap and recyclable plastic material. He wanted to make sure the dimensions were correct before he bothered wasting good material.

While that was going on, he took what he knew of the launcher and the railgun he had built back on Petrov and came up with a few designs for orbital defense guns. Of course, he had two arms and could split his attention, so with the other hand, he designed battery and capacitor banks.

Alexander had worked with over a dozen types of battery systems and probably close to a hundred types of capacitors during his time at Petrov. Now all that knowledge was going into designing the most energy-dense system he could come up with given what he knew. He was sure there were better designs out there since the stuff he had worked on was usually decades old by the time he saw it. It was still a significant step up to what existed on Eden's End, so he wouldn't complain.

Once the designs were complete, he sent them to the printers. The first railgun would take six hours to print, and it was only at the scale of a slightly large handheld rifle. Alexander wanted to test the device before he went and printed a full-scale model that would be nearly as long as the launcher.

He looked at the finished model. As far as designs went, it was not very inspired. The gun was a rectangular block with a hole in the center of the square end about the width of a thick pencil. It sat on a simple weighted and recoil-absorbing tripod. He had thought about adding the dish and loading mechanism like the launcher had but decided against it for the test. Those systems were easy to replicate, and he knew they would work. He wanted to ensure his weapon design functioned correctly. Manual aiming and reloading would have to be done for now. As for the design, he did that for ease of manufacture.

He would likely carry over the blocky design for any defense turrets made using the flechette rifles that Travers had mentioned as well. He didn't have the luxury of multiple processes for building weapons. He could print whatever, but he only had a few printers. And he couldn't tie them all up with printing weapons that may or may not get used. Once one of the manufacturing lines became free, he would set that to building the weapons.

After he inspected the gun to ensure it was functional, he printed out a dozen tungsten sabots. Using his limited supply of tungsten like that hurt, but it was the hardest material he had available. It would get replaced eventually by the workers mining the surface. The planet was rich in metals, along with other rare earth materials. Trace amounts of tungsten and harder-to-come-by minerals were already coming in with each load.

Alexander loaded everything up on a little robotic cart that looked like a topless golf cart. He had built the small vehicle to haul heavy loads around the station. Normally it was used to carry the replacement beams to the work sites where some of the engineers and locals were clearing up rubble and removing rusted beams to replace them with new ones.

As he was doing that, his door opened, and Travers walked in.

The man whistled as he saw what Alexander was loading on the cart. "Now ain't that the ugliest little duckling you ever did see. I always preferred function over form though. You going out to test it?"

Alexander nodded.

"Mind if me and my team tag along? It isn't every day we get to see a railgun getting fired."

"I don't see why not."

chapter 45

Alexander finished setting up the last plate of armored steel against the backdrop of a rocky outcropping. They were about half a mile from the facility, and nowhere near where any people or mining was taking place.

Alexander quickly crossed the distance separating him from where the gun was situated. He joined the twenty-odd people who had come out to see the test. Some of them were Travers' people, but it seemed like Damien, Lucas, and Gabriella had heard about the test and wanted to watch as well—not that Alexander minded the audience. The rest were just random mercenaries who were on their downtime and looking for any entertainment.

"So, you're making weapons now?" Damien asked as he approached.

"I'm testing weapons so I can come up with a design to build defenses," Alexander replied calmly to the man's question.

The man only grunted in reply, wandering away with his perpetual scowl on his face. At least Damien was predictable. Alexander might have been concerned if the man was suddenly excited that he was making weapons. The fact that the martial artist didn't seem to care one way or another spoke volumes to his character even if the man wasn't the most likable person.

He had gotten a briefing on Damien's history from Matthews and the Field Leaders; a decorated martial expert and de facto leader slash security officer for Eden's End. A rather impressive resume for a guy who seemed to dislike everyone and everything.

That briefing also included what the Hawks found on their initial sweep of the facility. From what he learned, the only guns the Hawks found were the ones they confiscated from a group of men—one of the men trying to shoot them when they first entered the facility. There were also a few pulse rifles that the Hawks had returned after Alexander and the locals had come to an agreement.

The fact Damien and his people had been able to repel or kill off pirates with only improvised weapons and a few pulse rifles was a testament to the man's ability to plan effectively with very little. Alexander could appreciate that fact, even if he didn't like the man all that much.

Alexander thought of producing more of the sonic weapons for the locals, something he would probably do eventually. When the Hawks left, there needed to be a capable group of security people to defend the facility. He only hesitated at the moment because he didn't know those people enough. He left figuring out who could be trusted for the Hawks as they trained some of the locals per his extended agreement.

Once they were trained up, Alexander should be able to print out pulse rifles for them. The devices were surprisingly sophisticated. He would not be able to get away with cobbling together a 20th century computer chip to replace the electronics in the rifles. Making the flechette, or CQB rifles as the Hawks called them, were orders of magnitude easier, but he didn't trust these people that far. He knew the pulse rifles were useless against him, but he couldn't say the same about the flechettes. In time, if the people there proved trustworthy, maybe he would produce better arms for them.

To be fair, Alexander would prefer to be building pretty much anything other than weapons. He wasn't naïve enough to believe pirates or other unsavory sorts would simply leave them be once he started actively building weapons in space. That was why he had gone straight into building the defensive railguns instead of focusing on designing and building the engines he wanted. Putting off defending the facility was simply not an option. It was best just to get it done as soon as possible and while the Hawks were still there to cover for the lack of defensive options.

The defenses were to protect Yulia, his operations, and the people on Eden's End, in that order. He didn't tell them that though.

Alexander arrived at the tripod. A slew of thick cables ran from the back of it to a box. The large bulky box was a series of batteries and supercapacitors with a wide umbrella of solar panels over it that produced the only shade for miles around. Everyone who didn't have vac suits was understandably crowded under the umbrella. So only Damien, Lucas, and Gabriella were standing in the shade. All the other mercenaries had their suits sealed and their visors set to reflective.

They didn't need it to breathe the thin atmosphere out there, but it did provide thermal regulation and protection from the UV radiation of the blue star, which the thin atmosphere did little to filter out.

Alexander's interface barely registered any heat, but the radiation would give someone a sunburn in ten to fifteen minutes. The locals managed by covering any exposed skin and wearing darkened goggles. He wondered where they got them.

He checked over the weapon one last time. Everything looked in order. The batteries were at full charge and everything looked good on the power pack. He entered a security code into the simple keypad and a slow whine began to build as the batteries dumped their energy into the capacitors. He used both because batteries could store power for much longer without it bleeding off, but they couldn't dump power as fast as a capacitor could.

As the whine built, he picked up one of the pencil-sized sabots and slid it into the open breach. Once it was inserted, he closed and locked the breach. Then he aimed the weapon at the first target two hundred yards down range. It was a ludicrously short range for a railgun, but he wasn't testing range right now.

The single layer of dense armor plate should have been equivalent to what the Hawk's augment suits might have. At least he assumed so after studying the things walking around the facility. He really wished he had an old-world equivalent to compare the augment suit's armor to, but he didn't.

Alexander dialed the energy output to twenty percent. With little fanfare, he yelled, "Firing!"

There was a click followed by a sensation of static as the capacitors dumped their energy into the railgun. The weapon kicked back along the shock absorber as a flash of light left the barrel, followed by a deafening boom.

He could see the two halves of the sabot separate and drop away, but even Alexander's enhanced eyesight wasn't quick enough to track the projectile. Fortunately, he wasn't trying to, he just needed to watch the destination. Almost instantly, there was a flash of light and a spray of molten metal from behind the target sheet. The round hardly slowed down as he noted a puff of dust on the distant hillside.

"A bit overkill," Travers stated. "Then again, that's kinda what railguns are known for."

Alexander readjusted the gun to the next set of targets. The first plate, while armored, was only about a quarter inch thick. The next target was two of the plates sandwiched together.

The tungsten penetrator at the core of the sabot easily tore through the two sheets at the same power output. He noted there wasn't any impact on the hill behind the target.

The third target was the same two plates, air-gapped to simulate front and rear armor. The round easily tore through the first plate, but when it reached the second, there was a bright flash of light. He wouldn't know the results until he inspected it after they were done, but he suspected the pencil lead-sized penetrator had either come apart or tumbled after going through the first plate.

There was no comment from Travers or anyone else.

He adjusted the gun again, this time moving to the targets at six hundred yards. It was the same set of tests so he expected similar results. It was similar, at least on the first target. The small dart must have lost too much speed to penetrate the dual layer of armor. There was a bright burst of sparks between the sandwiched sheets before the welds holding them together came apart, sending both halves crashing to the ground from the force.

"That's one way to do it," one of the mercenaries called out, earning chuckles from a few others.

The third test gave no real surprises. The dart tore through the first armor and exploded against the second. It should have gone straight through, but Alexander was beginning to think the penetrator was simply too small to hold together from the force of impact.

The third test was at twelve hundred yards. Before he ran that, he checked the batteries and capacitors. They were holding up fine, although they were getting slightly hot from the energy discharge. He made a mental note to add some sort of thermal management to them.

The third set of tests went about the same as the second. The only change was that the second target didn't explode apart and the flash from the third target wasn't nearly as energetic. The round seemed to be losing more speed than it should at that range. Was it a flaw in the aerodynamics of his design? It wasn't as if he had a step-by-step tutorial for designing railgun rounds. He just put something together based on what little knowledge he had.

For the final tests, he cranked the power output to the full one hundred percent. That was to test for any failure on the gun or batteries at full load.

The last target was a series of six plates with about six inches between them. They were set at the same twelve-hundred-yard range as the third test.

The three people huddled under the shade of the solar panels moved away as the whine built.

"Why's it making so much noise?" Gabriella asked in concern.

"I'm using the full power output. You may want to move farther away from the energy pack in case it fails."

The three moved away from the device. To be fair, the mercenaries moved farther away as well.

Alexander loaded the round. The air was practically buzzing with energy as the capacitors whined to release their stored power. He obliged them as he fired the gun.

The kickback was so forceful that if Alexander hadn't caught the weapon, it would have been launched back into the energy pack. Down at the targets, there was an increasingly bright flash as the round tore through the armored plates. The last target produced the brightest flash of light but also a series of bright orange sparks. This was likely the tungsten carbide shattering against the last armored plate.

"Alexander, behind you!"

He didn't need to turn around to see that the energy pack was throwing sparks as the heat melted the components inside. He did turn his avatar though, to assure everyone that he was aware of the issue. As he turned, he yanked the power cables out of the gun to prevent the internal components from being damaged by the surge of electricity.

He stepped back to join the others as they watched the pack reduce itself to a half-molten pile of slag. It could have been worse, he supposed. At least these weren't like the old lithium batteries that burst into nearly unstoppable flames. The energy just discharged into the surrounding material, heating it up and breaching more cells until everything was too hot to remain solid.

"Well, it looks like I have some things to work on. Shall we go see the results of these tests?"

"I'm going back inside before I get burned."

Alexander watched Damien and his group walk off. He just shook his head. Once they were gone, he went to join the other mercenaries who were already inspecting the closest targets.

He went straight for the third target in the closest row. The entry hole was a tiny thing, but the material it blew out the opposite side was impressive. The cone of molten material was about the size of a tennis ball. Considering the penetrator was the size of a piece of pencil lead, that was a whole lot of damage. The back plate had a nice spray pattern where the molten metal impacted and hardened, along with a series of deeper craters in the center, likely caused by the remnants of the dart.

The projectile had indeed broken apart. When he inspected the second test in the closest row, he found just a small hole bored through until the back of the target blew out. The first test matched the same pattern. He would need to check on where the round impacted on the hillside after he looked at the other tests.

The second row of tests showed a similar damage pattern. The sandwiched plates showed that the first plate blew out, which is likely what caused the plates to burst apart. There were signs that the dart had gone into the second plate, but it seemed to have exploded before making it all the way through, leaving a large crater and caving in the hardened material.

The third test was much the same, only with less damage. The tungsten dart didn't even manage to get through the two plates that were welded together. There was also less blowout, showing the speed of the rounds had become significantly reduced over the short flight time.

The full power test was interesting. It looked like someone had taken a plasma cutter to the plates. After the first plate, each showed multiple holes melted through from the material of the previous one. It was only on the final few plates that the material had cooled enough to weld itself to the plate instead of melting through. The last plate had a small dent from where the round finally shattered.

Considering how much energy he had dumped into the gun for that test, he had expected more damage. If he had used a larger penetrator, he probably would have seen better results. The small size of the one he used wasn't meant to transfer that much energy. He would look over his video later and determine the speed the projectiles were flying at. It would also help him determine why they were slowing down so much.

Before leaving the range, he walked over to the spot on the hill where the first round had gone. It would have been hard to spot for anyone else, but Alexander quickly located the tiny hole drilled into the tan surface of the rock. He couldn't see how far into the rock the penetrator had gone, but it had clearly gone quite far. What he did notice was the hole didn't have any indication that the fins impacted the surface. Had they been ripped off by the first impact? He filed that fact away for later. If the fins were being broken or torn off, it might explain why the rounds weren't working as expected.

With the tests over and his curiosity sated, he packed up the surviving components and headed back to the facility alone. All the other mercenaries had left some time ago, their interest waning shortly after the fireworks were complete.

As he made the walk back, Alexander realized that was the first time he had been alone in a long time. The last time he was truly alone was after Yuri up and left, and the first few weeks after he opened his shop on Petrov Station.

While he wouldn't give up his current life, no matter how hectic it had become, he was glad for the moment of peace and quiet.

CHAPTER 46

"Colonel Jun, why haven't we been allowed to depart yet?" Mingyu asked his STO contact and former Coalition shipmate. "I don't understand."

After reporting the pirate takeover, they had been sequestered in that damned military outpost for months. His crew's morale was at an all-time low thanks to being cooped up aboard The *Destiny*. It wasn't a luxury ship. Most of the time when they were on a long deployment, people were working and keeping busy. They didn't even have that now. The only spot on the station open to civilians was the lounge, but there weren't any more amenities than aboard his ship. He didn't even want to go into how the children and Headmaster Wong were faring.

Mingyu was pretty sure if he didn't do something soon, the man was going to go to the nearest STO officer and tell them he was kidnapped just to get off the ship and away from the kids who were even more cranky than his crew.

"Look, Mingyu, I'm doing my best. After you requested my aid with those *guests* of yours half a year back, I don't have nearly the same pull around here as I used to. Someone reported the training exercise to my superiors back on Earth."

He winced at that. "I'm sorry. If I had known, I wouldn't have called in the favor."

The Colonel shrugged. "I was glad to finally pay it off, even if it cost me the chance of moving up in my career. Something that was unlikely to happen anyway considering my previous time with the Coalition. The problem here is the STO is trying to hide just how bad this pirate infiltration was."

"It wasn't just Petrov then?" Mingyu asked in surprise.

Pirate attacks on border systems weren't exactly rare. It's why Petrov Station had hidden weapons systems, but a concentrated attack on multiple places at once was new.

"I shouldn't even be telling you this, but I feel I still owe you at least this much. Eight stations and three outer systems fell to the pirates on the same day. It was a well-thought-out, well-coordinated attack. From what I gathered, the STO upper brass are deciding if they even want to commit resources to retake these systems."

"That's ridiculous! They can't just let the pirates do as they wish, it will only make them push for more."

The man nodded. "I know that, and you know that, but the STO brass can't see beyond a spreadsheet. Right now, that spreadsheet says the cost outweighs the benefit."

Mingyu cursed, something he hadn't done in years. "What does that have to do with my ship and the people aboard?"

Jun sighed. "They were debating what to do with you as well. They are afraid you'll spread the word of what happened to other systems, requiring them to act for a change. I'm afraid they just issued a no-contact alert for you as of today."

"I don't understand. Is this something new in the STO?"

"It means no public station or planet within the STO is allowed to offer you docking or landing rights. The rule was designed to stop the spread of possible contagions. As you can see, they found other creative uses for it as well. They have also ordered the engineers here to disable your communication systems, except for a tight beam laser link for emergency use. I assume they have also flagged all your comm bands, so they no longer connect to Qcomms or relay stations either."

"How can they do this? We haven't done anything wrong!" Mingyu had been a standup individual his entire life, doing his utmost to live within the law, even when he found some of the laws to be nonsensical as well as a complete waste of time. Now he and his entire ship were being punished for it. How was that fair?

"I know, old friend. Unfortunately, I had no say in this order. When I tried to argue against it, they threatened to lock me up for insubordination."

"Thank you for trying. What am I supposed to do now? We can't stay here. This ruling is essentially a death sentence, without the bother of taking us to trial."

"Now you're just being overly dramatic. It'll be tough, that's true. But you can still do emergency docking and refueling at any Navy yard. There are also legitimate places outside the STO's borders that you can go. You asked me about a ship a few months ago?"

As if those places would be safe. Most were probably pirate hideouts masquerading as independents.

"Yes, the *Zephyr*."

Jun nodded. "You're in luck. A fleet station in Varlen pinged them, along with a mercenary ship heading for Y6X-3H2. If those are friends of yours, I suggest you start there. It's well outside STO jurisdiction so they would have no reason to uphold this order. It's likely safer than anywhere else you might randomly stumble across."

Things had become so hectic that he had forgotten about asking Jun to give him a heads-up on the ship if he could. He had been curious about where Alexander might have gone after learning he left on the ship. Now he knew. He didn't begrudge the man for leaving after how the Council had treated him. He would have done the same in his shoes. Mingyu wanted to apologize to the man and try to forge an actual working relationship with him if he could. That was before he was chased out of Gliese 667.

Now... *now*, it sounded like the system Alexander had gone to might be his only safe harbor.

Jun was correct, it would be difficult. Mingyu didn't even know where either of these systems were or what awaited him there. He gave it a fifty-fifty shot on whether or not Alexander would be happy to see him if he arrived, or if he would even be welcomed into the system. You didn't move outside colonized space because you wanted uninvited visitors.

If he had any other option, he would have picked it, but the STO ruling effectively cut him off from any allies he had that weren't stationed in military posts like Jun. He had few of those as it was.

The *Destiny* would eventually need service and repairs as well. The Navy yards would provide consumables because they were bound by law to aid any ship in distress, but even those would be at a premium. He winced at the thought of how expensive any repairs might be.

With a quiet sigh, he nodded to Colonel Jun and headed back to the *Destiny* to inform the crew they were leaving. If his crew didn't mutiny against him on that journey, he would consider himself lucky.

* * *

Alexander lifted one of the heavy beams in place as an engineer welded it to the one below. It had taken a few iterations, but he had finally come up with an acceptable design for a railgun emplacement.

It reminded him of old satellite dishes. The half-moon portion sat below the ground and acted as the weapons inclination adjustment and reloading system. Along the perimeter was a rotational actuator that controlled the rotation, obviously.

The reloading system was at the bottom center of the dish. It meant the weapon would have to point straight up for reloading, which wasn't ideal for aiming purposes but was the best method he could come up with at the moment. Placing it anywhere else in the pit meant the gun would have to lower itself and rotate back to the loading mechanism, then back to the target before it could fire again.

An autoloader attached to the back of the gun would eliminate that issue, but that added unneeded complexity and weight to the part of the gun that moved. Having the autoloader as a stationary component at the bottom center of the pit eliminated those issues and allowed the loader to store way more darts than it could if it was attached to the gun.

With his design, it only had to get back to the correct elevation. Doing it that way also allowed the gun to rotate the full 180 degrees vertically in the cradle because there weren't bulky autoloader components in the way.

Technically the weapon could even point down, but he had put limiters in to prevent that sort of situation from happening. He didn't want some accidental discharge going into the very delicate internals of the emplacement if the elevation system failed, or the cables to be ripped out if the gun got confused on orientation.

There were also some hard-coded limitations built into the program that Lucas had coded for him. It prevented the gun from firing at the facility, or while it was below the protective hatch that would protect it from the environment. Whenever they got it put into place, that is.

The limitations on the weapon did leave a blind spot in the defensive envelope around the facility though. After talking it over with the Hawks, Alexander implemented a second railgun design that would be placed above ground and covered with a dome. The smaller railgun emplacements were not much bigger than Alexander's first design test. The kinetic darts they delivered were about the size of a marker instead of the much smaller ones he used in his initial test.

As with the guns themselves, his ammunition went through a redesign. Instead of having fins that stuck out past the core, the rear tapered to a point and the fins maintained the original diameter all the way back. It looked like a pointed teardrop with fins. He didn't have any research to say which was better, but his tests of the new ammunition showed they didn't lose velocity as quickly, and they were still stable in flight. That was all that mattered to him.

The larger emplacement that he was working on fired kinetic darts around the size of a can of spray paint. That was a whole lot of mass requiring a whole lot of energy. With as much power as he was pumping through the railguns, they should be capable of hitting anything in orbit but not much beyond that. While not ideal, their main use was for shooting at ships in low orbit or anything trying to land that wasn't authorized.

If he ever got around to it, he might even be able to find a suitable explosive to pack inside the darts. He wasn't sure if the darts would do more damage as is or with an explosive inside them. That would take more testing to figure out later.

Alexander would have preferred to use a smaller projectile, but the static shielding ships used to deflect space debris were strong enough to redirect smaller projectiles. It added a considerable amount of counteracting force as well, which reduced much of a projectile's punch. The round had to be large enough to overcome both if it had any hope of punching through a ship's hull. He didn't have exact numbers, so he erred on the side of caution and went as big as he could. Captain Matthews said the size should be fine, so Alexander went with it.

He wished he had time to study the static shielding system to figure out how it worked. According to Travers, static shielding was mostly useless planetside. Something to do with power draw as it almost constantly had to push atmospheric particles out of the way. He still made a mental note to look into in the future.

The man welding the beam in place finished up and Alexander released his hold. The first railgun cradle was almost complete. A few more supports then the gun and power systems could go in. They were already built and waiting, it would just take some assembly. Alexander made that process as simple as possible—just moving them into position and sticking them together. It didn't even require engineers.

He wanted the design to be as simple and straightforward as possible because they needed to build six of the large railguns to cover all the blind spots around the massive complex. There would also be twelve of the smaller railgun turrets, two for each landing pad. Each entry would then be fitted with an automated turret inside that would drop down from the ceiling with two of the flechette rifles inside it.

Was it overkill? Probably. Did Alexander care? No. Well, he only cared that it delayed his actual engine-building work, but safety had to come first.

The security room was also getting an overhaul. Alexander pushed a few projects farther down his list and used his limited supply of advanced computer chips for the new defensive center.

All of the computer coding came from a very excited Lucas. When Alexander told him what he planned to do, the man could barely contain his excitement. Even the taciturn Damien seemed less unhappy about this project than most everything else.

Alexander was holding the final piece of the railgun mount when his radio buzzed. He excused himself and put down the support as he grabbed the radio.

"This is Alexander." He hadn't figured out a way to communicate via radio with his body yet, so relying on the small handheld units provided by the Hawks was the best he could do.

"Alexander, it's Martinez in the security center. Our sensors just picked up a ship jumping into the system. Figured I would give you a heads up."

"Um... Okay." He didn't know how to respond to that.

The Hawks were still in orbit, and they would deal with any hostile vessel that came through. If it wasn't hostile, they would tell him.

"Thanks," he finally said.

Maybe giving a radio to the person watching the asteroid cameras wasn't the best idea. Then again, it was infinitely better than having Yulia woken up every time a ship jumped in, and the facility alarms were triggered.

A few minutes later, he got another radio message. That time, it was from the *Talon*.

"Mr. Kane, It's Captain Matthews. We have received a tight beam comm message from the new ship. The captain claims to know you and is asking if they can approach the planet."

Someone who knew him was there? He had no clue who that could be, Jasper wasn't due back for a few more weeks.

"Who is the captain?"

"He says his name is Captain Mingyu Na. Ring any bells?"

Alexander paused. What the hell was one of the Council Captains doing all the way out there?

"Yes, I know him. I'm not sure what he wants from me, though. Is his ship capable of landing?"

"No," Matthews stated flatly. "It looks like a large mining ship if I had to guess."

"Tell him it is okay to approach. I will speak with him in a few days."

Matthews acknowledged the order and closed the radio connection. While he didn't think Na was here for nefarious purposes, there was the possibility his ship got hijacked in Gliese 667, or that he was being coerced somehow. Deciding not to risk it, Alexander urged the engineers to complete the first gun emplacement before the ship arrived. At least then they had some protection if things turned south.

It wasn't that he thought the *Talon* couldn't handle a single mining ship, he would just feel better not relying on them completely.

chapter 47

By the time Captain Matthews reported to him that Na was in orbit around Eden's End, Alexander and the engineers had completed the first railgun installation. That was thanks to the additional help from some locals and the simplicity of assembling the unit. He probably could have been halfway complete with the second if he hadn't stopped to ensure everything was working properly on the first.

It was one thing to model something, but he had learned that, until he built it, there was no telling if there would be unforeseen problems. It was a good thing he didn't continue because there were issues to work though.

The first had to do with how fast the railgun rotated and elevated. The preliminary test stripped out the precision gearing because he had forgotten to account for the masses in motion when writing the code that operated those portions. He would have asked Lucas to do that code, but he was busy with a much more important project.

Thankfully, he had five sets of spare parts. After cannibalizing one of the unassembled railguns to replace the broken parts, he reprogrammed the controller to reduce the speed by half. It wasn't an ideal solution to the problem, but redesigning the entire system wasn't possible for that installation. He also didn't want to have six different iterations as he was sure to find some way to improve with each assembled gun. For now, they just needed to work. Later on, he could create upgrades.

The second test went much better. The motors didn't tear themselves apart and the gun was capable of moving in all the axes that Alexander wanted. The issue that cropped up in the second test was how much the weapon wavered after it reached its intended angle. With land-based targets, that little bit of wobble probably wouldn't be too much of an issue, but at orbital distances, it could mean the difference between hitting the target and missing by hundreds or maybe even thousands of feet.

Another bit of code fixed that issue. He simply slowed down the last few degrees of motion to ten percent speed. That almost eliminated the wobble. He was starting to realize designing an effective weapons system was far harder than he thought. Already he had ideas on how to improve upon the design, and he hadn't even fired the weapon yet.

Speaking of firing, he radioed the security station. "We are ready for the first test fire," he stated.

"On it!" an excited Lucas replied.

A few moments later, the massive gun rotated straight up. There was a *thunk* as the autoloader rammed one of the sabots into the barrel and the breach shut. Then the gun rotated to point low over the horizon.

Their first test was simply to fire and see what happened. He didn't want to fire one into orbit just yet.

The whine of the capacitors had already been going since he first activated the gun. The sound dimmed slightly as the weapon recoiled. There was a boom followed by a hypersonic crack as the projectile disappeared into the distance.

Unlike his original test with the small railgun, that one left a visible trail of dust kicked up in its wake as well as a line of superheated vapor to mark its passage through the atmosphere. The shockwave was actually pretty tame, all things considered. He chalked that up to the tapered redesign of the darts.

Alexander clicked his radio on. "The first test is a success, reload and prepare for the second shot."

"Roger that," Lucas replied happily.

The barrel lifted again and the railgun was loaded with a second round. That time it was aimed higher. And he watched as the barrel slowly traversed to follow the target in orbit. That meant target tracking was working. It was one of the things Lucas had been tasked to code.

"Captain Matthews, we are ready for test two."

"All ships are clear, you are good to go for your test."

Alexander was using this opportunity to show Na that he had ways to defend himself if there was any tomfoolery about to go down. Their next target was one of the defunct spy satellites that the people of Eden's End had launched around the planet.

It would let him know the gun's accuracy as well as its damage potential.

He had to give the people there credit, disguising their satellites as asteroids was rather ingenious. Even Matthews had been impressed because he hadn't registered them as anything other than rocks until they took control of the facility's computers.

Alexander gave the signal to fire. The gun sent its round tearing into orbit and Alexander was nearly knocked off his feet by the shockwave that pressed down on him that time. He probably should be in the observation bunker like the rest, but he wanted to get a good look at the gun's workings himself. It wasn't like he was in any danger from the blast due to his lack of squishy bits and all that.

"Target miss," Matthews stated. "Looks like it passed a few feet behind the satellite."

Alexander sighed. Their orbital math must be off somewhere. He radioed Lucas to check on it.

"Oh, yup. Seems I missed one decimal place in the tracking code. Want me to prepare a follow-up shot?"

The man knew far more about coding than he ever would, but Alexander had learned Lucas could be a bit sloppy sometimes. Hmm, no.

Sloppy wasn't really the right description. Rushed maybe? No, that didn't really describe the man either. Slapdash was probably the best description Alexander could apply to the man. Lucas liked to code, but he preferred to move on to another project as soon as he finished the first. The code would be functional but tended to cut corners where the man was less concerned.

That was fine for simple things, but when accuracy mattered, it wasn't. To be fair, Alexander had gone over the math in the code with the man and had missed this issue as well, so he couldn't be too harsh on Lucas. He was still young, so there was plenty of time to get better and Alexander was already starting to see more focus on the details from the man.

"Switch to target three," he responded. The second target was getting too close to where the *Talon* and Na were parked.

The gun swept down after loading the third round and started tracking the next target. Alexander waited until it was within their firing window before he issued the order.

The gun sent the round hurtling into orbit. That time, Alexander watched the trail it left in its wake as it tore through the atmosphere.

"Target destroyed," Matthews radioed him a minute later.

He heard the engineers in the bunker cheering at the successful test.

Alexander smiled. "Lucas, round was on target. Congratulations! You can put the gun in standby mode."

He heard some more cheering over Lucas' radio. It must have gone on for a few minutes because that was how long it took the gun to rotate into standby and the hatch to slide closed on top of it.

Now he was ready to talk with Na.

* * *

Had Mingyu been the worrying type, he would have been pacing across his small bridge. As it was, he was sweating slightly. His sensor operator had picked up the weapon discharges from the planet and the subsequent destruction of one of the many asteroids that hung in orbit. He wasn't a fool. It was a declaration to tread carefully.

It was also rather pointless. Especially with the massive armed and armored troop transport shadowing them from behind. Like most civilian ships, the *Moonlit Destiny* wasn't armed. If it came down to it, they could repel boarders with their pulse rifles, but that was about it. The *Destiny* relied on the fact that mining ships weren't very profitable targets for pirates to remain safe.

Even if he wanted to arm *Destiny*, the STO was very selective of who they allowed to have weapons. Mercenary ships were one of those exceptions. However, not all mercenaries were equal. Harn's ship, the Devil's Bargain, was weaponless for example. However, calling Harn a mercenary wasn't doing the name justice. Harn had been more of a bounty hunter pretending to be a mercenary than anything else.

Soon after the tests ended, Mingyu got the radio call he had been expecting.

"I'll be in my cabin," he said quietly as he left his chair on the bridge.

Nobody responded to him as he left. He wasn't surprised.

Tensions had only continued to rise throughout the ship as they made their way through STO space and to that system. It had gotten so bad that he had been forced to confine a few people to their quarters after fights broke out. Now there was just an undercurrent of simmering anger and exhaustion among the crew. He was ready to beg or promise just about anything if this place would allow his people to disembark.

He pushed his cabin door open and the thing squeaked noisily—something it had never done before. The addition of the extra people on board and their extended trip had strained the environmental systems and moisture had started to build up, rusting anything metal. There were already a few systems that were on the verge of complete failure.

The door shut and he walked tiredly over towards the terminal to activate it. The holograph came to life and then split into two separate screens. One showed the captain of the mercenary ship. Matthews if his tired brain was correct. The other screen showed Alexander's avatar face.

"You look like shit," Alexander stated bluntly.

Mingyu couldn't help but chuckle tiredly. "I feel even worse. I know you probably never wanted to see me again, but I was given few options after pirates took Petrov Station."

Alexander frowned. "So they did take Petrov... What of the orphans?"

Mingyu wanted to smile, but he didn't have the energy in him to do so. "They were aboard my ship for a field trip when the station was attacked or, more accurately, when it was taken over. We barely escaped the system."

He told them what happened next and who he suspected had been in cahoots with the pirates.

"So you're saying your fellow captains were involved?"

Na nodded at Alexander's question.

"You know how this looks, don't you?" Captain Matthews asked.

"That I may also be in league with them," he stated with a resigned sigh.

The video froze for a bit and Mingyu assumed Alexander and Matthews were discussing stuff they didn't want him to overhear.

When it unfroze, Alexander spoke first. "This does explain some of the actions Sergei Zhang took against me. I could never quite figure out what his issue was. How did you find me anyway? I certainly didn't leave a forwarding address."

"I may be ostracized from STO space, but I still have some contacts. One reported to me that the *Zephyr* and Captain Matthews' ship had headed out here."

Matthews frowned at that. "That information should have been private. Who is this individual?"

Mingyu shook his head. "I will not be giving that information away. I'm sorry."

Matthews' frown grew even more pronounced, and his eyes narrowed. "We'll see about that. The Hawks have contacts too."

"Gentlemen... let's get back on track," Alexander interrupted.

Both men focused on Alexander.

"What is it you want exactly, Na? And none of this politicking nonsense that went on back at Petrov. I have no more patience for that."

"I would like you to speak with the leaders of Eden's End to request they allow my people time to rest. At least take the orphans and Headmaster Wong if that isn't acceptable. I'm willing to negotiate compensation."

The screens froze again for much longer the second time.

When they came back, Alexander spoke again. "You're in luck. I own this facility. Before we discuss allowing your people to disembark. What are you offering?"

With that question, Alexander had put all the pressure back on him. If he didn't offer an enticing enough deal the first time, there might not be a second opportunity. This was the worst possible outcome for him. He had been prepared for the worst though.

"I see you don't have any orbital infrastructure. I'm willing to offer my ship's services for free for a year. As long as you let my people live at your facility. After that, we can negotiate a new deal."

That was risky. It meant Mingyu was shouldering a lot of expenses.

"Do you have a shuttle?" Alexander asked.

Mingyu shook his head.

"Then how do you propose I refine the material you collect? As you have already stated, there isn't any orbital infrastructure."

"Do you have a refinery?"

"I have a smelter, why?"

"Even better. If you can get material into orbit, along with a smelter, I will provide you with plans for a simple transfer station. It won't be much more than refueling and topping off consumables, but you should be able to modify or extend it to include the smelter and an ore delivery hangar. As you grow, you could add a shuttle hangar. That's probably the extent the design I have is capable of, though."

Alexander paused again, but that time Mingyu could see movement on the screen still. *So the man was just thinking.*

"Why are you offering this to us? We didn't leave on the best terms."

"I care about my crew and the people aboard my ship. Do I need any other reason?"

"And what of your ship while your crew is planetside?"

"I will remain on board to make repairs."

Alexander shook his head at that, which surprised Mingyu. "No. Matthews, I think you can answer this one."

The captain of the massive troop transport smiled. "The Hawks will ferry you all down and then we will search your ship to ensure there isn't anything we need to worry about. If that search comes back clear, our engineers will effect repairs as needed. Mr. Kane has graciously decided to provide the components. So long as you provide him with all your design schematics."

If he wasn't so exhausted, he would have applauded Alexander's maneuvering. In one stroke, the man had managed to secure plans for a refueling station from him as well as the schematics for his entire ship. The man may not like politics, but he knew how to use it when it suited him.

Mingyu agreed to the deal without hesitation.

CHAPTER 42

Yulia kept shifting her feet nervously as she stood next to Alex. He said her friends from Petrov were coming to visit. She was so happy she didn't even wonder why they all traveled so far just to see her.

She was startled as a boom shook the air. When she looked up, she could see a glowing trail. Alex had told her what caused them, but she couldn't recall the reason at the moment. She let go of Alex's hand and plugged her ears as the booms started to get louder.

"You could have waited inside," Alex reminded her.

She just shook her head.

Yulia wanted to be the first to greet her friends. If that meant standing out in the awful-smelling air and the bright light, she would do it. Alex had made her a wide-brimmed hat and some neat goggles that made it so she didn't have to squint, but she could still smell the air even from inside her mask.

Once the other kids saw her goggles, hat, and mask, she was sure the kids from the orphanage would want some for themselves. If she asked Alex nicely, he would make them some as well... probably.

The shuttle flared its engines—she gave herself a little mental pat for remembering that term—and set down on the landing pad a distance away. Even with the goggles, she turned away as the hot wind from the shuttle landing blew sand across the area. A shadow fell over her and she realized Alex had stepped in front of her to block the remaining dust.

She smiled up at him. "Thank you, Alex."

He made his cartoon face nod.

Once the wind died down, she stepped out to the side to see the shuttle. The ship belonged to the Hawks, which was apparently some sort of bird.

She wished that planet had birds. She wanted to see a hawk, or any animal other than a rat for that matter. Alex had shown her pictures of Earth animals from the learning modules, but it wasn't the same. Her only experience with animals was with the occasional rat or bug on both Petrov and Eden's End.

The ramp to the shuttle lowered and she was about to run over and greet her friends when she felt Alex's hand on her shoulder.

"Let them get used to the environment for a bit before you bombard them with questions, okay?"

She nodded and held herself back, barely.

The first to step off the shuttle was Headmaster Wong. She was about to wave to the man but stopped herself. He looked tired. More tired than she had ever seen him look despite knowing him during a time when he was up for almost three weeks straight monitoring two sick toddlers after their parents abandoned them. Someone adopted the toddlers shortly after that and the man went back to looking normal again.

The rest of the kids shuffled out of the shuttle, looking much like they had the night she got hurt. Her instinct was to try to comfort the smaller children, but the older kids were already doing that even though they didn't look much better.

Finally, she waved. When nobody waved back, tears started to well up in her eyes and she sniffled. Had they forgotten her already?

Alex kneeled down next to her as the group trudged across the landing pad. "They have had a much rougher journey than we did to get here. Give them time. Your friends still care about you. I have an idea. Once we're inside, why don't you take them to the cafeteria? Get them some good food and then show them to their new home. Do you remember where it is?"

She nodded as she pulled up her goggles to wipe her tears away.

Alex smiled at her and gave her a warm hug. She liked his warm hugs.

The group was quiet as they moved into the facility. Headmaster Wong and Alex only shared a single nod. She wished she knew what it meant.

Yulia kept glancing back at the kids, feeling a bit awkward for some reason. She wished Sarah and Claire had been allowed to wait with her, but their parents had forbidden them from going outside.

"Headmaster Wong, I've asked Yulia to show the children to the cafeteria, if that's alright with you. You don't have to worry about their safety. The people here are nice, and the facility is patrolled by the Hawks. The children won't be able to get anywhere they aren't supposed to."

"Thank you, Alexander, and hello again, Yulia. I think that would be fine. Children, please go with Yulia."

Yulia smiled brightly as she turned to the kids, but most just gave her tired looks in return. "Um... follow me."

When everyone responded with a weird look, she realized she said that in English. She repeated herself so they could understand.

At first, she felt a bit self-conscious leading around all of the kids, especially the older ones. However, soon she started chattering away so she wouldn't have to think about it.

She heard someone in the back chuckle softly and say, "She hasn't changed at all." Yulia smiled when she heard that.

The cafeteria was in the Hawks' camp. She didn't get to go there often because Alex told her not to bother them unless it was an emergency. One of the times she had been there, she wished she could forget.

She stopped and saluted the guard, doing her best to mimic the expression a few of the Hawks had shown her.

The guard was one she knew: Zorina. The woman eyed her up slowly before looking over the trail of kids following her. When Yulia glanced back, she could see most of the kids were looking away from Zorina's scary expression. Yulia knew the woman was nice despite that. She turned back to glare at Zorina for scaring her friends, but the woman had a slight smile on her face, and she returned Yulia's salute.

"Miss Kane, what brings you by today?"

"Cafeteria!" she declared proudly.

Zorina nodded and waved them through. "Cook has stew on today's menu. Eat up."

With head held high, she marched into the camp with her arms swinging back and forth.

Now, Yulia had been hungry before, so she knew how awful it felt, but the kids from the orphanage practically inhaled the food and went back for seconds. Nobody said they couldn't and the cook seemed perfectly happy to serve them as much as they wanted, so she didn't complain.

After their second bowl, the younger kids looked about ready to pass out.

"Is there a place to sleep nearby?" one of the older kids asked.

"Um..." They had a place to stay, but that was quite a walk still. She didn't think the younger kids would make it that far and some of the older kids looked equally as tired.

The cook cleared his throat. "Ahem. Feel free to use the bunk tent. Everyone is on duty at the moment, so you won't disturb anyone for at least the next six hours."

"Thank you!" she said, hopping up from the table. "Follow me!"

Once all of the younger children were set in the cots, someone walked up beside her and placed his hand on her shoulder. She looked over and saw it was Markus.

"Hey, shrimp. Been awhile. I see you're doing okay?"

She scowled at the nickname but nodded her head when Markus smirked at her indignation.

"You can show us around after we get some sleep. We didn't get very good sleep on the ship."

"Sorry," she said.

"Why? Not your fault. Not anybody's fault."

"Can I ask why you left Petrov Station?" She had been curious, but Alex wouldn't tell her.

"It doesn't matter."

She knew what that meant. The only time Markus didn't like talking about something was when she asked him about pirates. Her gut churned at the realization and she felt somehow responsible because her parents had been pirates.

"You're it."

"Huh?" she asked, startled out of her thoughts by the words.

"I just tagged you. You're it." Markus smiled broadly at that before walking off.

She blinked in confusion for a moment before it hit her. "Hey! That's not fair!"

The older boy turned around and shushed her, making her clamp her mouth shut before she could yell again No tagging others during sleep, naps, or dinner, those were the rules. She kicked her foot against the floor and stomped out of the tent with a huff. She would find a way to not be 'it' after everyone woke back up.

* * *

Alexander waited for the children to disappear out of sight before he spoke quietly to Headmaster Wong. "Do you need to eat and rest as well?"

"I'll be fine until the children are settled. Thanks for asking though," the man grunted as he sat at a nearby bench. "Stars above, I never thought I would be planetside."

"You lived your entire life in space?" Alexander asked in surprise.

"My entire life aboard Petrov Station. Figured I would die there as well. I never had any need to leave. Yet here I am. I may not even be alive today to be thankful for this if it wasn't for Captain Na. Don't be too harsh with him, okay? The man's had it just as rough as the rest of us for the last four months."

"What happened exactly?"

The man shrugged tiredly. "Na might be able to answer that question better than me. I was on his ship with the kids doing a field trip when I got asked if they would like to take a quick trip. I wanted to say no, but the kids overheard and, well, you know how kids can be. I'm glad they changed my mind. Next thing I know, Mrs. Wu is filling me in on what's happening, and we are getting ushered into the mess aboard Na's ship and strapped in for violent maneuvering. I have never been more terrified in my life. More for the kids than myself, though."

"That's awful."

Wong nodded. "We survived, that's all that matters. What happened next was even worse. We got stuck aboard his ship for over two months at some STO outpost station. They wouldn't let the kids aboard the station at all, so they were cooped up on the ship that entire time. Then we finally left and came here. That took another month and a half. It was like I was raising fifteen cranky toddlers all at the same time! There was nothing to keep them occupied other than me and a few videos that were age-appropriate on the holo aboard the ship."

The man paused and breathed in deeply before coughing.

"Sorry about that, I'm working on restoring the air systems."

Wong waved away Alexander's concern. "I'll take this foul-smelling air over the recycled smell of body odor aboard Na's ship any day. I suppose I should see what the kids are getting up to. You have another guest."

Alexander had seen Captain Na and the rest of his crew arrive, so he didn't need Wong's head nod to point them out. Standing beside Wong was Eva Wu. He was glad the older woman had made it off the station.

He nodded his avatar and pointed Wong in the direction of the camp. He was sure the kids were still there. Then he turned and headed for Na.

Unlike the children, Na and his crew were escorted by Travers and his team. He waited patiently for the mercenaries to complete their search. He knew they had been searched before entering the shuttles, but the Hawks liked to be thorough. Alexander could respect that.

Once they were done, Alexander approached. "Travers, can your people show them to the cafeteria? I wish to speak with Captain Na."

"Sure thing, Alexander. Come on, follow along."

Alexander started walking away, forcing Na to hurry over and keep pace.

Once they were alone, he spoke up. "It doesn't feel nice, does it? To have your agency stripped away from you as someone else decides what's best for you."

The man sighed. "No, no it does not. I'm sorry for what we put you through."

Alexander stopped at the man's words and turned to Na. "Apology accepted. Now, tell me what happened to Petrov Station. Should I be worried?"

The man explained everything he had learned about his fellow captains and what occurred during the coup. He went into much more detail than he had during their brief video conference.

After telling his story, Mingyu slumped onto a bench and placed his face in his hands. "I don't even know what became of the rest of my family. Those bastards at the STO blocked every attempt we made to communicate. It shouldn't be possible with Qcomms, but obviously it is. They even destroyed my ship's communication gear before we left. The only way we could communicate was by tight band laser link which only the Navy still uses. If Captain Matthews hadn't been in a former Navy ship, I doubt he would have ever picked up our message."

"Why do you think the STO is refusing to attack the pirates?"

"Who knows? Politics, probably. Some asshole is likely up for election or reelection. Then this whole pirate uprising comes up, making them look weak. They are either trying to squash it or use it to their advantage to seem like they are cleaning up the mess out here."

Alexander frowned at that. "That's deplorable."

"That's the STO for you," Na snorted. "As for your question earlier, yeah, you probably should be worried. If the STO isn't going to come down hard on the pirates, it will simply embolden the rest of them. I don't know how many are on this side of STO space, but it probably isn't pirate-free. I assume that was what the weapon demonstration was for," he wondered, finally removing his face from his hands and sweeping back his unruly mop of greasy hair.

Alexander realized for the first time just how unkept and tired-looking the formerly pristine-looking man was.

"Something like that."

The man simply nodded. "Thank you again for allowing us to land. T– Things were getting bad aboard the *Destiny*."

"The *Destiny* is the name of your ship?"

"The *Moonlit Destiny*," Na smiled sadly. "My father named it in honor of my mother."

"How much time do you think your people will need to recover from this ordeal?"

"A month, at least. More if possible, but we aren't going to be allowed back aboard my ship until your friends give it a good once over anyway."

That was true.

"I'm afraid Eden's End doesn't have much in the way of amenities. What it does have is space. If any of your people need to be alone, there are plenty of places to do that. The Hawks will turn them around if they wander where they shouldn't. So long as they don't get into confrontations with anyone else or break any rules, they are free to do as they please while here. Just tell them to go by Petrov Station rules. Those should be close enough until they learn what's acceptable or not." Alexander paused. "I'll see about getting messages out to their families."

"You would do that for us?" Na asked hopefully.

"People deserve to know you and your people are still alive. Just be aware, both Matthews and I will be reviewing any messages that go out. I don't need the STO knocking at my door because someone on your crew decided to spill the beans about the invasion."

"That's more than fair. Thank you again, Alexander. I knew you were a good man after I sent Eva to speak with you. I just wish my fellow captains had seen it. Then again, if they were involved with pirates, it explains a lot of their rash actions."

chapter 49

LOCATION: PETROV STATION
SYSTEM: GLIESE 667
DATE: 2399

Harlow luxuriated in the plush chair as he bit into the ripe apple, savoring the sweet juice as it ran down his throat. The members of the Council sure did know how to live comfortably.

He let a little sigh of pleasure escape his lips. "It's been far too long since I've had an apple. Have you ever tasted one, Zhang? And I'm not speaking about the vat-grown shit you spacers call food, but a real planet-side grown apple?"

Zhang didn't answer; he only stewed. Harlow glanced over the wooden desk at the man chained to a small platform below. They were in the once prestigious Court of Affairs building on Petrov Station. It seemed fitting, but his little puppet wasn't in a very talkative mood which was a shame.

Harlow chucked the apple at the big man, hitting him in the leg. "I asked you a question. I expect an answer."

"No," the man growled in reply. "I did what you asked of me, why am I in chains?"

"Did you, now?" Harlow asked as he sat up. "When did I ask you to kill Kovalenko and Hoffman?"

"They would have reported your involvement in their trials."

Harlow laughed and leaned back again, kicking his feet up on the expensive wooden desk. "Unlikely. Those two idiots didn't know I was the one backing them."

"I thought you said—"

Harlow waggled a finger at Zhang. "You thought... see, that's where you went wrong, Zhang. I don't pay you to think. I pay you to carry out my orders."

The door at the end of the hall creaked open and Ingrid Liu walked in followed by a few more of Harlow's personnel who had infiltrated Station Security. Could it even be considered infiltration if the Council were the ones who hired them under his orders? He shrugged and looked at Ingrid. She stared back at him hungrily.

The woman was always a bit of a handful, but he knew what she wanted. Ingrid Liu wanted to be the sole family in charge of Petrov Station. When she had first approached him with her plan, he had been surprised she had figured out what ship he was hiding on and that she was audacious enough to come straight to him to suggest it. At the time, she wasn't aware that he was already undermining the station through Zhang, Kovalenko, and Hoffman.

"Ingrid, it's been far too long," Harlow stated as he got up and walked over to the woman, pulling her into a passionate kiss before pushing her back.

Ingrid hissed angrily, but not about the rough treatment. He would love to continue their reunion, but he had important matters to complete.

Harlow turned back to a very surprised Zhang.

"See, the thing you don't understand, Zhang, is that I don't put all my eggs in one basket. ...Do you spacers even understand that saying? Probably not. Doesn't matter."

Harlow paused in thought, not because he forgot what point he was trying to make but because he liked to build tension. It was so fun watching his victims squirm. "Where was I? Ah right. You failed me once, but I'm a reasonable man. I understand mistakes are inevitable. So I give people an opportunity to make amends, to correct their mistakes."

He sighed dramatically. "Then you killed Kovalenko and Hoffman, forcing me to move up my plans before I was ready, which allowed Na to escape. His loss isn't much of a concern in the grand scheme, the station is mine after all. But it irks me that your careless actions caused me distress. Do you know how long I have planned this takeover? A long time. And your little stunt put all that in jeopardy because you weren't afraid for me but for yourself. It's a good thing I had people in place already, if not, things might have turned out wildly different. That's failure number two. A foolish man might think that was just a coincidence. I didn't get to be a pirate lord by being foolish."

Harlow snapped his fingers and the four guards standing around Zhang began to beat him. Not with stun sticks, but with good old-fashioned clubs. The big man collapsed to his knees and Harlow raised his hand to forestall more punishment.

"I'm sorry, I swear I won't fail you again!" the man wailed in pain.

"I believe you," Harlow nodded. "In fact, I'll even let you go spend some time with Captain Yuchen and Captain Weiss. Neither seemed all that cooperative. Perhaps you can talk some sense into them. If you do, I'll forgive this transgression."

Another nod to the guards, and they began to drag Zhang from the room.

"Ingrid, Dear. Please go make sure Zhang doesn't screw this up."

She smiled, "I would be glad to."

After the woman turned, Harlow made a cutting motion across his throat with his thumb. The guard smiled and nodded.

Once the room was empty, Harlow dropped back into the chair behind the desk and waited for the large holo-screen to flicker to life. A scene much like that one had played out a few months ago. The lights outside the hatch started flashing and four flailing forms were launched out into space. The last of the families who controlled Petrov Station were now out of his hair.

He would have loved to keep Captain Liu around, but the woman was far too ambitious for her own good. She would have become trouble at some point. It was better to just get rid of her now and avoid it altogether.

All of the first steps in his plan were falling into place. His comm chirped as he was watching the last of the life leave the foolish Council members.

"What!" he demanded, annoyed at the interruption.

"I would think you'd be in a better mood now that your plans are in motion, brother."

"What do you want, Arkonis? I have more pressing matters to tend to than listening to you."

"Oh, nothing much. I found some information you might be interested in trading a favor for. That's all."

Harlow snorted. "What nonsense are you talking about? It would have to be worth more than my flagship for me to even consider offering you a favor for it instead of cred."

"Who knows?" his brother replied cryptically. "Last I checked, you were very eager to learn the whereabouts of that engineer that slipped through your grasp. I just happen to know where he is."

Harlow sat up. "How? Where?" he demanded.

He had learned about Kane back when everyone else had learned about the man, but unlike the imbeciles running Petrov Station, Harlow had seen his potential right away. The first giveaway was that Omni didn't get personally involved with useless people. They also didn't pay out hundreds of millions of credits for nothing. He also had access to information that none of the other parties involved did. Mainly the footage from the one Coal brother's implant that his man in Petrov's security wiped before handing the original footage over to him. He knew without a doubt that Kane had been building weapons.

Seeing his face in the doctored footage was a bit surprising. He would have beaten the mercenary to death for the insult if the idiot hadn't already met his fate in the cold embrace of space. Luckily, implants stored the original footage if someone had access to the hardware. His people had extracted the fake eye before the man tumbled out of an airlock.

If a man like Kane could create weapons and improve on Omni's designs, what else could he do? Harlow wanted him, and he was willing to go to great lengths to acquire his prize.

"Not until you agree," his brother said.

"Fine. Where is Kane?"

"He's in a system on the other side of STO space. The locals call it Eden's End. Some of Katalynn's people have raided the planet over the years. Small timers. Not much worth taking, and a large group of drifters have taken up residence in the facility where Kane resides. The contact who reached out to me said Kane let them stay. The man has a bleeding heart. Should be easy enough to force his hand."

Bah! Drifters were worse than rats. They scurried everywhere and stole everything that wasn't bolted down. Even that didn't stop them all the time. He hated them for the same reason he hated the other pirate lords, they took things that should rightfully be his. As for Katalynn, Harlow didn't have much to say about his female warlord counterpart. The woman had the personality of a brick and a face to match.

"Do we have anyone in the area?"

"I might have some, for the right price."

"You can take whatever you want from the facility. The only thing I want is Kane. Bring him to me alive and in working order, and you'll have your favor. Fail... and I might just find myself with one less brother."

Arkonis chuckled at that. "I don't fail. I already have a plan to get to Kane. It may take a bit though. He has some mercs running protection. Once they're gone, I'll move in."

Harlow was a patient man so he could wait. After all, he had waited many years to get to that point. He wondered what his younger self would say if he could see him now. Harlow somehow doubted the snot-nosed raider, drunk on his own invincibility and enough alcohol to drown a horse would have even considered anything. His younger self wasn't much of a planner or thinker. It had taken being stranded on a nearly dead planetoid for four months, after a failed attack against an STO battle group, for him to seriously reconsider his priorities.

* * *

LOCATION: FLEET HEADQUARTERS
SYSTEM: SOL

Admiral Clemont strode down the corridor, scattering Navy personnel as he moved with purpose. He didn't even bother returning the salutes as he made his way into the conference room.

There was a loud clamor as he opened the door. He let his gaze slide over everyone present as well as the holographic representations filling the other seats.

"Admiral on deck!" the guard at the door shouted.

The room went quiet as everyone who was there in person stood and saluted him. That time, Clemont returned the salute, then he nodded to the STO leadership who was attending remotely.

"You're late!" the Chairman stated at the announcement.

The door closed and the Marines standing guard exited the room.

"Apologies for my tardiness, representatives. I was receiving a last-minute update on the situation with the pirates."

"I doubt anything has changed in the last hour," the Chairman huffed in annoyance. "Please just get on with this meeting. I have an important dinner party to attend in two hours."

Clemont despised the current Chairman from Borrus. Then again, he didn't much like any politicians. They were too stuck up their own backsides for their own good.

"No further attacks," he stated as he sat down. "That doesn't mean the situation isn't fluid."

"You act like this is a war, Admiral. This is just the pirates acting out. They do this from time to time. Soon, they will devolve into infighting amongst their families like they always do. Then the fleet can push them back to their borders," the representative for both Malis and Malik, the twin planets in the Tau Ceti system, responded.

Considering Tau Ceti was the home system of Omni, he would have thought the representative of that system would be pushing for an all-out war. War meant more profits for Omni after all.

After a bit of thinking, he recalled a report stating Omni was receiving increased criticism for some of its actions. It might be something to look into. While he didn't care much for the monolithic manufacturer, his predecessors had burned the bridges for any other companies to even offer a competing product, even if that product might be slightly worse.

"The previous pirate incursions lasted days at most. This incursion has been going on two months already. It is also important to note that none of their previous attacks were ever as coordinated as this one. I believe we should treat it as a declaration of war and respond accordingly."

His reply received a few polite chuckles from the group of representatives. None of the Navy people present laughed though.

"The pirates are not the Coalition, Admiral Clemont. Those days are behind us. They reside on one rocky planet beyond the rim. To treat them as anything other than an annoyance would be to acknowledge they have actual power. We will not be doing that unless your purpose is to make us look incompetent. Or do you think a handful of ships are capable of standing against the combined navies of the STO?"

"They hold three former STO systems and eight stations, Chairman."

Clemont could see the man roll his eyes. "They took three border worlds whose navies were made up of Coalition expatriates and a handful of undefended stations. Those systems were likely filled with traitors already. I say let them suffer the hubris of their actions, then they might learn from this. Or is this thirst for revenge a result of the bloody nose they gave one of the smaller task groups?"

The Admiral froze at that.

"Yes, I've read the reports as well, Admiral. Yet you want us to declare war on them. The cost to activate our fleets and move them out there would outweigh the value of those systems. We should have let the Coalition keep them. All they do is drain our resources without providing any tangible benefit."

Clemont wanted to yell at the man and ask him whose fault that was. The STO leadership during the war had stripped almost all industries from the former Coalition worlds, forcing them to rebuild from scratch. It was done in the name of fostering a lasting peace, but he knew it had been done to ensure those planets never became a threat ever again. Given the choice, he might have made the same decision back then, and he hated that thought.

"So we just abandon them?" Clemont asked, doing his best to hide his irritation, but, apparently, it wasn't good enough.

"Watch your tone, Admiral. You can be replaced. Do you know the last time I spoke with the representatives of Zarinsk, Pravda, and Volnaya, Admiral?"

He couldn't imagine the planetary governors of those captured systems communicated with the STO very often. "No, Chairman."

"It was at our last summit. Do you know which governors contacted me after news of this attack made its way through the Qcomm network?"

He was forced to reply in the negative again, which seemed to be what the Chairman had been aiming for with his questions.

"Every other governor reached out to me except those three. Now what is more likely, Admiral? That the multiple Qcomm arrays on each of those planets were taken offline simultaneously, or that those two governors and the people in charge on those worlds are allied with the pirates?"

Clemont tightened his jaw but answered the leading question. "That they have allied with pirates."

None of the other planetary representatives seemed all that shocked by this revelation.

"Exactly. So now they get to live with the consequences of their actions for a time, but I never said we were abandoning those systems. I just don't see the point of expending resources to retake them at the moment. Like I said before, the pirates will likely collapse on their own in short order like they always do. Once that happens, the fleets will be in place to take advantage of their disorganization to recapture those worlds and arrest the traitors who turned them over to pirates in the first place. That doesn't mean we won't do anything right now. The representatives have agreed that we should increase the fleet presence in the systems on those borders by twenty percent. This will reinforce the border without leaving the rest of the systems undefended. Don't you agree?"

Twenty percent? That was two ships per strike group. He swallowed his pride and replied. "Yes, Chairman. I will start issuing orders to increase guards along that border. Is that all?"

"No. Another concern is these rumors that the pirate ships are displaying certain design elements of Shican origin. Can you confirm if this is true? I thought the last time a Shican vessel was spotted anywhere was in 2350."

"2358," Admiral Clemont corrected, earning a warning glare from the Chairman.

As for what the Chairman asked, he didn't believe it to be a rumor. One of the STO battle groups had encountered a pirate fleet of a similar size. The same one the Chairman so blithely stated as having received a bloody nose. While the ships engaged in battle were models from back during the war and not the newer ships that patrolled the core systems, what should have been a one-sided battle in the STO's favor had turned into a slugging match. That was unheard of in any previous engagement with the technologically inferior pirates. After losing two ships, the STO pulled back and retreated from the system, causing that system to fall to the pirates.

"Those rumors are unconfirmed at the moment," he stated.

That was technically true.

While the analysts were still pouring over the footage they received when the battered fleet made it back to the Navy yard, Clemont had already seen the footage of the battle. He was old enough that he had been in the last fleet engagement with the Shican in Varlen before the furry bastards retreated into the dark. The distinct sensor profile of Shican weapons fire was burned into his memory. He really hoped the analysis of the combat footage came back false, but he somehow doubted that to be the case. If his aging mind wasn't playing tricks on him, he would very much like to know how the pirates had gotten their hands on Shican railguns and missiles.

Every attempt to communicate with the aliens before they withdrew from that area of space had been met with hostilities. Had they come back, or had the pirates recovered a derelict ship for study? It wasn't out of the question. Studying a recovered Shican wreck was how the STO had discovered artificial gravity.

If the pirates had access to Shican tech, their threat would rise precipitously and they would be able to match the STO's current generation of ships. If he had free rein, he would take the first and second fleets and wipe the pirates out at their homeworld, leaving no survivors. Unfortunately, he was bound by his oath to follow the STO leadership's orders, no matter how much he disagreed.

He had hoped his tenure as Admiral would end in an era of peace, but it seems that would not be the case.

cHaPter 50

LOCATION: EDEN'S END
SYSTEM: Y6X-3H2
DATE: 2399

"Test forty-three," Alexander called out.

Everyone in the launcher control room let out a collective groan at that.

Getting the Low Orbit Launcher to even function had taken far longer than it took to install the rest of the orbital railguns around the facility. Had Alexander realized that before they attempted repairs, he would have stripped the entire thing out and started from scratch. Restarting would have been far less work, but it was too late to go back and do that now though.

The previous test, test forty-two, had resulted in the payload being shot out of the railgun like confetti. If he were trying to design a rail shotgun, he would have succeeded wonderfully. Unfortunately, he was trying to launch materials into orbit, so keeping it intact was sort of important.

He didn't even want to talk about the tests before that. Most of those involved tracking down system faults. Eventually, he got so sick of trying to hunt them down that he disconnected the launcher from the station power to eliminate the broken power flow problems entirely. That required him to print a new power cell for the launcher, but it was probably a good thing. His battery slash capacitor bank was far more stable and allowed for a much more repeatable power draw compared to the ancient systems in place before anyway.

That eliminated the power issue.

He wished he could say that was the only problem, but it wasn't. The rails he had manufactured to replace the old worn-out ones, turned out to produce a far stronger electromagnetic current for the same amount of power draw. Normally that would be a good thing since it meant less power was needed to launch the payload. If they had realized that issue ahead of time, they might have been able to stop what happened. The first live test blew the entire top half of the launcher apart. There had been an undiscovered structural weakness in the frame.

Thank god for the command room being situated behind a thick reinforced concrete wall. That little accident set their testing back an entire week and he was running short on time. Jasper was due to return any day now, assuming he wasn't delayed in STO space.

More importantly, they needed to have materials in orbit for the Hawks to start assembling a working refueling and refining station before their contract ran out in five months. That seemed like a lot of time, but it really wasn't. He had underestimated the difficulty of building a station in zero gravity. The Hawks' engineers were the ones who slapped some perspective into him. They estimated the station would take a full year to build, assuming materials were available and onsite. Alexander couldn't even guarantee he would have any materials in orbit at the moment.

The Hawks had given an all-clear for Na and his crew to return to their ship, but they were still relaxing after their ordeal. It would take them months to gather materials anyway. That meant the initial materials to build the station needed to come from the planet. That was fine because, without the smelter inside the station, any ore they brought would be useless.

Alexander had tried talking Matthews into using his shuttles to lift materials into orbit, but the man declined. Not because they couldn't do it but because the wear and tear on the drop shuttles to carry stuff into orbit would require them to be down for maintenance once a week. That was far too often to make them an acceptable alternative.

He supposed he could understand that. He was lucky he got the man to agree to bring the smelter into orbit when it was time.

Losing the smelter was going to be a pretty big blow to his manufacturing capability planetside, but he had the designs to build a refinery. While not as good as a smelter, the material produced by the refinery would be plenty strong enough for rebuilding the facility. To be honest, he wasn't utilizing even a tenth of the smelter's capacity with the mining being done planetside anyway.

However, he was getting ahead of himself. The smelter was still in place and turning out the material that would eventually turn into scaffolding that would go into orbit. The initial station plans were just a loose collection of exposed scaffolds along with some ion thrusters that would keep it from falling back into the atmosphere. The hollow rectangle design reminded Alexander of the types of stations built back when he was still human. All bare bones and utilitarian.

Before he got there, he needed to fix that stupid issue with the transport capsules. Having them come apart as they exited the launcher was not conducive to orbital manufacturing. The plastics that made up the majority of the capsules should have been more than enough to withstand the G-forces applied during launch. They were even stronger than what should have been available back when the original capsules were built. Yet something about his design was obviously not right.

Alexander walked out of the room and over to a nearby storage area where they had placed the old capsules until they could be recycled. He found the one that looked to be in the best condition and awkwardly carried it down the stairs and into the launch chamber.

The few local engineers that the Hawks had deemed passable were inspecting the launcher for damage from the previous test. The Hawks' engineers were busy repairing Na's ship and he needed the people living there to get familiar with the work anyway. If the rails were warped or damaged, they would need to replace them before continuing. That would set them back at least four hours.

He shoved the newly manufactured capsule off the loading platform and set the old-style one in its place. A few of the people looked at him as he did that, but nobody commented on the change. They were probably as sick of the tests as he was.

"Launcher is in working order, Alexander," one of the engineers called.

Alexander nodded to the man. He waited at the door to ensure everyone was clear before closing the blast door. Now that he had seen what happened when the launcher had a critical failure, he was glad the blast doors were there.

Everyone returned to the launch center. He nodded to Lucas—who had taken an active role as head of testing—and the man started the activation sequence for the launcher. A large holograph showing the inside of the chamber appeared on the blank concrete wall, almost making it look like it was see-through.

Everyone watched as the loader arm pushed the payload into the barrel along a set of rollers. Unlike his railguns, the launcher only had a set of locking lugs that prevented the payload from falling out the back as it raised its elevation.

Once it was loaded, it slowly started to rise. The gear-driven elevation system on the launcher was slow, but it was accurate. Eventually, it stopped, and the dome door slid open on the newly replaced concrete roof. Turns out the acid rain had severely weakened the concrete, which had caused it to break apart. The new concrete should be much more resistant to that, but it did make Alexander wonder about the structural integrity of the rest of the concrete encasing the facility.

With the door open, an alert blared through the room. Lucas pressed the launch button, and a five-second countdown began. He didn't know why the countdown was necessary, but it was apparently part of the original system coding–probably a failsafe in case they needed to abort the launch.

After five seconds, the launcher fired the capsule out of the barrel. The fact that it didn't explode into tiny bits right away, both irked Alexander and made him extremely happy. The display immediately shifted to an external camera that watched the payload rapidly disappear into the distance. The zoom on the camera tried to keep up, but it wasn't quite fast enough. After ten seconds of flight, the capsule collapsed upon itself, and the drag of the air pulled it down.

"Follow the descent," Alexander stated.

Whoever was controlling the camera, did their best until the thing vanished below the curvature of the planet.

"What was different about that capsule versus the new ones?" he asked, not expecting an answer.

"Did you see how it crumpled?" one man asked.

Alexander played back the video in his mind space. The man was right, it crumpled very strangely. "Does anyone have a saw or cutting tool handy?"

"Should be one down by the blast doors. Why?" another engineer asked.

Instead of answering the man, Alexander strode out of the room and down the stairs to retrieve the power saw. Then he walked into the room where they were currently storing the old capsules. He took the saw and cut the capsule in half, then into quarters.

The group from the launch room who had followed him, watched in silence.

Once Alexander had it cut apart, he separated the thick plastic parts, exposing a reinforcing mesh of metal hidden inside the thick plastic.

"Well," he said, spinning the piece around so everyone could see, "that explains why our capsules are falling apart. I'll print up a new one. Take a break, we will come back for test forty-four in the morning."

He walked out of the storage room, annoyed with himself. He should have considered the possibility that the capsules were reinforced. His oversight had cost them a full day.

Alexander knew he shouldn't be so harsh on himself. It wasn't like he had ever built a launcher or these capsules before, but he couldn't help it. A large portion of the success or failure of the project relied on him. One good thing that came out of that discovery was the fact he wanted to redesign the capsules anyway.

Their original design was meant to be picked up by a ship heading in the same orbital path as the capsule was on. It was fine for a ship leaving orbit, but it was not fine for a station that was being built in orbit.

The ideal orbit for a station was significantly higher than the orbital launch capabilities of the launcher. That meant either a shuttle would need to be in place to rendezvous with the capsule, or for the capsule to maneuver to the correct location. Considering he couldn't rely on the Hawks to be there to move the capsules after five months, he decided to design ones with small maneuvering thrusters built into them.

That requirement reduced the usable space within the capsule by an additional ten percent, but it also allowed the capsules to be much more useful, so it was a fair trade-off in his mind.

After entering his workshop, Alexander pulled up the schematic of the capsule he had been working on. The entire exterior surface was covered by a flexible weave designed to collect solar energy. Over the weave was a thin ablative layer designed to flake away in the vacuum of space. It was added to protect the sensitive nature of the solar weave from the harsh passage through the atmosphere.

Alexander hadn't designed the weave or ablative components, he had simply pulled them from other items he had worked on in the past. The ablative coating was a sort of hardened gel used in places that saw high temperatures for prolonged periods of time. The material canisters used by most printers utilized that gel to keep the canisters from melting as it turned the material inside malleable for printing. He just happened to remember the warning that this gel would break down if exposed to a vacuum and used that to his advantage.

The solar weave came from the few armor designs he had experience with. It was also used quite extensively in most vac suits to ensure at least a trickle charge during spacewalks or emergencies. He exploded the view of the capsule on his program and added a metal mesh. Then he wrapped the plastic back around it. He did have to redesign a few components and move stuff around a bit to get everything to fit again, but it all came together. When he was done, the design looked mostly the same on the outside.

Eight tiny ion thrusters were molded into the top and bottom half of the design allowing the capsule to maneuver. As far as thrust went, the back of the capsule had two ion thrusters: one on the top half, one on the bottom half. It wouldn't be fast, but it would be enough to get the capsule where it needed to be eventually.

His changes required additional space, but instead of further reducing the interior size by adding more padding, Alexander reduced the padding. It would mean he would have to reduce the size of any sensitive components he planned to launch. While not ideal, he couldn't add more padding because his scaffolding was already designed to take up the entire space available to maximize each launch.

He sent it to the printer and groaned internally at the projected time it would take. Six hours per capsule wasn't that bad, but the previous ones had only taken an hour each. He activated the rest of the printers that were large enough to print them and walked out of the room. There was nothing else he needed to do in the workshop as all the other machines were busy cranking out components for the facility, the station, or the automated defenses that were all still being worked on.

Alexander looked at his clock and realized it was almost time for the evening meal. He headed toward their apartment to make some food for Yulia. He hadn't seen much of his daughter since her friends had arrived from Petrov. What few times he saw her warmed him. She was laughing and smiling much more now, and she seemed to really enjoy showing her friends around Eden's End from what Zorina told him.

That was excellent news.

He had also heard a few families had expressed interest in adopting some of the children. Alexander left that to Headmaster Wong and Damien to figure out.

There was a lot of work to complete before he could start building engines or ships, but things were starting to come together.

chapter 51

The *Zephyr* jumped into Y6X-3H2 alongside one of the Hawks' gunships. Jasper wondered if Alexander or the locals would ever bother renaming the system as they did the planet. It just felt so impersonal to call it by the scientific designation.

Jasper was a few weeks behind schedule, but that couldn't be helped. Some of it was due to him being delayed because of the additional security thanks to the pirate attacks while leaving the core systems. The rest was from him loitering in Varlen until the patrol ship arrived to escort him. With the increased pirate activity, he had decided not to risk the crossing without some protection.

He was glad he waited. Two jumps past Varlen, they encountered an unknown ship running without a transponder. The ship fled at the sight of the gunship, but that was enough to tell Jasper that the outer systems were soon going to be far too dangerous to fly without protection.

As the two ships made their way to Eden's End, he got to see what his friend had been up to the last few months. While he had expected to see the Hawks' massive troop transport orbiting the planet, he did not expect to see the large mining vessel sitting alongside it. Unless his friend had suddenly been able to produce ships from thin air, he doubted this ship had been built in the system. That begged the question, who had come all the way out there to mine?

The transponder ping tagged the ship as The *Moonlit Destiny*, belonging to Captain Mingyu Na. It didn't take long for Jasper to recall that name. It seemed he wasn't the only one curious.

"What is a Council Captain from Petrov Station doing way out here?" Wilkes asked.

"I'm sure Alexander will fill us in, but I suspect the rumors we heard are true."

While nobody in the core seemed to know the extent of the pirate attacks, everyone was still talking about them. There hadn't been any concern when the topic was discussed though, which surprised Jasper.

"Captain, it looks like a station is already being built," Sierra commented.

Jasper returned his focus back to the sensor readout. What appeared to be the start of a small station was coming around the far side of the planet.

"Well... if that isn't a surprise." He hadn't expected to see Alexander focus on building a station for some time to come.

It seemed they had missed quite a bit since they left.

"Ping the *Talon* and let them know we're going to come along their opposite side from the *Destiny*."

A few minutes later, they got a reply confirming their orbit. A day and a half later, they coasted in alongside the *Talon*. They could have been there faster, but he wanted to conserve fuel as much as possible.

During their journey in-system, the crew got a bit of entertainment as they watched a live feed of capsules being launched from the surface only for them to accelerate into a higher orbit and drop their payload near the under-construction station. The capsules would then fall back into the planet and burn up. This happened every half hour on the dot. During their passage, the station had nearly tripled in size. Considering it was barely anything when they arrived, that wasn't all that much, but it was still impressive to watch.

"Is the shuttle loaded?"

"Yes, Captain. However, we are going to need the help of the Hawks to bring the larger items down."

He nodded and sent a message to Captain Matthews to see if he had any ships available. From what he could tell, most of the dropships were floating around or attached to the station under construction.

The man replied quickly. "We have one dropship on standby. I can let you use it for three trips."

There was only one large crate that time, so it wasn't an issue. The rest of the cargo could be carried down by his shuttle on multiple trips.

He responded to the man while Wilkes put the ship on autopilot. Everyone aboard was certified to maneuver the ship in case of an emergency, so he wasn't concerned about having his only pilot fly the shuttle. He could have flown it himself, but he wasn't nearly as skilled as Wilkes. When dealing with planetary landings, it was smart to use the best pilot for the job.

The ride down was just as rough as he remembered, but Wilkes put them on the pad with a gentle touch. They both glanced out the cockpit window. Wilkes whistled at the new constructions going up just outside the facility.

"Those look like some nasty weapons. I would hate to be some idiot trying to land here uninvited."

Jasper only nodded in reply. He knew Alexander had planned to build defenses, but he didn't know the extent of them.

"I think those are only the baby ones, look over to the left, that circle in the ground. That wasn't there when we left. How much you wanna bet that's a weapon emplacement as well?"

The circle in question was over half the length of his shuttle.

"That's not a bet that I'm willing to take," Wilkes chuckled as he began the shutdown procedure on the shuttle.

The entry opened and Jasper saw Alexander wave as he exited the facility to greet them.

Jasper waved back, but he doubted the man saw it through the auto-darkened glass.

He made his way to the back, which necessitated shimmying through the tight walkway between the stacks of crates. His people really had packed the shuttle as full as they could.

Once free of the cargo, he lowered the back hatch. His friend was there to greet him.

"Welcome back, Jasper! How was your trip?"

"Exhausting," he stated as he walked down the ramp to greet his friend. "Sorry about our delay, I hope it didn't cause any issues."

The face Alexander used to communicate shook. "No. I moved some things around and came up with some alternative solutions for other problems."

"I can see that. I assume the space station and mining ship are quite the story."

"You could say that. Na provided the plans in exchange for safe harbor for his crew."

"So Petrov was attacked?"

Alexander nodded. "From what Na tells me, it was more an inside job than an attack. Although he was attacked as he tried to flee the system. Then the STO quarantined their ship, making it impossible to dock at any public station in STO space. Someone told him I was out here, so he came out to see if we would allow them to disembark."

Jasper frowned at that. "Are you sure everything he says is true? I don't want to second guess your judgment, Alexander, I just want to make sure you're safe."

"I appreciate your concern. And yes, as far as we can tell, everything he said is true. His ship even has the scars to prove it was shot at. Not something I would expect someone to attempt just to try to fool us. With our new defenses, I'm not overly concerned by a pirate attack anymore. I'm not saying it won't happen, but we are far more prepared than anyone is likely to expect."

"I can see that," Jasper stated, glancing over at one of the turrets being constructed in the distance.

Alexander chuckled. "Come, let's get this stuff moved inside and I can show you all the changes. I think you'll be surprised."

* * *

It took over an hour to unload the shuttle, even with Alexander, Jasper, and Wilkes all working in tandem. They would pile the crates onto the transporter and when it was full, it would roll off to the secure storage room near his workshop.

Since he wanted to limit who had access to that room, he had installed robotic cranes that ran along the ceiling. They quickly and efficiently unloaded the automated cart so it could return for the next load. The cranes were much smarter than the stupid loaders aboard Petrov, thanks to the self-learning algorithm he built into them. He had learned more programming thanks to hanging around Lucas, but he still wasn't at the level where he could program anything too complex. The robotic arms reused the code from the robotic assemblers, with the addition of the self-learning functions.

He could have had Lucas program them, but he needed to improve his own programming. Doing it himself also ensured the code was safe and free of anything funky while also testing the new design he had implemented to build the cranes. So far the man hadn't done anything to make him think he would do something fishy, but Alexander was just being cautious by not relying on the younger Laront to do everything.

His new robots were similar to the old robotic manufacturing line, with their inflexible appendages that required rotational servos at the base, the elbow, and the wrist. Instead of the old geared joints, Alexander had replaced them with rotary actuators, much like he had with his railgun design. The cost in time and materials was quite a bit more, but he deemed it acceptable.

The accuracy of the actuator was far superior to gear drives because there was little to no backlash to compensate for. And when building parts with tight tolerances, he didn't want to worry about compensation errors.

It was complete overkill for the simple cranes, but after seeing how well the crane functioned, he was already incorporating the improvements into a new generation of robots meant to replace the engineers working on the space station. The new robots would be needed sooner rather than later to complete the station.

"Now that we have the ship unloaded, let me show you what I've been up to."

As the pair walked into the facility, the shuttle took off again. It would be a few hours before it landed with another load. That was plenty of time to tell Jasper what went on while he was gone and show him everything.

"Welcome to where the magic happens," he stated as they walked into the manufacturing center.

"Other than all the machines seeming to be constantly churning out items, I don't see that much has changed in here since I left," Jasper chuckled.

"True, but it's a good place to start. I'm currently producing parts for the defenses, parts for the facility repairs, and parts for the station. Oh, and I'm also printing out capsules to launch into orbit pretty much non-stop."

"We saw them on the way in. Are they only single-use?"

"Unfortunately. We are recovering some of the material when they crash down, but I can't afford to add a parachute or landing system without wasting even more space inside the small enclosures. It's annoyingly frustrating, but it's what we have at the moment."

"It seems to be working for you though," Jasper commented as he watched part of the clamshell take shape in the printer. "How are you launching them into space anyway? Did you get the launcher operational?"

"We did. And let me tell you, that was a pain."

Alexander told Jasper about the struggles with the launcher as they walked through the facility and toward the launch control. They were in luck, arriving just as the system was readying for another launch.

"We could launch faster if the facility transit system was intact. It takes my transporter fifteen minutes to drive across the facility to deliver a newly loaded capsule. Then another ten for the old crane inside the launch room to move it to the loader. Add another four minutes for the blast doors to close, and we just decided to launch every thirty minutes. It works out, though, since the engineers in orbit can only work so fast."

"I don't think you know just how impressive this is, Alexander."

Alexander shrugged. "Sure, it's impressive, but it feels so slow. There are so many things I want to work on that I can't even start until this is done, the facility is repaired, or the defenses are in place. It's frustrating."

"Everything you accomplished in a little over two months is impressive, don't get me wrong. That being said, I think you should take a step back and reevaluate your timeframe."

Alexander sighed. "I would love to slow down, but it feels like so much is happening beyond our system. I'm afraid if I do, something horrible will happen."

Jasper patted him on the arm. "Delegation is your friend. I can see you're doing some of that already, but don't try to spread yourself too thin. Focus on what is most important to you and have others worry about the rest. Speaking of what matters, have you been spending time with your daughter?"

Another sigh escaped Alexander. "Not as much as I would like. It turns out all the orphans from Petrov came with Captain Na. She's been spending quite a bit of time with them and the few friends she has made here. I didn't want to take her away from that."

"I'm sure she is happy her friends are here, but you are still her father. Take the time to make memories with her. I may not be a father myself, but I still recall the times my father spent with me. She will too."

After they exited the launch control room and got to a quiet spot, Alexander thanked Jasper. "Thanks for telling me that. I sometimes feel like the people here are afraid to tell me something or speak out like I might banish them or something. The Hawks, while good at their jobs and nice enough, tend to act like employees rather than friends. Some are better than others, though, but I doubt they even considered what you just told me."

Jasper laughed lightly. "That's what friends are for. You'll make more in time."

CHAPTER 52

After completing the last of the tour with his friend, Alexander did just as Jasper suggested.

"I need some people willing to unload some supplies from shuttles," he stated as bluntly as possible to Damien.

Over the last few months, Alexander realized the man preferred this approach to him trying to butter him up or resort to small talk.

"Why don't you just add it to the job board like the rest?" the man asked.

"Because it needs to be done as soon as the shuttle lands. If you know anyone willing, tell them I will double the trade allotment for this job. I need at least four people." Now that the additional supplies were there, Alexander had a bit more wiggle room with what he was willing to offer in trade, at least until it ran out. For now, he had plenty of credits to buy stuff from STO space, but that wouldn't last indefinitely if he didn't start making some money.

The majority of Alexander's trade supplies came in the form of medical treatments. Before, he had to limit medical services to only those willing to do the hardest tasks. Soon he would open that up to more people willing to work for him. For now, doubling up the trade allotment would allow anyone who accepted this offer to at least afford basic treatments.

He hated to have to ration life saving medicine like that, but he had no way to produce more. Everything pharmaceutical had come from off-world and it would for the foreseeable future unless some of the locals decided to go into the field. Alexander certainly had no interest in producing medications or drugs, but if someone else wanted to start a new enterprise, he wasn't opposed to that.

Unfortunately, that was likely not going to happen amongst the current locals. Most seemed uninterested in doing anything other than just living day to day.

To be fair, Alexander hadn't really gotten to know them all that much. There was still a barrier between him and the drifter population. They tolerated his presence, but they weren't all that accepting of him. He kept to himself unless he needed to interact with the people helping to repair the facility or taking up his jobs.

That probably accounted for the way he felt about the system he set up. Alexander hated rationing his medical supplies like some greedy jerk, but that didn't transfer to the rest of his supplies. He didn't owe the people anything. If they wanted something, they needed to earn it or trade for it.

The barter system he set up worked quite well. People would work to earn allotment credits which they could use to trade for whatever they offered. People could take advantage of it or simply ignore it completely if they wanted to and it wouldn't change anything.

The people of Eden's End could live their entire lives without having to interact with him at all if they chose to. He didn't charge them rent, taxes, or for stuff like water and power, so they had no costs associated with living there. Which was the same as it had been before he purchased the facility. That was beyond fair in his eyes.

He thought about charging for those things but decided against it. It would be much easier to entice people to come to that out-of-the-way system or stay there if living there was essentially free. It wasn't like he had any other amenities to entice people to stay at the moment, but there was a whole lot of free space available for people to live. Even with just over three thousand residents, Alexander could go an entire day without seeing another person if he was in one of the unoccupied sections. At its peak, the research facility could have housed eighty thousand people comfortably.

With everything so damaged and decayed from non-use, it could probably only house ten thousand without people having to cram in on top of each other. That would change as areas of the facility were repaired, but that was a long-term project that could take years to complete. He hoped the population would increase as well, once word got around.

Damien grunted and walked over to a comm panel and pressed the button. "If anyone wants to earn double allotment, meet Alexander over in Atrium D. Only four temporary positions available." He turned back to Alexander. "There. Now if you'll excuse me, I'm a bit busy." The man turned and walked away without another word.

Alexander picked four of the ten people who showed up in the Atrium to help unload Jasper's shuttle. It was too bad his friend wasn't able to stick around that time. The ship's reaction mass was being topped off by the *Talon* and, once the *Zephyr* was unloaded, they would be heading back to the core worlds until the danger settled down out there or Alexander could ensure safe passage.

The pair had discussed an ongoing delivery back before he left the first time, but things had changed since then. The space outside STO's territory was too volatile to risk traveling through alone. Alexander would not want his friend to risk himself or his crew for his sake either so there were no hurt feelings on his side.

The fact that the *Zephyr* encountered a ship without a transponder on their way back was disheartening to hear as well. Sure, the gunship had scared it off, but it was probably just an opportunistic pirate boarding ship.

From the intelligence briefings he received from Matthews, Alexander had learned more about pirates than he wanted to know.

For example, not all of their ships were armed. Some of the smaller ones were unarmed and built for speed. Those sorts of ships were used to chase down other ships and forcefully board those vessels. It turned out to be a pretty common tactic for the newer and younger pirates who were trying to get a start.

Unfortunately, just because some of their ships were unarmed, didn't mean they all were. Even the smaller pirate ships were armed more often than not according to Matthews.

Typical pirate armaments consisted of missiles or auto-turrets. The missiles were by far the more dangerous of the two, especially with static fields to deflect space debris. Most ships could deflect smaller and slower projectiles, but they could not outrun a missile even at full acceleration. The static field did little to mitigate the damage if one got close before detonating.

Just the threat of using one of those weapons usually got most captains to stop running and allow the pirates to board them in hopes of surviving. If the ships being boarded didn't have security, the crew locked themselves in the bridge, or engine rooms and let the pirates take what they wanted from the rest of the compartments until they were satisfied.

However, that didn't mean this tactic was always successful. Matthews had told him of plenty of instances where the pirates took the ship or crew hostage. If the hostages were worth anything, they ransomed them back, if they weren't or their contact refused to pay, the hostage disappeared as a slave inside the pirate strongholds. That was still better than what some pirates did to the crew when they wanted only the ship.

While missiles were used by some of the more successful pirates, the most common weapons in the pirate arsenal were autocannons or chainguns. While not as deadly as missiles, that didn't mean bullets fired from the auto-turrets weren't dangerous, they were. Especially at close range. Fill the static field with enough incoming ordinance, and you could overload it or drain the systems used to keep it powered. Once through the field, it didn't take much to punch through most ships or disable their lightly protected engines.

If an armed ship had encountered the Hawks gunship and the *Zephyr*, it may have concluded the risk was worth a fight. Alexander hated to admit, the pirates might be right. The Hawks' gunship used a rapid-fire flechette turret as its main weapon as opposed to an autocannon, but they packed around the same punch. It was just easier to fit more flechette rounds into a smaller space than it was for the old-style cased ammunition, which is why the Navy had switched to flechettes long ago according to Matthews.

Alexander hated to think what would happen if his friend came across a pirate ship that had railguns, Gauss turrets, or lasers. Matthews said he had never encountered a pirate with advanced weapons of that nature and said it was unlikely to happen, but Alexander didn't see any reason the outlaws couldn't possess more advanced weapons. He thought of how easy it was for him to make railguns.

All of the dark thoughts started souring his mood, so he turned his mind to something much happier. Now that he had delegated the unloading responsibility, he had some free time. He decided to fulfill the other promise he made to Jasper.

It took a few hours to print out the surprise he had in store, but he managed to complete it and get it assembled before the evening meal came about. Yulia strode into the apartment, whistling a tune and smiling wide.

"You look like you had a good day."

She nodded before climbing up on the stool.

Alexander handed her a plate of food while she busily recounted her day. This reminded him of their time back on Petrov Station. If he had some greasy parts partially disassembled on the counter, the image would be complete.

The girl practically inhaled her food while managing to still talk with her mouth full. He admonished her about manners and she apologized, only talking when her food was mostly chewed. A small win was still a win.

Once her plate was cleared, she got ready to hop off the stool and run back out with her friends, but Alexander stopped her.

"I actually have a surprise for you. Follow me."

"But I was going to play with my friends," the girl began to pout but stopped herself.

He could understand she wanted to play with her friends, but Jasper was right. He needed to spend more time with his daughter.

"Don't you want to spend time with me?"

"I'm sorry," she replied apologetically, lowering her head. "I didn't mean it like that, Alex."

"Why don't you ever call me dad, or father?"

She shrugged. "Dunno."

That meant she didn't want to talk about it. That was fine. He wouldn't push her to call him dad if she didn't want to.

She held his hand as they walked to the nearby atrium.

Very few locals used the atriums other than the one located where most people lived. He could understand why, considering how bleak and lifeless the large spaces were. Unless you wanted to play in the dirt or sit on benches, there really wasn't much to draw people to them. He had plans to fix them up, but they were low on the priority queue for repairs.

He led Yulia to an area off to the side that still had some working overhead lights and a large stretch of level ground. The place had probably once been a park or garden. As they rounded a concrete divider, Yulia's eyes lit up.

"What's that?!" she asked eagerly as she released his hand and raced over to the colorful playground that Alexander had assembled.

He joined her shortly. "This is a playground. That thing is a swing."

"What's a swing?" the little girl asked.

He picked her up and sat her in the plastic seat, before stepping around behind her and gently pushing her.

She immediately started laughing. "Higher!"

He obliged, giving her a gentle push. "Lean back while holding the sides and kick your feet out when you get to the top, it'll increase your height. Now tuck them in when you get close to the bottom. It didn't take long for Yulia to figure out exactly where to do this for maximum effect. "Good, you're getting it."

He stepped back and watched her as she laughed non-stop. He should have expected what came next.

On the next upswing, the girl cried out, "Catch me!" as she leaped from the swing.

Alexander was close enough to do that, but he did have a momentary bit of panic as she released the ropes. She landed in his arms and he absorbed her momentum before she could crash into him.

"Please be more careful, if I wasn't here, you may have hurt yourself."

She promised him she would be, but somehow Alexander didn't quite believe her. She was a bit of a daredevil.

He showed her how to use the other playground items: the seesaw, the merry-go-round, then the slide. He couldn't exactly use any of the equipment himself, but that didn't mean he couldn't demonstrate how they worked. She seemed to like the merry-go-round and the swing the best, probably because they went the fastest.

It was a bit sad that Yulia had no idea what any of those things were before he told her. He wondered if the other kids who lived there were the same way.

After playing with her for a good hour, she finally needed to rest.

"Can I show my friends this place?" she asked hopefully.

"Of course you can. I built it for all the children. Anyone who wants to come here can."

She rushed over and hugged his leg.

Alexander stroked her hair. "Unfortunately, I have to get back to work. You have a little over two hours before bed. I suggest you use that time wisely." He winked at her, earning a giggle in return before she hurried off to gather her friends.

"Thank you, Alex!"

Before he returned to his work, he looked over the playground one more time. The rubber padding underneath was hopefully sufficient to prevent any serious injuries. Luckily, the Hawks camp wasn't too far away so they could hear if anyone got hurt.

Other than standing there and monitoring the children, he couldn't think of anything else to make it safer. Since sitting there and monitoring them would likely scare the kids away and make Yulia upset with him, he didn't want that.

As he was walking off, he wondered what the Hawks had thought of all Yulia's screaming and laughing. Considering nobody came to investigate the noise, probably not much other than just a kid having fun.

chapter 53

Alexander sat down at a table a few minutes before the meeting was set to start. With the delivery from Jasper, the defense project wrapping up, and the repairs on the facility well underway, he finally had time to start the project he had come out there to start in the first place. It was time to discuss building his first engines, he just had some questions to ask Matthews and his engineers first.

It was too bad his friend Jasper and the *Zephyr* had left the system a few hours before. He would have liked to get his opinion on some of his ideas. With his friend gone, it would be quite some time before he saw the man again. While the parting was bittersweet for Alexander, he knew it was the right decision. There was no rational reason for Jasper to risk himself and his crew if he didn't need to.

The screen turned on, and Alexander saw two people. One was Matthews and he assumed the smaller woman sitting off to his side was likely his chief engineer.

"Good afternoon, Mr. Kane. As you requested, I have invited my chief engineer, Aria Sullivan, to this meeting. What did you want to discuss with us today?"

"Thank you for taking the time to meet with me. As you know, my original goal for coming out here was to start a company that produces spacecraft engines. A company I finally founded with the help of Captain Daniels. Blue Star Enterprises' big debut might have been delayed due to a few unforeseen factors; the missing equipment, the state of the facility, and the need to build defenses. Now I'm finally ready to begin designing my first engine."

Matthews nodded. "I am aware of most of your troubles, but how does this concern the Hawks? We can't provide you with any design specifications for the *Talon* if that's what you're asking. Even when it comes time for you to build our upgraded propulsion system, you would need to purchase the design from STO space."

Alexander waved away the man's concern. "No, nothing like that. I was more curious about why larger ships, like Captain Na's, use compressed plasma ejection instead of the more common fusion pulse drives?"

It had been a bit of a surprise when he saw that on the *Destiny*'s design schematic.

"Size constraints, mostly," the chief engineer of the *Talon* responded.

Alexander quirked an eyebrow at that. "I would think storing fuel would take up much more space than simply using up the reaction mass. Am I wrong?"

He wasn't quite that far in his engineering studies.

The woman shook her head. "At first glance, perhaps. But when you factor in the containment systems required to move the plasma from the fusion chamber to the engines, you lose quite a bit of space. There are other things to consider as well. The biggest consideration is the ability to enter an atmosphere. No ship equipped with a compressed plasma ejection system would be allowed to enter a planet's atmosphere. The temperatures are such that the exhaust plays merry hell with any combustibles near it. That includes the twenty-one percent oxygen mix of a standard atmosphere. It wouldn't ignite the entire atmosphere or anything silly like that, but it would create a huge fireball, potentially large enough to destroy the ship. While pulsed fusion still uses a fusion reaction, the individual pulses are far cooler than ejected plasma."

"Oh... Yeah, that wouldn't be good. Thank you for answering that question. My next question has to do with reaction mass. Doesn't plasma ejection reduce the overall reaction mass?"

"Of course it does, but most ships have what's called a fifty-year core," the engineer replied. "During reactor idle, the reaction mass would last for fifty years. This is standard across any ship capable of FTL. It can also easily be topped off since the fuel used to run the fusion plants is relatively safe. In–" the woman paused to speak with Matthews while the line was muted.

The man rubbed his chin in thought at whatever she had said to him before finally nodding.

The audio came back on and she apologized. "Sorry about that. Had to make sure what I was about to tell you wasn't part of our operational security. As I was about to say, in normal combat operations, that reaction mass would last the *Talon* a year. That is a year of constant maneuvering and fighting. Sitting about like we are now, we could go ten years or more depending on maneuvering needs. It's a trade-off for sure. Refilling reaction mass is more expensive than topping off the tritiated water, commonly referred to as super-heavy water and deuterium oxide also known as heavy water burned by the more common pulse drive, but compressed plasma ejection also offers more thrust. A ship like the *Talon* can't keep up with something like the *Zephyr* even with our more powerful engines, but it can still accelerate at a pretty decent speed. Since we don't need the speed as much as a smaller cargo ship might, it's not really an issue."

"Thank you for the information. It seems I still have a lot to learn."

The woman nodded.

"Any more questions for us, Mr. Kane?" Captain Matthews asked.

He shook his head. "Not at the moment. I think what you've told me so far has helped to point me to where I need to begin my efforts. Thank you."

"Good Luck, Mr. Kane. Maybe you'll even have something ready for us to see before we leave."

Alexander chuckled at the captain's statement. "No pressure then." He made his avatar smile.

The pair smiled back before the video cut off.

While it was true that this meeting helped narrow his design efforts, Alexander had already been leaning toward the more common pulsed fusion drives because they were... more common. It seemed like a prudent choice if he wanted to carve out a market share from the other giants. In time, he was sure he would branch out into the compressed plasma ejection engines, but that was still quite a ways off.

He chuckled internally as he thought of something. If the people from back in his time saw what the thrusters and the propellants they were using were capable of, he was certain they would have passed out in shock.

It was a good thing the elements needed to produce the fuel were easy and abundant in most systems with gas giants. Y6X-3H2 had two such planets, making gathering the elemental hydrogen and oxygen rather easy. Yup, the fuel used to propel ships at a fraction of the speed of light was water or a manufactured version of it: good old heavy water and super-heavy water.

Using an initiated fusion reaction to propel a ship was brilliant. It reminded him of a much more sophisticated version of the nuclear pulse propulsion concept he recalled from back in his day. He wondered if that theory was what eventually led to this design.

Pulsed plasma was similar to the compressed plasma ejection since it used the results of a fusion process as the thrust. It was why he was confused when he first saw the form of propulsion that Na's ship used. According to Matthews' chief engineer, Aria Sullivan, a ship with pulsed plasma could land on a planet because there was little concern of it igniting the surrounding air.

That meant the *Zephyr* could land on a planet if it wasn't so large. That also meant the *Destiny* was definitely too large to land so the issue of igniting an atmosphere was sort of self-regulating. It was probably a deliberate design choice now that he thought about it. Anyone dumb enough to try to take a large ship down onto a planet would blow themselves up.

He switched gears and focused on the fuel he would need. It was a good thing that the station Na had offered him came with the design specs for a fuel converter. Otherwise, he would have wasted quite a bit of time trying to figure that problem out.

Alexander left the communication tent and headed to his workshop. On his way, he could hear the excited laughter as the kids put the playground to great use. He couldn't help smiling at that.

Once in the workshop, he projected an exploded view of the Omni engines on the *Zephyr*, along with the Sinorus engines on the *Destiny*. Then he walked into the massive hologram and closely examined every part as he manipulated the images.

Alexander could simply rip their entire design off and call it good. He had no qualms about doing that anymore, but it was lazy, and he wasn't the sort to do things half-assed. Over the next six hours, he poked at parts, tossed others away, and redesigned every single component to ensure there would be no mistaking that this engine was an original design.

What he found was a bit surprising. Some of the Sinorus components seemed to be superior to the Omni ones. At first, he thought this was simply due to the different forms of propulsion involved, but when he looked closer at what the parts did, he realized they did the exact same job.

When he was done, he stepped back and looked at the diagram. He moved his hands back together and the parts moved until the hologram was a single unit. From the back, not much had changed. The thrust cones were shaped slightly differently, but it was hardly noticeable unless someone like Alexander looked at it. The main difference came in the other components. The exposed bits looked slightly melted or more organic in nature. It would certainly require more printer time, but if it worked it would be worth it.

He saved the file as Version One and loaded the simulation software he had purchased back on Petrov.

The simulation ran a whole three seconds before the hologram displayed a red fault message. He had to dig around to find what the fault was. It was claiming the combustion chamber temperatures had exceeded specifications.

"No first-try home run this time," he lamented as he tweaked the engine design and saved it as version two.

When the tenth test failed to produce a working design, he grew frustrated. He had nearly rolled back all of his changes and was almost back to the original Omni design. Gone was any Sinorus influence his design had carried before. Even still, the damn program was telling him the design wouldn't work.

He wondered if he was doing something fundamentally wrong until he had the idea to run the original Sinorus engine schematic through the simulation program. It gave the engine a passing grade but highlighted possible failure points. If Alexander hadn't noted those parts as superior to Omni's during his deep dive, he wouldn't have even second-guessed the program.

Suspecting something was up, he loaded the software onto a data chip and went to find Lucas.

It took some asking around, but he eventually found the man in the computer room as everyone called it. The room held the facility's servers. Much like the computer chips of that century, Alexander had no clue how those servers even operated. That was fine, he had Lucas for that until he got around to learning himself.

Speaking of Lucas, the man was sitting cross-legged on the floor with one of the servers in his lap. There were parts spread out all over the place and the man was listening to music while he soldered some components inside the case.

Alexander waited until the man was finished to get his attention. "Lucas, do you have a moment?"

The man looked over and smiled. "Oh, hey, Alex, what's up?"

The man had heard Yulia call him by that nickname and decided it was easier than using his full name. Alexander wasn't really bothered by it, he just preferred his full name. It sounded more... *regal.*

He held out the chip. "I'm having an issue with this software I purchased. I was hoping you might take a look?"

The man paused in his reach. Instead of taking the chip like normal, he took it like it was radioactive. "You bought this from STO space?" He grimaced, barely holding the data chip between his fingers.

"Where else would I have purchased it from?"

The man shook his head and set aside the stuff he was working on. He got up and walked over to his tablet that was blasting the music. The music suddenly shut off as the man pushed the metal disk into the device.

"I wish you would have come to me before running this software. You know there is a bounty out for me, right?"

"Yes. But what does this have to do with that?"

"Probably nothing. When I lived with my brother back on Helios, I freelanced as a coder."

"You mean you were a hacker?"

The man chuckled. "No, well, not exactly. Companies paid me to make programs for them. Programs designed to prevent their competition from surpassing them. They were often designed to transmit any improvements these new companies ran through the testing software that I built for the original company–under a separate third company's name, mind you."

Alexander sighed. "You did corporate espionage?"

"More or less," the man replied casually as he typed away at the pad. "I played both sides, though. I would always reach out to the companies that bought the software and offer to do a penetration test after their newest secrets were somehow leaked to their competitors. I would miraculously find their leak that nobody on their internal teams could, and they would pay me handsomely. This went on for five years until one of the companies merged with the original company I designed the software for. They realized what I had been doing and placed a bounty on me. The rest is history," he said as he pressed one last button before showing Alexander the screen.

"You know I'm not that advanced with code yet, just tell me what I'm looking at."

The man rolled his eyes and pointed to a line in the code. "This transmits everything run through this software to a Qcomm. It's a good thing we don't have one otherwise your design would have gone straight to the owner of this code."

That statement made Alexander extremely upset. Even out there, it seemed he couldn't get away from the grubby little mitts of the corporations.

"You're certain that nothing got sent out?"

"About as certain as I can be. Whoever wrote this shit code never thought the people using it would be outside the range of a Qcomm, so they didn't implement any contingencies."

"So you didn't create this one?"

Lucas shook his head. "Nope. There are plenty of other people like me in the core. Maybe not quite as talented." He puffed out his chest. "But they can still code something like this."

"Can you remove that code to make the program safe again?"

"Sure, but that's not gonna make it function."

"What do you mean?" Alexander asked in confusion.

"The code isn't only designed to trade all your secrets away. It's also designed to prevent you from making something better than the people who paid for this code to be written in the first place."

"Omni," Alexander muttered, causing Lucas to pause and turn to him.

"You're joking right?"

When Alexander didn't say anything, the man sighed. "Of course it's Omni. You don't do anything small do you, Alex? As for your next question, because I can already tell what you want to ask me, maybe. I might be able to make the program function correctly for its intended purpose. It's going to take me a few weeks to go through the code. I have to make sure I'm not screwing up any of the calculations. Rocket science is not my forte, so if I get something wrong it could make this entire simulation software useless."

"Please, do what you can." He glanced over at the disassembled server. "I'll trade you two supercomputer chips for the work."

"How can I say no to that," Lucas chuckled. "I'll do my best and get back to you as soon as possible... If you have any more software, bring it to me and I'll look it over as well. No need for additional payment."

Alexander thanked the man and walked out of the room, annoyed that he was once again delayed in producing a new engine design.

chapter 54

With his progress delayed until Lucas finished checking over the code, Alexander shifted his attention to other projects.

His main focus while he waited for Lucas was assisting with the facility repair efforts and preparing for when the Hawks would leave.

That date was coming quicker than he would like and there was still quite a bit of work to do. Making sure the refueling station stayed on track after they left was at the top of his priority list. Some of the components to ensure that happened were already in the queue for launch. Mainly the parts for the large robotic arms that he designed for capturing the pods. The rest he was getting ready to manufacture.

The robot arms weren't anything special, simply mimicking the robot assemblers he had in his manufacturing center. They were just much longer.

Alexander was still putting the finishing touches on the robots that would replace the Hawks' engineers when they left. He didn't want to create single-purpose robots—which would be an extreme waste of resources—but he also couldn't pack every conceivable tool known to man into one either, or that would make the things massive and impossible to build. He also had limited space to work with. If the robots were too big, it would make them impossible to launch into orbit with their current capabilities.

The design he decided to go with implemented swappable tooling. Each robot had onboard storage for up to four tools and could switch them out depending on the work it was performing. Three articulated arms, similar to the ones he built for his storage room robot, gave them the flexibility Alexander needed them to have. With the upgraded robotic appendages, he didn't need to worry about construction issues as much.

With the station being just a large hollow rectangle built from triangular scaffolding sections consisting of round pipes, it made it easy to clamp things to the interior. If he had to guess, it was probably why they designed the structure that way in the first place. No matter the reason, Alexander used the scaffolding design to great effect by implementing a series of rollers for his robot workers. He thought about making other designs that would work elsewhere but decided against it for now. It would increase the complexity of the robots and mobility wasn't currently needed. He just needed them to run along a set path like a train.

That didn't mean he wasn't thinking ahead. He designed the roller portion to be swapped out, just like all the other components on the robots.

The rollers securely fastened the robot to the two outer rails of the triangular struts, allowing it to move back and forth along that axis. That meant they couldn't move away from the side they were attached to, but it was fine. It did mean he had to build four of the robots, one for each side of the structure. The machines came with locking clamps, both physical and magnetic to ensure they wouldn't wobble around once they were positioned to start work. With two arms to hold the material in place, and a third arm to do the work, they should be able to complete the station ahead of the *Talon*'s Chief Engineer's predictions—or so he hoped, assuming no supply issues cropped up.

He sent the file to the printer and went to retrieve four of the advanced computer chips. His generic breadboard chips weren't going to cut it for the robots. Alexander had plans to build a computer chip manufacturing machine. Nothing that was capable of building the types of chips made today, mind you, but he thought he might be able to mimic the types of computer chips made in the 1980s or '90s with his current manufacturing capabilities.

He hadn't gotten time to work on that project yet. It was high on his list though because of the limited amount of advanced and super-computer chips he had on hand.

He input the code into the door's lock. The room had previously been secured with a biometrics lock, but obviously that didn't do him any good, so a simple alphanumeric touchpad had been added. It wasn't a perfect system by any means, especially with his automated carts having to broadcast the code every time they entered, but it kept the casual passerby out.

The door opened and he moved through the room until he found one of the padded cases with the chips inside. He picked up the case and carried it back to his workshop.

By the time he returned, the initial frame for the first robot had been printed and moved off the printer bed for the next to begin. He really did love automation.

Due to the constraints of the capsules, the engineers would have to assemble the robots once they were in orbit. Alexander had provided them with a detailed list of assembly instructions. They did ask about purchasing the plans for their own use, but he had to deny that request at the moment. It was mostly because he didn't have the design registered in STO space, so there was nothing stopping someone from stealing it. He didn't think the Hawks would do that either, but it was better to be safe. He also didn't want the attention quite yet. Especially considering what he learned from Lucas that day.

He opened up the insulated storage compartment where the chip would reside. Calling those things computer chips was a bit of a misnomer. They were essentially the entire computer, shrunken down to the size of a two-inch cube. Having all the complicated bits built into one component meant printers didn't need to specialize in building motherboards or memory or any of those sorts of things. It just had to build the connecting components.

It was a rather ingenious method. The computers could be ordered in all sorts of configurations as well. If someone needed a wafer-thin computer for say, a tablet, it could be manufactured. However, he had chosen the cheapest method, which was the cube.

Alexander had looked into a printer capable of printing the cubes along with everything else. As it turned out, there were printers capable of doing that, but they were massive things that cost more money than Alexander had gotten from the Omni payout. At that point, they were more like assembly lines than a single printer. The smallest one he looked at, out of curiosity, was larger than the refueling station he was building. It also had to be built in a vacuum for it to function correctly at the picometer scale those advanced chips operated on. He didn't even want to see what the requirements of the super-computer chips were. Those chips were expensive, and he only had ten of them.

The iridescent cube clicked easily into the housing of the robot and Alexander sealed the compartment. He heard the thing beep quietly before it went through its self-test cycle. He didn't have to worry about that code as it had been written by Lucas. The machine made hardly any noise as the actuators rotated. Then it beeped again and the console it was linked to showed an error.

It was an error Alexander expected to see. The message was simply letting him know there was nothing attached to the actuator assembly. Seeing no other faults, he put the robot in standby mode. Then he wheeled over one of the specifically outfitted capsules and lifted the robot into the foam padding inside.

It took the rest of the day to finish up the four robots as well as the other components that went along with them. He was glad the plasma welder only required a lack of oxygen to weld properly. It would have been an extra step to bottle inert gasses and then a real pain to have to constantly ship them into orbit to keep the construction on schedule.

A total of ten capsules were earmarked for delivering the four robots and their additional components. It would set back construction in the short term, but once the robots took over, that delay should turn around quickly.

With the robots complete, he set the printers back to making more capsules. The capsules still took far too long, but he had optimized the prints from six hours down to four by removing the foam printing and delegating that to a separate machine. It did mean he had to manually shape the foam to fit, but it still took less time overall.

If he planned on keeping the capsule launch method, he would probably get around to making a shaped mold at some point so he could free up the printer.

He piled two of the capsules on the cart and sent the wheeled vehicle off to the launcher. One more thing to check off his list.

* * *

"You're sure everything was removed?" Alexander asked. He was looking at the simulation software. His first iteration still showed a failure.

"As far as I could see," Lucas replied. "Could it be your design doesn't function?"

Instead of getting upset by the question, Alexander paused. It was indeed possible. He loaded in the Sinorus design and ran it. That time, it came back as fully functional, and it didn't show the warning errors on the parts that were more efficient than the Omni components.

He sighed internally. "It does indeed appear to be working. Thank you."

"Hey, don't mention it. I gotta say though, that first design looked wild. Like on the order of magnitude of being a pain in the ass to work on wild. You may want to consider that. I know if I took a look at that, I would be like, nope."

Alexander loaded up the third iteration. "What about this one?"

The man waggled his hand back and forth. "That looks slightly easier to work on, but I'm not an engineer. You may want to ask them."

After Lucas left, Alexander tested his later iterations. Everything other than the first, second, and third came back as functional. There was the possibility that the simulation software wasn't robust enough to recognize the extreme changes he made, but he decided to play it safe. Instead of going straight to the printers, he took Lucas' advice and loaded up the working designs into a holographic presentation. He needed a second opinion.

"Thank you for meeting with me again so soon," he said as soon as Matthews and Chief Engineer Sullivan came on screen. "I'm looking for an opinion on some engine designs if you would be willing."

The captain kept a composed façade, but he could see the small woman's eyes slightly widen at his words.

"It's not every day I get to take a peek at experimental engine designs," she stated in interest. "I'm free for as long as the *captain* allows it." She looked at the man pointedly, and Alexander could swear he saw Matthews flinch.

"Yes... We would be happy to give you as much time as needed," Matthews said diplomatically.

He nodded his avatar's face and sent the presentation to them.

It took hours for the woman to painstakingly go over every detail of the engines. She didn't have the design specifications, but Alexander assumed she had been around enough engines to know what she was looking at. It seemed he was right.

"This first one would be far too hard to maintain." She pointed at four components nestled into the interior. "It would require taking apart the entire combustion assembly just to get at these parts. Then you have to deal with radiation. If I was given a berth on a ship with an engine like this, I would quit. I'm sorry if that sounds harsh."

"No, not at all. I want your brutally honest opinion. What I make is going to eventually need to be serviced by engineers just like yourself. If it's too difficult to work on, nobody is going to want to buy them, no matter how much better they are."

"Do you have any numbers yet?" Matthews asked. While he didn't appear all that interested originally, he had come around.

"Not yet. I built these designs after the last time I spoke with you."

Matthews and Sullivan paused and Alexander thought they had paused the connection, but they were just staring at him.

"You designed *all* of these in five days?" Sullivan asked.

"Oh, no," Alexander chuckled. "It only took me a day to design them. I had to wait four days for Lucas Laront to fix my simulation software."

Chief Engineer Sullivan opened and closed her mouth a few times before she finally spoke. "I'm at a loss for words. You designed not one, but six working prototype designs in a single day?"

He decided not to correct the woman by telling her it had actually been ten designs but only six working ones. "Um, yes? But they are just simplified iterations from the first one."

She shook her head. "That explains why the designs look so similar. Still, if you can correct the component placement, and get some hard numbers, you may be looking at some serious contenders. This is a Class 3 engine, is it not? I don't think I've ever seen a Class 3 engine so compact."

"Um... It's actually a Class 4. Or more accurately, it's based on the Class 4 engines from the *Zephyr*."

"Alright," the shorter woman said, getting up from the desk. "I've had enough surprises for one day. Considering what you've told me, you should have no issues moving the parts to be more accessible. Hell, I suggest you expand everything out so it matches a standard Class 4's scale. Speed and efficiency aren't everything. If you make an engine that is significantly easier to work on while being as fast and efficient as current designs, that's a market as well." With those words, the woman walked out of the video and he heard the door shut.

Matthews turned back to him. "Chief Sullivan is correct. Saving time on repairs is sometimes much more important for certain people. Let us know if you need anything else, Mr. Kane." The man nodded one final time before the video cut out.

It looked like he had more design work ahead of him.

chapter 55

The next week went by rather quickly for Alexander. The station was starting to take shape with his new construction robots being run through their initial tests.

He did have to make some design iterations and launch those replacement parts into orbit, but overall, they were working out well. Engineers would then continue to monitor their work for the remaining time they were in the system, but they said they didn't expect any major issues.

Alexander hoped that was true. While the robots had some ability to repair each other, they wouldn't be able to do much if the central processors died on them or if the track wheels broke off and the machines floated away. The clamping system should prevent the second scenario from happening, but it was still a possibility.

With the station well in hand and the final railgun turrets going up outside the facility, Alexander was able to finally free up production time for his engine. Technically, he was manufacturing three different engines, all scaled down to one-tenth the size. That was still quite a large engine to build. The engine cones alone measured two feet across.

It was a testament to the ridiculous amount of power these engines produced that a mere three of them could push something the size of the

Zephyr across an entire star system in a little over a week if it pushed the limits of human endurance. Thankfully, most ships cruised at an average speed of 1g so trips took longer, but people were generally still alive by the end of them.

One g of acceleration didn't seem like much, but when it was constant, it added up fast. Then again, fast was relative when speaking about space. Depending on the size of the parent star and the planets in a system, it could take anywhere from a few days to over a week to cross between the closest stable jump points. The smaller the star, the weaker the gravity well and the closer one could get in the system without the field destabilizing. Planets also had to be accounted for. There was so much space between most planets that one could slip between their gravitational pull without too much issue most of the time.

From what Alexander learned so far in his engineering courses, pulsed fusion and compressed plasma ejection were the two main types of propulsion systems used for sub-FTL travel. Each had their advantages and disadvantages as well.

From speaking with the Hawks', specifically Chief Engineer Aria Sullivan, he learned that plasma ejection technology was still in its infancy. Alexander thought it had been around for some time, but apparently, it was only invented after the Coalition war ended.

Fusion reactors were delicate things at the best of times. The fact that someone figured out a way to pull out plasma from the reactor without destabilizing the reaction was a monumental achievement in and of itself.

Pulsed fusion seemed to be at the end of its useful life as far as improvements to the core technology went, but plasma ejection would likely only improve with each generation.

With that being said, Alexander needed to understand both technologies. It wasn't until much later in the module that he learned pulsed fusion had a strange bottleneck. The fusion process for pulsed fusion took place in a combustion chamber, but that chamber was open to space through the exhaust nozzle. When those types of engines tried to push past a certain maximum thrust output, a resonant hum started to form inside the combustion chamber. It wasn't enough to damage the chamber, but it was enough to disrupt the delicate fusion process.

That didn't mean people had given up on the older technology. He knew people were looking into the issue thanks to his exchanges with Dr. Lund.

Despite that issue, those three engines could push the *Zephyr* through a system the size of Sol in a little over five days using the closest stable jump points to Earth. If they wanted to take a scenic tour through the solar system, they could cross its entirety in twelve to twenty days depending on the planetary orbits. If they had to push the ship's maximum acceleration of 3.6g, they could do the crossing in a little over seven days. However, that sort of acceleration for that long would have some serious drawbacks on anyone aboard the ship, assuming they survived.

As far as he knew, humanity hadn't discovered inertial dampeners or anything that could reduce the effects of gravity on a person. Then again, Alexander had assumed artificial gravity plating wasn't real until he saw it. So maybe some of the fancier ships had the technology or it was a military secret, and he just wasn't aware of it.

He realized he was getting off track again. The engines were powerful—so powerful that he couldn't test a full-sized version on the planet without a specialized test facility. The scaled-down engines he printed consisted of an Omni, a Sinorus, and his new design. All of the designs he chose were from Class 4 engines to ensure the numbers were comparable.

Alexander had planned these tests weeks in advance. There was a pit much like the railgun pits outside the facility specifically designed and built for those tests. In a perfect world, these engines would be tested in a vacuum, but Alexander didn't have the time or patience to build a vacuum chamber long enough to keep the exhaust gasses from melting the lining. He thought about coating a chamber in heat-absorbing gel, but it was only rated for 3500 degrees Celsius. That was nowhere near enough to keep the plasma from melting everything around it. The pulsed fusion drive burned at nearly twice that temperature.

He suspected his pit would probably be rather worse off after those tests, but that was fine. He had plans to incorporate liquid cooling into the walls as well as electromagnetic containment to keep the plasma from getting too close to the walls on future tests. He figured if it was good enough to keep ship thrust cones from melting from the obscene temperatures involved it should be good enough to keep his pit intact.

The pit consisted of a simple steel liner with fire-protective matting stuck to the inside of it. The test rig had a mounting platform that allowed the engine to face straight up and a sensor plate that measured thrust. That design ensured the engine wouldn't go flying off if there was some catastrophic failure with the mounting.

It was also the most simple and straightforward design he could come up with. Alexander didn't want to waste a whole lot of time and resources on the first tests especially since he didn't need exact numbers. With the engines being scaled down, he wouldn't be getting that anyway. The only thing he cared about for this initial test was a side-by-side comparison of the three engines.

Before he could do that, he was running the parts that he could through the testing station he had built. It was a scaled-down version of the one he used on Petrov Station. While he couldn't afford to take a testing station with him when he left, due to cargo space concerns, he did purchase the plans to build one. He just hadn't needed it until now.

As the parts were running through the diagnostic tests, he moved over to the printer and pulled off another set of finished power banks. Ideally, Alexander would build a fusion power plant to supply the needed power to operate these engines, but he still didn't have the capabilities needed to do that. Instead, he resorted to printing out dozens of power banks.

The tests wouldn't run very long, so he didn't need to sustain the fusion reaction that turned the fuel into thrust. It would still probably take the power supply's complete charge to run each test though. So long as it worked, he was fine with that. The power banks were rather quick and cheap to manufacture.

That left the last issue he needed to overcome: fuel.

Matthews had stated he would provide fuel if Alexander needed it, but he wanted to do it on his own.

Finding water was easy. The facility had twenty-four wells that went down to a buried aquifer. Converting this water into rocket fuel was a bit more challenging. He already had the designs for a processing plant thanks to Na though.

It turned out that it was a bit complicated to make heavy water and super-heavy water. Both elements existed in small amounts on Eden's End, but mining them would be far too labor-intensive at the moment. He didn't need to do that though, because he already had the design for a processing machine that would do that for him.

That meant more power banks and a secure storage tank for the rocket fuel after it was ready. As a bonus, the fuel would come in handy when he finally built a fusion power plant for the facility. It wouldn't be as good as what ships used for their reactors, but it would get the job done.

Building the insulated and lead-lined tanks was taking longer than printing and testing the individual parts for his scaled-down rockets. The tank wasn't something Alexander was willing to rush, though. He knew heavy water wasn't radioactive, but super-heavy water was slightly radioactive. Given the quantities he was producing, he didn't want to worry about the radioactive liquid causing issues around the facility or making people sick down the line.

Then again, he was probably overthinking it. The people of Eden's End were likely getting a higher dose of radiation just by living there.

He looked over at the robotic arm that was welding two of the tank sections together. It was nearly complete and he would have to take the crane and remove it from the work area soon. The storage tank diameter was so large that it barely fit through the closest opening to the outside. He would have to roll it out himself since there were no delivery vehicles low enough to hold it without hitting the top of the door.

It highlighted another problem he was going to have to resolve at some point. Mainly, how was he going to build full-scale engines without them getting stuck in his workshop?

He knew the far wall of his workshop faced away from the facility. The easiest option would be to cut out that wall and put in a large door with an overhead crane. It went on his to-do list.

It seemed like every time he marked something off that list, two or three more things got added.

The machine beeped to let him know it was complete, and Alexander rolled the dual-layer ring section out of his workshop and down the hall to the transport path. It made quite the racket as he went, but there were few people in his section, most having decided to move to the quieter areas after he restarted production. He couldn't blame them. If he needed sleep, a noisy assembly line that ran all day every day a few hundred feet away would be extremely annoying.

The walls and doors were sound dampened, but with so much production going on, the large entry was left open most of the time as the transport carts retrieved items and zipped down to where the parts were needed.

Once outside, Alexander filtered out most of the glare from the star. He was glad he figured out that nifty feature after arriving there, otherwise it was often too bright to work outside during the peak hours of the day.

It took him ten minutes to roll the ring next to the secondary pit near the engine test site. A simple overhead crane with a hand-operated chain ran on rails that passed alongside both pits. He didn't want to expend a lot of resources for what was likely to be a temporary site.

After hooking the crane to the lifting points on the ring, Alexander pushed the unit into place over the pit. This was the last ring section going on the storage tank. The next part to come off of the assembly line would be the top. He lowered it almost in place before he headed down the spiral stairs that ran along the outside of the pit. Each level had a landing and he looked down at the one below where one of his automated robots was welding the outside layer together. He was already glad he had designed the robots for multiple applications.

Before putting in the guide pins, he examined the inner weld. There were no issues as far as he could see, but he did note that the robot was almost empty of inert gas for the welder. That was one major downside of welding in an atmosphere.

He pulled out his tablet and sent an order to his storage. Soon one of his carts would be along with a fresh supply of gas. He was starting to run low on the supply Jasper brought him on the last trip. Alexander hadn't expected to go through it so fast. He would likely have to build a machine to harvest the gas from the atmosphere sooner rather than later.

Another item got added to his list.

Alexander didn't have any plans for a machine like that, but he could probably figure it out. It wasn't like they could be too complex, people were filtering atmospheric gasses back when he was human.

As he was adding the alignment pins, he saw the orange flashing light overhead that indicated his delivery had arrived. He finished putting the last pin in before heading back up. On the back of the cart were two seventy-five-pound cylinders full of argon. Since he didn't want to have to go back out there until the top was completed, he grabbed both tanks and lifted them as he walked back down the stairs. He didn't even need to stop the robot. He simply set one canister down, removed the empty one from the cart attached to the back of the robot, put a full one in its place, and then did the same for the nearly empty one. There was no pause in the welding and no sign that it had lost shielding.

Alexander went back up with the empty bottles and put them back in the cart. It drove away and he finished lowering the new section into place.

* * *

It was finally time to test his model engines. Three days had passed since he finished the fuel storage and checked it for leaks. The processing plant had been pumping out fuel ever since, so he had more than enough to do his initial tests.

The first engine, the Omni design, was already in place and ready to go. Unlike the time Alexander stood outside the railgun pit to watch the tests, he was well secured in a bunker a few hundred yards away for those.

That day he was observing everyone else work and taking Jasper's words to heart by delegating tasks. The group of people who had signed up and trained for that were going through the last-minute checks. Alexander could have done it all himself, but if he ever wanted to compete with companies like Omni or Sinorus, he needed skilled and capable people behind him.

Of course, Lucas and Gabriella had shown up for that important milestone. Damien was busy with the Hawks, ensuring the last-minute training was completed with his new security teams. It would be up to that rather dour man to continue the training once the mercenaries were gone. Alexander had no issue with the man taking on that role, while Damien wasn't very likable he was focused.

Alexander knew why Lucas was there, the man was curious about anything technological, even to the point of staring at him sometimes. However, he never did ask about the robot body. However, why was Gabriella there? He didn't have a good read on the woman as he had only met her a handful of times, but she didn't come off as all that interested in technology or him in general.

It's possible she was only there to report back to Damien. He didn't mind, it wasn't like the tests could be hidden.

"Green across the board," someone said.

Lucas looked to him for the next steps, but Alexander simply smiled back. He had given the man an itinerary. If Lucas wanted to be the head of testing–which it sure seemed like he did–the man would need to figure some things out himself.

Seeing that Alexander wasn't going to give him a hint, the younger man sighed and dug around in his pockets until he produced a crumpled sheet. Alexander wanted to frown at the abuse Lucas put that poor sheet of paper through. Did the man not realize how hard it was to find suitable material in an alien world to make paper?

Since he thought about it, probably not. It wasn't like anyone used paper in that day and age. Alexander just liked the nostalgia factor of it. Plus, it was way easier to make paper than it was to make a new tablet.

After smoothing out the paper and glancing at what was written, the man tucked it away again. "Shunt fuel to the engine storage tank."

One of the operators pressed a few spots on a tablet and a red bar appeared on the holo display against the wall. Once the bar was full, the man disconnected and purged the line. It retracted behind an armored plate. Alexander had designed it that way to prevent any sort of explosion from back-feeding into the storage tank and bursting it apart.

Any explosion would be bad, but the small amount of fuel in the engine would only spread the radioactive liquid in a small area. If the storage tank burst, the entire area could become slightly more radioactive. At least the fuel wasn't explosive or flammable in its unfused state. That would be a nightmare.

"Test fire in five!" Lucas called.

After the countdown, Lucas pressed the ignition button. He could see people look around as a tingling sensation crawled along their skin. Even he could feel it.

"It's just the energy discharging into the fusion igniter," he stated calmly.

True to his word, a few moments later, a ghostly blue flame shot from the open pit where the engine was resting. Less than a second after that, the sound of the engine firing rolled over their bunker, causing a bit of dust to rain down.

He made a note to have the control center moved a lot farther away when he got around to testing full-size models.

The blue flame lasted fifteen seconds before it burned through the tiny amount of fuel it had been provided.

Alexander recorded the results, and the next two tests were prepped and run over the next eight hours.

The results were not what he expected, and he returned to his shop a bit annoyed. The Omni engine out-produced the Sinorus engine. There was no surprise there, but he thought his design changes would have had him way above either of the engine manufacturers or at least close. Turns out he wasn't nearly as proficient as he thought he was.

His engine performed so poorly that it failed halfway through the test. The time it did run for, it produced only a third of the thrust of the Sinorus engine.

Alexander had skipped over his first three designs and tested the fourth iteration—the first that the simulation software said would work. It did work if one could call that poor showing 'work.'

After arriving back in his shop, he marked that design as non-functional and began printing the other five. If none of them worked, he would need to step back and reassess what he was doing wrong.

CHAPTER 56

"Is it that day already?" Alexander asked Matthews over the video conference.

"We have a few days yet, but we are going to begin pulling our people back to the ship. I just thought you could use the heads up."

"Thanks for the notice. I wish you could stay longer, but I understand why you can't."

"You may see some of our people sooner than you think. I believe Travers and Jallen have expressed interest in coming back here once their contracts are complete."

Alexander put a surprised expression on his avatar's face. "Really? Why?"

Matthews chuckled, a rare thing for the no-nonsense man. "It's not for the scenic beauty, I can tell you that. I think it might have something to do with the free access to learning modules you have provided to the people who live at Eden's End. I've heard a few of our engineers expressing interest as well. Heck, even I'm interested, and my retirement is coming up soon."

"I honestly don't know what to say. I didn't think it was such a big deal."

"That's what I like about you, Mr. Kane. You are a generous sort of guy, a bit too generous I might add. If someone tried to do what you were doing in STO space, the company that made those learning modules would slap you with a lawsuit faster than you could blink. There isn't anything the monopolies hate more than losing their profits and sharing a learning module that is supposed to be for a single person with thousands would certainly cost them money. Getting their attention is not something you want."

"I'm aware," he muttered.

The captain nodded. "I figured you might be aware of that particular problem. Most people who come out here do it to get away from STO or the corporations for one reason or another. Just be careful who you allow in your little community. There are those who would gladly take advantage of you for this opportunity or try to take it from you by force. I can't even say for certain if the corporations wouldn't try something more unsavory. There is more than one corporation with its own private military forces. While I find the STO to be useless most of the time, being under their jurisdiction does have its benefits—benefits that you have waived. You have some decent defenses, but never assume they are infallible. That's about the only advice I can offer."

"Thank you, Captain Matthews. And thank your people for their stellar job here. Without them, I doubt half as much would have been accomplished this soon."

"Speaking of accomplishments, congratulations on your successful engine test."

Alexander grimaced at that. "It's not quite successful yet."

He had tested the rest of his engine iterations and found them all to perform far poorer than the Sinorus model, except the last one, which was almost a carbon copy of the Omni design with only a few changes to make it his own. Unfortunately, even that one didn't outperform the Omni engine.

"Yes, but the numbers are promising. You went from never having designed or built an engine, to having one that beats out one of the major manufacturers. You just need to take a step back and realize this. Do you think either of those companies got off the ground in only a few months?"

"No." He sighed. "I know what you're saying is true, it's just hard for me to accept."

The man laughed. "Considering all the crazy stuff you have been doing in the last nine months, I'm not surprised that failure is a hard concept to accept. Someone once told me that you learn far more from failures than you would ever learn from success, so fail and learn, Kane. If you keep at it, I expect when we return, you will have some of the most powerful and efficient engines around."

They discussed a few other topics, mostly the station, which was partially operational.

It was just the smelter and a storage area to contain the raw ore for now. He was still working on getting fuel storage and processing up there but the challenges of getting those components into space were significantly harder using only the launcher. It took redesigning the fuel storage multiple times before he managed a design that could fit into the capsules and be formed by his robots once it was in place. He hadn't gotten around to manufacturing those components yet.

He needed to make that happen soon though, especially with the Hawks leaving.

Na and his crew had gone back to their ship about a month before and were deep in the outer belt of the system, scanning asteroids for mining. They would need to come in for fuel eventually. If he couldn't get fuel up there, they would be stuck drifting or relying on their maneuvering thrusters to get around.

Alexander hadn't spoken to Na much during the last few months. The few times he had, the man had expressed his concern over what had become of his home. Na was haunted by the fact he ran away and left Petrov Station to pirates—not that his being there would have changed that outcome. Explaining that fact to him didn't help, though.

Alexander hoped that going back to mining would help take his mind off of things in Gliese 667. From the little news coming out of this 'Pirate Incursion' as the news outlets were calling it, little had changed since the initial attack. There had been a few more signs of pirates lingering around the systems that the Hawks patrolled, but that had tapered off a few months back.

The going theory from SAM was that the Hawks' continued presence in the area had made the pirates move on to look for easier prey. Captain Matthews agreed with the machine's analysis based on his personal experience with pirates.

With the meeting concluded Alexander left the meeting room. He had a lot of things to complete in the next couple of days before the Hawks left.

* * *

Yulia hid behind a crate, doing her best to remain still and silent even though her heart was beating super fast. She had managed to avoid them for the last few days, but they had finally cornered her in the atrium.

There were no more places to run. The playground was on the far side of the camp and it was open ground all the way to it. They would spot her as soon as she left cover.

She heard footsteps nearby and froze, a dark shadow loomed over her, but the figure didn't turn to face her.

Instead, the woman cleared her throat. "Your friends were redirected to a different area, I suggest you hurry before they figure out you aren't there."

"Thank you, Zorina," she said quietly before darting out from her hiding spot and towards the safety of the playground.

"There she is!" one of the kids yelled.

The chase was on.

Yulia pushed her short legs as fast as she could as the screaming, laughing group of kids chased her in the game of tag. She learned early on after arriving at Eden's End that, while she was shorter, she was slightly stronger and faster than some of the kids born there. Not by much, but it was all she needed to barely avoid the lunging hand as she dove onto the playground mat with a triumphant shout. "Safe!"

"That's not fair," one of the kids grumbled.

"Yeah, you cheated!" one of the mean boys proclaimed.

"Cheated, how?" she asked indignantly, putting her fists against her waist.

The boy was not intimidated by her actions. "You got that soldier lady to give us false directions."

"No rule against outside help," Markus replied in his broken English.

The two boys were about the same age and neither one seemed to like the other very much. She wasn't quite sure why, but she was glad Markus was on her side.

She stuck her tongue out at the other boy who she hadn't even bothered to learn the name of. "See! Besides, I didn't ask for help. People just like me more than you."

The boy snorted and turned away from Markus. "Keep thinking that way, princess. Let's go. I'm bored with this game anyway."

A few of the kids left with the older boy, but some stuck around. They didn't seem to want to play tag anymore, and the few left decided to run over to the playground equipment instead.

"Why did he call me princess?" Yulia asked the only person left.

Markus sighed. "You know what a princess is, right?"

She shook her head. Yulia had never heard the term before.

"A princess is a girl that comes from wealth and power. Since you are the robot's daughter, and he owns this entire place, you are the princess."

She started to smile at that until Markus burst her happy little bubble.

"It's not meant as a compliment. They are being mean because they don't have the same advantages you have."

"That's not true," she began to argue.

"It's not? Why was the playground built? Sure, everyone else uses it, but the robot built it for you."

"Stop calling him that," she huffed. "His name is Alex!"

Markus just rolled his eyes. "Fine. Alex built it for you. He also hired the mercenaries for you and him. I even heard that he told someone that the only reason he is defending this place is to protect you and him. He doesn't care about the rest of the people here, never has."

"That's not true! You take that back!" Yulia got so angry, she tried to kick Markus in the shin.

He stepped back and she missed.

"I'm just telling you what I heard. You know how rumors spread. Remember on the station? I taught you to keep your ears and eyes open. How have you not heard people talking about these things?"

She had been listening to people. Sort of.

"Most adults don't talk a whole lot when I'm around."

"Because they are afraid of what Alex will do to them. They are afraid of you."

"No," she began to cry.

"I'm not telling you this to hurt your feelings, but you should know how people, the kids, and adults all see you. Even—"

"Even what?" she demanded through her tear-streaked eyes.

Markus sighed again. "Even your friends, Sarah and Claire are probably only pretending to be your friends because they think they can get something out of it, or their parents do."

"You're lying!" She wiped away the tears. "Why are you being so mean? Is it because I got adopted and you didn't?"

For the first time that she could remember, she saw Markus get angry. "Fine, don't believe me. See if I care." Then the boy walked off, leaving her to stew in confusion.

There were only two people she could turn to for answers. She didn't want to ask Alex about that, he would think it silly and he was busy fixing things.

Yulia found Zorina removing some tent poles that had been driven into the dry dirt of the atrium. She paused at that.

"Are you leaving?" tears began to well up in her eyes again.

The woman looked up from her work, giving Yulia a piercing stare that made her wish she wasn't being such a baby. After setting down the poles, the woman walked over.

"We are. You knew we would eventually, why are you crying?"

"I thought it wouldn't be for a while longer," Yulia muttered as she looked away and wiped off the tears.

"Is that the only reason?" the woman asked pointedly.

Yulia shook her head. She found she couldn't ever lie to the woman when she confronted her for doing something she shouldn't have been doing.

"Tell me what bothers you?"

She told Zorina about what Markus and the other boy said.

The woman nodded. "Your friend tells the truth—at least about what people say. I do not know your friends well, so I cannot say if that is true also."

"Why didn't you tell me?" Yulia demanded.

The woman only quirked an eyebrow at the outburst.

"Please," Yulia lowered her head at her shameful tone.

"Since you asked nicely, I will tell you. It was not important to our mission. People always talk down about people above them. It is the way things go. Telling you wouldn't have changed this fact, it would have only hurt your feelings. Your friend Markus could learn a lesson in tact, he shouldn't have told you this either."

"Isn't it better that I know?"

"Is it?" Zorina asked in reply. "From what I can see, all it has done is make you angry, and upset, and shoved a wedge in your friendship with Markus and the other children. Are you happy that happened?"

Yulia shook her head slowly.

"Of course, you aren't. Let me ask you another question. Do the kids treat you differently?"

"No?"

"You don't sound very sure of that."

"No. Well, some of the older kids do, but they never much liked me to begin with."

"Then their opinions don't matter. If you are happy with how the other kids treat you, then that's all that matters. But if you think this is important, I will relay this issue to my Field Leader, and they can bring it up with your father."

Yulia paused at that. She didn't want to make a big deal out of it, that was why she had gone to Zorina instead of going to Alex.

After thinking about it for a bit, she shook her head. "No... I can deal with the other kids."

Zorina smirked. "Good. Let this be a valuable lesson, Yulia. Sometimes, you have to solve your own issues. That doesn't mean you can't seek help or guidance from someone older and wiser though." With a wink, Zorina turned Yulia around and gave her a gentle shove. "Now, I have work to do."

CHAPTER 57

A small two-man ship floated silently in the system, its passive sensors watching for any change. The boredom wasn't even the worst part, it was the smell. Their little vessel stank after having to sit out there and scout for two weeks. It probably didn't help that the individuals inside weren't the most hygienic at the best of times. Their circumstances probably wouldn't improve anytime soon either as they had another week of monitoring before another ship came to relieve them.

They couldn't even get drunk anymore because their booze had run out after two days in that pointless system. The two pirates slept most of the time, played cards, or fought until one was knocked unconscious, which would have been the better outcome if the loser hadn't been forced to take the winner's shift watching the sensors.

Merkel gently touched his eye where Zarrick, that bastard crewmate of his, had given him a shiner the night before by sucker-punching him. While Zarrick got to sleep, he was stuck on double duty. The only thing worse than sleeping in that tin can was being awake in it. Merkel hated watch duty and even though he was supposed to stay alert, he nodded off a few times. Those naps didn't last long despite the fact he could barely keep his eyes open. The pain in his face kept jerking him awake. When he got back, he would find out who he pissed off to get that shitty assignment and stick a knife in them. Nobody deserved that bullshit.

As he was nodding off again, the console began flashing, jerking him back awake. It took him a moment to focus on the display. That didn't help. He was forced to use his shirt to rub the grime off the screen to even see what the alert was for. If it was one of those damn patrol ships again, he was going to scream.

What he saw was three distinct jump signatures. Hard not to see them, they were blasting the entire system with their scanners as they flew through. No pirate would do that.

Their ship was drifting dark with only emergency power on, and they were placed near an asteroid in the inner belt. The chances of the three ships spotting them were virtually nonexistent unless those ships got way closer, but he knew they wouldn't. They had picked that spot specifically because it was outside the travel lane of the scout ships. Well, technically their boss, Arkonis had chosen that spot.

Merkel doubted he would have thought about positioning himself so far away. When he ran down ships, he wanted to be as close as possible to a shipping lane so he could get the jump on his quarry.

He didn't bother waking Zarrick. Once those ships transitioned through the system, he would get them moving. If Zarrick questioned it, he would just say they got relieved early so he could claim the bonus their boss was handing out for being the crew to spot the mercs leaving. That was assuming he could hide the ships from his crewmate, which probably wouldn't be hard since Zarrick was a moron.

The last time Merkel had relieved him to take watch, the man had turned the console off because he said the buzzing sound was annoying him. How the idiot expected to detect anything with the console and passive sensors offline was beyond him. His crewmate didn't seem concerned.

Merkel watched as all three ships burned hard toward STO space. That was good. He figured roughly a day and a half, they would be out of the system and he could report to the boss. Then maybe he could finally get in on some real action.

* * *

"Boss!" the communications man yelled. "Scout ships back."

Arkonis shoved the woman off his lap and sat up in the bridge chair. "They best be reporting good news. If they left their post early, shoot them."

Nobody batted an eye at that.

"They say the mercenaries pulled out three days ago."

"'Bout damn time!" Arkonis clapped his hands and laughed. "Call in everyone, it's time for a big score!"

He got up from his seat and grabbed the affronted woman he had shoved aside.

The woman took a swipe at him, and he chuckled as he dodged the fist. She was certainly no delicate flower like his brother preferred. No, she was a real woman, a pirate, just like him.

"Call me when we are underway!" he yelled back into the bridge as he led the angry woman back to his cabin.

* * *

"If our informant screwed up these orbital paths, I'll string the bastard up myself when we land. Make sure you double-check the math."

The contact had sold them information on how many people were down there, the types of defenses in place, and even a general location of where they were. It was a bounty of information Arkonis would kill for on any raid—not that he was about to trust someone who was willing to sell out their own people for a measly hundred thousand credits.

"I will, boss! Although, our friend here knows what'll happen to him if he tries to fudge the numbers, don't ya?" The pirate enforcer smiled a gap-toothed smile at the man chained to the pilot's station.

The man nodded frantically and the rest of the crew laughed.

Their pilot had been an acquisition last year along with another ship. Arkonis had trained pilots, but it was hard to beat a former STO Navy pilot. He had been on some vacation in an outer territory when the headhunter descended upon the hapless vessel. The man took a bit to break before he fell in line, but his days of defiance were over. It was also much quieter now that the man didn't have his tongue to flap around.

"Jump in ten," his enforcer called out. "Alert the rest of the fleet to wait ten minutes and to stagger their jumps. I don't want any hot-headed bastards giving our positions away. We need to deal with their weapons before they become a problem."

"Orders sent."

Arkonis smiled as the stars twisted around them, and they vanished from the system. When they reappeared two hours later, they were facing a large gas giant, far enough away that their field hadn't been destabilized too much.

"Report!" he ordered.

"We are exactly where we expected to be, boss, right behind the largest planet in the system. If the orbital chart was correct, our target planet should be on the opposite side of the system. There's no way they could pick up our inbound jump with the gas giant masking it."

"Good, set a trajectory and go dark. We will coast in nice and slow. Once we see nothing has changed, we'll launch our present."

The ship moved on an intercept course for Eden's End. Soon other ships joined them as they jumped into the same area. As they closed the distance, their passive sensors began to get a better visual of what awaited them.

"Looks mostly the same, but the station is much larger than our informant claimed. I don't see any armaments on it. We are still too far out to tell for sure."

Arkonis frowned at this, he didn't like surprises. "Show me the station."

A grainy image appeared on the holo display. Arkonis almost laughed when he saw the thing. "It's a refueling and dumping station. I doubt it'll have weapons, but that does help us out. Anything else to note?"

"Nothing we can see. The same asteroids where they hid their cameras are floating in orbit. No ships around the planet. Our man did say an ore hauler had entered the system, but I'm not picking it up on our passives. Maybe it left with the mercenaries? Can't imagine why it would stick around."

"Once we engage, turn on active scanners. I want to know everything in this system."

He really needed to invest in better passive sensors, a more updated system could pick up active transponders in passive mode, but the cost irked him.

The slow passage across the system was nearly unbearable, but they needed to get closer to deliver their gift.

After a day, he finally heard what he had been waiting for.

"We're in range to fire."

"Well, let's not keep them waiting," Arkonis smiled widely.

The ship shuddered multiple times as missile tubes opened up and the rails launched their payload at the slowest possible speed. A total of twelve missiles left the ship, two for each orbital railgun installation. Thirty seconds later, one last missile left the ship. The ship was on an intercept course for the planet, and the missiles would coast ahead of them, slowly gaining distance to arrive ahead of them. When it was time, they would light their engines and streak toward their targets.

The people of Eden's End would see the weapons at that point, but by then it would be too late. Assuming their inside man had done his job correctly, there wouldn't be a single orbital railgun left standing. Arkonis hedged his bets though. That was what the last missile was for. If it wasn't needed, it could be retrieved and set into safe mode again.

It was a shame he had to destroy the powerful surface weapons, he could have easily repurposed them for his flagship. Then maybe he could carve out a chunk in his brother's new empire or get rid of him and take it all for himself. Arkonis smiled. It was good to have goals.

* * *

Alexander was working on his engine design when the facility shook slightly. Then it shook again and again. He quickly realized it was the railguns firing. An even louder boom shook the facility a moment later, followed by two more before the facility alarms finally went off. He heard the smaller railguns burst to life, their muted booms shaking dust off the walls as they sent hypersonic darts at something.

The overhead speaker crackled to life but fell silent almost immediately as all of the power cut out.

As soon as the power died, a red warning flashed across Alexander's internal display.

[WARNING EMP DETECTED!]

All of that happened in the span of twenty seconds. His mind quickly parsed what was going on and he decided he needed to make sure his daughter was safe. He rushed out of the room to find Yulia.

The entire facility was eerily quiet until emergency lights and power started to flicker back to life. He tried the small radio he carried, but it was dead. He wondered how he was still alive. An EMP should have shut him down. Especially one powerful enough to disable power in the facility. The fact that the guns had fallen silent was not a good sign.

"Pirate attack! Get to the shelters!" someone screamed over the comm system as it crackled back to life.

Red flashing lights and alarms began to blare across the complex as people rushed to safety.

"Alexander, report to security," Damien said over the comm, obviously replacing the hysterical man from before.

Dammit! He didn't have time to rush to security, he needed to find Yulia. He quickly realized she could be anywhere. Without knowing where to start, trying to find her could be a waste of very precious time. Quickly debating the pros and cons of trying to track down his daughter, he turned down the next path and raced for the security station.

Yulia was smart, she would go to her shelter area and Damien would not have called on him if it wasn't important.

He arrived at the security room a few minutes later. "What's going on?"

"Pirates hit three of the orbital railguns. We took out the rest of the missiles, but the bastards set off a nuke in orbit," the man stated grimly. "The resultant EMP forced a system reset."

"The external defenses!" Alexander said in realization.

With the facility's ancient computer core in the process of being rebuilt by Lucas, Alexander hadn't seen the point of connecting the new guns to the facility's power grid. That and the cost of running that much high-voltage cable to the gun pits had made it a low priority. It had been much easier and more efficient to hook up his batteries to an array of solar panels. The batteries for the guns stored enough power to empty the magazines, so recharging them quickly wasn't all that important for him. He was regretting that decision now.

"All down. Your fancy new internal defenses as well."

"What do we have for weapons?" Alexander asked instead of freaking out.

If he could get out there, he could reset one of the guns.

"The pulse rifles should still work. However, they won't do much against pirates with nukes."

"If they were willing to nuke the facility, they wouldn't have detonated it in orbit. They want something, and my guess is that something has to do with me."

Damien grunted in agreement. "If I thought the pirates would simply leave us be if they got to you, I might be inclined to step aside and let them."

"How very shrewd," Alexander responded coldly.

The man shrugged. "If they wanted me and it would save the rest of the people here, wouldn't you do the same?"

Alexander's silence spoke volumes.

"I thought so." Damien smirked slightly. "At least that makes you human."

"You need more weapons."

"Preferably, but I doubt you have time to print more even if the printers came back online."

"They didn't," he replied. At least he hadn't bothered to check on them before he left to search for Yulia before being called there. "We have CQB rifles at all the entrance turrets. Get your people down to the entrances and have them pry the turrets open. The rifles should be easy enough to remove, but they aren't exactly set up for standard use. Still, it'll be better than trying to stun the pirates."

The man nodded and sent out another communication over the station comm. "We can only hope people are in those areas. It's not like they can communicate back with us unless they get to a nearby terminal."

Alexander nodded, but the man just looked at him. He realized his holo-projector was burned out in the attack. Not that again, he groaned internally.

"Do the best you can. Do you know where Yulia might be or how long we have?"

"She would have headed to her designated bunker. I don't have enough people to send them on a wild goose chase looking for her if you think she didn't... I'm sorry. As for when the pirates arrive, no clue. We don't exactly have an uplink to our satellites anymore. My guess is they would have waited well back of that detonation though. So ten to fifteen minutes before ships start descending from orbit would be my guess."

The man's rebuke over his daughter stung, but he was right. It didn't make Alexander want to punch him in the face any less, though. Before he could do something rash, he stomped out of the security room. It was no time to start a fight.

"Where are you going?" Damien asked.

"To try to reset one of the railguns. Unless you think the pirates will simply sit back and let us kill them while they have a ship in orbit overhead."

The man had no response to that and Alexander picked up speed as he raced down the hallway as fast as his servos would carry him. He had never gone full out with this body, it was time to put it to the test.

As the walls blurred past him, he focused on the problem at hand. There was no tunnel leading to the railguns, which meant he needed to head outside. He had separated the gun pits from the rest of the complex to protect it in case the weapons failed catastrophically. He never figured the failure would have been caused by pirates.

If they survived that attack, he would need to address that oversight as soon as possible. Having to go onto the surface to fix a weapon platform while under attack seemed like a monumentally stupid idea. Alexander hoped he could reset the connection to the turret or that little stunt would be a complete waste of time.

The exit door came up fast and Alexander was forced to slow as he encountered his first obstacle. The door control was burned out. He ripped a panel off the wall with a screech of tearing metal and reached for the manual release. The ratchet-style mechanism was slow as hell, but he was glad it was there. After thirty seconds, he finally got the doors open wide enough so he could pass through.

The sun was beginning to set and Alexander could see the remnants of the electromagnetic disturbance over the facility from the detonation. The shockwaves resembled an aurora, it would almost be pretty if he didn't know what caused it. He didn't stand around to admire them as he raced across the landing pad and toward one of the railguns.

As he quickly covered the distance, he could see two black clouds on the far side of the facility and one on the closer side. He zoomed in on the closest cloud. There were broken solar panels and the twisted wreckage of the gun sticking out of the destroyed weapon installation. They had indeed managed to target the guns—thankfully, not all of them. The thin lines of smoke rising in the distance must have been the remaining missiles.

He quickly added them up, including the three impacts he heard. There were a total of twelve. Someone had used enough weapons to ensure two per gun. If the smaller guns hadn't come online, all of the weapons would have been turned into twisted scrap. There was no way the bigger guns could fire and reload fast enough to stop two missiles simultaneously.

That meant someone knew about the defenses. Had someone betrayed them?

With that chilling thought, he pushed his body even harder, getting angry orange lights popping up in his vision. He ignored them.

Alexander thought about trying to get the landing pad guns back online, but he only had time to reactivate one gun. While the landing pad guns would deter any landing for a short time, the turrets wouldn't be able to do anything about the ships in orbit. Sooner or later, the pirates would destroy the smaller gun and come down.

As he neared the pit, he thanked whoever was on duty in the security room for being diligent. Any delay and the guns may not have even activated and he would either be sprinting toward a burning pit or a sealed weapon hatch.

Alexander jumped down the service ladder at the side of the gun, falling forty feet and landing with a loud boom as he hit the grating at the bottom of the pit. The metal caved in below his weight, but he simply yanked his legs out of the hole and ran to the main breaker.

He flicked the breaker back on, but all he heard was a loud buzzing sound coming from the power supply. There was no sign of movement from the weapon overhead.

He quickly thought over the problem.

The buzzing meant the power was working. The capacitors would need time to recharge from the batteries since they were designed to dump their energy into a grounded connection if the breaker tripped so they didn't damage the wiring. However, there should have been enough power to move the gun. The fact it wasn't moving meant the fuses in the gun itself had popped. Since all of the power for the gun and the rotary mechanism went through those fuses, he needed to replace them to get it working again.

Alexander designed them to be sensitive to power spikes to prevent any damage to the weapons. It seemed he would need to redesign them to take into account EMPs now.

He flipped the breaker back off before he ran over to a nearby cabinet and tore it open since he didn't have time to enter the code. He grabbed two of the massive replacement fuses and hurried over to the gun. Normally the weapon would be in standby mode for changing those out. The fact it wasn't in that mode would have been a real issue for anyone who wasn't an eight-foot-tall robot. That was another design flaw he would have to correct in the next iteration.

Alexander yanked the service panel off the weapon and pulled the blown fuses out, replacing them with the two new ones. Then he ran back over and flipped the breaker back on. The gun jerked into motion, and he nearly sighed in relief before it settled back into storage mode.

"What? No! Move, dammit!"

When he looked at the maintenance terminal, he saw the gun was resetting due to numerous faults being detected.

He cursed himself for having built these fail-safes into the gun as he climbed the ladder back out of the pit. The gun would take time to ensure all the systems were working properly before it would activate again, but they didn't have time.

As he exited the pit, he could already see the telltale streaks of shuttles descending from orbit. Without enhancing his vision, he could even see a ship slowing as it fired its landing and takeoff thrusters to maintain a stationary orbit over the facility. The ship had to be quite low for him to see it without zooming in.

There was no more time to get any other guns working. Alexander rushed back to the facility door and shut it behind him just as he heard the flare of engines.

CHAPTER 52

"Alex!" Yulia shouted as she ran into his workshop in a panic. He wasn't there. The place was as quiet as everywhere else. She had been heading home from classes when the lights went out. Then the voice on the speaker said there was a pirate attack. She knew she should have headed straight for the shelter, but she was afraid to do so alone.

Shortly after she called out, the voice of the scary security guy called Alex to the security room. Now that she knew where to look, she did her best to hurry over there. It was a long way to the security station from Alex's shop and before she got there, the building shook around her, sending her falling to the ground.

She screamed and tucked her head in her hands, fearing the worst, when she heard footsteps.

"There you are!" a familiar voice called.

Yulia peeked through her arms and saw Markus running towards her.

"You were supposed to go to the shelter, why didn't you?"

"I—I was looking for Alex. Why didn't you go?"

The boy sighed and picked her up off the floor. "I had a feeling you weren't going to follow instructions. When I heard them called to the security room, I came this way to stop you. Do you think he would be happy to know you weren't heading for safety?"

She shook her head, not meeting the older boy's gaze.

"Let's go."

Markus pulled her, but she resisted. "What about Alex? I need to find him."

"No," Markus said in annoyance. "He's busy, and we're kids. We'll just get in his way. Now come on, or I'll drag you."

Yulia didn't want to be dragged so she hurried behind Markus as fast as she could.

Loud booms started to echo through the halls and Markus stopped at an intersection, cursing under his breath as he looked for where to go.

"I don't know this section. Which way to the closest shelter?"

"I only know where my designated shelter is," Yulia admitted in embarrassment. "And that's near atrium B."

The boy cursed again, and Yulia wanted to tell him to stop or Headmaster Wong would give him a talking-to, but it did feel like a time that cursing might be allowed.

"We need to find someplace safe. Someplace the—" Markus' words trailed off as loud shouting came from down one hallway.

The shouting was followed by a series of loud pops that echoed through the halls and a buzzing crack that made her tense up. She remembered that sound from the attack at Alex's.

"This way, quickly," he whispered as they ran in the other direction.

* * *

Zade chuckled darkly as one of the shuttles impacted the landing pad faster than it should have and exploded. "More for us!" he yelled to the cheers of his crew.

He would have preferred that shuttle to have been Arkonis' that way he could have taken over the crew, but it wasn't. That was unfortunate, but there was still a chance the man would get himself killed down there. The old bastard was going on forty-five. He was a relic and should have done everyone a favor and gone down in a raid a long time ago.

Arkonis was also a coward who liked to run raids from the rear instead of getting his hands dirty. The pampered little prince might as well have moved into STO space and lived there if he wanted safety. This place was too big for him to hide behind his other teams that time, though. Other than skeleton crews left to monitor the ships in orbit, everyone was down there. Maybe he could accidentally fire a grenade in his boss' direction. It was certainly an option.

The ship flared its thrusters hard and Zade grunted under the pressure. He didn't black out though. If he did, someone on his team probably would have shot him in the back at the first opportunity and taken his place as the leader of his crew. It was as it should be: the weak should be culled and the strong should rule.

Even with the extreme deceleration, their landing was a hard one. The planet's atmosphere was so thin that he was pushing his luck with a ship that large. He had the biggest crew besides the boss' and he would be damned if he wasn't taking everything he could from that miserable rock.

It better be worth it because the cost of that nuke had come out of everyone's share.

He checked his armor. Unlike the grunts, his was the best money could buy off the black market. It had military-grade armor plating and even had minor augmentation making it nearly as good as the mech suits the STO used. He smiled and lifted the heavy grenade launcher. Since he liked to lead from the front, he got to breach the doors.

What better way to lead than with a big boom?

The ramp lowered and his crew hollered in glee as they followed him off the ship. He almost paused when he saw the turrets, but if they had been active, they would have shot by now.

"Maybe that nuke was worth it after all." He smiled wickedly as he let a series of grenades fly toward the entry at the far end of the landing pad.

A satisfying series of explosions rattled the thin air before the tone changed.

"Door's open, boys!"

His crew streamed past him, hoping to be the first to claim a kill or something good. Zade just stuck the launcher on his back where it magnetically attached before he drew his minigun. He spun it up, smiling widely at the sound before he joined his people who were already forcing their way inside and firing on whoever was dumb enough to resist.

The only thing he heard was the buzzing crack of pulse rifles. He shoved the broken door aside and his people hit the deck as the defenders all turned to look his way. The bullets from his minigun tore through them before they even had a chance to fire more than a few blasts his way.

One man held a strange weapon and fired it at him, but the flechette ricocheted harmlessly off his armor. In annoyance more than anger, Zade hosed the man down and kept the trigger pulled as he stomped forward, turning the man into a red paste on the ground before he finally ran out of ammo.

He tsked in annoyance and unlatched the weapon and the ammo canister, dropping it by the door. He picked up one of the rifles from his dead men, replaced the magazine and his team stalked forward looking for more targets.

* * *

Alexander felt more than heard the next explosion as something came down just outside the door he was at. At first, he thought maybe the turrets came back on, but when no further explosions happened, he realized that wasn't the case.

Then he heard muted gunfire and booms. This was followed by a long series of shots from some fully automatic weapon. The people in Eden's End had nothing comparable to that and he knew that things were going to get much worse if he couldn't come up with a solution.

He made for his workshop as fast as he could go. There were parts in there. Maybe he could put together something to help.

Alexander crossed an intersection when someone shouted from down the hall and a hail of bullets came his way. He was moving so quickly that they missed or slammed into the walls behind him.

[WARNING HOSTILE FIRE DETECTED!]

Alexander wanted to roll his eyes at the stupid message. Of course, he knew 'hostile fire' was detected. He tried to will away the message, but it stayed front and center for a bit before it seemed to go away on its own. 'What? No defensive mode, or ultimate badass mode?' The mind space didn't reply, it never did. He saw no changes to the other readouts, most of which he still didn't understand.

He took the next turn, ensuring the people who were now chasing him couldn't get a clear shot. He still wasn't convinced this body was bulletproof, and from the sounds of it, the pirates had much heavier weapons. He had spotted one of them wearing an augment suit with something large strapped to its back. That single pirate could take on this entire facility without issue.

His workshop came into sight, and he ducked inside and shut the door before locking it by placing a piece of scrap barstock in the track to jam it closed.

Alexander quickly looked around for something he could use to fight back with. The workshop had accumulated quite a series of failed tests and components ever since the smelter had been moved into orbit. However, one thing caught his eye.

It was the railgun from his very first tests. He dragged it out from the pile of scraps. The cables were still connected to it, but it had no power source. Since it was offline during the EMP, it should be functional. How was he going to power it?

Alexander scanned the room for any batteries or power banks, but there were none. Then he looked at the flashing warning light for the station alarm.

"Power is power," he muttered as he dragged the weapon over to the wall just as someone started pounding on his door.

He worked as fast as he could to modify the internal capacitor of the gun so it would only discharge when he was ready. It wouldn't be a very high-power shot, but with any luck, it would work. Alexander just needed time.

* * *

"Doors wedged shut," one of his people stated.

Zade didn't have time for that shit. A closed door meant there was likely something valuable behind it.

"Move!" he yelled as he backed away from the door and pulled the launcher off his back again.

Each explosive cost a hundred credits, which is why he mainly used it for breaching, but he had a good feeling about that door. The first blast rocked the hallway, sending dust and debris flying, but the door was stronger than it looked. The explosion had dented it quite heavily though, so one or two more would get them in.

The third time was the charm as he heard the metal shriek in protest before it blew inward. He hoped it didn't kill anyone inside. He wanted to do that personally for making him waste his time and money.

Zade stepped through the blasted opening and saw a treasure trove of high-end electronics and manufacturing equipment, but his eyes focused on the robot at the far side of the room—the one they had been chasing. Arkonis had told them to be on the lookout for it as it had something to do with the person they were there to capture. That didn't mean he couldn't disable it, though. He smiled, as the thing wasn't even facing him. He flicked the selector to burst fire and shot off three grenades.

They screamed across the room… and stopped.

* * *

Alexander would have blinked if he had eyes. He heard the attempts to get into his shop and knew it was only a matter of time until they would succeed. Once the door blew open, he watched them with a part of his focus as he put the finishing touches on the railgun he was hiding from view.

He hadn't expected the man to fire three grenades his way as soon as he entered or the message that popped up when they flew his way.

[WARNING THREAT DETECTED!]
[COUNTERMEASURES DEPLOYED]
[DEFENSE FIELD ACTIVATED]

The messages popped up so fast that he couldn't even react. A static hum built around him in the time it took the grenades to cross the room. The three grenades slammed into the field and simply stopped about a foot in front of him. Alexander was shocked by this. He expected them to maybe be deflected by this strange defense field. That was not the simple static field ships used to deflect space debris. It was bordering on a freaking forcefield.

A stray thought entered his mind. If his body had something like that, how the hell had it been damaged in the first place?

It seemed everyone was just as shocked to see that as he was because the pirates stopped and stared. It was a good thing Alexander's mind worked much faster to process the new situation. He plucked the three explosives out of the air and chucked them back toward the pirates.

Unfortunately, there must have been some sort of timer or proximity awareness fuse on the weapons because they detonated far short of his target, tearing up the room. The explosion had the additional effect of knocking the pirates out of their shock. As they recovered, they quickly opened fire at him.

The strange field stopped every bullet, but he saw the man with the augment suit was getting ready to fire again after having adjusted something on his weapon.

Not willing to risk a second round of explosives, Alexander stepped aside, exposing the railgun.

It was already loaded with a spare round he found in the same pile he dug it out from. The man with the grenade launcher had just enough time to realize what was facing him before Alexander touched the exposed wire to the firing mechanism.

The crack of the hypersonic round was deafening inside the workshop and the blast of its passing kicked up dust and sent loose parts scattering around the room. Fortunately, it found its mark and passed effortlessly into the man's armored front.

Alexander was worried about the round going through the facility walls. Turned out he needn't have worried. Much like his early tests, the round failed to penetrate the back side of the armor. Unlike those early tests, there was a squishy human between those plates. The energy had to go somewhere. The man exploded like a water balloon as shards of tungsten flew out the sides hitting three more pirates who were standing next to him.

The sonic boom and resultant human explosion had done a significant amount of damage to the pirates as well, leaving the few survivors groaning on the ground.

Disconnecting the gun, Alexander hurried over to make sure they didn't get back up. He took no comfort in picking up one of their rifles and dispatching them, but it had to be done.

He grabbed a small rolling cart that had been knocked over during the fight and loaded the pirates' weapons onto them. Even the grenade launcher was loaded onto the cart. Once everything was piled on top, he pushed it out through the opening and toward the next entry point.

He didn't know if his new defense field would stay active forever, so he needed to make it count while it was.

chapter 59

Arkonis ground his teeth in annoyance from inside his powered armor suit. He had seen one of the shuttles go down as his shuttle was landing on the far side of the facility. The crash was likely due to pilot incompetence. He was certain all the people aboard were dead. If the pilot had somehow survived, he would have shot the man anyway.

Their deaths were inconsequential since there were always new raiders on Haven willing and able to join a crew. Hell, he could even pick up more raiders on the other pirate outposts scattered around the outside of STO space, but a shuttle... A shuttle cost *him* money. No matter what his crews might like to think, everything they used belonged to him.

He made a mental note to replace the leader of that crew. His third in command preferred to play captain instead of raiding and never got his hands dirty unless he had to or was ordered to.

Arkonis preferred to let his people do as they pleased because it kept them happier most of the time, but it seemed he had been too lenient. Perhaps he needed to take a more hands-on approach like his brother. His life would be so much easier if all of his crews were led by thick-headed idiots like his second-in-command, Zade. Zade might be a loose cannon and a threat to his role as leader, but that's what made him such an effective pirate. Idiots were much easier to control.

The shuttle touched down and his people raced toward the door to force it open. Unlike Zade, who he could already hear firing into the facility, Arkonis preferred an approach that damaged as little as possible. He could make money from even unexpected things like door controllers, so why damage them if he didn't need to?

By the time he strode into the building, his people had already dealt with the few guards at this entrance. He had picked this side specifically because it showed the fewest signs of activity. They would have quite the trek to get to where the action and likely the best loot was, but he didn't care. He got a cut of everything anyway and he only had one other goal there.

"Send out the seekers, I want to know where our quarry is."

The man he addressed nodded and dumped out a sack of orb drones. Then he began tossing them into the air after activating the little devices. Someone dragged over a crate the defenders had been using to hide behind and Arkonis took a seat on it while his people monitored the drone feeds. He wasn't about to go searching the place on foot—it would be like looking for credits in an asteroid belt.

The building shook and everyone turned as dusty air blew past them. It wasn't a strong breeze, but this place shouldn't have any breezes.

Arkonis knew a shockwave when he saw it. "What the hell was that?"

"I don't know, Boss."

Arkonis turned to the man, and he flinched. "Find out!"

The local idiots shouldn't have any active weapons systems after his EMP, but if they got one of the external railguns working, their liftoff could be in danger.

"We managed to triangulate the point of origin," the tech said.

Arkonis focused on the projection that moved to the front of the holo display. It showed a scene of carnage. An entire team of pirates; dead inside a room filled with expensive-looking manufacturing machines. If he wasn't mistaken, the charred armor lying on the ground—covered in gore—belonged to his second in command, Zade.

The drone zipped to the back of the workshop where a cobbled-together railgun sat near a set of exposed wires from the local power grid.

"Pack it up. We're leaving," he stated as he began to stand.

Before anyone could reply, there was a loud crack followed by a much stronger shockwave. That time it originated from outside the facility.

He rushed out the door and looked up in the sky, just in time to see one of the ships hovering in orbit burst apart as something slammed into it. It was one of the smaller pirate ships but still.

Arkonis pressed the radio button on his suit. "Move the fucking ships out of orbit! They have a railgun online!"

There was no response to his command, but the ships started getting smaller quickly. The idiots should have been paying attention the entire time. They would have seen the gun activating.

The ships weren't fast enough. The massive ground-based weapon fired again, sending the hypersonic round tearing through yet another vessel.

Arkonis screamed in inarticulate rage and stormed back into the facility. He couldn't order the ships in orbit to fire down on the surface, those idiots were just as likely to kill him as they were to hit their target.

"Find me the godsdamned control room. NOW!"

* * *

When Alexander finally heard the orbital railgun fire, he let out a quiet sigh of relief. The attack wasn't over by any means, but the one working gun would limit the pirates' options.

He was approaching another gunfight. It was clear by the growing sounds of weapons firing back and forth.

When he rounded a corner, he spotted a group of twenty locals behind a makeshift barricade. They had somehow gotten their hands on some of the pirates' guns and were using them to keep another group of pirates pinned down at the far side of the hallway at an intersection. What he wasn't expecting to see was Eva Wu leading the defense.

The woman must have heard him coming because she ducked away from the battle and leveled the gun she was holding on him. "Alexander!" she exclaimed. "Why are you out here? You should be with your daughter."

"I could ask you the same thing."

"I'm just doing my part," she stated casually.

"I can see that." He glanced down at the gun she was holding.

She smirked. "This isn't my first tussle with pirates." She glanced over at his cart, "And maybe not yours either."

"They attacked my workshop, I got lucky. Do any of your people need guns or ammo?"

She whistled, the sound cut through the noise of battle and three people dashed toward them in a crouch as the return fire subsided for a bit.

"What's up, Eva?" one of the men asked.

"Distribute the weapons to anyone who needs one. Top them off with any ammo that's compatible."

One of the guys attempted to lift the launcher, but it was way too heavy. Alexander walked over and easily picked it up, earning some whistles of approval from the gathered people.

"How many rounds you got for that thing?" Eva asked.

"I'm honestly not sure. I kinda just stuffed everything on the cart and hurried over to the closest fight."

They quickly counted out ten rounds.

"If you don't mind, could you clear out the far end of this hallway with them? I fear some of the pirates are trying to flank us, but if we leave this spot, they will simply rush the barricade."

"Gladly," Alexander said, walking over to the barricade without a worry.

Eva tried to stop him, but he watched her pause as the pirates started firing on him. Their bullets seemed to stop in mid-air until he passed, and then they fell to the ground, all their momentum lost. He aimed the large grenade launcher down the hall and fired three times.

The pirates either didn't realize what was going on or were too stupid to seek cover. The hallway went eerily silent after Alexander's exchange.

"What was that?" Eva finally said, running up to him.

He shrugged. "Just a feature I learned about recently."

The woman looked like she wanted to know more, but she simply nodded. "Uh-huh. Thanks for the help. Now we can start pushing the pirates back. Maybe we can even link up with more security teams."

"I'll leave you to it. Like you said, I should be looking for my daughter."

"Good luck, and stay safe, Alexander."

"You too, Eva."

* * *

"Sir, we found something!" one of the techs exclaimed.

"If it's not the weapons control room, it better be damn good!"

"It's the little girl—the one you said we could use as leverage."

Finally, some good news. That damn railgun had been firing every twenty seconds, and he was unsure of the status of his fleet because these damn walls were disrupting radio communications.

"Where?"

The man presented a map with a glowing path. "Two of you guard this door. The rest, with me."

If he couldn't find that control room, a hostage would be an acceptable alternative.

His people raced through the winding halls of this massive complex, avoiding or ambushing defenders when they could, but the resistance was starting to increase as they made their way deeper inside. Instead of running into teams of defenders with only pulse rifles, they started running into scattered groups of locals with scavenged pirate weapons. He knew they were pirate weapons because the vast majority of them had kill tally marks on them.

Arkonis was so angry that the raid was going sideways he crushed one of the weapons in his augmented grip.

"We're almost there. Pick up the pace!"

The girl in question and a slightly older boy with her were running for all they were worth since spotting the drone trailing them. However, they were children. They couldn't outrun adults forever.

His raiders came around a corner and he spotted his quarry just turning down the next hallway. He smiled wickedly and raced after them, not bothering to wait for his people who were far slower than he was in his augmented armor.

He rounded the corner and slowed to a stop.

The kids were running toward another target he had been looking for. The robot.

Cursing, he rushed forward. A useless cargo robot was no match for his state-of-the-art armor. He doubted even the STO military had armor as advanced as his. Hell, he knew they didn't. When the STO turned down the outrageously expensive contract for that armor, the company that made it turned to the private sector for sales. Plenty of corporate bigwigs wanted the best of the best—they actually made more money that way. It was easy to get them to sell a pair of the suits to him. More specifically, his shell company.

It was clear the company he had purchased the armor from had not done their due diligence and looked into his company's records. His company's records wouldn't have passed even minor scrutiny. Maybe they did and simply didn't care since most STO companies only cared about money. They didn't care where it came from.

He almost laughed when the robot told the children to keep running.

The thing raised the grenade launcher it had taken off of his second in command at him and pulled the trigger.

When the weapon failed to fire, Arkonis laughed. "Best armor and EW suite money can buy. Don't worry, though. I'll make sure your adopted daughter remains alive and mostly unharmed. You just need to turn yourself over to me."

Arkonis didn't know or care if his words had gotten through to the man behind the machine. His EW module had probably fried the dumb thing's electronics already, but he would know that his daughter had been captured. That would be enough.

Arkonis went to skirt around the inert robot when a hand shot out, wrapping around his bicep. He was jerked to a halt so fast it felt like his arm had almost been ripped out of its socket.

"W-What?" he asked as the robot lifted him into the air with little effort.

"What did you say about my daughter?"

Arkonis didn't have time to respond as the robot smashed him against the floor like a child throwing a temper tantrum with a stuffed animal. He groaned as the armor started spitting out damage notifications in the HUD.

"Nobody will lay a finger on my daughter... *ever*!"

Arkonis pulled his pistol out and fired it point-blank into the robot's torso. He wasn't sure why it was still active, but the armor-piercing rounds should have been enough to damage the robot so he could free himself. Then he could finish it off.

The bullets ricocheted off whatever material the exterior of the robot was made of, only leaving small chips on the surface.

Before he could fire again, the robot crushed his hand around the gun and swung him into the wall with a reverberating boom. The impact gel absorbed some of the damage, but he coughed, and blood speckled the inside of his armored faceplate. If he didn't free himself or disable the damn robot, he wasn't going to last long.

Then the sweet sound of gunfire erupted. He smiled despite the pain. His people had arrived.

* * *

Alexander held the armored man, his rage over the man's threat not yet quelled. Fortunately, he wasn't blinded by it like he had been when Yulia was injured aboard Petrov Station. He kept one eye on the fleeing pair of children. When he saw the pirates rounding the corner and raising their weapons, he stepped into the hallway to block any possible bullets from hitting the kids.

The pirate hung loosely in his hand, but even he was saved from the bullets as Alexander's defense field stopped them. It was good to know that it wasn't unbeatable. The three small dark spots in his vision proved that.

When the kids finally turned another corner, Alexander focused on what was to come next. He wound his arm as fast as he could and threw the armored form at the pirates before he rushed forward.

What happened next was not a fight.

He stood there, surrounded by dead bodies. The pirates hadn't even lasted a full minute after he crashed into them. The armored one had taken the most effort to kill, but he had been knocked senseless after Alexander hurled him like a baseball into the pirates. Even then, it took effort to ensure the man inside the armor was dead, but the crushed helmet was enough proof for him.

Alexander was still angry despite the threat being eliminated. He was angry they had dared to try to harm Yulia and angry that they had forced him to kill. They needed to die, he knew that. That didn't bother him. The fact that the universe seemed to be conspiring to change him into something he didn't want to be was what pissed him off.

All he ever wanted to do was find out how he ended up in that body and have a pleasant life. Then the corporations got involved, stealing his invention and forcing him to reevaluate his goals. Alexander hadn't even had much time to do that when mercenaries attacked him and injured Yulia all to get their greedy little hands on a few weapons, so he had to reevaluate again. The universe wasn't done with him yet. The Petrov Station Council decided to stick its nose into his business.

He should have been more angry about all of that, but each setback only pushed him to greater heights. If it was only him on the receiving end of that bad karma, he probably wouldn't have been nearly as upset, but they intended to harm his daughter. That was unacceptable.

It was clear by the man's words that they were there specifically for him. It put to rest any doubts he had that there was a traitor on Eden's End.

Alexander could still hear the orbital railgun firing, which meant the attack wasn't over yet. He decided to catch up to Yulia and Markus and find a safe spot for them while the rest of the facility was cleared.

Chapter 60

The *Talon* was pushing as fast as possible back to Eden's End. They had been halfway to Varlen when Matthews was woken up by a high-priority ship comm. He would have preferred a hostile attack than the actual issue they had woken him up for.

One of the techs responsible for reviewing Qcomm messages going out from Eden's End had failed to enter the comm data into SAM for analysis since he didn't see anything out of the ordinary in the messages. It wasn't until an after-action review was performed by the head of analysis that SAM pointed out the suspicious nature of the messages. It didn't take the program long to decode the conversations.

They had come from one of the drifters living on Eden's End. When Matthews read the decoded messages, he ordered the *Talon* to use the closest planet for an orbital slingshot back the way they came. The tech who failed to do their job was going to be scrubbing floors and toilets until the *Talon* returned to Ganos. Then the Hawks' leadership would decide if he got sent back to remedial training or released from the company for that gross oversight. That man's eventual fate would depend a lot on whether they were too late or not.

In his updates with HQ, they simply told him to "Go above and beyond for Mr. Kane." It wasn't hard to figure out why after he started sending in his monthly field reports, and he was more than glad to oblige.

He liked Kane, and most of the crew liked the man as well. It was rare to come across someone so talented and honest, yet humble as well. The Hawks' leadership knew a good investment when they saw one. If it wasn't for the pirate incursion, they would have stuck around and maybe even rotated out with their sister company to ensure constant security for the system.

"How much longer until we emerge into normal space?" he asked, doing his best to hide the worry in his tone.

"Less than a minute, Captain," the crewman replied.

He pressed the all-hands button, and an orange light began to strobe throughout the ship followed by a short klaxon. "We are about to emerge from FTL, strap yourselves in for combat maneuvering. This is not a drill. I repeat, this is not a drill."

The warning was unnecessary. His people had been ready and in position for the last hour, but it paid to make sure.

"Lockdown the bulkheads and finish venting procedures."

Every door across the massive troop transport was sealed shut and he could hear the quiet hiss as oxygen was pumped from the rooms and into the storage tanks.

Matthews reached up and clicked the button that would seal his helmet.

"Five seconds," the same crewman from before said.

"All weapons are green," the Chief Weapons officer stated over his suit radio.

The ship emerged into normal space—the entry far rougher than usual because they had pushed the warp exit much deeper into the system's gravity well than was normally advised. He knew from experience that the ship and the drive could take it. Even if the bubble destabilized, the ship probably would have been fine. The people on board, maybe not so much.

Matthews had never been on a ship that experienced a warp field collapse, but it was a topic of discussion in flight school. The premature collapse of a warp bubble would have made the turbulence they felt at that moment seem minor by comparison.

The ship was racing towards Eden's End but, even so, it took a few minutes for their sensors to collect the data of what was happening at the planet.

"There are fifteen contacts in low orbit above the planet. No transponders, Captain."

Dammit, they were too late to stop the pirates from landing.

"Any signs of debris in orbit?"

The planetary railguns should have done a number on the pirate ships.

"The sensors are picking up some debris, but it's not enough to indicate a ship. The sensors are also picking up multiple signs of smoke from the surface. There is also residual radiation from high in the planet's atmosphere. SAM indicates a nuke was detonated?"

That last one came out as a question from the stumped ensign.

Matthews wasn't surprised. Nuclear weapons weren't in common use since before the Shican war.

It sounded like the pirates attempted to destroy the surface weapons. When that failed, they set off a nuke outside the atmosphere as an EMP to clear the way. Even as a student of military history, he hadn't heard of anyone using a nuke as an EMP in well over a hundred years. There was no point when more sophisticated methods existed to temporarily disrupt electronics.

That didn't even answer the question of how the pirates got their hands on a nuclear weapon in the first place. The STO sure didn't use them, and even the Coalition had never bothered with the weapons during the war. Matthews gritted his teeth. While the existence of the weapon was concerning, how the pirates got their hands on a nuke wasn't important at that moment.

"Tell the PDC crews that I don't want a single missile getting anywhere near us. Tell the main battery crews to open as soon as they have a firing solution."

If they had one nuke, they might have more. Better to be safe than sorry.

"The pirates have spotted our jump signature. They are beginning to accelerate for a higher orbit."

"Weapons fire from planetside detected!" another of the bridge crew cheered.

"Calm down," Matthews chided. However, he smiled as he watched the smaller pirate vessel burst apart from the single impact.

He had never mentioned that fact to Alexander, but his railguns were complete overkill for most things. A ship like the *Talon* might be able to shrug off a dozen of those massive rounds, but smaller ships like gunboats and Corvettes simply weren't built to take that sort of kinetic impact and survive. Matthews was of the mind that it was always better to go for overkill than underkill, though. In that case, it seemed to have paid off.

The ship shuddered as the main guns fired. The *Talon*'s weapons may not be as large as Alexander's, but he had twenty-four of them.

"Tell the missile crews to target the largest ship. I guarantee that was the bastard that launched the nuke."

Moments later, four streaks zipped past the *Talon* before tiny points of light flared to life as the missiles closed in on their target.

Two more ships burst into expanding clouds of debris from the planetside guns before the *Talon*'s weapons arrived on the scene. There were no explosions as his weapons tore into the weaker shielding on the rear of the pirate ships.

The pirates tried to escape the planet's gravity or curve around to the far side to avoid the oncoming fire, but they had been stationary when the *Talon* jumped in and were at a distinct disadvantage. Two more ships died as their drives gave out and he watched in satisfaction as they began to plunge into the atmosphere.

The *Talon* rocked hard as return fire impacted its thickly armored front.

"Minimal damage to report, Captain. They are using autocannons."

A burst of fire exploded between him and the fleeing pirates.

"One of our missiles was intercepted. The other three have engaged electronic warfare countermeasures and evasive maneuvers."

"Splash two," the officer said a few moments later.

He witnessed the third explode as it hit a piece of wreckage. The fourth made it through and exploded near the large pirate ship.

"Heavy damage to the pirate ship, but they are still maneuvering. Six inbound missiles detected."

A hail of PDC ammo flew to intercept the missiles while the Gauss cannons continued to spit death at the fleeing pirate ships.

The *Talon* was moving so fast that he needed to maximize the damage they inflicted before overflying the pirates. If they didn't kill or chase off the pirates before that happened they would be vulnerable to an attack from the rear. There was a reason why high-speed interceptions like that were inadvisable.

"Enemy missiles destroyed. The main ship is attempting to accelerate to a safe jump distance."

He pressed the comm button and spoke calmly into his radio. "If that ship escapes this system, I will be severely disappointed in all of you."

Every gun capable locked onto that larger ship and began to fire. Three more missiles flew out as well. Missiles were expensive, so they normally only used the bare minimum in a combat situation. Since the captain said he was going to be disappointed, it was time to pull out all the stops.

The enemy ship did a valiant job trying to stop the missiles, but another one struck the engines, and the kinetic rounds easily punched through the ship's static field and armor. He knew they were dead in the water when he saw the ship start to drift sideways.

"The rest of the ships are jumping away, Captain."

The fact that the pirates had risked a jump so close to the planet surprised him. They wouldn't have gotten far with the unstable warp bubble, but by the time the *Talon* picked them back up on sensors, the ships would have plenty of time to jump properly.

"How many escaped?"

"Only three of the fifteen, Sir."

Matthews grunted in annoyance. "Slow us down and get the dropships ready to disembark. I want to ensure there aren't any surviving pirates. What about conditions on the surface?"

"Scans show one debris field on a landing pad and four other ships down there. It also looks like three craters where gun emplacements used to be."

At least they hadn't been caught completely unaware.

"Any communications from Eden's End?"

"Negative, Captain."

It was likely their comm gear was down due to the EMP strike.

"Tell the dropship teams to split into two groups. I want one aboard the ships and the other to scour Eden's End of these filthy bastards and find anyone who survived."

With fifteen ships full of pirates, he had little faith that anyone was left alive down there. Getting revenge was the best the Hawks could do, and he would take that failure to his grave.

* * *

It took hours to slow the *Talon* enough to swing back around toward the planet. By then, the planetary gun had gone silent. Nobody aboard Travers' dropship knew if that meant it was out of ammo or that the pirates had finished off the defenders. Either way, they were going in with full kit and the heavies were leading the charge. There were no half-measures that time.

The dropship shook as its bow-mounted flechette turret tore into the pirate ship on the landing pad. The ship had tried to take off when they saw them coming. It was a little too late to run though—not that they would make it far without a jump drive. Even if they somehow made it past the dropships, the *Talon* would shoot them out of orbit.

The ship was likely still on the landing pad because they were afraid of the orbital railgun picking them off. That was the only smart choice the pirates had made today.

The enemy ship lost power and crashed off to the side of the landing pad, cracking the frame and leaving a large furrow in the dirt until it came to a rest. That was a bit annoying. It meant his team would have to clear the ship before they could go for the facility. Unless…

"Pilot, when we land, rotate so you're facing the pirate ship."

"You read my mind, sir."

The shuttle touched down and his people stormed off the ship, the heavies swept their much more powerful flechette cannons back and forth looking for hostiles. No pirates poked their heads out, though.

With the landing zone clear, they all rushed through the doors that had been blown open.

As Travers rushed inside, he had to skid to a stop before he ran into the back of the augment suits. "What's the hold-up?!" he demanded.

One of the heavies gestured down the hallway.

Travers poked his head from around the large, armored suit to see a barricade of metal crates and a whole lot of dead bodies on this side of it. An older woman he recognized but had forgotten the name of poked her head from around the corner.

"You're a little late for the fireworks, boys."

That got a chuckle out of the rest of the people behind the barricade pointing weapons their way.

Travers had removed his helmet after they learned the people had repelled or killed off the rest of the pirates. When he radioed it in, he wasn't sure if he or Captain Matthews was more surprised that the people down there had driven off the pirates

He followed Eva Wu—that was the older woman's name—down a hallway. People thanked him for showing up and for the training the Hawks gave them as he walked past.

"You're certain they're all dead?"

Considering what he saw at their entrance, he didn't doubt the woman's words, but it was possible they missed a few. Pirates liked to run and hide.

The woman snorted. "Trust me. Alexander was in quite a foul mood after the attack, he personally scoured the entire facility. If there are any pirates left, it's only on the shuttles. Alexander and Damien both agreed that it wasn't safe to try to board the shuttles since there was no cover."

"What were you planning to do then?"

"Nothing. If they tried to leave, the one working railgun would have shot them down. If they tried forcing their way back inside a second time, we were ready for them. The decision was to let them starve in their ships and in a few weeks check to see what remained."

It was a very clinical tactic, but considering there was no place to survive on the surface, it was probably the safest course of action.

"How many survivors?"

The woman looked at him out of the corner of her eye. "Hun, don't try to sugarcoat your question. Ask what you want to ask."

Travers cleared his throat. "How many died?"

"We suffered eighty-six casualties. Most of those came from the two augmented pirates. One bastard had a grenade launcher and a minigun. Alexander took care of both of them."

Travers paused. "Alexander did? How?"

"I'll let him explain that to you if he decides to. Now come on, we're almost there."

They entered Kane's workshop or what was left of it. The place looked like a bomb had gone off and most of the robots and machines were damaged to one extent or another. Alexander was over by one of the printers, removing components from it and putting them into another one. The repaired printer hummed to life as they approached.

Alexander turned toward them, but he was without his usual holographic face. The robot body he used was far more unsettling without the face.

Travers' first instinct was to run when he saw it. He squashed those feelings ruthlessly as he held out a hand. "I'm glad you survived."

He could almost sense Kane's easy smile as he reached out and shook the offered hand.

cHaPter 61

Alexander was notified of the arrival of the new ship. Due to their uplink to the satellites being offline, it wasn't clear who they were until they started firing on the pirates in orbit. If it wasn't for the facility's sensors, which were designed to monitor the local star, they may not have even known another ship arrived. Even then, the consensus was split on it being someone there to help, or another faction of pirates.

He was glad to see it was a friendly face. "While I'm glad to have the Hawks' assistance once again, why are you back?"

"You'll need to speak with Captain Matthews about that. All I know is I was ordered to clear the facility of hostiles and the ships sitting on the landing pads. If you're saying the facility is clear, I think it's time to clear some ships."

It took less than two hours for the Hawks' ground teams to clear the vessels. There were not many surviving pirates, and the ones who had survived were certainly not equal to the Hawks.

Alexander stood next to Travers as they watched a single dropship touch down. Out stepped a man he had only seen and spoken to over video comms.

"Mr. Kane." Captain Matthews offered his hand and Alexander shook it. "I make it a rule not to step off of the *Talon* during operations, but with your communications being out and the sensitive nature of this discussion, I decided to come speak with you myself."

"That wasn't really necessary, Captain."

"I felt that it was. Is there a place we can speak quietly, Mr. Kane?"

"Yes, follow me."

Normally he would have simply headed to his shop or his apartment. The shop was a mess thanks to the firefight. It wasn't exactly private at the moment either. He had hired a group of locals to clean the place up and watch over the one working printer as replacement components were built. On the other hand, his apartment was occupied by a little girl who was grounded for not following the evacuation plan.

Alexander was relieved to see Yulia and Markus were safe, but that didn't excuse his daughter's reckless actions. He knew that being a parent meant punishing a child in certain circumstances, but that didn't make him feel any better about having to do it. Regardless, Yulia needed to learn that certain actions have consequences.

To be honest, the girl looked relieved to be home, and it wasn't like Alexander had simply abandoned her at home alone while he worked to fix all the damage from the attack. One of the tutors who helped with her language lessons agreed to watch her. It was the woman's way of thanking him for driving off the pirates and saving her husband. Alexander didn't know the woman's husband, but he thanked her for her assistance anyway.

The tutor wasn't the only person who tried to thank him. He didn't think he did all that much, but it was clear the battle had shifted sentiment towards him quite drastically. When he put out the request for people to help clean up his shop, he got more people than he bargained for. Not wanting to send anyone away, he assigned twenty to his shop and split the eighty others into four separate groups to help remove the bodies and clean up elsewhere.

The dead citizens of Eden's End would get proper burials, whereas the pirates were going to be tossed into a waste furnace. It was a fitting end for the vile bastards.

"We can talk in here." Alexander typed in the code to his storage room.

Matthews stepped inside, but Travers simply took up a position outside the door. Alexander would have shaken his head if his holo-projector was working. Instead, he simply stepped into the room filled with crates and closed the door.

"I'm afraid we don't have any conference rooms. At least none that are in any condition to be used as such."

"This is fine. I'm not the type of man to beat around the bush, so I'm going to be blunt. The Hawks fucked up."

"Um..."

Matthews lifted his hand. "Please, let me finish." When Alexander didn't say anything else, the man continued. "It was our job to ensure the safety of this facility. As we were returning to STO space, our SAM discovered someone was sending coded messages through our scouting ships to pirates. When I learned of this, we turned around immediately to warn you. Unfortunately, we were too late."

Alexander had suspected there was a spy, but he had no evidence to even begin to figure out who had sold them out. That all changed now.

"You have a name?" was all Alexander could ask while his anger simmered restlessly.

The name the man gave was not one Alexander knew. It was a minor relief that it wasn't anyone with any real security there, but that fact barely kept him from storming out of the room to personally punish that individual.

As his rational mind reasserted itself, he spoke up. "Please have your people work with Damien Laront. We need this man alive to answer questions."

Matthews nodded. "I was hoping you would say that." The captain pressed a little comm badge on his flight suit's arm. "Travers, work with Eden's End's security to apprehend a man by the name of Draven Holstein. And keep it quiet."

"Copy that, Captain."

"So, that's it then?" Alexander asked.

He knew the Hawks couldn't stay; they had commitments back in their home system.

"Normally, yes. You know we can't stick around for more than a few days, right?"

"I figured as much. You coming back at all probably saved a lot of lives. Thank you for that."

"Like I said, we screwed up, so we needed to correct that issue. From what I saw, you did a pretty good job of taking on the pirates all by yourself."

"Not good enough," Alexander stated bitterly. He would have frowned if he could. "The defenses I set up were completely overwhelmed by one attack. If I hadn't managed to get that one gun back online, we would have been at the pirates' mercy."

"There is no such thing as a perfect defense." Matthews sighed. "I would have recommended spreading your defenses out into orbit, but you simply didn't have the capability to build anything in the timeframe you had available. Your railguns should have been more than sufficient to deal with a normal attack. That's another thing. Fifteen pirate ships don't just attack one location without reason. Do you have any idea why they were here?"

"For me. They tried to take my daughter hostage."

"Is she okay?"

"She is uninjured, but I'm not sure if she will sleep well after what happened."

Matthews nodded. "Considering what I've seen you do in such a short time, it makes sense the pirates are interested in you. The *Talon* will be leaving once we capture and question the spy, but I've been authorized to leave one of the gunships for you to use for another three months. It's the best I could do."

"Thank you, that's more than generous. Can I ask why?"

"I would think that is obvious, Alexander." He was taken aback by the man using his first name. "The Hawks' leadership sees a relationship with you and Blue Star Enterprises as an important asset—a mutually beneficial one."

"I don't know what to say."

The reserved captain chuckled. "Don't say anything yet. Neither one of us has seen any benefit from this relationship. Once that happens, I suspect both of us will be happy to have each other."

Alexander extended his hand. "I guess that makes The Hawks of Ganos, Blue Star Enterprises' first official customer."

The man accepted the gesture with a grin. "I guess it does."

Matthews comm beeped and Travers spoke. "Captain, we have him."

"That didn't take very long. Well, now that we are done here, let's go have a discussion with this bottom feeder and find out why he sold out everyone here to pirates."

"They were only after me," Alexander reminded the man as they exited the room.

Matthews shook his head. "You don't commit that many forces for one person. Every man, woman, and child here would have ended up dead or as a prisoner."

Alexander didn't want to think about that, so he changed the subject. "Do you know if Captain Na survived?"

"The *Destiny* is fine. They were in the outer belt on the far side of the system when the battle kicked off. Once they realized it was pirates, they did the only thing they could and made for a jump point. They didn't jump, though. They waited to see what the pirates were doing. Once they saw us attacking the pirates, they started to head back in. His ship should arrive in another day with a load of ore. The station was unharmed in the fighting, and it must have been far enough away that the EMP didn't knock its systems out. That reminds me." The man reached into a pocket on his vac suit and pulled out three crystal cards. He handed them to Alexander.

"What are these?"

"Those are the fusion activation crystals for your new ships."

"My new what?"

"There were three surviving pirate ships. They're yours now. They are a bit banged up, but they should be serviceable. You also have the surviving shuttles on the ground and two large piles of debris that roughly resemble shuttles. You can do with them as you see fit. I suggest refitting at least one as soon as you can to run shipments to and from the surface."

"But you disabled them, shouldn't the Hawks be claiming them or something?"

"That's not how it works. Since we are still technically contracted to you until we return to STO space, everything we do is for your benefit. Even if we had returned to STO space and came back, we wouldn't claim these ships. Their transponders have been disabled or removed, meaning we could only use them for scrap. You, however, could use them as picket ships inside the system. I wouldn't use them to patrol between here and STO space until you get a legal transponder code for them though. The STO would shoot on sight."

As they neared the confinement cells, Alexander heard yelling. "Answer the damn question! Who did you sell us out to you useless sack of shit!" The yelling was followed by a wet thudding sound and they both picked up their pace.

The scene that greeted them was about what Alexander expected to see. Damien was purple with rage and practically vibrating with barely constrained violence. Considering the condition of the prisoner, it wasn't as constrained as maybe he wanted it to be. The man strapped to the chair had one eye swollen shut and a badly cut-up lip. Blood dripped from Damien's fist which was clenched so tight it had turned white.

"Damien!" Alexander yelled.

The man whirled on him and looked like he was ready to throw punches at Alexander. To his credit, he didn't. "This piece of garbage nearly got everyone here killed. Are you going to stop me?"

"How do you expect to get answers from him if you knock him senseless?" Alexander asked instead of answering the angry man's question.

"We should just put a bullet through his head and toss him with the rest of the trash."

"What would that accomplish?" Matthews asked as he stepped around Alexander, earning Damien's glare as well.

"It would be one less piece of shit, wasting air."

"And we would be clueless if more pirates were on their way, wouldn't we?" Alexander asked pointedly.

The man ground his teeth together. "This bastard isn't going to talk, but if you wanna waste your time, be my guest."

Alexander had been hoping to convince Mr. Holstein that they would let him go after he answered their questions. It was a long shot, and he knew it, but Damien's words made that tactic impossible. He sighed internally and mentally prepared for what came next.

He walked over and crouched down less than an inch from the bruised man's face. Despite his predicament, the man still flinched back at his approach. Alexander didn't enjoy using his appearance like that, but he would use it to his advantage if he had to.

Alexander used the little trick he learned to warm up his exterior to keep Yulia comfortable while in his arms. Only this time he sucked all the heat out of his hand, making it uncomfortably cold to the touch. Then he ran it along the man's leg and up his side like he was inspecting a piece of beef at a market. The man yelped at the freezing cold touch and tried to move away, but Alexander didn't let him. Touching the individual responsible for so many deaths made him feel disgusted. There was an urge to just smash the man's face in and be done with it. He barely suppressed the urge.

He could understand how Damien felt. If they hadn't threatened Yulia, he probably wouldn't do something like that, but his anger hadn't fully subsided after the attack. He was struggling to get a grasp on the first fully realized emotion he had felt since waking up. He didn't count the blind rage he fell into back when Yulia was injured mostly because he lost complete control back then.

In the calmest, most emotionless voice Alexander could come up with, he spoke to the man. "You have two choices, Draven. Neither of them is good, but one will end your suffering far faster than the other. Who did you sell us out to and why did you do it?"

chapter 62

In the end, the implied threat was enough to make the traitor talk, which was a relief.

Alexander had already done enough things in the past few days that he would rather forget. If he could trade those new memories for some of his lost ones, he would have done so in the blink of an eye.

The man's reason for doing what he did was as disgusting as the man himself. He was a degenerate gambler who had fled STO space after racking up a debt he couldn't afford to pay back. When he realized there was a chance to pay off that debt and return to STO space, he jumped at the opportunity and reached out to an old contact of his who acted as a go-between for him and the pirates. All it took to get the man to turn on everyone there was a promise of a ride home and what amounted to fewer credits than it would have cost Alexander to rent his small shop space on Petrov Station for a year.

Alexander found it hard to believe that someone could be so cold and callous to do such a thing or how he thought it was a good idea to trust pirates to keep their promises. Draven didn't come across as very smart. He came across as a sad, pathetic man whose only goal in life was to get back to gambling.

Alexander didn't stick around to watch the remaining interrogation, but he knew what the end result would be. The man willingly worked with pirates, what did he think would happen? Alexander didn't feel so much as an ounce of remorse for what awaited Draven, which surprised him. Not that he thought he should care about that useless waste of oxygen, but his feelings had been jumping back and forth rather hard since his run-in with the pirate who threatened Yulia. It had gotten so bad he almost wished he hadn't awakened them. ...That wasn't true. While the emotions were inconvenient, he felt more human now than he ever had before.

He still couldn't tell if he had a full range of emotions, but some were certainly better than none.

Having those emotions brought about an intense feeling of disgust for the actions he took to break Draven. Alexander knew logically that those feelings were misplaced, but he never wished to have to do something so vile again. Acting like that, even for a short time, made him feel dirty, like he had somehow stooped to the level of the pirates. He should have left the questioning to Damien and Matthews, but he had a personal stake in the matter. With Yulia's safety on the line, he wasn't willing to be a bystander.

Matthews stepped out of the room a few minutes later. "Are you okay?"

"I—" He was going to feed the man some empty platitude but decided against it. "I will be, eventually."

The Captain of the *Talon* gave a single slight nod. "You did what needed to be done. Nobody will fault you for that."

"I know. I just wish it hadn't been necessary in the first place. All I ever wanted to do was find someplace safe for my daughter and get away from the corporations. Now pirates are after me."

"I would like to tell you everything will be fine, but I don't like to fill people with false promises. Your defeat of this group will certainly leave this area of space rather quiet for a time, but the name Draven gave us is a well-known pirate. Arkonis Anazi was pirate royalty and the brother of Harlow Anazi, an infamous pirate warlord. I doubt the two were close so it isn't likely he will take the death of his younger brother personally, but you never know with pirates. I was more surprised to hear someone from the Anazi family was even out in this sector. The Char family are the ones who are usually found in this area of space, specifically, Katalynn Char. The Anazi family controls Haven, which is on the opposite side of STO space. If I had to guess, they are probably the ones who attacked Petrov Station."

"This Arkonis Anazi was here? Which one was he?"

Matthews pulled up his tablet and flicked to a picture. "Here's a picture of him. The DNA scanner said this was his armor." The man flicked to the bloody armor worn by the man who threatened Yulia.

The man got what he deserved.

"What now?" he asked.

Alexander's only real plan was to rebuild the defenses, improve them, and try to get back on track with his other projects. He could certainly use the opinion of someone with experience.

The man put away his tablet. "Now... now you get to claim the bounties. There were quite a few that the STO will be more than happy to know are gone."

"Can you claim them?"

Matthews quirked an eyebrow. "Why would you want the Hawks to claim them?"

Alexander gestured around. "I don't want to draw any more attention here than I already have. Arkonis may have come here for me, but I don't think he did it on his own initiative."

"Are you certain?"

"No. But I find it highly suspicious that all of this seems to lead back to Petrov Station. Someone there must know what I can do. For all I know, the entire Anazi family could be after me."

"That seems like a bit of a stretch, Alexander. Then again, I have seen you do some remarkable things in nine months, so maybe it isn't as implausible as I think. I'll make you a deal. I will only agree to turn in these bounties if you provide your corporate account to send the money to."

"Can't you just use the money to pay what I still owe you for your services?"

That seemed like the best option to him. It also didn't leave a trail straight to Blue Star Enterprises.

The man chuckled. "I think you're underestimating the bounties on these pirates. These are people who have been stalking the space lanes for decades. Arkonis alone was worth a hundred million credits. You also took down his second, third, and fourth in command. Those all total up to another hundred million. Add in the small fry that got tagged by ship cameras during their past raids and you might be looking at yet another hundred million, it's hard to say. That's three hundred million just in bounties. If you sell that armor that Arkonis was wearing, that would probably net you another three hundred million."

Alexander would have started coughing if he had a mouth, but instead, he just stared at the captain, which wasn't very effective since he didn't have his hologram. "Why is the armor worth so much?"

"I don't know who made that armor, but I can tell you that it is state-of-the-art electronic warfare gear. That alone is surprising to see, but that's not why you could get three hundred million for it. At most, armor like that would cost fifty million to purchase outright—which is a ridiculous sum for something like that—but there are people who pay for that type of stuff.

"The reason you can get three hundred million is because the company that built it will pay you that much. They will do this just to keep it from becoming public knowledge that their armor was sold to a known pirate. The STO tends to frown on black-market arms to the point of arresting entire companies until they can sort out who sold the armor. Even if they were somehow innocent, which I doubt, that would put a black mark on their company and nobody would buy from them ever again."

"Isn't that blackmail?"

Matthews shrugged. "It depends on how you word the request. The world isn't black and white, Alexander. It is many shades of grey. You just need to learn to live within them. If you don't want to deal with the logistics of it, let the Hawks handle the problem."

"That seems like a risky venture. Won't that get you in trouble if the company finds out?"

The man smirked. "No. We have our own black ops team. We'll pass it off to them to do the dirty work."

"I somehow feel like you shouldn't have told me that," he muttered, earning a chuckle from the grey-haired captain.

"Everything I told you has already been cleared by our leadership. Like I said, they want a close relationship with you. Just don't go spreading that information around."

"I wasn't planning on it. You said that armor is state-of-the-art. Shouldn't I keep it and try to reverse-engineer it or something? Seems like a waste to just give it back."

"I would recommend against that. The material might be worth studying, but you only need to take a small sample of that. As for the rest of it, don't bother. Some systems will alert their manufacturers when they get tampered with. For a suit like that, I can almost guarantee it has other protections built in as well. Get rid of it, earn a large chunk of credits, and be free of the hassle. Besides, knowing you, you could probably build your own suit in a few years given what I've seen you do. It would probably be better anyway."

"I'm familiar with the practice of companies hiding shit inside their products," he said in disgust. "Alright. Have your people take the suit and sell it back to the manufacturer. I already got a good look at it anyway, and I gotta say, I wasn't impressed. Can you do something with that money for me instead of just depositing it in my account?"

"Sure. As far as I'm concerned, it's your money, we're just holding it for you."

He told the captain what he wanted. The man didn't seem all that surprised by the request.

"Could take a while, but that should be doable. We can set up the delivery for when we return. With the pirates acting out, I don't know how long that will be, but let's assume a year at the earliest. That will also be close to the time the *Talon* needs to go in for its regular maintenance anyway. Since you have a station now, we can just do that here. If you happen to have some fancy new engines ready to go by then…"

This time Alexander chuckled. "I'll see what I can get done by then. Thank you again for everything, Captain Matthews. I look forward to seeing you in a year." Alexander held his hand out and the man shook it.

"You can call me Archie, it's short for Archibald. Stay safe, Alexander, and good luck with your company."

He walked the man to the exit and watched as all the Hawks' dropships lifted off as one and roared into orbit in formation.

Alexander was immensely grateful for having employed the mercenary company. He doubted another company of mercenaries would have come back after learning of their mistake. Things would have turned out much differently in that case. The pirate ships would have realized sooner or later that only one railgun was online and simply blown it up. Then destroyed the entire facility and called it a day.

Alexander glanced over at the crumpled wreckage of a ship about two-thirds the size of the *Zephyr*. It was going to take months to clean up the wreckage. At least the stupid thing was off the landing pad. He turned to the other distant pads that he could see from his spot. There were four shuttles on the two pads within his view. If that stayed true for the other six landing pads around the facility, that meant he now had sixteen shuttles.

He looked into orbit and focused until his vision telescoped to show him the ships up there. He wasn't sure zooming in like that would work, but he figured if he could magnify an area in his vision, he could probably do that. His view was mostly blocked by the hazy yellow atmosphere but, he could see the sun glinting off the ships. Even so, they were tiny specs in his vision.

Captain Matthews' people had moved them to a Lagrange point between the planet and the largest of the four satellites that orbited Eden's End. He wasn't sure what to do about the ships. They would probably come in handy at some point, but certainly not in their current configuration and not without serious repairs. It might be best to strip most of them for useful parts and feed the rest to the smelter. He would need to go up there personally and inspect the ships to figure out what would be best.

He tried scanning the sky for the *Destiny*, but it was either on the far side of the planet or too far away to see. He could clearly see the *Talon* hanging in space even without his enhanced vision. The ship was just that massive.

Alexander watched the tiny twinkle of lights from the dropships as they entered the troop transport. He continued to watch it as it started accelerating away.

With his new friends gone, it was time to get back to work. Alexander turned and walked back into the facility, his mind full of ideas.

cHaPter 63

BOOK 1 EPILOGUE

A third pirate ship jumped into the system. Much like the previous two who had arrived a few hours earlier, it was venting atmosphere but to a lesser degree.

The *Epsilon's Dawn* watched all this through its passive scanners, the same as it had when the fifteen-strong pirate fleet had been here a week ago. None of the ships had ever detected its presence in the system. It wouldn't have been a very good experimental covert ops ship if it had been detected.

"Sir, the three ships are finally moving to cross the system."

Vitor quirked an eyebrow at that. "Only the three? I wonder what our friends ran into? Wait for them to get deeper into the system's gravity and then set an intercept course. I want to find out firsthand."

If there was a new threat out there, he needed to report it to the Navy command.

The chase was rather anticlimactic from the Dawn's perspective. Three shots from the ship laser disabled the fleeing pirate vessels before they even realized they were being followed. It could have been pure luck, but Vitor guessed the ships were short-staffed.

* * *

"Come in," Admiral Clemont said as a knock came at his door.

Vice Admiral Fletcher, the head of Navy Intelligence poked his head in. "Do you have time for a report, Admiral?"

Clemont cleared the work from his terminal and waved the man in. "I assume it's important if you came personally?"

"It could be. Our AI analysis hasn't determined if it requires action yet or not. Do you remember Project Cobalt?"

Clemont had to think for a minute. The Navy had thousands of projects going on at any given time and he couldn't remember all the code names. That one did ring a bell. "The stealth ship made from recovered alien tech? I thought they mothballed that project over a decade ago because of the difficulty and cost of producing the elemental carbon that made up the exterior?"

"Officially, it was," the man stated.

Clemont grunted. "Let me guess, it went into the black ops budget?"

"I can neither confirm nor deny that." Fletcher shrugged.

"Fine, it's your ass on the line if they do a budget review. What of your non-existent ship?"

"We deployed a ship for testing about a month ago from Varlen. The initial deployment was supposed to be just a shakedown test, but they jumped into a system that had a buildup of pirates. The Captain of the *Epsilon's Dawn* decided to shadow the group of fifteen ships inside the system to see what they were up to. We believe the lead ship belonged to Arkonis Anazi."

"As if his bastard brother wasn't a big enough headache with him capturing stations and systems... Is this a prelude to another incursion?" Clemont asked.

"I don't believe so, sir. The report I got this morning says the pirates jumped out of the system heading farther from STO space. It's not unheard of for pirates to do that to skirt our border patrols, but they were already three systems out. You don't normally see fifteen pirate ships together unless they are raiding something big."

"Raiding something? What's even out there?"

"Nothing but a few leftovers from the Expansion. We thought maybe they ran into the Shican, but the pirates my people captured claimed they assaulted a planet and were driven off by a large ship and planetary defenses."

"Someone's building an outpost beyond the rim?"

That seemed like a foolish venture, but every few decades, someone got it into their mind to strike out on their own. Most either came crawling back or never returned.

"I believe so. Varlen reported that a mercenary company by the name of the Hawks of Ganos was contracted a little over nine months ago. They were seen escorting a small freighter by the name of the *Zephyr*. That freighter and the Hawks' scout ships have been seen multiple times since then in Varlen. It's obvious that the gunships were keeping the route from Varlen to this Y6X-3H2 system clear for transport. An Alexander Kane purchased the old research facility on Eden's End, formerly known as Y6X-3H2-4 so they must have deep pockets."

Clemont frowned and pulled up the system, flicking it over to the holo display so he could get a better idea of its location. He zoomed in on the display until it showed the system along with the edge of where STO space ended.

"That system is almost two weeks travel outside of our border. Is it possible this person is funding one of the other pirate families? Maybe the Anazi clan decided to cut them off before they could get started."

"It's possible but unlikely," Fletcher noted. "The Hawks would have followed STO mandate for pirates. They are the premier mercenary company for Ganos so I doubt they would risk their reputation by doing anything illegal."

"If they are so important to Ganos, why are they still out there? Surely they got recalled when the planetary governor started crying about the pirates at his border. As if there weren't ten systems between him and the systems the pirates attacked." Clemont shook his head.

"They were according to the Qcomm messages we intercepted. It seems like their original six-month deployment was extended before the recall order. They should have passed through Varlen a few days ago, but they didn't. The pirate attack could certainly explain their delay."

"What do we know of... what did you say his name was?"

"Alexander Kane."

"Yes, what do we know of him?"

"Nothing. His background is a complete fabrication. I didn't even need the AI to tell me that. There was some issue between him and Omni, but Omni ordered all records of that deal be sealed. The only other information we have is that he adopted a little girl from Petrov Station around eleven months ago and then left the station shortly after."

"I don't like it," Clemont stated as he sat back in his seat. "Kane may not be a pirate, but Petrov Station fell to Harlow around the same time. Now this man is attacked by Harlow's younger brother even though he relocated to the opposite end of STO space? That is no coincidence. They want this man, why?"

"We're not sure. The AI doesn't have enough information to produce an answer."

"Get it," Clemont ordered. "Put the *Epsilon's Dawn* to use and find out why the largest pirate family wants Kane."

* * *

Harlow was in a foul mood for a variety of reasons. The first was that his push into STO space had been stalled for the last few months. There had been a few skirmishes between his fleets and the STO, but the battles had been rather even since the STO Navy had reinforced their fleets with newer ships.

That wouldn't last long. Soon his first real warships would be coming off the secret shipyard he had built. Those ships wouldn't be deployed to the front right away, though. He needed to consolidate his power among the family and finally take control of all the pirates from Haven. Once that was done, he could triple his fleet size and start hammering the STO fleets back.

That left his other problem. His bastard brother Arkonis had yet to contact him. He should have been back by now. Harlow reached out to his spies on the other pirate worlds and outposts, but they reported no sign of his brother.

"If that scum-sucking shit ran off with my prize, I'll scour the fucking galaxy until I find him, then I'll flay him alive and string him up as a warning to others not to fuck with me!" he cursed.

Arkonis running to one of his hideouts was a definite possibility if he had learned about how useful Kane could be.

Harlow's guards didn't comment on his outburst. They knew better. It had only taken a few removed tongues until the rest learned to keep their mouths shut, but at least they learned.

While Harlow would love nothing better than to chase his brother down personally, he had more pressing matters to deal with. He flicked through his comm and brought up a contact.

"What do you want?" the haggard voice on the other end responded.

"Get your ass up, I have a job for you."

There was a grunt from the other end. "Ten million, non-negotiable. And I want my payment upfront, Harlow."

"Fine, but if you fuck this up or think of running, I'll come find you myself, Dalton."

"Whatever. What's the job?"

"Find my brother, Arkonis. If he's still alive, find out what he did with a man named Alexander Kane. If my brother is dead, find Kane and bring him to me alive."

"Is that all?" the man asked in annoyance.

"The information on his last known whereabouts will be in the info packet along with your payment. I want this done as fast as possible."

The line went dead, and Harlow ground his teeth. Dalton was a prick, even by pirate standards, but he went at a problem until it was resolved.

In an even worse mood, Harlow stomped out of the residence he was using as his base aboard Petrov. The place was almost nice enough to make him forget he was in this shithole of a station, almost.

He made his way to the Qcomm room to see if the engineers he captured aboard Petrov had any luck with their little project. The station Qcomm was still offline, but he had access to the one his people stole and modified years ago. Otherwise, he would be just as cut off as everyone else in that station.

"Give me some good news, or I'm sending one of you out an airlock!" he yelled as he entered the room.

He smirked when everyone shot to their feet and stiffened at his declaration. Harlow picked one poor bastard at random and pointed to him.

The man swallowed. "W-We managed to pull a few schematics from the system before they shut the network off."

Harlow snapped his fingers and two of his guards grabbed the man and dragged him out of the room. It wasn't that he was upset, he was happy they managed to get anything, but he needed to break the will of those new slave engineers. He preferred his slaves to be too afraid of disappointing him to think of rebelling. Getting rid of one to bring the others in line was a cheap expense.

"How many, exactly?" he asked another man.

That wasn't the first time he had tried pulling schematics from the net. His first test had been in a tiny mining outpost. Once the slaves out there bricked that network and failed to gain any useful knowledge, he spaced that entire station along with the crew he sent over. It was mostly to cover up what he had been up to. Not his wisest decision, but he had been rather irate at the time.

"A d-dozen or so. We even managed to get a Class 4 engine design from Sinorus," the man added hastily as Harlow turned his way.

Everyone knew the Sinorus designs were junk, but an engine schematic was an engine schematic.

"Congratulations, the rest of you get to live another day. Transfer the schematics to my ship. I have business elsewhere."

It was finally time to trade in his cobbled-together ship for a new one his people were building based on the ship the Shican had gifted him twenty years before.

Who would have thought a drunken one-on-one fight in an interceptor vs whatever the Shican equivalent was would have earned him the respect of the elusive aliens? Turns out they respected personal strength and not the useless platitudes and peace gestures of the STO. As far as he could tell, the Shican didn't even have a word for peace in their vocabulary—not that they communicated with him much.

It was no wonder the STO had never made any progress with the feline aliens, and they likely never would. He chuckled at that thought. His fortuitous encounter with the Shican twenty years ago was a secret he would take to his grave but only after he used that knowledge to carve out an empire in his name.

Want another exciting story to keep you busy?
Check out *Survivor's Descent* by TAL Deason!

Andrew was a thirty-year-old engineer living his best life until millions of alien orbs fell from orbit and altered reality itself.

Three years later, they activated a system that turns existence into an unforgiving trial. Power comes from combat, adaptation, and staying ahead of a world that no longer tolerates weakness.

With no way out, Andrew must learn the rules while the rules are trying to break him. Guided by advanced artificial intelligence, a small group of allies, and a mysterious, dilapidated alien spaceship, he faces the same demand as everyone else.

Get stronger.

But strength alone will not save Earth. Conflict is spreading across the galaxy, and rebellion threatens to drag humanity into a much larger war. Even if Andrew wins every fight, failure on a greater scale could still mean extinction.

To save his world, he will have to grow beyond anything he ever planned to be.

Available now on Kindle Unlimited and Audible!

Thank you for reading a MoonQuill original novel. More exciting stories can be found on at www.moonquill.com.

We would greatly appreciate it if you could take a moment to leave a review. Each one helps the author and supports their ability to continue writing fantastic books for everyone to enjoy!

Scan the QR code below to subscribe to our mailing list and be notified of new releases. You'll receive a few e-books for free!